FLANDERS

Ace Books by Patricia Anthony

COLD ALLIES
BROTHER TERMITE
CONSCIENCE OF THE BEAGLE
HAPPY POLICEMAN
CRADLE OF SPLENDOR
GOD'S FIRES
FLANDERS

FLANDERS

a novel by

Patricia Anthony

ACE BOOKS, NEW YORK

FLANDERS

An Ace Book
Published by The Berkley Publishing Group,
a member of Penguin Putnam Inc.,
200 Madison Avenue, New York, NY 10016

The Penguin Putnam Inc. World Wide Web site address is
http://www.penguinputnam.com

Book design by Erin Lush

First Edition: May 1998

Library of Congress Cataloging-in-Publication Data

Anthony, Patricia.
Flanders / Patricia Anthony.—1st ed.
p. cm.
ISBN 0-441-00528-4
I. Title.
PS3551.N727F58 1998
813'.54—dc21 97-33120
CIP

Printed in the United States of America

10 9 8 7 6 5 4 3 2 1

The existence of any major newspaper represents a daily miracle. Only those who have worked on one can understand the canny skill, diligence, and sheer plow-horse labor which goes into putting out each edition. So here's to the *Dallas Morning News*, where I held a fifteen-year "temporary" day job as a classified advertising phone rep. My long-suffering supervisors always seemed proud that a novelist could rise from the ranks of classified; in truth, I am proud to have been one of the crew.

Thanks to Joe Mayhew, who checked this novel's Catholicism; and to Charles Meister, who helped with the book's Judaism.

Spring 1916

One

March 2, off the coast of England

Dear Bobby,

It grieved me to leave you, considering how mad you were. It's just that I am not cut out to be a homebody. Ma knows that. Don't you recall her saying as how she had to tether me to the porch to keep me from straying? Well, I'm past my toddler days and the neighborhood's bigger, and war or no, I could not pass up a trip to Europe. Besides, the hostilities will be over by fall.

Make me two promises: First, take care of Ma and watch her close. If she's feeling poorly, she will never give you a hint of it. Second, don't let Pa come on the place. I know you don't recall him well, but he has the disposition of a junkman's dog. And mind that he doesn't come courting Ma. I suspect she harbors a weakness for him that may override her Christian virtues.

Don't fret for my sake, either. When this is over, I'll settle down, finish my studies, and spend the rest of my life doctoring lumbago. Still, come to find I sorely needed a vacation. Maybe when I get back stateside I won't mind those tight-assed Harvard Congregationalists.

But I miss my English literature classes, especially as I am within sight of Shakespeare's "sceptered isle." It galls not being able to step foot where Keats walked. I'd like to see one of Wordsworth's daffodils. I feel an awful longing to hear a nightingale. Tomorrow I sail the channel to France and, like as not,

I'll spend that trip as I did from New York to here—with my head over the rail, bestowing a free lunch on the fishes.

Didn't see any submarines on the way. In that, I was luckier than those poor souls on the *Lusitania* who probably never realized they were dying as an example of bastardly German gutlessness.

Kiss Ma and tell her not to worry. Assure her General Wood's battle lessons will come in handy. Remind her that I graduated at the top of my class, way over all those Yankee boys who cannot shoot straight and who complain mercilessly when they are made to shit in the woods. The general always did say that he perceived in me the *élan* for battle, and in a real man's war, spirit is all that is needed to win.

Yours in brotherly affection, Travis Lee

P.S. I knew it, for folks had told me; but I hardly believed until I saw for myself—the cliffs of Dover really *are* white. Yesterday I stood at the rail in the pouring rain until long after we had left them behind. How can I begin to tell you about Dover? It's a chalk line God drew to separate gray from green, breakers from earth. Seeing it, I don't know why William the Conqueror didn't just put down his sword and take England captive with his eyes.

MARCH 18, FRANCE, REST AREA

Dear Bobby,

The postman finally caught up with me, and it was no child's play to find me, either, since my location has moved about. The Brits put me first in one battalion and then in another when they saw how well I could shoot.

"Good God, Yank," Captain Hodgeson said to me the other day at target practice. "Do you realize that out of five bullets, you have shot five perfect bull's-eyes?"

I speak fluent Texan around the limeys as they enjoy it so, and are not hurtful with their joshing like the Yankee boys. Anyway, I scratched my head like I was puzzled and said, "Did I ruin that target, sir?"

Captain Hodgeson then called up Major Woodhouse to

see, and both officers asked me to fire once more, which I proceeded to do. Now it appears that, after a semester of introductory grenade tossing and an advanced course in trench-digging, I am to be a sharpshooter.

"Where did you learn to shoot like that, Private?" the major asked.

I told him, "Plinking squirrels for Ma's varmint stew," which delighted the two of them so that they had me repeat the phrase again and again for a succession of other officers. But my own jest was my downfall, for it caused me to ruminate upon those times before Ma started raising those fancy goats of hers. I was somber for the remainder of the day. You do not recall how strapped Ma and I were after Pa left us; how we lived off grits and yard greens and possum, like poor coloreds. Still, now I am filled with a sense of superiority. The English may have seen war, but I have lived with Pa, so I have seen Hell. Therefore I will always be hardier than they, and if that was all the inheritance that drunken bastard will give me, I suppose forcing me to become a man is enough.

Anyway, it is always good to hear laughter, no matter if the source of it is sorrow.

I cannot tell you where I am, but suffice it to say that it is a pleasant and verdant place in France. Here green has no overtones, not like in Texas where dry is always pushing through. Nailing France's grass to its brown earth are massive chestnut trees and elms as stately as Gothic cathedrals. Oh Lord, Bobby, the flowers—all colors, and everywhere you look. Europe has such a tender and civilized countryside.

I wish you were here.

Fondly, Travis Lee

MARCH 21, FRANCE, REST AREA

Dear Bobby,

You must not tell Ma, for it would send her entire praying circle to their knees, but the Tommies took me into town and got me knee-walking drunk.

At some point that night I found out that they don't like being called "limeys," and I informed them of my personal objection to "Yank." After another few tots of French brandy I went to echoing some of the more choice selections of their speech like: "Not by 'arf" and "Gotcher mouf on yer, ain't yer?" I tell you, they may have invented it, and it might even be named after them, but their language doesn't bear much resemblance to English. After a few minutes of my aping them, a private from Lancaster started shouting, "Oos iff it, Yank? Oos iff it?" or something like, which I immediately parroted. He began a pushing sort of fight. I beat a retreat and went outside to find an outhouse. There I searched and searched, and the more I looked, the more urgency I suffered. In desperation, I crept around the side of the inn and unfastened my pants. I was joined by a drunken French private who spoke no better English than the Tommies, but who parley-voued well enough in gestures to let me know that he was of the opinion that he could piss farther than I. Little did he know that I was not only possessed of a sorely laden bladder, but I was a sharpshooter besides.

"Give it your best shot," I said.

He let loose at an innocent bystander duck who took cheerfully to the shower. The striped cat that I chose was not so sanguine. I laughed so, I fell into a nearby ditch. I was told that the Frenchman attempted to get me out; but since I was unwilling and he too was drunk, he walked off and left me, forgetting to inform my sergeant where I was. There I lay until my mates stumbled upon me the next morning. The officers had assumed that I had deserted, and it was a trial explaining my hardshell Baptist upbringing. I told them, "Don't y'all get me to dancing, then, for I ain't used to that, neither; and God only knows what I'd do."

They would have put me in the clink had they not found me such a caution. Had I not been such a dead-on shot. The sad thing is, last night I came to find out what lures Pa to the bottle, and I wonder if I shall discover in myself the same gloomy thirst. Promise me, Bobby, to stay away from liquor, as it gives a short-lived sort of glee, and you don't remember the best parts.

One thing you might try, though, is pissing on a duck, as they seem to enjoy it. You might also try pissing on the Jennings' calico cat for something of the opposite reason.

Yours in sin, Travis Lee.

APRIL 2, FRANCE, RESERVE AREA

Dear Bobby,

Yesterday my new captain, Miller, ordered me to go with the new subaltern; and so the pair of us shouldered our packs and set off down a poplar-corridored lane, toward what destination I could not discern. As the lieutenant was a Scot he could not, in understandable English, tell me, either. After an hour's pleasant stroll, we came upon what looked like a crude bar ditch, with a few soldiers lining one side and peering off across an orchard.

Right then the lieutenant throws himself down, yelling, "Four in! Four in!" The Tommies lining the ditch begin to shout, "Hed doon!" And then I heard wasps buzzing.

The lieutenant waved frantically. "Yer bloody ignorant Yank! Fritz is four in!"

I dived headfirst into the ditch. Soldiers and packs and curses were propelled every which way. When we got untangled, I saw that the lieutenant was ordering me to ready my rifle, which I did. There were only a few Boche, and they were lurking about the trees in the apple orchard, plinking at us haphazardly. My first shot dropped one, an outcome which took me by utter surprise. I saw the helmet sail off the German boy's head. I saw him go down. Regret so overwhelmed me that I nearly vomited, an enterprise which, considering the close confines of the trench, would have earned me a pummeling. Luckily I must have only winged the man, for to my relief he soon sprang up and fled east through the trees, his fellows behind.

I have read of battles, and Granddaddy de Vrees talked enough about Shiloh to make me think I'd been there. This seemed like a puny encounter, without much glory. Still, I think that I shall like this war, as there is a sort of silliness to it.

When the battle was over and the Germans had run off through the apple trees, the lieutenant clapped me on the back. The corporal gave me a tot from his ration of rum. We lounged about and had a smoke.

The trenches are less than I thought, and the war is, too. I was prepared to go face-to-face with spike-helmeted ogres and damnable cowards. I understand why the old soldiers, the ones who have been here for a while, have an odd pity for the enemy. You shall see—very soon the Germans will lose heart altogether and run home, and the disagreement will be over.

I'll travel a bit then, and see more of Europe. I need me enough memories to last through all the tedium of adulthood—for I realize that I must grow up eventually. There are enough scrub oaks and mesquites in my future; enough mockingbirds and grackles to make me forget the larks. The afternoon in that ditch smelled of moss and history. I sat and listened to the Tommies bicker over their game of cards. Apple blossoms drifted across the meadow like snow. In some other bar ditch well removed from us, a German sang a ditty in a lilting tenor, so high and pure a sound that it near brought tears to my eyes. The sun lay down, gently dying, in the soft grass of the orchard. I stood guard, and I would not have shot him for it, but my Fritz did not come back to retrieve his helmet. Evening settled with calm, chill indigo. Stars emerged. Oh, Bobby. How I love it here. Even after the warmest days, the nights are cool as salvation. Lieutenant sent someone into town to fetch dinner, and we ate crusty bread and hard cheese while the silent parliament of night convened. As I closed my eyes for sleep that night, I saw the German fall and fall again, in showers of petals, in the tranquil beauty of the meadow.

I shall soon have to overcome my squeamishness, for killing

is why I came. But the first deer I ever shot was so sloe-eyed that I sat down and cried over him, too.

Forever stout and bravely yours, Travis Lee.

APRIL 4, FRANCE, REST AREA

Dear Bobby,

Well, I am unmasked for an academic. Captain Miller came upon me today as I sat alone, reading from my Keats.

"Why are you not at the YMCA pavilion?" he asked.

"Noisy," I told him. It was getting noisier all the time where I sat, too, what with the bees buzzing like sluggish bullets through the nearby clover and the captain making have-to conversation.

"Are you having problems with the others, Private? Any complaints you care to unburden yourself of?"

I took it upon myself to needle him a bit. "Yes, sir. Matter of fact, what with the rifle cleaning and all the grenade training, there just ain't enough quiet time to read, sir."

As is usual with the Brits, Miller failed to get the point. "Well, idle hands, what? Practice sharpens skills. Besides, our enlisted chappies are illiterate, or the nearest thing to. Books simply fail to interest them."

Well, I tell you, that rubbed my fur wrong-ways. "You joshing me, sir? Somebody swore up and down this book has pictures of naked women."

It wasn't meant as invitation, but he sat down on the grass by me, anyway. As I said, the Tommies are always mistaking my intent. They howl with merriment at my anger and bristle at my good humor. God only knows what would happen if I'd up and kiss one. "Lieutenant McPhearson tells me you acquitted yourself well the first time under fire."

"Um." I went back to my reading.

It was a damp day, and the Tommies do better with the chill than I do. I pulled my greatcoat up around my neck.

" 'The owl, for all his feathers, was a-cold.' " Miller has melancholy eyes and the stuffed-shirt British sort of voice that sounds like he's eating mush; but that troublemaker grin of his gives him away.

I closed the book, marking the page with my finger. " 'The hare limped trembling through the frozen grass.' "

" 'And silent was the flock in woolly fold.' "

There I was, in another pissing contest.

I recalled the next line easy. " 'Numb were the Beadsman's fingers, while he told . . . ' "

" 'His rosary!' Too easy, Yank. 'And . . . and . . . ' Oh, bugger it!"

In pissing contests, it helps to have a full bladder; it's essential to know your Keats. " ' . . . and while his frosted breath,/Like pious incense—' "

"Cheating!" He snatched the book out of my hand. "You'd just read it!" He opened the book at the marked page and surprised, he read the title: "*Endymion*?" He looked at me then—not like an officer on a soldier, nor even like a rich man on a poor. "Good memory, Yank."

"Travis Lee."

"Travis Lee Stanhope. Good God. How inutterably quaint."

"Ma worked on it."

He handed me the book. "Travis Lee. So I find that you are not quite the rube."

"I can pass in a pinch."

"Um? Ah. Yes, I see. Well, you shoot. I have been made well aware of that. You have ridden horses too, then, I take it?"

"Bareback like a wild Indian. And if you will forgive me, sir, you don't sit a horse for shit. Although you ride some better than Major Dunn, who I expect got the crack up his ass from being throwed so often, if I may be so blunt."

He relished the comment about the major like spun sugar candy. "Please, Private Stanhope," Miller said, smacking his lips, "promise me that you shall always be blunt. So tell me. Were you acquainted with any wild Indians, there in Texas?"

"Ma's half Cherokee."

He took to that, too. "How charmingly American of her. Which side?"

"Her ma come across the Trail of Tears and stopped when she got tired of walking. Hell, she was always tired after that, for Granddaddy de Vrees sired fourteen children off her. He sired more off a widder woman he knew, more off some boughten slaves. It fair shames me to admit to it, sir, but half the boys in Texas—white and colored—are relatives of mine."

"Really."

"Uh-huh. Granddaddy stuck it in everything it pointed at. Ma always tells me I favor Granddaddy de Vrees, and she don't mean it kindly, sir."

The captain guffawed so loud that he embarrassed himself. Right quick, he clapped his hand over his mouth. He peered about, then shrank back against the bole of the elm. "Shhh, Stanhope. Please be less entertaining. We must take care that no one hear us. In case you were not aware, it's frowned upon for officers to consort with the enlisted."

Well, Bobby, about that time I started asking myself, "Why me?" and hoping I hadn't given him the wrong idea. It struck me that consorting might have overtones, for, as Uncle Cecil was always fond of warning me, you know the predilections of those poetry readers.

It started to rain—not a downpour like it might have in Texas, but a soft, refined European sort of rain. He didn't make a move to get up. I didn't either.

His tone was as mannerly as that shower. "Stanhope? Do tell me: Why on earth did you join?"

"Well, sir, it's a long damned story. Won myself this scholarship first. Wrote an essay for some old Harvard alumnus as to why Harper, Texas needed a doctor. Ma'd been craving a sheepskin for her wall, and I got that first one just to please her. I'll earn my license, I guess; but there's a load more study goes into doctoring. Before I settle down I need something just for me: a couple of spoonfuls of adventure."

Miller smiled cheerlessly. "Ah, yes. Of course. Adventure." He looked quickly away, down to where the road grew tired and petered out in mist. " 'Mother whose heart hung humble as a button/On the bright splendid shroud of your son.' "

"What, sir?"

"Stephen Crane. *War Is Kind.* Please remember that some courage is mere idiocy. Learn to keep your head down when the Boche fire, will you? And you might also acquaint yourself with your own fine American poets." He got up. I watched him amble across the pasture, worry's weight bowing him.

I have made myself a promise, Bobby, that the captain's warning will not spook me. I inherited Granddaddy's obsession with the ladies; and like him, when my pecker at last gives out, I plan to die in my bed of disagreeability and old age.

Love, Travis Lee.

APRIL 9, FRANCE, REST AREA

Dear Bobby,

Well, I have seen my first aeroplane and was nearly shot by a Canadian. His name's Pierre LeBlanc, but don't let that fool you, for he has only a nodding acquaintance with French. Even the Tommies speak the language better than he, and their vocabulary's no more than a Texan's *chinga su madre.*

As soon as I came into the company, the Tommies threw LeBlanc and me together. See, this particular Canuck was born on a horse ranch up near Alberta, so as fellow yokel colonials, the Tommies naturally figured we'd have a lot in common.

Yesterday all of us were in the barracks. There was rain outside, a leaking roof within, nothing but housework to do. LeBlanc looked up from cleaning his rifle and said, "Lose my company, and they throw me in with an untried asshole of a captain. The bastards are doing their best to kill me, eh?"

The Tommies said nothing because talking about destroyed units is bad luck. We're a green company and an even greener platoon. Among us, only Lieutenant McPhearson and Corporal Dunleavy and Sergeant Riddell have seen battle, and they don't like to talk about it much.

Anyway, I took it upon myself to defend Miller. "Oh, strikes me he's smart and careful. Rather have that in an officer than one who's got more balls than sense."

LeBlanc jumped to his feet. Mind you, he had his loaded rifle in his hands—pointed downward, but still. "You have a point to make about the Third Canadian?"

I put up my hands real quick. The barracks was quiet except for the hollow drip of rainwater into a nearby bucket. The Tommies were eyeing us both.

"Didn't mean nothing by it, friend," I said.

"You're not my goddamned friend." All of a sudden he went to shaking hard, trembling like he had the fever. It scared the fool out of me. "I'll tell you. I'll tell you what," he said.

"Take it easy." I spoke to him patient and slow, the way I always talked to Pa when he was drunk.

"Shut up," he said. "And listen. You listening?"

"Yeah. All right."

"They sent us into Kitchener's Wood at midnight, eh? Dark and wet as a whore's cunt, and we fixed our bayonets and went, not knowing where the hell the Germans were. The Frogs didn't have the stomach, eh? And the Tommies were bumping into each other in the dark. The Canadians, see? We pushed them back."

"Okay. That's good," I told him.

He wasn't having any of it. "Shut up. You don't know. It was last April. End of April."

"Yeah. Okay."

"Shut up," he said again, and this time I did. "The weather was nice. Later it rained and all there was, was mud. But it was a pretty morning when we climbed down into the trenches. Later that afternoon we could see it coming. We could see it for a long time, coming across the pasture slow, like fog rolling in . . ."

"Private LeBlanc," Lieutenant McPhearson warned.

It shocked the hell out of me when LeBlanc snapped, "You don't know! Shut the hell up!" And it utterly bewildered me when Lieutenant went quiet. LeBlanc was still holding the rifle, and I began to wonder if the lieutenant was scared to take it away. "Piss on your bandolier, Stanhope. Piss right on it. That's what they told us. And so I did. And before it hit, the gas smelled good, sort of like spicy pineapple. Then my eyes started to sting and I put my wet bandolier up to my face. Funny, right? Don't you think that's funny? Breathing through your own piss? I would have eat my own shit, too, see? Would have eat yours. I would have done anything. Up and down the trench, men started barking, a terrible hard barking, like choking dogs. Then all of a sudden the firing along the line stopped. Jesus. It got so quiet. For weeks I thought that everybody but me'd turned and run. But piss on it, right? Right? That's what the Brit officers told us, and they should have known. Still, I feel a tingling in my throat. My chest starts to hurt bad. The captain yells, 'Up top!' and the few of us left scramble up the parapet, right into the bullets. The boys who are hit fall in the trench again, down into the gas. Ricky and Danny and Dennis and Jean Claude. And there they are in the bottom of that goddamned hole, clawing at the dirt and turning blue. But we held, didn't we? We pushed the Boche back. That was the important thing. The whole world was dead and the battle was won and everything smelled like pineapple. Goddamn it to Jesus and Mary fucking holy shit." He threw down his rifle and walked out into the rain.

Into the silence, Sergeant Riddell said, "Never you mind, boys. I've walked through gas, 'aven't I? And Lieutenant McPhearson, too. I can tell you the masks work. Captain Miller may be a Jew, but don't let that worry you, either. You'll see. When the time comes, he'll stand shoulder to shoulder with us, stout as any white Christian officer."

It fair shook me. A Jew. Now I understand why I never see Miller with the other brass. And why, when he was looking for company, he only found me.

Still, how could the Tommies know by looking? Miller seemed like an ordinary man. I mean, I can pick out a colored, even if he's high yellow. I can pick out a Mexican. The only Jews I've seen were in cartoons, and they didn't look at all like Miller. How could the Tommies know for sure?

And what's against him anyway, more than an idol-worshipping papist, I mean? And this army's full of papists. Jews, papists, they're all of them the same—all walking that long road to Hell. And so what? I have the suspicion Lutherans and Church of Christers will end up sucking flames. If God's fair, the Congregationalists will, too. I figure that, despite "Once saved, always saved," I'll meet with all of them there.

Later, the rain let up and I walked out of the barracks. Down at the stables I saw LeBlanc. He was standing by an officer's mount—Captain Hawkins's, I think. A bay gelding, like a hundred others. Just any horse. And he was so patient, standing tethered there, LeBlanc hanging on to him tight as a man drowning, his face buried in that brown satin neck.

I walked past the YMCA pavilion. Across the way, a squad of Frenchies marched through a stand of trees, in their horizon-blue uniforms faint as smoke. High up, in a calm azure lake between clouds, a glint of color: an aeroplane. I thought of how lonely the pilot had to be, nothing but wind to hold him.

Still, I guess I'm flying now, aren't I, Bobby? Strikes me Miller is, too. And Pierre LeBlanc, just because death put him there.

I sure do miss you,

Love, Travis Lee

APRIL 11, FRANCE, REST AREA

Dear Bobby,

Miller came by the practice field yesterday, all swagger stick and attitude. "Stanhope," he said. "Put down your rifle. I wish to see you at once." He turned around and walked off, leaving me to follow, wondering what the hell I might have done to set his temper off. We arrived at the stables, where a group of officers were sitting around a table drinking cheap red French wine and scratching their balls and speculating about what was happening where people were fighting actual wars.

They shut up fast when they saw Miller and me. Miller began to shout orders: "Bring my horse up!" Then "Wilson!

Might I borrow your mount? The private here is to ride mine. I wish him to check my gelding's wind."

One of the captains tapped stick to cap, then went back to his conversation, all the time eyeing us like he was trying not to stare.

When they brought Captain Wilson's gray around, Miller climbed up and left me to mount his long-legged sorrel. That gelding had to be near seventeen hands high. I'd never mounted from one of them women rider blocks, but I swallowed my pride this time. Even then I had a hell of a time getting up, since my hobnail boots were too slick for those steel stirrups.

I swung a leg over that limey excuse for a saddle. Before I was settled, Miller barks, "Fall in!" Damned if that gelding didn't start sauntering across the paddock—with only half of me on him.

The officers around the table nearly pissed themselves laughing.

I held on best I could. Then I hear Miller call out, "Stretch high! High!" and the gelding commenced to backing. About the time he reached the middle of the paddock, he started up on his back legs.

I jerked that gelding's head hard right, grabbed me an ear and twisted hard. I surprised the bejesus out of that sorrel. He took to snorting and crab-dancing, and then to standing stock-still in place, waiting to see what I would do next. I crooned to him, the way Grandma de Vrees always taught me; and only when he started to quiver did I let go.

I looked up. I had everybody's attention. The officers weren't smirking anymore.

"A Cherokee trick, is it, Stanhope?" Miller looked cat-in-the-birdcage satisfied.

That's when I got that it hadn't been my respect he was after. "Yes, sir. Biting the ear is better, but pinching will do."

"The stirrups bother you?"

"Can't keep my feet in them, sir."

He climbed off the gray, came and fastened my stirrups up under the saddle's gullet. It was odd, sitting and looking down as he helped me. There was gentleness to his touch, a humility to his gesture. I figure it was by way of a public apology and a private thanks.

He never looked at me. When he was finished, he walked over and climbed up in his saddle. He called for the paddock gate to be opened, then he trotted the gray through. I clapped my legs around the sorrel's belly and followed.

At the road, Miller let the gray have his head. We cantered past chattering knots of soldiers, past artillery shells nestled in their open boxes like brass eggs. There is a magic to riding, you know, Bobby? An enchantment, even astride that jackrabbit sorrel and that slick little postage stamp of a saddle. When we were clear of the lorries and the road stretched wide and empty, Miller cried out, "Put heels to him!" and we flew into a dead run.

The race was just for the intoxication of it, I guess, for once past the next turn of the road, he halted. He turned to me, and his face was flushed. "Close your eyes, Stanhope. No, don't gape at me so, old man. I'll take your reins."

He kicked the gray close and nearly tore the reins out of my hands. Then he gave me one of his rascally grins. "Close your eyes."

Eyes shut tight, I let him lead me. The thud of steel on clay softened; dry leaves crackled under hoof. The chill of dense shade washed my face. The air went damp and rich with the scent of horse and forest. A crow cawed, startlingly loud. Soon the wind freshened and the dark behind my lids went ruddy and hot sun prickled my skin.

"Look," Miller said.

I opened my eyes. Before me stretched a meadow of crimson, as if God himself had bled there. A breeze sent flower heads nodding. A current shivered through the poppies and blew a confetti cloud of white butterflies upward.

"I thought you should see it," Miller said, "before it is gone."

I dismounted and waded knee-deep into that calm scarlet sea.

His quiet voice came from far behind me. "We are to move

out the day after tomorrow," he said. "I could not let the flowers die unseen."

I turned. Astride his horse and at least twenty feet away, but his stare was as assertive as a hand. "Sir?"

He ducked his head. "Yes. Well. I suppose we should go."

Still, he sat where he was, sat so quiet that it seemed he had given up on breathing. I walked to the sorrel and hesitated. There was no convenient rock wall, no fallen tree trunk. Finally Miller awkwardly, and without meeting my eye, dismounted to give me a leg up. Close as we were—chest to shoulder, my knee planted in his hands—I could feel him tremble. His face was high-colored, his skin so hot that his heat baked right through my trousers. As soon as I was up, he sprang away, clearing his throat.

"Right you are," he said. "Just a bit of sightseeing. Hope you enjoyed it."

He mounted the gray. There we sat, considering each other across a gulf of rank and questions.

Miller's a gentleman, I'll give him that. A poetry lover, as Uncle Cecil would say. All that time, Bobby, he was hoping. And when it came down to it, he was so smooth that he asked and then accepted my rejection without either one of us having to say a word.

Those dark eyes of his went even sadder. "I'd best get Wilson's mount back to him." Suddenly he wheeled the gray and cantered back to camp.

Knowing that he's a light-stepper disgusted and shocked me for all of ten minutes; then I decided, unless he tries proselytizing some, I don't really care. Long before I came, this company set fast as concrete. Everyone else is runoff. There's no sticking place for me, who'll always be a stranger; nor for Miller, who they look down on; nor for LeBlanc, who no one understands. I wish there was some way for me to tell Miller that I need him—not in the way he'd like, but in the simple way humans need each other.

When we got back to the stables, Miller dismounted and handed the gray's reins to a groom. He thanked me coolly for testing his mount; then he walked away, the other officers' eyes following him. At first I thought they knew about his predilections, but his secret's too dark and Miller is too discreet. I was right. When he was out of earshot, I could hear whispers: ". . . right school, but good God, how could they have taken a sheeny," and ". . . whole outfit's rotten with kikes, bad as the Boche army."

Damn those Brit officers. Those soft faces, those softer hands. They remind me of those Harvard Congregationalists. I'd rather kill me some limey officers, frankly, than any poor helpless Germans.

I'll keep this letter until I see you again, because—for poor Captain Miller's sake—I daren't send it through the censors.

I remain yours in outrage, Travis Lee

APRIL 20, FRANCE, ON THE ROAD

Dear Bobby,

Granddaddy de Vrees should have told me about the marching. Understand, Bobby, that to secure some glory you have to get from Point A, where battle isn't, to Point B, where things are going on. I never imagined the tedium.

I'd been off my feed the day before, and achy like I was coming down with an ague. The ague never hit. The next day started off well enough: everybody finally marching to war, each platoon singing, me having to learn the ditties in a hurry: "Oh, Landlord, Have You a Daughter?" and "Mandalay." Then the pack gained some weight, and the straps started to bite into my shoulders, and the hobnail boots, which never fit me worth a damn, rubbed blisters onto my feet.

We marched on and on, not singing anymore. We stopped for lunch, and afterwards, just to break in my boots, we marched some more. Everyone looked tired. One of the battalion's supply wagons lost a wheel, and our company was ordered to stay behind and guard it. The rest of the companies marched on.

It wasn't just the wheel that had gone bad. It was the axle, and it took three hours to mend. We hurried to make up the time. LeBlanc, who isn't a big man to begin with, looked to be collapsing in on himself, pressured by fatigue and fury.

How many picturesque churches can you pass without them looking the same? Miller rode up and down the line of our bent-backed shuffling company, throwing out a sympathetic word here, a joke there—a cutting horse watchful of the herd. He would not meet my eye.

When the sun began to lower, the wheel failed again. We bivouacked that night where the wagon broke down, deep in a dripping forest; and some of us slept in a charcoal shed and some slept in a smokehouse. It rained, and the damp brought the fragrance of long-eaten hams from the smokehouse's walls. I dreamed of food and thought I heard thunder. The next day we found the bridge five miles up had been blasted. Despite our songs, war had gone on and men had died. We passed a dray mare with her two back legs blown off and a mercy bullet between her ears. Then we marched by two Frenchies, one with a splendid handlebar mustache, his eyes glassy with surprise. His horizon-blue uniform was stiff and so maroon with blood that for the life of me, I couldn't tell which part of him had been wounded.

Nobody talked much. We looked over our shoulders for the next several miles. Except for that capricious death, there was no other sign of battle. We stopped to eat in a woody copse by masses of white flowers—so many blossoms that it seemed like we'd stopped in snowdrifts. My stuffy head and aching muscles had turned into a full-fledged cold. I couldn't smell the flowers. I couldn't smell my rations. I sneezed.

Miller put guards at the perimeters, told us to keep our talk down and to set no cookfires. The dappled woods spooked me. I could see the others' eyes dart here and there. My boots had not turned comfortable and the pack was just as heavy; still I was ready to leave that place. The missing bridge took us five hours out of our way.

Poplar-bordered lanes. Churchyards with their dead sleeping under tapestries of pink winecups. Bluebottle flies buzzed us like enemy aeroplanes. By the time the sun sank, I sank, too. I couldn't breathe. My feet hurt.

Lieutenant told me to "Gi' up, mon. Can ye not gi' up?" Me grumbling and pretending not to understand. "Up! We ma' meet w'the battalion," he says.

"Let the Boche shoot me. Save them and me both the trouble of marching."

Little baby-faced Abner Foy laughed. "Captain's sent Sergeant ahead to find us billets, hasn't he. And maybe there's a barn with warm straw waiting, and a farmer's daughter for the cuddling. So off yer bum."

I got up and we went on. Sergeant had found us an abandoned farmhouse, half its roof caved in from a shell. I dropped my pack in the kitchen and lay down on the tiles. Above me, the ceiling gaped open to twilight. That evening when I closed my eyes, I saw Ma's face before me as plain as if she had been standing there. I could smell her, too: that mix of camphor and rosewater soap.

Something punched me in the side.

Miller's toe. "Up! Up, damn you! Get those boots off at once, Private! Sergeant Riddell!" The bellow brought Riddell on the double. "See that this soldier washes his feet and dries them thoroughly. Tomorrow, Private Stanhope, make certain that you put on a pair of clean socks, two pair if need be. If that does not solve your problem, speak to Sergeant Riddell here, and he will arrange for another pair of boots."

There were quick salutes and "Yes, sir"s all around, and then Miller was gone, leaving Riddell looking at me helplessly.

There weren't any goddamn extra boots.

Still, Riddell helped me get my boots and socks off. He clucked at the bleeding and oozing blisters. " 'E's right, the captain is. Ain't a man in this platoon what ain't got sores from double timing, but you takes the prize, Yank. 'Ooever requisitioned these boots for you did you no favor."

He washed my feet and then salved them. I was too tired to eat. Riddell, who knew his way around weeds, went out and picked me some.

"Look what I found, Yank!" Riddell held up fistfuls of yard greens, and he was beaming ear to ear. "Ribwort and agrimony. 'Course you can always find ribwort. No luck to that. But the agrimony's a trick, ain't it."

He wrapped the ribwort around my blisters. For my cold, he made me chew the agrimony stalks. I fell asleep where I was, the bitter taste of that agrimony in my mouth, the night sky above, the murmurs and snores of men all around.

The next day my cold was better, but I couldn't put my boots on. Riddell looked worried.

"Hell," I told him, "I didn't know what a shoe was till I was fifteen. I can go barefoot. Let me go barefoot, all right?"

He stuffed bunches of agrimony into my pack until I ended up looking like a hay wagon. He shook his head. "All right, then. But best you don't let me see you marching wifout your shoes. Mind the captain and Lieutenant don't see you, either."

I tied my laces together and slung the boots over my shoulder. The bare dirt between my toes was a frolic, something like playing hooky. I'd come out the door and was hiding behind Riddell, keeping my head low, when Major Dunn rode up, his ass bouncing in the saddle and him pulling every which way on the reins and yelling, "Damn him for a nag! Whoa! Whoa!" The horse stopped so quick that he nearly sent Dunn over his head, a sight I would have paid American dollars for. And then he wasn't yelling at the horse. He was screaming at Miller.

"Your orders were to meet us at Conty! Did you not understand that? If I give a junior officer some responsibility, I expect in return a bit of self-reliance. Need I wipe your bloody arse for you? Need I? Why, when I arrive at Conty, do I find everyone billeted but you? Colonel Caraway asked, and not very politely, where I had mislaid you. Can you not read a blasted map, Captain?"

Poor Miller, ramrod-straight astride his sorrel gelding, his face as emotionless as an Indian's. Dunn shouting him down in front of his own men; the major's fury accompanied by Miller's soft "Yes, sir"s and "No, sir"s and "Sorry, sir"s.

"Sorry will not do, Captain. 'Sorry' leaves dead men in the field. 'Sorry' leaves battles lost."

"Yes, sir. But the wagon broke down again."

"Damn you! I will not have excuses. You may well have a problem on the road. Many of us do. But you are expected—no, you are required—to carry on. If your wish is to be a British officer, Miller, then kindly begin to act like one."

"Yes, sir. Right you are, sir."

Then those glacial eyes swung around the unit, and Dunn pointed right at me. "Captain! What is that man doing barefooted? Barefooted!" he screamed. "Is that the sort of army you will give us?"

Everybody in the unit was turning. Miller was frowning tight-lipped. And then right quick he was explaining, "An American, sir. From Texas. He was having a spot of trouble with his boots . . ."

Dunn's cheeks went brick-red. "Order him to put on his boots at once! You people may put up with such slovenly habits, but I will not have it."

Quietly and urgently, Miller was saying to me, "Your boots, Private. Please."

"Not *please*!" Dunn shrieked so loud that his mount flinched. "Not 'If you would be so kind'! Order him, Captain. If you cannot control your men, I shall see you stripped of your commission."

I went to it quick as I could, with Miller calling out, "On the double, Private!" By the time I got my boots on, I was fair panting from the pain.

Dunn said, "See that it does not happen again." And then off he rides, one hand on his pommel, the other grasping reins and a handful of horse.

"What an asshole," I said under my breath.

Sergeant Riddell turned, frowning. "None of that," he said, but his lips were trying to curl up at the corners. "Needs a bit of respect. Well, 'e's the major, isn't 'e. Nothing's to be done about it, Yank. You'll have to keep the boots on."

Riddell helped me up; then he walked beside me, toting my rifle. As we marched, he picked weeds from the roadside.

"Meadowsweet," he said, holding up a bunch of white flowers that smelled good as Heaven. "For your grippe, if it comes back. Best thing for fever, meadowsweet. That, or white willow bark. There's them that swears by white willow, but me? I likes the taste of meadowsweet best. Me mum's a healer, ain't she. Got her own medicine garden, like. Got to know me way around plants, I did. Your feet, Yank?"

I had stopped because I couldn't make my feet move anymore. A few of the company had halted to look back. My boots were leaking blood out the laces.

Then LeBlanc was there. "Jesus, Mary, and Joseph. Sit down! Sit for Christ's sake *down*! Take the boots off."

Riddell's voice was cautious. "Orders are—"

"You can shove the goddamned orders up this shitting army's ass!" LeBlanc jerked the bayonet off his rifle. Riddell and the others stepped back, round-eyed.

LeBlanc knelt by me and, gentle-gestured as Miller, pulled the blood-soaked boots and socks from my feet. He used his bayonet to cut holes in the sides of the leather, then handed them back. "Think you can you put them on?"

I managed to lace them. LeBlanc helped me up. My bloody toes stuck out to either side; my torn heels protruded from the backs.

"Take a few steps," LeBlanc said.

The half-boots were as ugly as Aunt Alice, but they felt good. Hearing the slow plod of hoofbeats, I looked up. Captain Miller was contemplating us.

"Well," he said, fighting a smile. "Carry on."

When Miller had ridden out of earshot, LeBlanc said sourly, "Carry on. Jesus. D'ja hear that? Carry the *merde* on. That's the only order they know in this turd of an army." He shoved his bayonet into its housing and marched down the road, never looking back to see if the rest of us were following.

Two

April 25, the trenches

Dear Bobby,

Three days ago we arrived at the place we're supposed to get "hardened." It was late twilight and we were marching in file when Miller and another officer came galloping by, barking, "Off the road. Keep moving."

When the horses had passed and it got quiet again, I could hear it: a low, far-off rumble—as full of threat as a coming Texas thunderstorm.

Riddell raised his head like he was sniffing the wind. "Shelling."

Foy turned, his pallid face a glimmer. "Gor."

"Keep marching," Riddell said.

It was near dark by the time we saw it, the fire through the trees. Lieutenant told us to put our packs down and take a rest. LeBlanc leaned against a tree and took out his smokes. I snuck higher up the hill to watch, and most of the others came up with me. I lay there in the sweet-smelling grass, the earth quivering under me; and every time there was a bright air burst, we made Fourth of July noises.

It's beautiful from a distance, war. Artillery glittered and sparked along the horizon. The strikes struck cloud-high blossoms of fire. Green flares sailed the night like drowsy fireflies.

I heard Abner Foy say, "I wouldn't be afraid, not me."

Then Riddell's laconic "Shit your britches first time in a shelling. Or piss 'em. No shame to it, man. They all do."

Foy again, in his mosquito-thin tenor. "Not me."

Riddell's soft "Well, still. I shit mine, didn't I."

No one spoke after that. From our safe perch, we watched the goings-on. I put my head on my arms and, despite the show, went to sleep. I dreamed you and me were in the house, Bobby. Outside, dark clouds were rolling in and daylight was failing and the afternoon was turning green. The air was hushed, breathless, and as heavy as water. I looked for Ma, running from room to empty room. I couldn't find her. When I turned around, you weren't there, either. There was a cyclone coming.

Love, Travis Lee

APRIL 27, THE TRENCHES

Dear Bobby,

The next day we spent in a real barracks, and that night we marched a long ways across the pockmarked earth—cussing the dark and stumbling—to go down into our first trench.

I knew we'd arrived when a call rang out, "Green troops coming."

The sky was overcast. No starlight from above, no cookfires nor companionable lights from below. Going down in that trench was like walking into my own grave. "Care with the firestep, boys," an unfamiliar voice said.

The trench stank of dead rats and burned charcoal and old cigarettes. I hit bottom and slid in mud. Wet squished into my open shoes. Another step, and I was on the dry plateau of a duckboard. I groped for the nearest wall and found something soft instead.

"Watch the hands, lad," a voice chuckled. "Only me wife has permission to grab that."

I moved away, sliding in mud again, tripping over someone's pack.

"What platoon?" another voice cried out.

Foy's whispered "Fourteenth" struck up an answering chorus of laughter.

"No use being quiet now, is there? And the Boche miles away."

Then from the gloom, an educated voice. An officer's voice. "Fourteenth? You here?"

"Aye, sir. Lieutenant McPhearson here with the Fourteenth."

"Ah. Good, Subaltern. Excellent. Corporal Jeffers will lead you to the front line."

I heard Foy say, startled, "Front?"

Heavy footsteps clattered along the duckboards; and an answer came, too—unexpectedly close. "They gives the posh duty to the new troops, they does. Everyone here, then? Eh? It's Corporal Jeffers asking, so best speak up."

Jeffers was answered by a wary chorus of "Yes, sir"s.

"Follow me, boys. Instead of traveling the overland way, so to speak, we'll be going up the communications trench, 'cause I'm of a mind today to be gentle. If you want to keep 'em on you, duck your heads."

Jeffers lit a lamp, and we fell in more or less behind, went zigzagging down the main trench, then into a slit that was barely coffin-wide. He called back happily, "Is this the platoon with the sheeny company commander and the cowboy and the Canuck?"

There wasn't much sound except for the wet sucking of boots through the mud, no touch except for the cold press of earth. Then I heard Riddell's "Yes. We're that platoon" from behind me.

"Well, best bring your cowboy up. He's to sharpshoot, but he's to harden himself first in the forward sap."

"Not tonight!" Riddell squeezed my shoulder. He leaned forward and whispered in my ear, "Chin up, Stanhope. When you 'as to go, I'll go with you."

Anxiously yours, Travis Lee

APRIL 28, THE FRONT LINE

Dear Bobby,

Jeffers wasn't joshing us. Front line is the posh duty. No shells, just the waiting and the rats and the occasional spat of machine-gun fire. They are so close, Bobby; close enough so that you can smell their cookfires. You can hear orders barked in German and smell the stench of their shit.

The others in the platoon are learning how to mend the barbed wire. Me, I sleep through breakfast and lunch, and as the sun goes down I squeeze myself through a narrow slit in the mud. Ahead is an old shell crater, good enough for listening. All evening Riddell and I sit and listen, Bobby. We speak to each other in whispers. We piss into empty cans.

The elms and the poppies are gone. What's left is a barren countryside that might never have been leaf-gentled. The only thing that moves in No Man's Land are the rats. At night when we stand guard I can hear them skitter and it spooks me. I think they are Boche sneaking up.

When the moon's full I can see the rusted briar patch of the German wire and a marker I make as the Boche forward sap: a tree blasted down to its roots. I hear mutters sometimes in that direction.

The death of the land bothers Riddell. "Me mum says the earth takes care of its own, but see what we done 'ere, Stanhope? And all up and down France the same. I never gave a farthing-sized fart for nothing French, meself. Don't like their food nor their fags nor their liquor. But this fair makes me want to cry. I know me mum would go all over tears, 'ow she loves the plants and all."

"Yeah. They took something pretty and made west Texas out of it," I said.

He shushed me. "Voice down, now. Sometimes you 'ears things."

"I don't understand German."

He shook his head wearily. "Oh, Stanhope, not me, neither."

"I mean I don't understand what they're saying. I could overhear them telling the Kaiser's pecker size, sir, and I wouldn't know what they were saying for shit."

"Oh. Well. That doesn't matter now, does it. Understanding, I mean. I don't mean the size and all." Riddell winked.

"Foreign Office might 'ave themselves a cackle. But it's not the understanding, Stanhope, see? It's the listening."

"Uh-huh."

In the dead of night we drink muddy-tasting chlorinated water from our canteens. We listen. Not fifty yards away, Germans chatter, they laugh, they probably cuss as much as we do. And when the moon sets, it takes with it the silver glimmers on the puddles. It leaves behind a brooding dark. It's then I'm glad that Riddell likes to talk. I'm glad the Boche laugh and fart sometimes. Still, three days listening and all I can tell you is, the Kaiser has a tee-ninsy pecker, Bobby. The size of your little finger. Bank on it. Tell all your friends you heard it straight from the source.

And speaking of little peckers, hear tell that Major Dunn got throwed and broke his leg. Not enough wounding to pull a Blighty and get him home, but it'll lay him up and out of our ways for a while all the same.

Well, the platoon has learned to accept me. I guess I go down like the apple and plum jam and the chlorinated water. Three nights together, I've gotten to know Riddell real well. I respect him. I even love him in a way when we're in the shell hole and dark's fallen all around us. But hours listening to Riddell's mum stories, learning more about weeds than I'd ever care to; three nights of hearing Germans grunt as they shit, and belch as they eat. Light-stepper or not, I wish I had Miller to talk poetry to. Hell, I'd let him put his hand on my leg.

I didn't mean that.

Yours in terrible boredom, Travis Lee

APRIL 29, THE FRONT LINE

Dear Bobby,

Last night Abner Foy woke up screaming. Rats had run over his face. One had bitten him on the cheek and he was bleeding. When I opened my eyes I saw him sitting bolt upright, slapping at himself. Riddell was trying to calm him down.

" 'E's gone now. Look, Foy. Look about, why don't you? See? Little bugger's gone. Everything's fine. I'll make you a sticking plaster of woad an' you'll be right as rain. Have some comfrey in me pack, but best not, seeing as how that's a filthy bite from a filthy creature, and we don't want it to go oozing and green."

Silver-tongued Sergeant Riddell. He set Foy to whimpering again.

The rats are all over the trenches, Bobby. They are born and die behind the wattles. They leave their filth and rotting stench behind.

By the time Foy finally shushed that evening, the rest of us were wide awake. Foy eyed us, one by one. He looked so silly with that steely gaze and that baby face and that weed-mulch plastered on his cheek. "Bullets and shells I can take brave as any. But it's just them rats."

Lieutenant told us, "Settle it doon, now. Gi' ye tae sleep," and we buried ourselves under our blankets. In the light of the candle I watched Foy. He was sitting, rifle in hands, his eyes on the wattle wall. He was still sitting his lonely sentry when sleep took me.

It takes me by surprise now, Bobby. One minute I'm wide-awake, thinking about home, maybe. Reciting Shelley in my head. The next instant I'm sucked into dark. Is this the way dying is to be? Shit. Please don't tell me this stinking hole is a peek into the grave.

While the others were snoring, I dreamed of home. I was somewhere near the Perdenales and the hill country's muscular spring had come. The knolls were a velvet gray-green, the hollows dusty with bluebonnets. Limestone extruded like bones. The dream was so real and the place so damned familiar that it seemed more like a memory.

I was standing, smelling deep of the cedar, when I noticed someone coming down the hill. They were too far away to recognize, too faint to put a name to, but I knew for certain that I was acquainted with this person, Bobby; had known 'em ever since I was a little kid. And as I watched the figure come down past the pecan trees, through lemony sunlight and mottled shade, I realized in a dream-sure way that the person was coming for me. Emotion came on me so strong that even thinking on it now sets me to shivering.

About then Lieutenant snapped me out of sleep with his usual cheery call: "Five o'clock. If ye want yer breakfasts, it'll be oop an' off yer arses!"

Anyway, it was a strange dream, Bobby. One chock full of passion. For the life of me, though, I don't know what passion it was.

Love, Travis Lee

MAY 3, THE FIELD HOSPITAL

Dear Bobby,

Don't fret. I'm better. Just a shrapnel cut on my back, and it's knitting. The fever's gone, and I don't see strange things anymore.

It was the night after Foy's rat, and we were still in the rear trenches. Most of the men were mending socks; and those who knew how to were writing letters home. So quiet a night that if you listened hard, you could hear the first shell coming in. The 8.5 had a soft voice, like an imaginary whisper.

I knew I was hearing true when Corporal Dunleavy cocked his head. "Artillery."

The whisper grew to a howl and Sergeant's eyes went white-rimmed. "Eight five! On us!"

Even inside the dugout, we ducked. At the open door, night thundered. Somewhere down the trench, fire flashed and men cried out.

The Boche had found our range and suddenly the whole world was screaming. Shells pounded the rabbit-hole where we hid. The earth danced. The explosions shook me down to my core and set my bones to jittering. Sergeant was yelling something. In the unsteady light of the candle Danny Boatman sobbed. Huge, hulking Charlie Furbush crouched next to me, his hands plastered to the sides of his head, his eyes squeezed shut and leaking tears.

The shelling went on; as demented as Pa when he was drunk.

You see? It wouldn't stop, Bobby. The shelling just wouldn't stop and the walls kept closing in and I kept seeing the roof collapsing. That's the worst part. I could have stood it if I hadn't thought that any minute the roof would come down. And so when there came a pause in the shelling and Danny Boatman ran through the door, I ran with him.

Lieutenant McPhearson was at my heels, jerking at my bandolier. Outside the dugout the air was sweeter, the sound of the explosions pure, the inferno of the shells as bright as flashing day. McPhearson dragged me to my knees and we knelt together in the firestorm.

"Back in, ye bloody fool!"

"Dugout's collapsing!" I yelled back.

He shook me. Reason dropped into place. My heart was pounding something fierce. My belly was sick with panic. I saw his disappointment and felt a fair bit of shame.

"You'll return to the dugout, Stanhope, or I'll put a bullet in ye meself!" Then the lieutenant was on his feet and scrambling down the trench yelling, "Boatman! I'll have ye oop on charges! Boatman!"

I snuck back to the dugout. No one, not even Riddell, paid any attention to my return. I'd left behind my helmet and gas mask. Outside, shells whistled and screeched. The earth shook. The explosions came fast and furious. The noise above our heads was a solid thing, a ceiling you could reach out and touch.

Soon McPhearson came back, Boatman in tow. I didn't want their company; still McPhearson sat Boatman, my albatross, down by me. Smoot and Dewberry covered their heads with their blankets. Trantham, empty-faced, rocked in a corner.

Sometime during that lunacy, Sergeant made tea. Dunleavy and LeBlanc ate quietly and alone. The shelling let up, the explosions coming farther and farther apart. In the aftermath my ears buzzed something fierce. After a bit I could hear, in the brief lull between shells, nervous coughs and mutters from our platoon, the moans from luckless soldiers, the shouts of passing stretcher bearers. Boatman leaned his head back against the filth-encrusted wattles and closed his eyes.

I listened to the individual strikes, even though I tried my best not to. The whistles get louder and louder until your nuts try to crawl up into your body. Your hair stands on end, Bobby. You're so damned afraid that this one's coming for you.

I'm terrified of dying. I never knew that before. The others are, too. I can see fear in every face—even LeBlanc with his pretense of disdain, even Trantham with his terrible vacancy. There we sit, crowded together in a rat-infested cavity in the earth, and wait. We wait lonely, because nobody wants to admit they're scared.

The shell that hit us was like any other—the whisper, the howl, the skin-crawling anticipation. But when the blast came, the noise was so stunning that my nose gushed blood.

I don't remember much except that the wind planted a hand in my back and shoved me. I remember trying to shout for help and sucking dirt into my mouth, instead.

I swear there wasn't any sensation of traveling from life to unconsciousness nor of going from unconsciousness to home; but that's where I was—on that hill by the Perdenales. And she was there.

I knew her as well as I know you. Maybe somehow even better. Her hair was loose and buttery with sun. Her smile was so sweet that it cut me.

They say that I looked peaceful as they took me away on the stretcher. They say I lay still as they stitched me up, and that I gave them no trouble. I don't remember that; but I remember that the blue of her calico dress matched her eyes.

The dugout they took me to was shelled, too; and for a while it was pretty thick. All I know is, while I stayed on that hill I felt safe; and when I came to a few hours after the shelling had stopped, my ears didn't work anymore and my back hurt and I had started a fever.

I heard they pulled Danny Boatman from under the collapsed wall, but not soon enough. Lieutenant didn't make it, either. When Sergeant Riddell dug McPhearson's body out, word is that he cradled him on his lap and bawled just like a baby.

Next day they moved me. I must have gone a little crazed from the fever, 'cause I could have sworn that I saw Danny Boatman walk through the hospital, up and down the rows. I even tried to call to him, but he paid me no attention. When I told a nurse he was there, they gave me something for the pain.

When I could hear better, Captain Miller came by. He stood tapping his swagger stick on his boot and looking anyplace but at me. "Well, Stanhope," he said. "Well." He stared hard at a table of rolled bandages. "Not quite a Blighty. Up and about soon, eh? And rejoining the old Fourteenth."

"Yes, sir."

The angry slap of stick against his boot. His lips tightened. "Riddell ended up with McPhearson's bloody gramophone, you know. Soldier's last will and testament. One record, and Sergeant must play it. The same blasted Elgar symphony, over and over. Good God, Stanhope. Elgar."

Whack of leather against leather. Blows so violent that they had to have stung. Miller's jaw worked. "Elgar." He shook his head and walked away.

Elgar. Could be worse. When I was in the forward sap, all the Germans listened to was Schubert. Still, I know exactly how Miller feels. Nothing is more stiff-upper-lip and carry-on-boys than Elgar. I bet you LeBlanc hates him like Mary Hell, too.

Tomorrow they're releasing me from the hospital. Five days later we move out, north I hear. Some idiot of an orderly threw out my comfortable boots, thinking they'd got ruined in the explosion.

Never you mind this letter. I'll get over my scared and get on with it. You eventually have to, you know.

Travis Lee

MAY 4, THE FIELD HOSPITAL
Bobby,

Got your excuse for a letter today. Goddamn it, don't you tell me about how she feels sorry for him. Don't you try to tell me how old and helpless he is. More than once I've seen Ma with blood running down her chin, all huddled up by the wood stove, cowering like a whipped hound. Shit. Don't you think she was helpless, too?

If she's contemplating with another part of her anatomy, then you be the one to use your head. I'm warning you and Ma both: You'd best get him out of there. If Pa wants any argument, let the 30.06 do your debating for you. Make sure he understands your meaning, boy, for I've had enough of his bullying ways; and if he's still around the place when I get home, I'll kill him.

Travis Lee

MAY 5, THE FIELD HOSPITAL
Bobby,

I dreamed about Pa last night. We were in the dugout together, just the two of us; and the Boche were shelling. It was a murky place, black except for a single candle. I could just make out his eyes and hands—Pa's worst parts. He was taking off his belt and he was saying in that low dangerous voice of his, " 'Pears you're sassing me, boy. You sassing me?" Me in a gloomy corner of a darkened room; Pa the monster. Above my head bombs were falling; but soft and terrible I could hear Pa hiss: "You sassing me?"

Jesus. Lying here I've had time to ruminate about life, and I understand something about myself—why I took the whip to old man Krause the day he tortured that barn cat of his; even why I came to Europe to fight—I've been trying to slay the monster, Bobby. I can't kill me any goddamned bombs, so I'll just have to kill Pa if I see him. You tell Ma that.

Well, well, well. Of all the people to come visit. A few

minutes ago, LeBlanc was here. He sat down beside the bed, lit himself up a cigarette and then offered me one. We smoked for a while, and when a Belgian nurse told us to put them out, he said, "Up your rosy red ass."

She went away. "Not a nice thing to say to a nun," I told him.

"No one better to say it to, eh? Except maybe it's up her ass with Father O'Shaughnessy. Or maybe Corporal Dunleavy's more his game. Goddamned micks. They'll fuck anything. That's how they take over places. Spread like weeds. Seen it happen, eh? Back home it's got so you can't fart without gassing an Irishman. These bastards here are probably IRA: O'Shaughnessy, every one of them. A little arsenic in your potato soup, Stanhope, just in case the shells don't get you? Think about that. Hey. People are talking about how you and Boatman and McPhearson were the only ones who quit the dugout. It's like the three of you knew something, eh? Trantham's fucked."

LeBlanc's cigarettes are unsmokable—strong and French. "Trantham? Was he hurt, too?"

LeBlanc lit another cigarette off the butt of his first. He didn't offer me another. "Not so's you can see, but next time they pound us, he's going shell-shocked for sure. He crapped his pants and then just sat there in it, even when the shelling was over. Goddamned Dunleavy had to inform him that he was stinking up the dugout with his wet brown *merde*. And you see that look on his face when the eight fives were dropping? Oh, yeah. Soon we'll be seeing that stupid little smile all those poor bastards get, eh?—like their brains just took a Blighty. You ever walk into East-6? That's where they store them. Locked away from the rest of us, so's we don't get ideas on how to duck the war. Assholes."

It's an interesting adventure, talking to LeBlanc. Most times he doesn't say much, but when he does, it's him that does the talking and you that do the listening, except for the detours in his conversation where you're forced into asking questions like: "Assholes? Those shell-shocked folks?"

"Nah. The doctors. They don't think it really happens, you know? Shell shock. Think they're phonies. Sometimes just for the fun of it they'll send one of them back. Saw a man walk out of hospital once, right into the trench and straight over the parapet. There he goes, wandering off across No Man's Land, smiling that shit-eating grin like he was out picking daisies or something, everybody shouting at him to come back and him not listening, until Fritz mowed him down. Cut him in half with a Maxim."

"Damn."

"Damn right. They're all against us. Nice shoes, Stanhope."

"Uh-huh. Somebody throwed my good ones away. You carve me another pair?"

"Just to watch the major's ass pucker." LeBlanc leaned his head back and blew a smoke ring. "I'm ready for a good fuck."

My mind sort of froze on that.

When I didn't take the bait, he asked, "What shape's your *bâton* in, Stanhope? Want a little?"

All of a sudden I was fighting to keep my head above an undertow of questions: Was LeBlanc, like Miller, a poetry-lover? If he wasn't, why the hell had he come by to visit? Just what were we talking about here? He didn't give me any clues, so I said cautiously, "Pecker's just fine, and thank you kindly for asking."

"You and your shrapnel got the company a day's leave. There's a whorehouse in town. If you're up for it, I'll meet you by the YMCA pavilion at sundown."

Oh, Bobby. Up for it? Wound or no, the acreage south of my belt sure is. LeBlanc walked away without saying another word. Now I been lying here thinking about things. And thinking. And thinking. Lord God almighty, Bobby. Real French whores.

I'll finish this letter later. The doctor's coming down the row. I figure he's about to release me, stiff *bâton* and all.

Yours in great anticipation; and I mean what I said about Pa, I really do. Travis Lee.

MAY 7, THE REST AREA

Dear Bobby,

Hide this letter from Ma. Hope you hid the last one as well, or she'll be pressing you to tell her the outcome of my excursion.

The day of the last letter, LeBlanc was waiting for me at the pavilion. We stopped by the blue-light tent to pick up some army-issue rubbers, then we double-timed it—me in the new boots he carved me—all the long miles to town.

The walking was easy, the day overcast and damp. The air smelled of rain and flowers and flourishing late spring. I drank the air and let LeBlanc jabber.

He's an interesting fellow, LeBlanc is. A person of strong opinions. Irish should be occasionally shot, he says, to keep the population down. "Otherwise they'll overrun the countryside like a buncha goddamned rabbits and start one of their shitting famines."

As part of their ordination, Catholic priests' nuts should be surgically removed. "They took an oath, eh? So what's the use to them? Maybe that'll keep their hands out of kids' pants."

"Huh. Seems you know all about this, LeBlanc. You were raised up Catholic?"

Right quick, he says, "Stanhope, fuck you and your goddamned ugly sister."

While we passed a stone wall—one that sprouted some of Riddell's meadowsweet from its crevasses and was polka-dotted with orange lichens—LeBlanc told me that horses should be kept out of war. On that opinion, I agreed.

"I hate to hear them scream," he told me. "I hate the way they keep trying to run when their legs are broken in two and flopping or when their guts are dangling out. Jesus, Mary, and Joseph. I've heard them cry, eh? They cry like a baby or something. Times I've sat right down and cried with them."

"I don't have a sister," I told him.

He said, "Shithead. Say, you're a country boy. You ever have a horse?"

"Lord knows I rode and broke enough."

"No, asshole. I mean did *you* ever have one? Your own horse."

I shrugged. "Had a meaner-than-cat-dirt Shetland pony when I was too young to know any better. Throwed me once, and then kicked me for good measure. When I got up, damned if he didn't kick me down again. Then I got me a real sweet little quarter horse dun mare. Gave her to my brother when I left for school. He rides her once in a while, just to keep her gentle."

"Horses are better than we are," he says.

I think about it a while. I consider the Shetland pony. I think about my little mare. I say, "I know."

Well, Bobby, it took us a whole hour of walking to get to that one-bar, two-whore town. The line into the whorehouse was three blocks long. Three companies including my own were there. From his station at the end of the line, Rudolph Pickering watched LeBlanc and me walk up.

"Whores any good?" LeBlanc asked.

Pickering took a swig out of his wine bottle. "Pranging tarts is always good. A religious experience," he said. "How's the wound, Yank?"

One place ahead of Pickering, Marrs turned around. "Don't tell no one you seen me, now. I got me a nice piece at home. Pretty as a rose and a churchgoer. You, Yank? You got yourself something like Miss Lillie Langtry? Have some brandy. Makes the waiting easier."

I took the bottle. "Hear tell she fucks around."

Marrs's eyes widened.

"Miss Lillie Langtry," I explained to his evident relief. It appeared to me that Pickering and Marrs had been hitting the bottle pretty good.

"So. The whores worth the wait?" LeBlanc asked.

Pickering abruptly shrieked, "Your piece is a churchgoer, is she, Marrs? My cock's Church of England."

Several men up, someone started to tell a joke, his voice rising over the general mumble: "That reminds me! So . . . so . . . Oh, yes. I have it now. A priest goes into confession with a parrot on his shoulder, and the penitent says . . ."

Loud cries of "Heard it!" and "Oh, bugger off! Bad joke from the start."

"I haven't heard it," I said, but no one was paying attention.

Three more men joined the line. LeBlanc stuck his hands in his pockets and bounced on his toes. "Take shitting hours, this."

The new men, a trio from another company, had brought armfuls of bread and cheese. I asked them if they knew the joke about the priest and the parrot. They said they didn't. They passed food around. Pickering knocked Marrs over the head with a baguette. Marrs dropped theatrically to his ass.

"Goddamned bunch of immature kids," LeBlanc said. "Hey, Stanhope. I'm going to find better pickings. How's about you?"

I expected resentment from him when I said, "I'll stay. I've a mind to hear that parrot story," but he simply shrugged and walked off.

Marrs fell twice trying to get up. Finally, he gave up and sat there on the cobbles, his mouth open. "Fascinating boots, Yank," he mumbled just before he passed clean out.

By the time I was halfway up the stairs, Pickering and I had finished his bottle. I recall things in flashes: someone yelling, "Queue up, then! Queue up!" and me shouting, "Lord God almighty! Will somebody just for shit's sake tell me that story about the parrot?" Then me feeling sick at my stomach and trying to find a bathroom. Pickering pulling me back to the stairs.

"Got to poke the tarts, Yank," he said. "Otherwise, what good is it?"

"What good is it?" I screeched with ill-conceived and fathomless delight. I turned to the puzzled men behind me. "What the hell good is it?"

I think I sort of passed out. In dogged allegiance to the British idea of "queue," the men behind me grabbed me by my belt and dragged me up the stairs.

When I came to again, Pickering was coming out of a door,

buttoning his pants. He grasped me under the arms and hauled me up. I couldn't find my direction for shit.

"There, Yank," he was saying. "No, no. Not that way. Girl's in there."

I ran into the jamb and banged my nose. Blood gushed. Seemed like I'd been having a time with my nose lately.

"Blighty!" someone laughed.

Pickering's hands on my shoulders, me walking into the shadowed room. The smells of old, cheap perfume and sweat and sex. There she was, Bobby, lying all spread out. Those thighs of hers just went on and on; pale and lumpy and huge, like cheap cotton-wad mattresses. She had a pretty pink ribbon tied around her throat.

I hollered out, "Heifer!"

The whore seemed confused. Pickering kept asking, "What? What is it you're trying to tell me, Yank?"

"Heifer with a ribbon!"

"Can't get your pants down, then, Stanhope? It's a crown in the box there, chap. Five shillings, or she won't go."

The men behind me asking, "What's it? Can't get his blue light on? Be a chum, man, and put it on for him."

Next thing I know, I woke up thinking that I was being smothered. My face was wedged in the Valley of the Shadow between the whore's sour, marshmallow breasts. My pants were down around my ankles, and I was positioned between those thighs, my pecker aimed more or less in the right direction.

Someone was dragging me off her; me all the time asking, "I come yet? Hey. Did I come?"

"You've had time enough for three men, mate. It's off with you," a new and very sober voice told me. Then I was rolling down the steps, falling easy and happy and loose-limbed. I ended up at the bottom, my face resting on top of a boot.

"I come yet?" I asked.

The line moved slowly, inexorably. The boot went away. My head dropped to the cobbles. I found myself staring down the sidewalk to the door of the bar where Captain Miller and one of his subalterns were walking out.

Miller came and stood looking down at me. "Stanhope? Your nose is bloodied. Your privates are showing."

Drunk, but it did not miss my notice that Miller was scrutinizing my pecker. I lunged up and made it all the way to my knees. The army-issue rubber was dangling, a telltale wad weighing its end. I pulled my pants to my waist.

"And I do believe you're quite drunk."

"Sir."

"I say, Stanhope! Have you been with a strumpet?"

"Oh, sir." Guilt made me heartsick. In my stupor, I figured that finding me whoring had irredeemably hurt his feelings. "Shit. I'm sorry, sir. It's not like it's anything pers—"

The swagger stick struck fast as a rattler. It caught me at the base of the throat. Not to hurt, but to stop words.

His voice was even. "That will do." And then he called back to the bar, "Sergeant Riddell! I've a little lost lamb for you!"

Riddell came out, clucking worriedly. Next thing I remember was sitting with Riddell in the barracks. Except for a pot of brewing tea, we were alone. He was playing McPhearson's gramophone and waxing poetical about Elgar.

" 'E's a beacon of truth, ain't 'e? Fair knows the heart of it. Pluck and valor and all that. Like Kipling and that poem of 'is. What is it, now?"

I shook my head, and the movement nearly toppled me. My hangover headache had started. "Dunno."

" 'Course you do, you all the time reading your poems. A real scholar, like. You must know fair everything." He cast a soulful look at the ceiling. " 'Into the valley of death rode the six hundred.' That one. What's it called, now?"

My lips didn't move too well. "Dunno."

"Still, makes it all worth it, don't you think? I mean about dying and all. 'Spite of what some says. If you can just die for something decent and upstanding. That's what it's all about, innit?"

God. Not the usual Brit quirk of speech, but a true question. And what desperation it held. When I looked up, Riddell was crying. I opened my mouth intending to say something comforting, but fell asleep instead. I never heard the rest of the parrot story.

Travis Lee

MAY 8, THE REST AREA

Dear Bobby,

Strange what you told me. It's hard imagining those sharp eyes of Pa's going blind. In his glory days he could flat pick out sin, Bobby. Sins of the flesh and sins of the mind. "You're thinking up deviltry, boy," he'd tell me. Omniscient, omnipresent. All of creation hung on his mood. When Pastor Lon preached about God's terrible ire, it was Pa's scowl I pictured. I figure if God has each hair of our head numbered, He's nothing we can hide from. And for me, God was always Pa.

God scared me a lot in those days. They say none of us can know the end, but I used to I think that if Hell existed I wouldn't get flames: I'd spend eternity hiding inside Ma's old dark wardrobe, trapped with the stink of mothballs and nervous sweat.

So I got to figure your letter is a lie, Bobby. Pa can't be going blind from the moonshine. It would break every universal law. You write to tell me he's got whupped in bars so often that he's crippled up now. Don't let him fool you. One day he'll stop limping and his eyes will go keen. He'll stand ramrod-straight and he'll take off his belt. He always wears a big buckle—you ever notice?—the better to bruise with.

I took a walk today past the hospital and saw the shell-shocked: cots of staring men, fingers plucking, always plucking at their lips, all with dazed smiles—men stricken stupid by fear. The company priest, O'Shaughnessy, was with them. He was sitting on a cot, holding a man's hand. Not talking. Not preaching. Just touching. It was nice, in a way. When he got up, he saw me standing there.

His voice was quiet, not like Pastor Lon's, who seems to be always working on his Sunday delivery. "Do you have need of me, my son?"

"Not a Catholic, sir."

"Well, I'll be here for more than Catholics now, won't I. You're the Yank, I take it."

"Yes, sir."

We stood close, there in the ward of the lost. The barracks was pungent with the smells of carbolic and rubbing alcohol, but not a wound in sight. O'Shaughnessy had shucked his uniform for a long black papist dress and purple silk scarf. He was wearing a comfortable smile. "Calling me 'sir' makes me feel more the officer. I'd prefer 'Father.' "

"Can't call you that," I told him. "You got another choice?"

He took my arm and gently steered me outside. The sunlight was dazzling. Birds chattered in the gathered trees. A clear sky, but the wind smelled of coming rain.

The fresh breeze teased the hem of O'Shaughnessy's skirt, toyed with the ends of his purple scarf. "Thomas, then, if you've a mind. Some Protestants have a problem with the 'Father,' and calling me by my first name is no offense, to be sure. What faith are you?"

"Not much, sir. Sorry. Reverend Tom."

"Why the lack of faith . . . ah, Private Stanhope, isn't it?"

"Travis Lee."

His eyebrows rose. "You were the one injured. And those to either side of you killed. Was that not enough proof of God for you, then?"

"He's a son of a bitch for irony, ain't He, pastor?"

"Pardon?"

"God. Like those men in there, smiling so ferocious that you'd think they feel joy, but the joy they feel hurts like holy hell. Any minute that joy's going to come exploding out, and when it does, it'll kill them."

A puffball cloud came over: flawless white at its top, a soft rabbit-gray at its bottom.

"Did you ever stop and think, my son, that because these men felt so much fear, God took them to someplace kinder?"

"No, sir," I said. "I don't."

O'Shaughnessy has an intensity to him that's disturbing.

Only the rumble of thunder—softer than any artillery—brought his head up and took his eyes off me. He squinted at the sky. "Great good heavens. What time is it getting to be? Nearly three," he said, checking his watch. "Dear, dear. I'm due to meet with Colonel Caraway, and he's not one for waiting. Travis, is it? We must talk again sometime." He had a nice handshake—not the Baptist preacher pump I'm used to.

"Don't want to be prayed over, Pastor. I've been prayed over before, and it never took," I told him, and that's about the truth of it.

Someplace kinder. That only happened once. And it wasn't God I was with, but a calico-clad girl. All the times I hid as a boy knowing Pa was going to come in after, all the times I listened to Ma beg him to leave her be—God never took me away, Bobby, and I asked Him lots of times.

Early evening I was sitting enjoying a smoke when I saw Miller walking with O'Shaughnessy. Their heads were together and they were speaking quiet—the pastor with his head bent, like he was listening to sin.

LeBlanc sat down on the steps beside me. "Look at 'em. Captain better keep his pants buttoned, eh?"

That brought me bolt upright in a hurry. What LeBlanc said next eased the startlement out of my spine. "You can't trust micks. O'Shaughnessy'll go hunting for some balls to play with."

Above us, clouds had gathered, and the late afternoon was fast becoming night. A damp breeze misted my face. Cool for nearly summer. Sweet weather, still I knew a storm was coming. "You believe in God, LeBlanc?"

"I believe in a good fuck," he said. Then he said, "I believe in horses."

I watched Miller and O'Shaughnessy, shoulders touching, fade into the gloom. What were they talking about so seriously? Not God, surely. Why, God isn't a serious thing at all.

Next morning all of us would move out, agnostics and believers together. I said, "I believe in horses, too."

Travis Lee

MAY 9, ON THE ROAD

Dear Bobby,

We made poor time to the billeting area, marching in a driving thunderstorm, pelted by bullets of rain. Wind bent the poplars this way and that. My wet pack weighed me down. Waiting for Miller and O'Shaughnessy and the subalterns at the end of the march was a warm farmhouse occupied by a cordial-looking farm family. For the other two hundred and forty of us there was a leaking stone barn and a hayrick—no place to build a fire without unintentionally barbecuing some milk cows.

We cleared a spot and heated a Tommy cooker, for all the good that did the cold tea. Sergeant sent Smoot and Dedoes to the field kitchen's tent. They brought us back dixie cans of bully beef and hard biscuits, and not near enough of that.

When we griped about the food, Smoot chortled, "It's the motto, ain't it? Eat Less to Save Shitting. Get it? Eat Less to Shave Sitting," and then he'd howl so with laughter that I knew he'd been in the rum ration.

I chipped at my biscuit with my bayonet. Foy, disgruntled, was all for stealing and eating a chicken. He would have, too, except that Riddell got wind of it. He grabbed Foy by the scruff of his neck and bellowed, "Thieving, is it? I'll have no thieving 'ere! You'll do nothing in this platoon but that you'd do for God and King."

By the time Riddell was finished dressing him down, Foy was pale and shaking. LeBlanc sidled up to me. "Riddell took McPhearson's shouting place, you notice? Wants Miller to name him lieutenant, I figure. McPhearson's ass always puckered for God and country, too. Say. I heard we were going to get a green lieutenant, but a whizzbang landed dead in his lap, so to speak. Platoon's screwed. Speaking of which, your whore any good the other night?"

"Not as I recall. Your pecker find a resting place, LeBlanc?"

He shrugged. I pounded the biscuit until a piece broke off. I put the bread chip into my mouth and sucked a little flavor from it. Outside, the rain went on and on. Pickering found himself a barn cat to play with and laughed when it turned up its nose at his bully beef. The air smelled of cows and mildew. Through the chilly blue dusk I could see the welcome glow of the farmhouse windows. I wondered how Miller was faring, and if he had bread and cheese and wine, and if he was enjoying the company.

Late spring, but it was cold in that barn. I hiked my coat about my shoulders and had started writing you this letter when LeBlanc leaned over. "Hey. You're always writing to people. What is it with you, Stanhope? You got some pussy waiting?"

"Not unless my brother's changed in new and interesting ways. Anybody at home for you?"

"Nah. All dead and buried. But that's the secret to life, you know—dying. Jesus and Mary. Just look around at the idiots here, Stanhope. They really think that one day the army'll let 'em go home. You and me, we never had any illusions, did we?"

I don't know, Bobby. I break off pieces of life and suck what flavor I can: the memory of Ma's drop biscuits, the sheen of my mare's hide, delicate-hued as a doe's. The tastes of chili and cornbread. The hot straw smell of high summer.

Just a fool, I guess. Travis Lee.

MAY 11, ON THE ROAD

Dear Bobby,

When we left the barn there was sunlight and mud; and as we went, we tiptoed as careful as we could through the farmer's kale field. The 10th Platoon started up a song that Miller soon shushed, not from critical sensibility but from caution. We passed signs of battle: a row of saplings that had been mowed down like the troops at Shiloh. Their stumps were shattered but still standing—their fallen branches like surrendering arms.

We stopped for lunch in a meadow embellished with grassy

shell holes and cheerful yellow flowers. While we lounged, one of our aeroplanes buzzed us and everyone waved. The pilot waved back before flying on. I lay back on the damp grass and thought of how free I could be sailing through that silence of air. I don't know, Bobby. Is it better to go out and meet death head-on, or wait for it to come in and get you? Maybe I should have given myself the choice and studied flying. That pilot might have been an American himself; and nothing special, just any farm boy from Ohio, any city kid from New York.

A shadow moved between me and the sun. From a height, a round face looked down. "Sentimental me, but I can't help thinking that aeroplane pilots are closer to Heaven," O'Shaughnessy said. "And that to gather that man to His bosom, God need only reach out His hand."

From the grass next to me came LeBlanc's acid "Crashed and buried, though, eh? In the end it's the goddamned ground that gets 'em."

I suppose LeBlanc was hoping for an argument. O'Shaughnessy ambled away. Next thing I knew, Riddell was scowling at the both of us. "It's a smart mouf on the pair of you."

"He did it," I said right quick.

LeBlanc elbowed me.

Riddell *tsked* and shook his head. "And you a good Catholic lad, too. Sister a nun and all. Well, me mum raised me Church of England, didn't she. But I've noticed it's not our C. of E. chaplain what goes out to comfort the wounded with the bullets whizzing and the shells flying. It's that papist. And for all his idol-worshipping and Mary silliness, well, in the end it's 'im what has the pluck. So watch what you say, lads, or you'll have my boot up your bums."

When Sergeant walked away, I told LeBlanc, "I thought your family was all dead."

LeBlanc sat up. He tore off a stem of pasture grass and stuck the end in his mouth. I asked him, "Well, are they?" but he got to his feet, grabbed his pack, and wandered off to where the rest of the platoon were gathering.

That night we bivouacked in an abandoned chateau, its walls untouched by war, its interior stripped of furniture and paintings, its owners months or years gone. Outside was an herb garden, wild and overgrown. All during that long afternoon Riddell wandered, beaming, through its scented tangles. Later, I saw Miller and O'Shaughnessy seated in the freckled shade of a garden bench, deep in conversation.

"There goes an interesting bit of work, Father," Miller said as I passed. "A cowboy and literary scholar."

I turned around. They were eyeing me.

"Most of the lads will be getting off their feet now, won't they, Travis, me boy? After the long march, I mean."

"Well, Father, I do believe Stanhope's enjoying a bit of sightseeing. He likes sightseeing, don't you, Stanhope? France is new to him, you see. And if you will take care to notice the boots . . ."

"Ah! And what fine boots they are."

"Dislikes shoes intensely. That's because he's part wild Indian. Stanhope! Recite us a bit of poetry. I'll start one for you, shall I? 'O wild West Wind, thou breath of Autumn's being . . .' "

I had to take that shit from the Harvard Congregationalists, but I wouldn't take it from him. Heat rose in my face. Before my rage turned billy hell loose, I stalked away. I could hear them laughing all the way to the house.

Just before dark we heard shelling, muffled and far away. I thought about the farm family of the night before: craters marring the familiar places where war had brushed past. I spent the night in a grand ballroom that smelled of nothing but dust. In the dark our lowered voices echoed along the arched and painted ceiling. I wondered where the wealthy family had gone, and if it was hard to go so completely from a place that you leave nothing, not even scent, behind.

The house was too big for me: wide open, with no crannies to hide in. I don't know, maybe I got too familiar with dark, tight places to ever make much of a pilot.

I went to sleep soothed by the murmurs of the platoon and the low booms of distant shelling. I dreamed about a graveyard, terraced and old, with peeling whitewashed steps running up and down. Low plaster walls outlined the graves, while at their heads sat attentive marble angels. Cypress stood quiet vigil at the borders: candles with melancholy green flames. Some of the graves were mounded with paper lilies, Bobby, and some had roofs of glass; and down in those beds little girls in frilly white dresses slept, encircled by dusty flowers.

It was peaceful. I fell asleep mad at Miller, but woke up not caring a bit, for those graves were soft and deep, perfect little hidey-holes; and the graveyard was so quiet, seemed like nothing could go stalking there.

Does the earth always get you? Maybe, if you end up in a graveyard like that, even falling out of the sky to reach it might not be so bad.

Love, Travis Lee

MAY 15, STILL ON THE ROAD.

Dear Bobby,

It's getting worse. Can't tell you all of it. Miller's under pressure from high up. Yesterday he rode by and I caught him eyeing me. His position here is shaky, and he probably figures I can't be trusted to keep his secret. Shit. Me telling what I know. Wouldn't *that* bring him down.

Two days ago he sent Marrs and me out to forage for water, and we found a quaint pond with swans and then we found some picturesque Boche. They'd broken the line to the south, and Miller had sent us down to meet them.

The incursion was only about ten men or so. Marrs got a bullet in the butt, which sounds a lot funnier than it looks. We scrambled up the bank of the pond, swans flapping and honking. We ran, him bleeding down his leg. We never fired back a shot.

Why is it all of a sudden that I scare Miller? Does he feel he has to shut me up? I need to tell somebody, and I hear what's said in confession can't be repeated. Still, would that really be smart? All I know is, Bobby, I can't trust Miller's orders anymore.

Travis Lee

SUMMER 1916

THREE

JUNE 18, FLANDERS, THE RESERVE TRENCHES

Dear Bobby,

Sorry I haven't written, but the army's kept me busy. Three days up, three days back, three days in reserve. When I'm "up," my job is to run along the front-line trench, jumping on the firestep and looking for targets. The other sharpshooters need a man to compute range and bearing. Me, I always find my target, and I find it alone.

See, Bobby, the Boche stick their heads above the parapet once in a while. Some have to, for standing sentry or fixing sandbags obliges them. Some get lazy and just plain forget that I'm there, or forget where the parapet ends. Riddell keeps bets on how many I'll take down that day. When the boys in the company win, they give me spoonfuls of their jam or stuff their folks sent from home. I finagled myself in with Dewberry, our rumwallah, so everybody can bet with their issue jiggers, too. The work's not bad, really. The Boche fall clean and sudden, just like bottle targets at a fair.

The bad part comes on the third day when they pull us back. The rear trenches are sons of bitches, the dugouts cramped and wet and leaking. The walls are sandbagged mud. They shell us nearly every night. All that stands between us and the explosions is a slab roof "elephant" of poor-fitting iron.

The first night I was there I was picking lice and listening to the whizzbangs when from behind me came a ringing uproar loud as all of Judgment Day. I jumped up so fast, I knocked my head against a bunk.

Sergeant calmed me. "Well, 'course it's loud, lad. It's our own artillery, ain't it."

Our own artillery. Good. They're giving some of the same back, like I give bullets. Still, I get tired of the noise. Trantham must have, too. Last week we were in the front trenches, mind, just the front trenches, when we heard the Boche start up their big guns; and even though everyone knew they were aiming for the rear, Trantham went running out of the dugout, up the ladder, and straight into our own wire. I don't know where he thought he was running to, but that's where the Boche sniper got him. You couldn't expect us to go out and fetch him down, so Trantham hung like a piece of windblown trash on a fence. Flies landed. It rained and washed the blood and drove some of the flies away. It rained harder, and we went into the dugout and left him dangling. When night fell, Marrs and Smoot cut him down.

Later I thought that I caught glimpses of him on the wire, hanging skin-tattered, the way dead cows look if you leave them awhile. Since then, I've dreamed of the pretty graveyard with the dusty paper flowers and the rain-stained angels. From beyond the cypress I hear a voice calling for help. It sounds like the voice might be Trantham's.

Lucky I don't dream of everyone. We've lost eighteen out of our company; but except for Trantham our platoon is more or less intact. We had us a new lieutenant for about a week. Forget his name now. A Boche sniper took him with a head shot. It's the damned scopes they have, Bobby. Any asshole could shoot with a scope. I told Riddell to get me one, and then I'd show those Boche. Shit. I could take the Kaiser from here.

You never told me if you got Pa to leave. Is he needing a white cane and a dog yet? You know what I've a hankering for is some of Ma's molasses cookies. You never send me anything, Bobby. Why is that? Must be because you're a no-account little son of a bitch. Why don't you send me something? I'm hungry all the time. The others get packages from home. It's the only thing we have to look forward to;

It was slow going, but I reached eighty-six when he told me to stop. Then we stood around and waited a while.

"Sir?" asked Dunleavy.

Miller said, "That will be all. Harter? Dismissed." The batman put down his mending, got up, and followed Dunleavy through the door, closing it quietly behind him.

Miller never took his eyes off me. "You are skirting the edge of drunkenness. Next time I might have you shot."

"Sir."

"At ease. You're an interesting problem, Stanhope. I did not give you permission to sit."

My leg ached something fierce from where Dunleavy had thrown me down. "Yes, sir."

"You are perhaps the most amusing person I've ever known. And your cloddishness does not serve to completely disguise your intelligence."

"Thank you, sir." The roses bothered me—they were a faded dusty color, as if the flowers had been too long away from sun.

"It was not meant by way of compliment, Private. I intended to point out that you are smart and perceptive; and therefore I believe that you will take this suggestion in the manner in which it is meant: Do not spend so much of your free time around Private LeBlanc. He is a bad influence. I see that surprises you."

It shocked holy hell out of me. "Sir. Can I speak frankly, sir?"

"I was under the assumption that this is a friendly talk, Stanhope. Not quite a dressing-down."

The dugout smelled of Earl Grey tea. A kettle sat on his primus stove, a plate of sugar cookies by it. If it was a friendly conversation, he would have asked me if I wanted a cuppa and a biscuit. I could near taste those cookies of his, Bobby. Sugar glistened like ice across their tops. They were yellow with butter, the way Ma likes to make them. I imagined my teeth sinking into the soft dough, crunching through that hard sweetness.

"So what is it, Stanhope? I'm attentively waiting."

"Who am I supposed to talk with, sir? I mean, if it's not LeBlanc, who else?"

"Um. Odd. I was not under the impression that LeBlanc was acquainted with the English Romantic poets. Is he?"

"No, sir."

"Then what is his attraction for you?"

"Well, sir, he's funny."

"Funny."

Miller saw everything. Hadn't he seen the humor in LeBlanc? "That boy cusses up a storm, sir. And he'll flat say anything that comes into his head."

"I see." Those watchful eyes. Not like Pa's, but something in them scared me. Abruptly he said, "Sit down."

My leg gave out. I aimed for the chair and collapsed, leaving Miller shaking his head and smiling. Well, I amused him.

"Stanhope? I will tell you something in confidence. LeBlanc did not join the Canadian forces willingly. He was running from a spot of trouble. No. Don't ask. I will give no details. But other than his brush with the law, I also find him—as did his fellow Canadians—insolent and surly to the point of boorishness. He does not follow orders and he fails miserably to get along well with others. He is an excellent killing soldier, but a poor excuse for a man. You are not. I need your cooperation, Stanhope. You would do me the favor, please, of helping your platoon run smoothly."

"If you need me so bad," I asked, "then why the hell did you try to kill me?"

Not as much guilt as I'd hoped for. The skin between his eyebrows creased. "What are you talking about?"

"That time you sent Marrs and me for water, sir, and the Boche were waiting, and Marrs got shot in the butt. You had to have known they would be there."

"Is that what you've thought? Good Lord. I . . . Why would I take it in my mind to kill you?"

"You'd know best, sir."

He sat back in his chair and regarded me, perplexed, like

my face had just sprouted a hairy ass. Finally he said, "You are the best sharpshooter in the battalion. Because of you, my company totals are extraordinarily high."

"Yes, sir. I'd heard that."

"So how did you come by your odd conclusion?"

"Somebody in Ninth Platoon told Dewberry who told Thweat who told Smoot that you'd gotten an updated message about enemy positions, sir."

There was a pencil on his desk. He picked it up and toyed with it a while. "Do you know what I am, Stanhope?"

And so I said, "Sir, I'm real glad you brought that up. This ought to be right out on the table, far as I'm concerned. It don't matter to me one way or t'other, and I want you to believe that, sir, I really do. Also, I want you to know I have never once spoke about you to nobody. Way I feel, it just ain't nobody's business. I considered at the time that you were a real gentleman about it, and didn't push or nothing. And you don't go flaunting it, not like some I've seen. I like you. I really do, and predilections aside, I think we ought to get together more. Not suggesting we . . . but, hell, a good conversation about literature every once in a while wouldn't hurt nothing, right?"

The pencil tapped the desk firmly. Once. Twice. "I am a Jew."

The roses on the wall were dusty, like the flowers in the little girls' graves. A Jew. Simple short words; still, I couldn't quite understand what he was telling me.

"And as a Jew, Stanhope, I am disliked and distrusted by many of the other officers. It is more difficult for a Jew, you understand, to establish an army career, as I fully intend to do. I will succeed here, Stanhope. Despite them. Despite you. Despite Private Pierre LeBlanc. I would prefer, however, if I had your good will."

I nodded. "Sir."

"Needn't be so lackluster about it."

"Sorry, sir. It's just . . ."

"Well, right you are. All settled." He got up. I did, too.

"Do take a biscuit with you, Stanhope. My mother sends them." When I bent to select one, he said softly, "A long way, America. Difficult to mail things, without them going bad."

The compassion in his voice. It surprised the hell out of me. And because it was so unexpected, it was needle-sharp with hurt, too. Tears came. I didn't dare straighten up.

"I will give you an order that you may not care for."

Gaze still on the cookies, I said, "Sir?"

"I wish you to counsel with Father O'Shaughnessy."

I blinked away the last of the wet and turned, my cookie fast in my hand. "I'm not a papist, sir."

"Neither am I, but I'm not thoroughly convinced that O'Shaughnessy is quite the good little Catholic, either."

The cookie was damned tasty. I'm to meet with O'Shaughnessy day after tomorrow. Confession is sacred, Miller assures me; but what does he want me to say? Should I confess how I lie in my cot and think about him? Not the way you're thinking, nor the way he'd like; but just wondering what he's doing, if he's reading or maybe what he's eating. Oh, shit. That doesn't sound like something a normal man would do. I've never had a problem. Ask around, Bobby. Near every lady in town—married or single—could tell you that. Still, do you think there's something about myself I haven't learned? I hope to God not.

Considering everything I've said here, I believe this is a letter I'll hold onto until we see each other face-to-face.

Travis Lee

JUNE 23, FLANDERS, THE REST AREA

Dear Bobby,

A comfortable cot, a tent over my head, but still last night Trantham walked my favorite graveyard. At least I think I heard his voice. I yelled back, loud as I could, "Couldn't expect us to go get you!" but he kept calling, calling, and I don't know if he was calling for me, or for his ma, or for somebody just to for Christ's sake go out and take him down off that barbed wire. He sounded so lost, and the dark by the cypress is so deep, like the shade in the thicket where I used to take Imogene Blaylock so I could sweet-talk the drawers off her; a place so secretive that you felt you could hide from God.

It was in the safe, bright morning of the reserve area when I asked O'Shaughnessy about my ruminations; and I was pure scandalized when, instead of answering, he took a cigarette out of his tunic pocket and lit up. He offered me one. They were expensive English smokes, smoother than the half-manure ones I'd gotten used to. The damned cigarette was so good that we just walked and smoked for a while.

It was leafy summer in the reserve area, with everything that had been budding a month earlier in full flower now. Nature was pushy and prosperous. Larks circled, singing up the sun. My counseling time with O'Shaughnessy had got me out of a session of rifle cleaning and enforced sock mending. Having some time to myself without shells and bullets or busy work was pure glory.

"Can one hide from God, I wonder," O'Shaghnessy said. We passed under an ash's cooling splash of shade. "Or does He come in to gather you up?"

I thought of Pa and got a chill up my spine for my trouble.

He must have caught sight of that. Come to find, nothing misses O'Shaughnessy's eye, like nothing much misses Miller's. "That disturbs you, then? The persistence of salvation?"

"Just that you ought to be able to hide somewhere, Reverend."

"Ah. Ought one? And would you hide from forgiveness or from damnation? What terrible sins are you guilty of, my lad?"

"Not *my* goddamned sins," I said. It's tough when you get took out from your hidey-hole; but maybe it's worse to be lost in the place Trantham is. "I dream sometimes about Tratham, Reverend."

We passed a hedgerow where a troupe of acrobat stalks balanced flower heads like white plates.

"I seen Boatman once, too."

"Do you think it's ghosties you're catching sight of?"

Trantham's lost-sounding call.

"No shame nor terrors in it. I've seen them meself, lad. Ah! And what a reaction to confession! Can an Irishman not believe in ghosties?"

"You can, I guess. I don't know if I want any truck with them."

To one side, a velvet green pasture; to the other, a sleepy stagnant-looking bayou, the kind you'd go catfishing in. I wondered if they had channel cats, and then for a minute I imagined I could see old Charlie Whalen with one of his cane poles and that blue tick hound dog of his, and I got to missing home so bad that it felt like memory was burning me inside-out. I wanted to see a friendly black face, Bobby. I wanted to hear the music of Charlie's kids' laughter. It ain't natural for a Texan to go off living someplace without coloreds and tortillas, catfish and tamales and cane poles.

"Travis. What is it you're afraid of?"

"I'm in a damned war, sir. Jesus God almighty. Isn't that enough? And, look. Thanks for getting me out of cleaning duty, but with all due respect, don't go pretending there's something between us just to get up next to me. I don't plan to tell you much of nothing. Next thing I know, you and Captain Miller would be making more fun."

He looked utterly stricken. "Ah, lad. Was it our laughing at your shoes, then?"

There were spotted milk cows in the pasture and a calf with buds for horns. I thought of the innocence of white-faced Herefords; the rambunctiousness of Ma's fancy goats.

"Come now. I'll be giving you my sincere apology. *Mea culpa*. There. Is that enough? Now I've a mind for a bit of conversation, Travis, and Captain says you're quite the philosopher. Would he be lying, then?"

"Look. I don't know."

He whispered sadly, "Whose sin is it, Travis? What terrible thing are you hiding from?"

I was anxious all of a sudden; memory itching at me bad. "I don't know."

I started back fast.

Behind me came O'Shaughnessy's voice. "The first time I was in a gassing, I nearly took my mask off, for I saw ghosties: German and English and French. Oh, but there's a great many ghosties here."

His voice was getting fainter all the time; still, what he said sent a shiver of cold right through me. I stared hard at the dead calm surface of the bayou where no fish jumped, no dragonfly hovered.

"Travis!"

I didn't stop. I couldn't.

"Tell me the sin, Travis, for I fear you'll be seeing the ghosties, too!"

I have these dreams, Bobby. They're only dreams. Besides, there's no sin left to punish. It was over long ago. The best thing to do is forget. Christ help me. Why can't I just forget? Pa's going blind, Bobby. He can't find me anymore.

Travis Lee.

JUNE 24, THE REST AREA

Dear Bobby,

Major Dunn is back, and on crutches. Hear he goes around telling everybody who'll listen that last year the king got his fat self throwed by General Haig's chestnut mare, so Dunn figures as how he's in good company. Today he called us in for a little talking-to. We stood at attention by the YMCA pavilion while a sweet light rain was falling. I watched the foliage near me shiver under the gentle blows of the drops.

Dunn talked about duty and honor and of how virtue was expected from us, seeing as how we were in an insolent and discourteous place. It was all very well and good, he said, for a Frenchman to go around doing wickedness, but the English must set an example. He called our battalion, that bunch of whore-fucking lice-infested bastards, "Guiding Lights." He rambled so that this particular Guiding Light got tickled. To shut me up, Dewberry stomped hard on my foot.

When the flowery prose all ran out of him and Dunn finally

dismissed us, I ducked Corporal Dunleavy's stare and double-timed it to the meadow where our company team, the Jam-Pots, was fixing to play Captain Dunston-Smith's Maconochies.

Marrs caught up with me there. "Lay you half a crown on the winner, Stanhope."

Knowing our players, I took the Maconochies. I watched both sides kick hell out of that ball. The game didn't make a damned bit of sense.

Surrounded by a crowd of ass-kissing officers, Major Dunn was grinning like a fool. "Sound body; sound heart," he was saying, like their idea of football could drive back the Boche.

Smoot ambled up, eating peaches out of a tin his ma had sent him. He passed the can around. "Think it was the Frenchies, meself," he said.

Marrs, chewing open-mouthed on a peach, told him, "Nobody I knows would do it."

I poked my fingers around in the syrup, fished myself up a slick bite of fruit. "What?" I asked.

"What Dunn was preaching about." Smoot took the can from me. He laughed. "Had to be pitch-dark for a poke like that."

Marrs flushed, angry. "Not proper subject for a giggle, Smoot. Bashed her eye out, I hears, and her a grandmum."

The problem talking with Brits is being lost in conversation all the time. "*What?*"

I got their attention.

"What the hell you boys talking about?"

"Well, it's the old lady, ain't it," Smoot said. "That French old lady that got beaten and worse."

Marrs shook his head. "Wasn't you listening, then? We been talking it up in the tents."

"Our little Yank's been skulking about the side of the billets drinking his winnings, is what. Why go sneaking your drinks, Stanhope? 'Fraid them temperance ladies back home will see?"

"Shut your goddamned mouth, Smoot."

Smoot pushed me. I pushed back. Marrs stepped in between. I saw O'Shaughnessy giving us the eye.

"Anyway, had to be dark," Smoot grumbled. He lifted the can, drank the syrup. "I seen her. The one who ran the bakeshop. The one with the yellowish gray hair that stood up like a brush all 'round. She had a great bloody wen on her cheek. Even the fat whore's a sight better. And the sod nearly beat her to death just to get his bird in. So who was the buggering bastard? Was he blind? Or did he have great sodding bad taste? I says it has to be a Frenchie. Wouldn't be one of us. Was you drunk enough to give an old lady a tumble, Stanhope?"

Goddamn him for asking me that question, for all of them staring at me, waiting to hear my answer. When Smoot passed me the peach can, I shoved it at Marrs and went back to the tent.

To my disappointment I saw that Riddell was there. He was listening to Elgar, his eyes closed, his expression blissful. At my entrance he raised his head. "Stanhope. Best mind your manners about Major Dunn. Major's after excuses, ain't 'e. I know Captain's a Jew, but 'e's a bit of all right. I won't have you cocking things up for 'im."

I went to my pack, got out my canteen and my dog-eared, musty-smelling copy of Shelley.

"You mind what I said?"

"Yes, sir. Going back out to watch the game, sir."

"Must take your rum with?"

That went all over me like a cold-water shower. "Look, Sergeant? Can I speak frankly, sir?"

Riddell shrugged. "Bloody 'abit with you."

"I don't know what you folks expect. And it's not like I drink a lot, not like you boys do when you're kicking up your heels. Hell, I never touched a drop before I came here, but you were always pushing it on me, remember? I figure you didn't want me to notice I was sitting in a hole getting shelled, or you didn't want me to notice I was being fed shit. A little swaller of rum every once in a while don't affect my aim, sir. Don't I shoot enough goddamned Boche for you?"

In the corner, Elgar played on in a proper and upstanding major key.

Riddell lay back down, closed his eyes. "You're such the Yank, Stanhope. Always fighting a revolution, even one you've just concocted. Seriously lad, me mum 'as a recipe to 'elp the craving. When you want for it, ask. But don't let this go on, for as it sits now, I can picture the day that you'll end up arrested and thrown in the glasshouse, or worse, me or Dunleavy will ask you out for a summary execution."

He wants to put a scare into me. But hell, Bobby, it's not like I get drunk or nothing. Not like Pa. It's just that I'm hungry and cold all the time. Seems, too, like I'm either scared shitless or bored. *They* drink and nobody says Jack Shit about it. There's nobody here to talk to, Bobby. Lord, how I miss home. I hear the rain sometimes when I'm half asleep and think it's a creek flowing clear and clean through limestone. I smell onions cooking and imagine it's a pot of pinto beans starting. Damn it. It's not like I'm fall-down drunk or nothing. It's not like they make it sound. The rum ration is just a little something to keep my mind off things, Bobby, that's all. It's just a little something to do.

Travis Lee

JUNE 26, THE RESERVE TRENCHES

Dear Bobby,

It was Sunday when we started back. Each time we leave the safety of the reserve area I want to grab hold of the earth and not let go.

They held church before we started the long march. I stood by a crumbling stone wall near the YMCA pavilion and listened to a choir carol that damned lie: "A Mighty Fortress Is Our God."

That's where O'Shaughnessy caught up with me. He'd shucked his British Army uniform for that black dress of his, and he was wearing what looked like a girl's lacy nightgown over it.

"Well, isn't it a perfect symbolic sight I'm coming across: God and men within, Travis Stanhope without. 'Tis your choice, lad. God and those men would accept you."

He was the brightest thing in the world that morning. The linen shone like sun on snow. His skin was so pale and cheeks so ruddy, his face glowed like a lantern. "You're all dressed up to go out, Reverend. Don't you have something to do?"

"A dismissal, is it? But Mass is over. *Missa est.* You have a grand romantic loneliness in you, Travis. It's that you needn't, is what I'm saying."

A pert little sparrow lit on a nearby branch. Not a Texas sparrow, but near enough.

O'Shaughnessy said, "Have you noticed that the world is full of symbols, Travis? Of course you have, you loving poetry like you do. And did you know that Martin Luther gave us that lofty hymn you're hearing? But Luther was a terrible wastrel of a man. He threw away the finest parts of the Church: the symbols."

Way beyond the pavilion, I could see LeBlanc standing. He was looking my way, probably wondering why I'd been snubbing him; why, this near eternity, he suddenly found himself alone. Men die here. They lose their arms, their legs, their minds. There shouldn't be any fretting over Martin Luther or bad influences. In Flanders, nothing matters much.

O'Shaughnessy clapped his hands. "A boy of few words, I see. We must discuss Emily Dickinson one day. A fine, precise use of words she had. Keen as a paring knife. We Irish love the language, but it's our habit to run on and on."

The hymn ended, and following on its heels came the doxology. I picked up my pack and settled its load across my shoulders.

"And a heavy weight it is, Travis," O'Shaughnessy said, "with the sin of rum filling your canteen."

I threw the pack down. "Goddamn it! So that's why Miller wanted me to talk to you! Well, you can just tell him to keep his damned nose out of my business. I won these watered-down excuses for rations fair and square. So I add a couple of drops to my canteen. So what? It cuts the taste of the chlorine.

Besides, you don't have no right to talk. You're the one who gives out wine to folks, and to little kids, to boot. The church where I grew up, it was grape juice. I've seen how you papists work. You smoke. You drink whiskey. Don't you try to put no hellfire and brimstone on me."

He laughed. The company began filing out of the pavilion into the light. I shouldered my pack and hurried fast as I could away.

An hour later Uncle Miller called us into formation and I was glad to go. We were shelled all the way back, but it was such a slow metal rain that we didn't bother to take cover. We walked, listening to the whistles as they came down, flinching at the crumps and spurts of dirt when they hit. Light artillery, and you could hear death coming so slow that you could step out of its way. We stopped to rest with shells falling all around; and when we got to the trenches, we found that the cooks had fixed bubble and squeak. Riddell rhapsodized about it so, that it must have been to him like Ma's venison chili is to me.

"All that's needed is bangers or a bite of toasted cheese, maybe an egg sandwich."

And down in that slime trench with the stench of shit and the rot of old French corpses, the rest of the platoon agreed. Bubble and squeak. Tasted like death to me.

I dreamed about Trantham and the graveyard last night. He was calling something pitiful. I started to go get him, but the place beyond the cypress was too dark, like the spot where the world ends. I yelled for Trantham to come out. He didn't. God, Bobby. He's in the place ghosties come from.

Travis Lee

JUNE 28, THE RESERVE TRENCHES

Dear Bobby,

Pickering thinks they'll be sending us over the top soon. Him and Smoot are having us make jam-pots and Battye bombs, 'cause there aren't near enough real grenades. Old

Uncle Miller's been bearing down on the inspections, and yesterday he cut poor, shy Marrs a new asshole for having dirt in his gun.

Something's for sure going on. There's rumors all up and down the line, and I hear tell that when we left the rear area, Riddell left his precious gramophone and Elgar behind.

Keep Ma's church group praying hard, 'cause you just can't never tell.

Travis Lee

JULY 2, POSTCARD FROM THE FRONT

Dear Bobby,

We moved out a few days ago. Got us some new trenches. They aren't half bad. Food still tastes like what you get mucking out the chicken coop.

Kiss Ma for me, Travis Lee

JULY 2, FLANDERS

Dear Bobby,

One day we'll sit down on the front porch swing. We'll have ourselves some lemonade and crack us a bowlful of pecans. When the sun goes down, we'll light the coal oil lamps and listen to the frogs croon by the stock tank. We'll count June bugs. Some easy evening when we're together again, Bobby, that's when I'll give you this letter.

On the last night of June we went over the top. It was still that morning, but by afternoon the wind had kicked up.

"Don't like that wind," Foy said. "Coming straight at us."

Unless the wind changed, Fritz would use gas.

Marrs wrote a last letter to his girlfriend. "How many Maxims you think?" he asked, and tucked the letter in a pocket near his heart.

"Lots and lots. Why, you'll have blood all over, that way," Pickering said. "She'll have to wash it to read it, Marrs, and the ink will all run."

Dunleavy snapped, "Shut up. Fasten that webbing."

I checked my ammunition, checked it again. My hands shook, and I hoped no one could see me trembling.

Pickering punched Marrs in the side. "Just don't get shot in the brain, like you were last time. As soon as they start firing, Marrs, sit your plump bum down."

Quiet. I never heard the world so quiet. Standing shoulder to shoulder with a thousand men, but not a cough, not a mutter. Then from that hush came a low mosquito buzz. Everyone looked up. Overhead was an aeroplane, one of Fritz's. The batteries set up a thumping barrage, over as quick as it started. It was a little yellow plane, Bobby, tiny as a toy; and it went down in silence, painting a thin black line of smoke down the blue wall of the sky.

When the sun was low and the light was brassy they ordered us up the communication trench, jostling, single file. The hole stank of last year's corpses. Behind us our own big guns rang out for the fourth time in as many hours. As the sun set, British fire lit up the gray dusk.

Whispers approached up the trench. A hissed "Stanhope!" from Smoot in front. "Forward companies ready, pass it on." I turned to Marrs and gave him the message, and the message was carried back to waiting officers by a thousand voices, one by one. The earth shook. The walls of the trench crumbled. Dirt spattered us. I fingered my gas mask just to make sure it was there. I clutched my rifle tighter.

The Boche couldn't survive that shelling. Nothing could. The Tommies gave them earthquakes of artillery, geysers of dazzling fire. I pictured the Boche cramped together in their small dark places, terror-stricken by noise. God, Bobby. The bright, dreadful beauty of it. I wondered if the barrage that had killed MacPhearson and wounded me had looked as awesome from a distance.

In too short a time—but it had always seemed so far—we were at the front-line trench. Riddell barked: "Fourteen here, sir!" and I shouldered my way into the crowd. The sun had set. The only light was the flickering orange glow from the English shelling. Dunleavy handed out the rum ration—unwatered this time—a scant jigger for each. A jigger. And I wanted so bad to get drunk.

Riddell climbed halfway up the ladder and took a quick peek through the trench periscope. I would be climbing that ladder myself in a minute or so. I'd go sprinting across a place only fools set foot. I doubted I was brave enough, and that scared me even more.

Strange, Bobby, seeing yourself as a feeble collection of meat and bone. A bullet could stop me in a heartbeat, shrapnel silence my brain mid-thought. Gas could burn my lungs; I'd drown in my own juices. And I would do it to myself, just because I'd climbed a goddamned ladder.

Riddell barked out an order: "Masks on!"

The mask smelled of new leather; the valve tasted like old pennies. The goggles made me half-blind. I tucked the hem into my collar and wondered if I had fastened it well enough.

A hand touched my back. In the flashing light of the barrage I turned and saw the insignia. Miller, only the sad eyes in his goggles recognizable. He squeezed past me.

The Boche returned fire, a lackluster, light artillery. Above No Man's Land star shells burst into pale greenish light.

Time. Miller was at the ladder and we were going and there wasn't any time. Cold settled in my lungs and I started to shiver hard. Around me a collection of faceless waiting men. Smoot—I think it was Smoot—fiddling with his bandolier.

Miller's hand lifted to the rungs. Another deep-throated barrage, then the sharp icy shrieks of the whistles and Miller was up the ladder and gone, another soldier behind him, another.

I touched the wood. I'd lose strength at the last minute. I wouldn't have the heart. I wouldn't be able to make it up the ladder, and they would call it a Blighty and send me home. One, two, three rungs. The ladder shuddered under my weight. Ahead was our wire and the holes our sappers had cut. Beyond, the lumpy expanse of No Man's Land.

It wasn't real. Nothing was real, not the battle litter that made me stumble, not the rat-a-tat-tat of the machine guns, not me. Especially not me.

Soldiers ahead broke into a run, so I did, too. Was anyone beside me? With the goggles, the sides of the world were gone. There was a slow rolling yellowish fog on the horizon, and all of us were running to it. I sucked air and wondered if the metal taste was the valve or fear or if I was drinking gas.

The fog bank swallowed Miller. I stumbled into the mist after him. Was there anyone beside me? Was I running in the right direction? I could be heading back toward our lines. I'd be safe. No. I'd be caught and court-martialed. God. I could be running on the diagonal and never reach the other side.

The low hum of falling shells. Tooth-rattling blasts all around. And then a figure through the fog, one of O'Shaughnessy's ghosts.

No, just Smoot, the eyes behind his goggles wide. He tripped over something and went sprawling. I pulled him up and we ran on. We ran until a furious ratcheting of machine-gun fire sent us diving for the nearest shell hole.

We kept our heads down. Around us, bullets slapped the dirt. Should we be stopping here? Would we get in trouble for this? The gas was so thick at the bottom of the shell hole that it had to be seeping through the canvas sacking. I sucked air through the metal straw of my mask. My throat tightened. My lungs ached. I was already dizzy. Smoot stayed where he was, hugging the ground, so I did, too.

The wind picked up. The fog thinned, dark smoke billowing. Someone threw himself into the hole with us.

"What in bloody 'ell'r—" Riddell. He paused, sucking air furiously through his mask's valve. When he spoke again his words were muffled and strained. "—you doing?"

I saw Smoot hesitate. Then he spit out his valve and said, "Waiting."

"For bloody what?"

Not me. I wasn't about to answer. There was too much goddamned gas. My teeth bit down on the valve, the metal sending a shiver up my spine.

Smoot said, each word a risk, "Well, they're firing . . . at us, aren't they."

" 'Course they're firing . . . at you! Christ! You a . . . nutter or sommit? 'Course . . . they're firing." Riddell took a Battye bomb from his pouch and threw it.

The Battye bombs. The grenades. The jam-pots we'd spent time making. Under fire, we'd forgotten.

I chucked a few toward the machine-gun emplacement. Smoot did, too. We either got the Boche or he moved, for the Maxim went silent. Shells kept falling.

Up and out of the hole, back into dream. People moving ahead. The dying glow of the flares cast green fire down bayonets. My gas mask was heavy. It made my world tiny, cramped, and hot. The breeze blew; black tarry smoke thinned. I caught the tastes of pineapple and pepper. Chlorine.

Gunfire, not the spit of Maxims but the pop-pop of rifles. Riddell fixed his bayonet and started to run. Smoot did too. I tripped and fell over a corpse with a coal-shuttle helmet. Where was I? What was he doing here? Then the breeze blew the smoke to me. Smoot had left me behind and I was alone. Where were the Boche trenches now? I didn't know what else to do, so I got up and went on.

The flares had gone dark. The only light was that from the explosions. A Maxim started up, this time from a different direction; and I found myself a crater and took cover. Someone was in the hole with me. Not much more than shadow, his gas mask gave him a pale lollipop of a head. To my left an orange flash, bright enough so I recognized the eyes in the goggles. Smoot was watching me.

I reached out to touch him and my fingers sank. My hand was up to the wrist inside his guts and he was still alive and moving around a little; and even when I wiped my hand on my pants and wiped it and wiped it I could still feel the wet heat of his insides. It took everything I had not to throw up in my mask.

What did Smoot expect me to do? I wasn't a doctor yet. He kept looking at me and I could see the hole in his belly now and his dark glistening liver and his pale guts dangling out. Jesus. How could he be wounded and live like that? Where was Riddell? He was the goddamned sergeant. Riddell would go find a weed for him.

My chest felt jittery inside, like I was going to laugh.

He was trying to get his mask off. I spit out my valve. "No! Shit! No! Don't do that." My mouth went searching for my valve again, like a baby hunting for a teat. I took a hurried breath that tasted of pineapple. "Gas in the hole . . . All right. It's okay." Jesus. Chlorine. You didn't feel chlorine happening. You didn't know for sure it had worked until your own lungs started to drown you. "Stretcher's coming."

Guts hanging all down his leg.

"No! Don't look." I sucked in a thirsty gasp of tin-flavored air. "Just pulled . . . yourself a Blighty." Around me bullets punched the dirt.

Smoot's weak fingers tugged at the mask. I'd have let him take it off if the gas would have killed him any quicker.

Since we couldn't talk, I lay down beside him so that I could look him in the eye. I thought if I was dying that's what I would want somebody to do. He reached out and held my hand. He held on tight, and I let him. His fingers were cold. I lay there until the whine of incoming shells started coming farther and farther apart. I stayed until the Maxim went still. By then Smoot was still, too. His eyes were fixed. I pried his stiff fingers off me, stood up, and started walking.

I walked around shell holes and through a ruin of wire. I nearly fell over the German parapet. Except for the bodies, the trench was empty. Nearby, fires smoldered and cast a tense and uneasy light across the corpses.

Down the trench, Tommies were milling. We had taken the forward Boche position, and the sun was coming up.

Miller was there, his gas mask off, regrouping to move forward. The shelling had stopped except for mortars. When I took my mask off, the air was cool. The breeze smelled clean and safe, something like the air after a bad storm. Then it was up and over the muddy parados and the long tiring slow charge to the Boche rear, at a walk. Feet moving: That was all I knew. I didn't have the strength to lift my rifle, to hold my bayonet in position. I was so tired, I didn't care if they killed me.

We arrived in the afternoon and found the rear trenches

deserted. Miller said we could stop. I sat with LeBlanc on the parapet of the Boche trench and drank the tea Pickering made our six platoon survivors: Foy and Riddell, Marrs, me and LeBlanc.

"Assholes," LeBlanc said. "Goddamned Brit artillery falls short all the time. If they hadn't been using those American sawdust bombs they would have killed the rest of us. Hey, Stanhope. Here's to American capitalism, eh?" And he drank a toast. "Jesus, Mary, and Joseph. What do you think, Stanhope? Think we should have kept advancing? Miller was for it. Half his company down, but he borrowed some balls from the old Fourteenth. Christ knows, Dunleavy didn't need his anymore. Think Miller was trying to prove something? Stanhope? You listening?"

I didn't know what to say. The world was strange there on the other side. I could hear the slow thump of my heart. The remains of that morning's sweat lay clammy on the nape of my neck. I was happy, Bobby. That's the strange thing. I felt life so keen—why didn't I feel death any sharper? All the platoon but six. Smoot's blood was caked under my nails, and I used my penknife to clean it. After a while LeBlanc went away.

We rested, and after O'Shaughnessy blessed the corpses, the cadre was ordered up. They buried our dead; then they buried the Boche. They sent the handful of tired-looking prisoners to the rear. Some of the Boche didn't seem to know what had happened, and had to be led away.

That evening in an intact officer's dugout Captain Dunston-Smith found a piano. He sat and played Chopin. The music drew Miller and me and three men from another platoon. We all stood, tired and mute, listening to etudes.

It was odd in those tumbled-down trenches that we'd won. Where the dugouts were still undamaged, we found books and letters and pictures: odds and ends of the lives of those who had retreated. Most of the ones who stayed died when the earth caved in. Some died from simple concussion, and we found them gathered in their dark holes, curled up like little kids sleeping, blood caking their nostrils and ears.

We slept, and I didn't dream, and the next morning Command issued sandbags. We're to rebuild the trench. Looks like with the ghosties is where we'll stay.

Travis Lee

Four

July 5, the reserve trenches

Dear Bobby,

Hope you had a happy 4th, little brother! No hot dogs nor red, white, and blue here, but I had me a celebration anyways. Yesterday morning we were all sitting at the back latrine: me and Marrs and Pickering. I was having a good sit-down myself, not the yellow squirt I get when the water's bad, nor the dark goat-turd pebbles I get when the food's not plentiful enough. No, this was a great, glorious golden cigar of a turd that felt fine and upstanding coming out, a British sort of turd. Major Dunn would have pinned a medal on it.

An orange sun was chasing the last of the night, and the breeze felt good on my bare ass. My balls were free and happy. Pickering must have been in a good temper, too, for he called out, "Hey, Stanhope! You know what day it is? Come on, Marrs. There's no better place for it than the privy. Let's sing a bleeding revolutionary ballad for our Yank."

And damned if he didn't start singing a pretty fair tenor rendition of "The Star Spangled Banner," complete with farts in all the right places. That boy is possessed of a rare and wondrous talent.

Everyone joined in, and there we were, our bare butts in a line, our voices lifted. The Tommies fell to la-laaing pretty quick, but even when I got to the high parts, I still remembered the words.

Captain Miller rode by with Dunston-Smith, and they

reined their horses and lingered awhile, laughing. I couldn't rightly stand up, but I saluted, anyway. The sun brightened the clouds in glowing bands. Birds warbled. It was a good shit, Bobby. I tell you, it was one of the best.

When it was over, we went back to the trenches. A few whizzbangs came our way, but it was a half-hearted effort. We dug more bodies out of the trench, already bloated, skin gray as their uniforms and spongy. Maggots were moving around in them.

There must be Boche left in the walls, Bobby, for the smell has settled in all the trenches. The stink draws black clouds of flies and, try as I might, I can't help but wonder what the flies walked on before they landed on my Maconochie. Only if the stew's hot enough, can I force it down.

I found out that Dewberry pulled a Blighty—a bullet in the thigh. A good wound to go home with. He was a good and friendly rumwallah, and I'm glad for him. Dedoes's gas mask got torn, and he went home wheezing and blinded. Carver lost both legs. Starks will have to learn to make do without a right arm. The rest are dead—Dunleavy crushed to pulp when one of those American dud bombs fell on him.

I haven't dreamed of the graveyard in a while, and maybe that's for the best.

Marrs and I sorted through the litter in the dugouts. I found a portrait photograph of a sweet-faced lady in a feather hat; a half-written letter to "Mutter" in spiky Gothic; a copy of Goethe's *Faust*—other people's memories, moldy and stained. I opened one envelope and found a letter folded carefully around a lavender stalk. The missing Boche must have carried it with him a long time. The flowers had crumbled; only the brittle stalk and its perfume remained. Lavender. I sat down right where I was, closed my eyes, and sniffed the paper a while.

Marrs was the right one to go attic-cleaning with. Pickering or Foy or LeBlanc would have asked me what the hell I was doing. Marrs didn't. And when I refolded the letter and started to put it on the respectful pile of mementos we were gathering, Marrs said, "Why'nt keep that letter, then? Ain't like he'll be needing it."

The envelope makes a warm homey place over my chest. I take it out sometimes, just for the smell. I puzzle over the German. The lavender reminds me of fine ladies with hoop skirts and parasols. The script is flowery. You can touch the fondness there.

When we were finished piling things up, Riddell told us to throw it all away.

"Chuck it?" Marrs asked, and he sounded heartbroken.

"Well, stuff's rubbish, ain't it?"

So we dug a hole and packed it with odds and ends of cloth. We nestled the memories inside, and covered everything carefully with earth. Marrs crossed himself. We bowed our heads and Marrs said some Latin: a *Pater Noster*, he told me, and an *Ave Maria* thrown in for good measure. Over it we planted a grave marker so the Boche could find it when the war was done.

"It ain't rubbish," Marrs said firmly when we were finished; and that was the best blessing of all.

Today was a rest period, but Dunn got a bee up his butt and had us organize a game of football. We were all tired. The Tommies were complaining of the heat. Dewberry had been the Jam-Pot's best goalie, Dunleavy the best forward. Still, the team played as well as they could. They chased that ball and chased it until Phillips, from 10th Platoon, kicked it over a jagged piece of shell casing and it sprang a leak. Both teams stood looking down at that deflating ball like it was a dying calf or something. It pissed Dunn off, and he stalked away grumbling. When he was gone, both teams sat down right where they were and took off their shirts. They wiped their faces and passed around a canteen. Everybody grumbled about the temperature. I told them about the summer you and me had to sleep in the creek just to keep cool. I told them how the cows died of sun stroke in the pasture and birds fell out of trees. They must be tired of my Texas stories, for they threw dirt clods at me. Despite the have-to football game, a good time was had by all.

Hope all your shits are fine ones. Travis Lee

JULY 8, THE FRONT LINE

Dear Bobby,

The replacements came, and every time a mortar shell falls within earshot the new boys go scurrying for cover. Pickering, serious for once, told them, "Wear your legs out that way," and the new boys looked at him so horror-struck that Foy and me near pissed ourselves laughing.

We didn't gain much by our battle, I discovered. The Boche fell back to the same fortifications they had advanced from last year. They're dug in comfortable now. That's why Dunn didn't want to press the attack and Miller did. Well, it's possible Dunn was right. We were pretty wore out, and might have been easy pickings. But lately the Boche have been sneaking up close. They planted a few Maxim emplacements, and they're busy starting a new forward trench I do believe. They have them a fine communication trench, for I haven't got many clear head shots. Sometimes I catch the forward diggers.

We got us a new and obliging rumwallah, but Marrs and Foy and Pickering refuse to bet me anymore. Those new boys of ours, though, have yet to down a whole ration of rum. Riddell is teaching them how to keep their rifles clean; Marrs, the best way to crack lice. I teach them the unfairness of odds-taking. They're too damned young for this.

For the first time in weeks I dreamed about the cemetery. It scared me, too, for I looked down and saw Smoot in one of those glass-covered graves. Smoot, preserved in a bell jar.

In this dream the rest of the platoon was lost and I needed to find them. They were my responsibility, Bobby. It was me who knew the place. And even though it still holds surprises, I had walked every terrace of that graveyard, had looked into the downturned face of each and every rain-stained cherub. So I ran those paint-chipped steps, calling out the names of the missing. I hurried breathless and anxious through marble winter forests. When I came to the end of the gravel walk, the dark stopped me.

Something was bad there beyond the cypress. Maybe it was

our deaths, maybe it was the Boche's; but the dark was stranger and emptier now, and I couldn't hear Trantham's voice anymore.

I ran away, back down the twisting path, calling for Dunleavy and Birdsong, Thweat and Furbush and Highwater. I ran past wilting wreaths and faded ribbons and solitary stone angels kneeling. I rushed, frantic and stumbling, on the painted plastered stair. Below me was a domed marble mausoleum, its rusty iron gate open. And there she stood, a gold and blue breath of mercy: the girl in the calico dress.

When I came to her she put her finger to my lips, sweet and gentle-like, to shush me. "They're resting," she said.

I'd found them. They were in the mausoleum, all of the platoon. The place was beautiful, with its fluted, cracked columns. I knew it would be cool and quiet inside, and that the air would smell of lavender. Outside, vines twined the walls and birds hopped and played among the leaves. God, they must have loved sleeping there.

I started to tell her that I wanted to rest, too, maybe just put my head down for a while. But she knew; and she held me, not the way a pretty girl would, but the way Ma always used to do—me small in the fortress of her arms.

And in the dream I knew I was finally free to go, because she'd take care of them for me. It was nice knowing that she'd be there, watching over. The dark's so damned near that it's easy to fall in, and so deep that you'd drown. She knows that, too. She knows everything: about Pa outside the wardrobe, about the loudness of shells and the bruising shock of bullets.

I woke up filled with a wide deep calm. Boche corpses stank in the walls, but that didn't matter. Somewhere outside the dugout a machine gun stuttered and then went quiet. A passing sentry laughed. I took the letter out of my tunic pocket and in the dank black cave of the dugout I sniffed the lavender. I think it smelled like her.

Yours, Travis Lee

JULY 12, A POSTCARD FROM THE FORWARD TRENCHES

Dear Bobby,

Everything's fine here. The weather's warm and dry, and all the Tommies are getting sunburned.

Hope this finds you happy and in good health. Kiss Ma for me and thank her for those angora socks she knitted. They'll come in handy this winter.

Love, Travis Lee

JULY 12, THE FRONT LINE TRENCHES
A LETTER FOR ME TO HOLD ONTO

Dear Bobby,

Two days ago Riddell called me into his dugout. LeBlanc was there, too. "Major Dunn wants more patrols," he said. "So tonight the pair of you are going on a stunt, under my command. Remember: 'Eads down, mind each other but don't lose sight of me, no noise to draw fire. And if the Boche send up star shells, find yourselves a 'ole to 'ide in. Just a bit of a tramp, then, and we'll come back and have ourselves a cuppa."

When we were dismissed, LeBlanc followed me down the trench. "I been with Riddell before. He's gutless. Let's have us some real fun, eh? Make sure your sheath knife's sharp."

It was hard to imagine anything with knives being fun.

"Come on. You're not a goddamned tit-sucking baby like Riddell and the rest of 'em, are ya? Hey, I tell you, there's nothing like it—looking somebody straight in the eye while they die. They squirm like bugs, you know?"

I said, "Uh-huh," like I'd done that so much I was plumb tired of it.

"I can trust you, Stanhope. The rest of them are a bunch of wet cunts."

Trust me? We were ordered to face No Man's Land together, and he hadn't bothered to ask why I was politely trying to get away or even why I'd been ignoring him lately. But then LeBlanc's not a man after honest answers.

"Let's do it, eh? I know right where the forward sap is. Two Boche at the most. One for each of us. We'll pretend we got lost, that's all. Riddell's too stupid to know any different. Shit. Come on. Whaddya say? It's easy. You sneak up behind 'em, jump on their backs, and shove their faces in the dirt like this—"

It happened so damned quick. He whirled me around and slammed me against the sandbags. I banged my nose. Air exploded out of my lungs.

His body was close and hot against mine. In my ear he whispered, "You prick 'em a little."

Something stuck me in the side. God, that knife was sharp; like the Bowie we keep to castrate the billies.

"You slide it and fish around till you hit a lung. That's so's they can't scream. Slice their liver to get 'em bleeding. And when you feel 'em go weak, you just turn 'em over . . ."

He flipped me so we were face-to-face. His eyes were hectic. "You ever see a dog die of distemper, Stanhope? That's the way old Fritz shakes under you. At the last minute their eyes get wide and scared 'cause they know what's happening and they can't do a thing."

The Mad Hatter delight in him.

"Better than a good fuck," he said.

He let me go. I staggered away, wiping at my mouth. He laughed like he'd just told a joke.

I felt the need for people—maybe a witness or two—so I hurried on down the trench to my dugout. He followed. When we got there, Pickering asked LeBlanc to stay and have a cuppa. "Come and join us, why don't you? We'll do it up right, just like home. I'll play Mother, shall I?" Pickering set out the field cups and an old potted meat tin for LeBlanc.

I sat as far away from LeBlanc as I could and drank the tepid tea that Pickering fixed on his Tommy cooker. He didn't really visit, but LeBlanc was still sitting there, wordless and solemn, when the kitchens sent up dixie cans of meatless stew. I couldn't eat. Pickering watered a biscuit with his ration of Jam Of Uncertain Origin. He added a few currants his wife had sent. He stirred the whole mess in an old tin and passed the mush around.

A Maxim started up a surly rat-a-tat-tat that ended when the sun set. We lit a candle and played a game of cards. LeBlanc left for God knows where. After the card game, Marrs and Pickering and Foy rolled themselves in their blankets and went to sleep.

I sat and sharpened my sheath knife. I took all the metal pieces off my uniform. I blackened my face with burnt cork till I looked like a vaudevillian. Then I had a smoke, counting my fingers the amazed way folks do when you come into the world, not the way you'd think you'd do leaving it. When the others started snoring, I snuck me a couple of jiggers of courage.

Sooner than I expected I heard LeBlanc's hissed "Stanhope!" at the open door. My stomach flip-flopped. I got up so fast, I nearly fell back down.

Riddell was waiting outside in the trench. "Ready, then?" he asked.

I didn't have enough spit in my mouth when I said, "Sure," and the word came out cracked in two.

LeBlanc elbowed me. "A good fuck, eh?"

Down at the bend of the traverse, Riddell went up the ladder. No whistles. No masks. Over the top in silence this time, and into limitless dark. This was the place, the dark beyond the cypress, and maybe when you fell in you found yourself in LeBlanc's lunacy. I crawled blind, hearing cloth scrape against dirt, pebbles rattle. Was that LeBlanc ahead of me? I figured that he could see through the thick night—for I knew my dream graveyard, but he was a native here.

Cold rusty metal pricked my cheek: the barbed wire. So soon? A twang as wire gave under the bite of cutters. Riddell's whisper to my right, "Through 'ere."

By faith I followed his voice. I crawled, my cautious hands fumbling over trash: empty tins with sharp edges, jagged rusting shrapnel, a burst and ruined canteen.

A fast sputter from the Maxim made me hug the moldy ground. The Maxim's fire was followed by an answering flurry of shots from our side. Head down, I kept moving through LeBlanc's nothingness.

I touched something slimy and wet that gave off an overpowering stench of rot. A corpse. I wondered if the Boche had shuddered when LeBlanc's knife went in; if he had trembled like a man fucking. No. This thing was too small, too furry. I crawled over the carcass, and left a trail of stinking death down my tunic.

I heard quiet movement to either side of me. Metal litter snagged my chest, my legs. I would have thought I was dead, if not for that.

Then Riddell's disembodied whisper. "Stop 'ere."

And LeBlanc's "Sure. Forward Boche sap's not far."

"Leave it."

"Yeah. Right. But I could take 'em."

"Leave it."

"Let Stanhope and me have a little fun."

"I'll bust yer arse for you, Private."

The Maxim barked again. A rising whistle and a quiet pop. Star shells burst above our heads and No Man's Land shone green.

Riddell ordered tensely, "Down! Down!"

The sergeant and I rolled into a nearby crater. Above us gunfire rattled: the Boche's and ours. The night turned loud.

"Where's 'e?" Riddell's voice was so strong, so normal, that it startled me. "Where's bloody LeBlanc off to, then?"

"Don't know, Sergeant!"

He grabbed my bandolier and shook me hard. "Where's 'e off to?"

The big guns started up—thunder along the horizon. And I thought: The boys in the reserve trenches won't sleep to-night.

"I'll find him."

I don't know if it was the rum or the dark that made me crazy; but I dropped my rifle and wormed my way up and over the lip of that hole. I went scrabbling through the green night, trailed by Riddell's call of "Stanhope! Come back, yer blockhead!"

On my belly, elbows first. The flares had dimmed, their glow brightening only the edges of things: the curve of a cast-off coal-shuttle helmet, the outline of a rotting boot.

I had to stop LeBlanc, Bobby. I don't know why, other

than war even with all its mess is cleaner. War happens in noise and blasts of fire. It takes you down capricious-like, not caring.

I heard his chuckle before I saw him. "Stanhope? Stanhope, that you?"

A rattle to my left, the clink of an old tin can. He'd go for the soft spot between my belly and short ribs—the tickle spot. I stared so hard that my head swam, but still I couldn't see him. The light from the flares was nearly gone.

His voice came much too close. "Stanhope?"

If I didn't answer, he would stop my words forever. "Yeah."

"Grab my hand."

I did. There was something wrong with it, a sick kind of wrong. It was too slack-fingered, too flaccid-fleshed. All loose. Jesus God, Bobby. I was holding his hand, and there wasn't any arm.

My stomach understood before my brain did. Pickering's tea came gushing up my throat.

LeBlanc snickered. His voice came from a couple of yards away. "You coming, Stanhope?"

All the way back to the trench I'd get to thinking about the feel of that Boche's severed hand, and I'd have to stop and vomit again. LeBlanc got a kick out of me.

We were lucky. The Boche sniper must have been asleep that night, or the dark that LeBlanc brought with him was too murky for the Boche to see through. Nobody shot at us. When we got back to our side, Riddell marched us straight into Miller's new quarters. The dugout wasn't as plush as in the old trench. No Grecian columns, no vines. Just a cot and a scarred table and a chair where Miller sat, looking out of sorts and sleepy.

"Disobeyed orders, sir," Riddell said. "The bof of 'em. Private LeBlanc 'ere worst."

Miller looked LeBlanc up and down. He studied him a long time. "You're in a bit of disarray, Private."

The front of LeBlanc's uniform was soaked with blood. Gore splattered his face, his hands. There was blood on my palm too, and quick as I could, I wiped it on my pants.

LeBlanc said, "Sir. Got me a forward sapper, sir."

"Um."

Riddell said, "Told him not to go mucking things up like that."

Miller raised an eyebrow.

"Well, it's a custom, like, ain't it, sir. I mean, the Boche is ordered up No Man's Land, and us, too. We listens to each other, and then we goes back. A gentlemanly thing, that. But 'ere LeBlanc goes sneaking up after 'em, and with a sheath knife, what's worse. They'll be thinking we're savages or sommit."

"I see. What have you to say for yourself, Private?"

"Should have been two sappers on duty. I don't know where the other bastard went, sir. I looked for him."

"Well. Right you are. A week's cut in pay should do. See to it, will you, Sergeant? And Stanhope? What is your latest infraction?"

Riddell said, "Went after 'im, sir, after 'e plain as day was told not to."

"Yes, well. I see. A week's pay for the pair. I would think that puts the situation firmly in hand. You're dismissed. Ah, Stanhope? A moment, please. Thank you, Sergeant. That will be all. Close the door on your way out, will you?"

The Boche guns had long ago stopped. The night outside was quiet now, so quiet that I could hear the cautious thump of the door closing.

"Father O'Shaughnessy tells me that you've been avoiding him."

"Sir, I ain't seen him lately."

"He says that when you do, you walk the other way."

"That ain't so."

"O'Shaughnessy says it is."

"Sir? Why do you take O'Shaughnessy's word for everything? Okay, he's a reverend and all, but that's not to say he don't lie. Why, we had us a Holy Roller preacher down to Fredricksberg who fucked all his church ladies. When he come, he'd even go to yelling in tongues, 'Ollie ollie ollie,' like they do. Now I'm going to tell you again, sir:

O'Shaughnessy may have seen me, but I ain't seen him. Why can't you believe that?"

"Because," he said, "you are an untrustworthy sot."

Plain walls, but he had put a picture up. The lady in the photo had the smooth good looks of the wealthy.

"And you're a goddamned liar, sir."

The girl in the photo looked at me so sad. She had Miller's dark eyes. His sister?

"Either that or you're stupid," I told him. "And with all due respect, if you think what I did tonight is worth the same fine as LeBlanc, well, then you're so dumb you can't find your pecker with both hands and a road map." I cleared my throat and added, "Sir."

"What did you do tonight, Private?"

"Hell, sir. That boy's flat crazy. He got up close and cut the hand off that Boche sapper. Give the damned thing to me."

Miller contemplated me, his gaze as steady as that girl's on the wall. "You have not yet answered my question. For one thing, you and LeBlanc both disobeyed orders. I believe you disregarded them because you had been drinking, which is why—"

"No, sir! Not drinking one bit, sir!"

"But LeBlanc went out and killed an enemy. Why should I fine him and not you?"

"I didn't touch a drop. Not one drop. And, well, I know *my* conscience is clean. All I did was go out and try to stop that boy."

He sat back so fast in the chair that it squeaked. "Did I not order you to stay away from LeBlanc?"

"No, sir. To my recollection, you just suggested that, sir. And I took your suggestion to heart and treated it like a real order, sir, I really did. But goddamn. We were out on patrol together. What the hell else did you expect?"

"Well, if you have a problem with comprehension, Private, I shall give you plain and simple commands. First, you are to meet with Father O'Shaughnessy at his earliest convenience. You are valuable to me, and I will not lose you to your own follies. Further, you will avoid Private LeBlanc unless specifically ordered otherwise."

"Look, sir. When I joined this unit, Sergeant Riddell kept throwing LeBlanc and me together."

"Sergeant Riddell has not been made fully aware of Private LeBlanc's situation."

"Goddamn it, sir. You're smarter than this. LeBlanc went out there and plain cut that German boy up. What about us, sir? What about the rest of the goddamned platoon? What if he gets mad at somebody? How quick do you think he'd be to take that knife of his and—"

"That is quite enough!" Miller slapped the table. He shot to his feet. "You will speak of this no more; neither to me, nor to anyone in your platoon. Further, you will never attempt to subvert Private LeBlanc's activities in any way. The man is the battalion's most decorated soldier. He has the M.C. and Bar, for God's sake. As he is a true soldier and you most decidedly are not, I will not have you interfering with him. I will certainly not have the rest of his fellows distrusting him. Is that understood?"

I stood straighter. "Yes, sir. I guess. You need him out there making a name for the you and the company, and I understand that, sir."

"Blast and damn! You insubordinate . . ." He couldn't come up with a fitting noun, I guess, for he went to sputtering, like Dunn does when he's mad. "I put up with your impudence because you demonstrate your lack of manners and common sense merely in private; but do not push the boundaries of my good will. Is that clearly understood?"

"Yes, sir."

"Dismissed. Bloody hell. Get out."

"Thank you, sir."

As I turned to go, the woman on the wall eyed me. Miller's tired voice made me pause.

"Stanhope? Never again come between LeBlanc and his prey."

Odd choice of words. A perfect choice, really. Miller may have his faults, but he sees through the bullshit. I've known bad dogs like LeBlanc, and probably Miller has, too. Well, he may think that dog of his is trained, but turn your back and that thing'll pure-D kill you.

Travis Lee

JULY 13, THE RESERVE TRENCHES

Dear Bobby,

So Pa found Jesus. The preacher called, the choir sang "Just As I Am," and Pa picked up that cross and walked down that aisle. Don't you believe a word of it. Pa's full of love stories, full of you're-my-boys and let's-just-you-and-me-go-fishings. He'll cry and hug on you when he's sober, and he'll beat on you when he's drunk.

You want to know why he left us? I guess you're old enough for some truth. Back when you were about three years old I got to figuring I'd have to kill him. For twelve years I'd seen how life worked, and by then I knew there wasn't no way we could all survive together. So I got the 30.06 and followed him one night, tracked him all the way from our house to Odette Johnson's. See Bobby, Pa was sleeping around.

Poor Odette. She used to be a good-looker. And I never figured it was her fault. It wasn't nothing personal—not that she was messing around with him, and not even that she was a colored gal. I just needed a place to ambush him, Bobby, a place where he would have his guard down. A place to kill him where his blood wouldn't dirty Ma.

I found me a cedar outside Odette's door, and I hid there for a while. I can still remember the clean smell of that cedar tree, the oily smell of that gun. When the moon rose, I cradled the rifle and walked careful as I could up her wood steps. I tiptoed past her kids—all tucked into the same feather bed. I went down the dark hall and found her on the four-poster with Pa. The coal oil lamp was burning low, and they were sleeping. On the nightstand was one of them little wood animals Pa liked to carve, when he wasn't taking a belt buckle and carving on Ma's face. It was a cat, and he had took and darkened the wood with walnut juice, so the color came near to Odette's. The face was like hers, too: that pointy chin, those wide eyes. A pretty thing, that cat. I guess he must have liked her.

They were sleeping so peaceful, not curled up together, but peaceful and apart all the same. When I cocked that rifle, Pa's eyes flew open. Odette sat up quick, blankets falling. I remember her white rimmed eyes, the shock of seeing her naked. I'd never in my life seen anything as soft-looking as Odette's velvet brown nipples.

She whispered real tense-like, "Not my babies, Travis."

I took aim at Pa and he bolted, bare ass and all. He threw himself through her open window, and I could hear him crashing and stumbling through the underbrush, cussing me all the way down the hill. Odette sat there, shaking. She was holding the sheet up over her, like she'd just noticed me staring. I was confused. Hell, I don't know which disappointed me more: Pa's running, or the disappearance of those titties.

"Travis Lee?" she said.

I said, "Yes, ma'am?"

"Please don't go hurting my babies."

I left, and by the time I got home, Pa had come and gone. He knew I'd finally gone hunting him for serious and wouldn't stop until it was done. Ma never forgave me for that.

I think of Pa whispering in Ma's ear, in Odette's, in mine, how he loved me, just me. How I was every good thing in the world. How proud I made him. Does he tell God that?

And does God believe him? I know He's omniscient and all, but I figure He must. Ma believed Pa, and she knew about Odette and her light-colored baby. They both knew about all the others. Pa wasn't as energetic as Granddaddy De Vrees, but Granddaddy didn't drink, didn't smoke. I guess moonshine made Pa only a fair to middling alley cat.

To this day I have never told a woman I loved her, for I can't tell no lies. I talk about how their hair's gold as early spring wheat or their eyes are gray as mourning doves—all that sweet talk they like. But I don't lie to them. I don't think that's right.

So you tell all them church ladies to be careful. Might as well tell God that, too; for he'll talk about taking Him fishing, but God'll never set His ass on a river bank with Pa, they'll never bait a hook together. You tell God that for me.

Travis Lee

JULY 15, THE REST AREA

Dear Bobby,

Well, I had my little meeting with O'Shaughnessy. He wanted to walk, so the two of us set off down the lane. He's a bandy-legged sort, but he can move fast. We went sightseeing in Flanders, saw a lot of it—its white-painted red-roofed farmhouses, its stocky windmills, its spotted cows and white cows, and egg yolk-yellow flowers blooming in neat bouquets. He stopped by a tranquil canal, and I stopped by him. Goddamn if he didn't drop his pants.

"Who's your favorite poet, lad?" he asked.

Shit. He was a poetry-lover, just like LeBlanc had warned me.

He shimmied his shorts down, kicked them off, and kept on talking. "Captain says you like the English Romantics."

"Not when they're *too* romantic," I told him.

He pulled off his shirt, and there he stood—except for his socks, buck naked. Then he noticed me staring.

"Travis, my lad. You'll not be having *thoughts* now?"

"No, sir!" I said real quick. "Not thoughts. Nothing like that, sir."

He picked up his pants, rummaged around in the pockets, and came up with a bar of soap. Then he tender-stepped through the deep grass and waded waist-deep into the canal.

"Haven't you been swimming in the all-together, lad?"

That water, dark as it was, looked inviting. I shucked my uniform and tippy-toed through the reeds. Europe was safe, I knew, but I couldn't help looking all the same. You grow up, but you never get away from habit. Hell, I'd spent my whole childhood being watchful of cottonmouths.

The water was cold. It smelled of silt and algae. I jumped up and down. Water splashed. He passed me the soap. I scrubbed and watched bubbles float the black surface. Around us, daredevil dragonflies zipped and hovered.

"Keats," he said. "That would be your favorite."

"Shelley."

"But Captain says you've a fondness for *St. Agnes's Eve*."

"Well, I bested him at it once."

That quiet water, the reflected clouds drifting. The sky seems close here, Bobby. Home, it's so big you can't ever hope to catch it. But here, even if the day is bright, the sky bends right down to you, tender and considerate-like.

"Are you lonely here without your family, Travis?"

Lonely? Not with that obliging sky. Sun warmed my shoulders like a shawl, but the rest of me was freezing. My balls had shrunk up to the size of pigeon eggs. At the rest area they'd give us one of them army showers, but it'd been months since I had me a real soaking bath—so long ago that I'd gotten used to the smell of my own stink. Now that I was clean, I didn't want put on that sweat and death smell again. I waded to shore, grabbed the clothes I'd been issued two days before, and brought them back with me for an extra washing.

"Well? Are you? And is there not a girl waiting at home for you, lad?"

My teeth chattered. "A bunch of girls are waiting for me, Reverend." I looked around for a couple of good rocks, and it took me a while to find them, for Flanders is a soft-fleshed place without much skeleton. "Fact is, the female half of town had themselves a crying spell when I left for up East. That's because I'd done some serious study in the art of making a woman happy. Hell, any man can learn if he wants. See? You start by loving on them real slow." I pounded my clothes. Stones clicked. The lather on my hands felt slick and smooth as cream. "Then you do something new and you say, 'Feel good?' and if they say 'No' then you try something else, and you ask, 'Feel good?' What you're going for here is for them to start panting and crying out 'More, Travis Lee! Do that some more!' That's when you know you got yourself a keeper.

After a while of experimenting, you get yourself a repertory going. I been working on my repertory ever since I was thirteen years old."

My whole uniform was lathered now. A flat island of gleaming spume spread out around me. Foam sailed in flat boats of white down the slow current. I looked up. O'Shaugnessy was staring.

"Oh, sorry, sir. Shit. I mean, sorry. I plumb forgot."

"That is the most amazing confession I have ever heard."

"Lord, I'm sorry, sir. I shouldn't have said nothing."

" 'Feel good?' is it?" He went to laughing and trying to slap his thigh, except that he was waist-deep in the canal. He went red in the face. He splashed water and laughed some more. "Merciful Lord! A self-taught man."

"I wasn't thinking about your, you know, Reverend. I'm really sorry."

"My?"

"Your, you know. How you can't. I reckon I don't mean 'can't,' but how you folks aren't supposed to, I guess, have any fun and all."

That tickled him no end. He laughed so much, I was afraid he wouldn't ever catch his breath.

"Hey. You ever think about it, Reverend? You know?"

He wiped his eyes. "Ah, and you've got a smooth way with changing the subject."

I got out and spread my clothes on the sweet-smelling grass. I lay down beside them and let the sun beat the tiredness out of me.

O'Shaughnessy got out, too. He shook himself dry like a dog. "Yes. There are times I think of it," he said. He plopped himself down on the grass next to me and crossed his legs at the ankles. He clasped his hands behind his head and peered up at the clouds. "Apparently not as much as you. Did you leave them crying for you at Harvard? For I've heard you're studying medicine there."

"Not no more." I didn't know it till I said it, and the freedom in those words set me to soaring. "No," I said, and started to grin. "Don't think I'll be going back."

He rolled over on his stomach. His shoulders were already pink from the sun. His eyes were quietly troubled. "And why would that be, lad?"

"I spent all my goddamned time there in Harvard being pointed at and whispered about. I never fit in."

He gave me a lopsided grin. "And so you joined the British Army."

"Well, soldiering helped me decide a few things. Going back for one. Not being a doctor for another. A couple of weeks ago—that time we took the Boche trenches, you remember? I landed in a shell hole beside a man. He was wounded real bad, and there wasn't no way I could help him. All night pinned down there, looking at that blood, listening to him hurting. No, thank you. I don't want to spend my life doctoring, for there's some wounds you just can't heal."

Near me, a tangle of broad leaves and spikes with purple flowers all around, delicate as a lady's petticoat. The wind was still, the air hot and breathless. One of the leaves was shuddering.

"Do you mind what you've just said, lad?"

A bumblebee. It pulled its fat ass up and over the leaf, then sat there, winded and resting.

"Travis." So soft a question. "Haven't you always been something of an oddity, then?"

The bumblebee, legs thick and yellow with pollen, took to the air and wove a slow, awkward path among the flowers, looking, looking.

"And you come here, where you are the rarest oddity of all. Isn't it that you go seeking after uniqueness?"

The bumblebee was too big for its aspirations. It landed, and knocked a petal loose. The flower tumbled, lacy and startlingly lilac, down onto dark green leaves.

"I don't fit nowhere, sir."

"Ah. I imagine that in Texas your intelligence set you apart. Did all around you seem to have blinders on? Was that it? Then traveling to a place of intellectuals, and finding it no home to you, either. Tell me, for I have a bit of curiosity about it: What is it you love in Shelley? Would it be the brightness in him?"

The brightness of Shelley, the low hum of the bumblebee. The air smelled of growing things.

"For there's a brightness in Wordsworth, too, although not so powerful a beam." O'Shaughnessy lifted his hand and wrote across the sky, " 'Trailing clouds of glory,' isn't it? The part that is the flame. Shelley would have been a unique man, I imagine. There's some of the same in your own transcendentalists, although Thoreau lived a brighter life than he wrote. Now there's the dark side, too, the ghostie side Poe knew of. The drink brought it out of him."

I sat up quick. The bumblebee wandered away through the stalks.

"Does talk of drinking scare you?"

I patted my uniform. "It's late. Clothes are dry. We should get going."

"No? Well, is it the talk of ghosties, then? They're not as Poe saw them, really, for he was looking through the darkness at the bottom of the bottle. They're not goblins, Travis. Most are like you, just lads searching for home."

I got up and started getting dressed. My shirt was wet, my pants were clammy, my puttees were two sodden wads.

O'Shaughnessy got up, too. "The first time I clapped my eyes on you, I said to meself, 'Thomas, now there goes a lad with a gift.' You see, those that possess the sight recognize it in others. Don't be afraid of the sight, lad. That's the brightness of Shelley you'll be seeing."

I have dreams. And a graveyard that's a gift of my imagination. About me the wind blew. It rustled the leaves. Cold made me shiver.

"For I saw ghosties when I was but a wee thing," O'Shaughnessy said. "I saw me gran, and her in the grave a year. I saw me brother, the one that drowned."

I buttoned my shirt so fast, the hem ended up crooked, buttons out of place. "You ready?"

"Listen to me, Travis. Don't turn away, lad. That time we

were gassed and I felt like running, I was afraid only because there were so many of them. Thousands. And they were so lost. Sudden death confuses souls, and it was the bewilderment of those spirits that frightened me, for I'm a doctor of sorts as well, and there are wounds I cannot heal, either."

"I dream sometimes. Hell, everybody has dreams. That's all there is to it. Now we better go," I told him firmly.

He nodded. "Yes. I suppose we'd better."

We started walking that long way back to the unit, past soggy emerald fields and red and white villages. Near a solitary abandoned farmhouse beaten down by war, we found Riddell. Sergeant was sitting on a low brick cistern a few yards from the road, and he was staring hard at the ground.

I only stopped because O'Shaughnessy halted. He called out, "You look to be of a mood this afternoon, Sergeant."

At the voice, Riddell started and looked up. His face was red, his eyes puffy.

O'Shaughnessy picked his way through the roadside weeds. "What is it, man? What's happened?"

"Oh." Riddell shrugged. "Me mum died is what."

I gave him a lame "Sorry to hear that, Sergeant," and he nodded.

"Well, she was took quick, and that was a blessing."

I murmured something stupid about how much better that was.

He wasn't listening, anyway. "They says it was 'er 'eart. She was sitting at table and keeled right over. My sister thought she'd gone into a faint, isn't that funny?"

"We should all go that easy," I told him.

O'Shaughnessy put a hand on his shoulder. As if that gentle touch had broken his back, Riddell sagged. "Oh, bless 'er. It's just that I should have gone first, shouldn't I. I mean, with the war and all. I never expected it to be me mum. Who'll I fight for now, then? What's left to go 'ome to?"

Riddell thought he had it bad? At least he had a home once. I never did. O'Shaughnessy was right: There never was anyone to talk to in Texas. And here? Why, I fought just to stay alive. Strange. I would have thought honor and duty had more stick-to-itiveness than adventure.

O'Shaughnessy sat down next to him. "Tell me about her," he said.

Oh shit. What time was it? The sun was already starting its long slide down the sky. I felt sorry for Riddell, but I was tired and hungry, and we were going to hear about Mum.

"An 'ealer, me mum. Smart as a whip, 'onest as the day. Knows 'er 'erbs upside and down. Nettle, for instance. Now there's something people pulls up and throws away, Father. But there's nothing better for the dropsy than stinging nettle. The juice strengthens cows' milk. Stops a nosebleed, too. Mum knew all of that and more. And pretty? Mum was small and delicate, like a wild marjoram bloom; so dainty, it scared me to hug her."

"She loved you," O'Shaghnessy said.

"Oh." A breathy, awestruck sound, a faraway look, as if her love spanned all of Europe. "Not by 'alf. It was 'er taught me everything. Cowslips all over this place, you know, and that was 'er favorite. Plain little flower, it is. Overlook it, if you're not careful. But she made a tea for nerves, and compresses for the 'eadache. It was 'er taught me never to throw away."

"And a valuable lesson it was."

"Was that. Just because something's common, well, it can still be important, can't it."

They talked on, sometimes it seemed at cross purposes, sometimes with such a private meaning that I couldn't quite catch on. But, simple as the words sounded, immortality stood behind them. I finally sat down on the grass. Sun streaked through a nearby stand of trees, threw lemony light over Riddell and O'Shaughnessy—splashes of grace.

Riddell cried some more, then wiped his eyes. He talked about Scotch broom and dandelion, about colt's foot and feverfew. I lay down on shaded grass that still smelled warm from the sun and watched white butterflies flirt with a hedgerow while Sergeant Riddell wove a quiet funeral wreath for his mother.

When Riddell was finished, O'Shaughnessy said, "I remember when me own mother passed on. It was hard, and me being a priest. I know that you're not of the Faith, Sergeant, but all the same, I'll pray for her when I say the Mass."

I rolled over on my back. One lone butterfly floated upward, teased through the tree branches, free and on its way.

" 'Tis important to remember her, I think. To say a few words. For knowing she's in a better place doesn't help with the hurting. There. There now. I know. It's all right. I know." The ugly sounds of a man's weeping, and over that O'Shaughnessy's simple and eloquent comfort. Finally, "Would you be wanting to pray with me now, lad?"

"Thank you, Father."

High up, where the butterfly drifted, a commotion of branches and birds singing loud. I thought about Ma, and what sort of wreath I'd weave her. Stern heart-ribbons, I guess, plain and strong. Nothing fancy.

I dozed off during the whispered prayer. O'Shaughnessy woke me and helped me to my feet. I woke dazed and bleary-eyed, confused to find myself in a meadow.

"Will you be coming with us?" O'Shaughnessy asked Riddell.

I saw Riddell's tear-swollen face and remembered.

"In a bit. I'll splash me face first. Get presentable. You go on, then." He stuck his hand out at me. "Thank you for coming by, Stanhope," he said, like we were standing around in his parlor.

I shook his hand, told him again how sorry I was, and got polite murmurs in answer.

Back on the road, O'Shaughnessy said, "I saw me mum after, you know. Me da, too. Wouldn't doubt that Sergeant will see his. Mothers come back to check, to tuck you in of a night, and see that you're eating well. Is yours alive?"

"Alive and kicking and ornery as ever."

"And your da?"

"He's a son of a bitch."

The breeze brought with it a faint reminder of the sea. I was hungry all of a sudden. Restless and ready for a drink.

"Would you be wanting to talk about him, lad?"

I told him, "Not ever."

When I got back to the rest area, I left O'Shaughnessy and found the rest of the platoon. Pickering said he wanted to visit the town whores, so we went to the blue-light tent and then we walked to town together. There were four whores in the whorehouse, all of them ugly; but I fucked the tar out of one all the same, hammered her so hard that she got to complaining. I threw an extra five shillings in the cardboard box and left. Pickering and me picked up Foy, and the three of us went out drinking together. In the bar, a Belgian soldier shoved me and I coldcocked him. Foy, who's a corporal now, had the balls to give me a dressing-down, and him every bit as drunk as I was. Pickering made us leave before the Belgian came back with his friends.

As soon as my head hit the pillow, I was asleep. Wildflowers were blooming among the marble angels now: yellow flowers in little bouquets and lilac ones with long lacy stems. All around the graveyard the trees—dark and secret with leaves—had fruited. Everywhere you looked there was life, Bobby. It hung heavy and pregnant from the branches. In the sunny spaces, it sprouted high and wild. Life, God, plentiful as the seeds in a woman. And through that fertile graveyard bees circled, their legs thick with golden creation.

As I stood there, I noticed Dunleavy standing beside me, looking out, too, on all that life. Funny. In the dream I didn't remember that he was dead particularly, but I remembered real clear the angry way we had left each other. It seemed he had forgotten, though, for he was grinning ear to ear.

He shook my hand and said in a loud, boisterous voice, "I'm much better now, thanks. Much, much better."

There was pink in his cheeks. His grip was strong.

"Much better," he said. "I'll be going now." And then he walked away. You know what, Bobby? I don't think I'll ever see him again.

Love, Travis Lee

JULY 17, THE RESERVE TRENCHES

Dear Bobby,

I want you to tell Ma something for me, Bobby. Find you a time when the house is quiet and supper's not waiting and tell her that Travis Lee forgives her. I know she's been waiting for that a long time.

See, when Pa was home, it was him who took up all her space. He was so big and she used herself up just surviving, so there wasn't nothing of her left for me. Then came the fancy goats and scrabbling for the next meal. It was a hard time, and she was too busy for mothering. I want her to know I understand that.

Also, tell her I understand why she went to spoiling you. Hell, by the time Ma had a minute to herself, I was already too growed up to be loving on. You were perfect: six years old and a cherub-faced hellion.

I never begrudged you anything; never faulted Ma for not standing between me and the belt. Seemed like growing up, Ma and me were kept as prisoners in the dark. But still, we were together.

Reason I'm thinking on her is that Riddell is still mourning his mum. You can see it in his face, in the way he walks. He doesn't talk much lately, doesn't laugh. Some ways, I don't think he'll ever get over losing her.

You couldn't ever call Ma gentle or sweet. She wasn't made as delicate as a wild marjoram flower; but she raised herself a pair of strong boys. Neither one of us will be giving up on life after she's gone. I want you to promise me something, Bobby. Before this week is out, you tell her thank you for me.

Travis Lee

Five

July 22, the forward trenches

Dear Bobby,

Yesterday I'd gone to Support to visit the medic. A headache was all it was, remedied easy by an aspirin powder. On the way back I was alone, threading my way up the communications trench, when I turned a corner and came upon a Boche. It took a heartbeat for me to believe what I was seeing. You understand, Bobby? There was a Boche in the trench. A Boche, just standing there.

He was so young and he looked so lost that I never even shouldered my rifle. He was wounded. There were great blossoms of blood all across his belly, and his helmet was off. I wondered how he had got misplaced so bad, and if he wasn't scared to death. Then he raised his head and looked right at me. He had guileless brown eyes and a baby face and pudgy hands, so new to the front that he hadn't had time to get worn thin and hard. Lord God, he was a pitiful sight. Young and sorely wounded. His right hand was missing.

I took a step forward and he started fading. When he went, he went misty-like. I could see the dirt wall of the trench through him. I called out for him to stop, but I wasn't quick enough. He was gone.

I went back to my station at the firebay. I set up my ammunition and rifle and started looking for targets. I missed two easy shots. That's when I asked the new lieutenant, Blackhall, to send for O'Shaughnessy.

"Want to pray over your aim, eh, Stanhope?" He laughed.

"Please get him, sir. And permission to take a short rest period."

Blackhall's a small man with a face like a suspicious monkey. "You're shaking. That won't do for a sharpshooter. 'As you been drinking? For I 'ear rumors."

"Sir." And I was near tears when I said it. My voice was unsteady. "Sir," I whispered, "please call him."

Blackhall started barking orders. I sat down on the firestep. I could see Marrs out of the corner of my eye. "You sick?" he asked.

If I'd tried to answer, I'd have started boo-hooing.

"Stanhope?" Poor solicitous Marrs. "You all right, then?"

Pickering's jovial "It's that bloody dysentery. Don't shit here, Stanhope. We'll make you clean the firestep."

Gatlin, one of the new boys, saying, "What's the matter with 'im?"

"Dysentery. You want to carry him, Gatlin? I'll take his top half, you have his bottom."

Footsteps boomed along the duckboards and everyone got real quiet. A hand clasped my knee. O'Shaughnessy said, "Travis." He bent down to look into my face. "Will you be needing me?"

When I nodded, he took my arm and helped me up. He asked Marrs to take my rifle, for I couldn't hold onto it no more.

"Crikey!" Marrs cried out. "What'd the medic say, Stanhope? What'd 'e tell you?"

Pickering asked in a voice stripped of humor. "You really sick? Anything we can do, Father?"

O'Shaughnessy waved their questions away.

We walked, Bobby—walked along the front line and down the trench past where the Boche boy had been. We ended up in Miller's dugout. It was empty but for the batman. O'Shaughnessy asked him to leave.

I sat down on the ground and bawled—not caring who might be listening. I cried because I knew it had to be ghosts I was seeing. I cried because I was scared of dying, because I felt so damned sorry for that Boche. I cried for everything, I guess.

O'Shaughnessy sat down next to me and slipped his arm around my shoulders. The holding wasn't as good as Ma's or as the calico girl's, but it was holding all the same.

"I hear you can forgive things."

"Tell me, lad," he said.

"I hurt a woman." I don't know why I told him that part, it was a small thing, really. "She didn't have nothing to do with why I was mad, and loving someone, even a whore, ought to be a happy thing. But I fucked her so hard, sir. It was fury I seeded her with. I squeezed her arms and titties till I bruised her black and blue and she was begging me to stop. When I didn't, she started crying. I really hurt her. I don't know why I did it, sir. I been asking myself that."

Miller's dugout smelled strangely empty, no life nor death to it.

I wiped my eyes. "You going to forgive me, or what?"

"Are you contrite, then? For both your sins? For 'twas not only the beating, my son, but fornication, too."

My shoulders slumped. I was nearly too exhausted to move my mouth. Twenty-three years old and so goddamned tired. "Sorry for hurting her. Yeah."

"So there is that much heavenly rejoicing, at any rate. And do you sincerely promise not to do it again?"

I nodded. My back ached. My arms felt too weak to lift.

"Well, then! If you were of the Faith, we should have a proper penance."

There was a map on Miller's wall with lines of red pins and lines of blue. Red to the west. So it was us who were bleeding.

"At least beg for forgiveness, Travis. Can you do that? Apologize to God."

"Yes, sir."

It was cool and damp in that dugout. I remembered when Ma would take you and me down to the root cellar when there was a cyclone brewing. There were spiders lurking around the jars of canned corn and black-eyed peas. When Ma'd light the lamp, you'd go to screaming. I thought how nice that was, screaming over spiders, and never having to scream over Pa.

"He hurt my ma, sir."

"Who was that, Travis?"

"My pa hurt my ma, sir. After I hurt that whore, I went out and started a bar fight. Pa was fond of bar fights, too. I had an uncle always said women turn into their mothers and men turn into their daddies. Do we have to, sir?"

"I think you needn't, if you have a mind not to."

"I took a thirty ought-six to him."

O'Shaughnessy gave a long sigh. "And did you kill him?"

"No. But I tried like hell."

"Ask God to forgive your anger."

"Yes, sir."

It was safe there in Miller's dugout, the cyclone brewing.

"Lad? Failing was not a sin."

It's good to know that, I guess. Miller walked in on us about then. When he caught sight of what was going on, he started to leave. I got up, dusted my pants, and told him O'Shaughnessy and me were finished. I thanked him for the use of his dugout and asked if I could have the time until dinner off. What I didn't tell him was that I couldn't shoot nobody, Bobby. Not that day.

Miller was real nice about it. He asked if I was well, and I told him I was. He asked after you and Ma—he'd heard about Riddell, I guess—and I told him y'all were just fine. He insisted that I take me some cookies. Three big hazelnut cookies. They were so good that I finished them before I ever got back to the forward trench and told Blackhall about the orders. Then I went in and lay down in my cubbyhole.

We sleep like mud dauber wasps in the dugouts here, Bobby: honeycomb holes in the walls, sandbags all around, a plank over me that my nose nearly touches. Earth to three sides, snuggled up close.

Marrs came in and asked if I was all right. I said I was. After a while he left me alone.

I wasn't all right. I won't be for a while. I never told O'Shaughnessy the very thing I needed to: about LeBlanc and the way he killed that Boche. Was it really him I saw in the trench, that sapper? Or was guilt just stirring up my imagination? If I was really seeing a ghostie, it sure beats hell out of how I imagined things work. The world is topsy-turvy right now, Bobby, and that scares the shit out of me. One thing, though: All this time I'd been thinking only about the horror of what LeBlanc had done. It took the Boche to make me feel the pity.

Travis Lee

JULY 27, THE RESERVE TRENCHES

Dear Bobby,

The last night we were forward I woke up to the noise of explosions. I thought we were being shelled until I remembered that we were on the front line.

Somewhere down the trench I could hear Blackhall shouting, "Fix bayonets!"

I ran out of my dugout. A bogeyman stood in the dark gully of the trench. His face was blackened, his uniform sooty. He was aiming a rifle at me. He fired, and in the dim glow from the dugout's door I saw the pale puff from the barrel, heard the bullet go buzzing past.

Another shadow figure leaped over the parapet. I took to my heels. See, all that time I was thinking the first Boche was a ghostie, Bobby. When I knew for sure he was real, it was too late to grab my rifle. Behind me I heard Pickering's dismayed shout, "What bleeding luck!" I heard the pop of rifle fire, the crack of grenades bursting. The air went thick with gunpowder smoke.

I darted around the corner of a firebay, ran through a traverse. Ahead, men had come out of the dugouts and were milling, confused.

I screamed, "Encroachment! Encroachment behind me!"

Riddell shouted, "Where were the sentries, then?" and, "Get me my Very pistol!"

"Help Pickering, Sergeant! Please! Pickering's back there! And oh God, Marrs!"

Some of the new boys spooked. They started chucking Battye bombs. Sergeant told them to stop, that they might be killing our own. He got them in line and had the front boys fix bayonets. They went charging around the corner and out of sight.

Boche in our trenches. Our small contained world coming to an end. There was no place to run from the Germans, so I went charging back toward the encroachment. All around me, men were up on the firesteps, shooting wildly into the dark. Sergeant's Very lights went up. Flares went up next, bursting like pale green meteors. The firing from our side crescendoed; and with it, the fast steady chatter of the machine guns.

In the next traverse, a Boche was waiting. I didn't see him until I was on him, and then it was too late. Before he had a chance to fire, I'd run him down.

We fell, tangled together, struggling. He fought, but I punched him hard, wrested away his gun. Straddling him, I looked down. He was bleeding from the mouth and grunting something in German. It took me a while to realize he was trying to surrender. He was just a goddamned kid, Bobby. Probably not old enough to grow a good beard.

"You all right, Stanhope?" From the dark of the corner came Riddell's bland question.

I got up, holding the Boche rifle. I grabbed the boy's hand and pulled him up, too.

"Good work."

We were alone in that traverse, just the three of us: the boy with his hands over his head; me holding the boy's weapon, Riddell holding his. Above us, the flares and Very lights were burning out.

"Is it over, Sergeant?"

Riddell was staring at that boy so strange. "Bit of rum luck, ain't it," he said.

"Sir?"

"Foy's wounded. Tucker and Redding is dead."

It happened so fast I guess I couldn't have stopped him. Riddell lowered his rifle and stepped forward quick, just the way you do in practice. And as if that boy had no more meaning than a straw dummy, he ran him through.

The German boy looked surprised. His arms dropped, and he grabbed the bayonet so tight that his hands squirted blood. He didn't have the strength to pull the blade out; and when Sergeant twisted the rifle the way you're supposed to, that Boche boy made a sound. I don't guess it was a word. I'll never know. He dropped to his knees like he was praying.

A few of the men caught up with us—like me, too late to do much good. The boy was already curled up, holding his stomach. Blood pumped between his fingers.

"Lucky I come along when I did," Riddell said. "Else Stanhope 'ere would 'ave got it."

The boy died before the stretcher bearer arrived. Everything was all right. I suppose it was all right. Three of our platoon dead, but it was the sentries and not me who got in trouble. They found our own forward sapper with his throat slashed. I reckon LeBlanc has started his own private dirty war.

Everything's settled back down, but I'll never feel safe sleeping in the trench again. I figure no one will. Still, we sleep, we eat, we shit. We pour over and over our letters from home. Days now, and nobody's said a word about me running, or the way that Boche boy in the traverse died. I sure didn't dare speak up, for I looked into Riddell's face real careful that night, Bobby. Sergeant may not know what's waiting for him at home, but one of his questions has been answered: I don't reckon it's love for his mum nor any Elgar sort of duty, but Riddell's found himself something to kill for.

Travis Lee

JULY 29, THE RESERVE TRENCHES
Bobby,

I'm asking too much of you? I'm asking too *much*? Bobby, I don't want to hear about how things are tough. You're the coddled one of this family. You've nearly always had three square meals a day, as much red meat as you wanted. Always had a roof over your head. So you have to care for the goats and clean up after Pa. So what? You're the one who asked him in so he could puke on your floor. You're the one wanted him around so he could shit the bed. If you don't like it, put him in the goddamned barn. Burn it down, and put him and you both out of your misery.

Just a word of warning, boy: Don't you go asking Ma to run the business and tend to Pa, too. You're fourteen goddamned years old. You're near six foot tall. Time enough for you to take on life. I was setting fence posts and gelding stock and changing your diapers by the time I was ten. By the time I was fourteen, I was negotiating loans with county bankers by day and plowing their wives at night.

The Tommies call me "old and bold," because I can finagle things. I get out of duty when I want, or nick extra rations. I've settled in to war just like I did to school.

I thrive. That's the secret to life—not dying, the way LeBlanc believes. Poor old LeBlanc thinks there's no Heaven nor Hell, just a big old Nothing. Seeing as how he relishes killing, I think that's the after-death choice he'd pick. Sometimes I start to believe in Nothingness, too, leastways when I start crediting my dreams as real and I start thinking about that black place beyond the cypress. But I tell you this, Bobby: Whatever's out there, Hell or Limbo, I'll thrive.

So I don't want to hear you whining on about how I was supposed to become a doctor and make lots of money to support you and Ma. You got to learn, like I did, to get by. Fact is, after this is over, I'm sending your butt straight out of Texas. Go to California like you've always had a mind to, for I'm coming home to kick you out of the house. Then I'll stay and take care of Ma, the way I always have.

Ma's the one who's worked hardest; and every time I'd come home from school she'd have herself another bad wheezing spell. I talked to Riddell about her, and here's what he says to do, if it's not asking too goddamned much: Find her a bunch of Joe Pye weed, hang it up and dry it out real good. Steep a tea from it and make her drink that every day.

Make sure you have licorice and horehound on hand; mustard plaster in case her chest starts filling up. Don't let her have any milk nor cheese nor coffee. Also, she don't need to be getting out in that hot sun. Please, Bobby, just take care of her a little, just till I can get home. That's all I'm asking. A mother's death leaves a gaping hole in you. When Riddell started talking about that Joe Pye weed, he went to crying so bad it'd break your heart. Nobody will ever love him like his ma did. Nobody'll ever pamper him when he's sick, or hug him when he's scared, or make that damned bubble and squeak just the same way. Nobody. Not ever.

I've been thinking: All I got besides Ma is the calico girl, and she's just this side of a maybe. The idea of being alone scares me worse than shells. So you keep Ma well until I can get home. Keep her safe, for I'm coming soon as the war's over. No gallivanting around Europe, no more vacations, no more adventure. And when she's fighting to take her next breath, you do all the things I used to: Boil her some well-water with camphor, rub her throat with eucalyptus salve. Tell her Travis Lee's coming home quick as he can.

Travis Lee

JULY 31, THE FRONT TRENCHES

Dear Bobby,

That goddamned Blackhall made me shit wallah. I can't believe it.

"Straighten you out, Stanhope," he said. "Report to Riddell. He'll be expecting you. You're to help Nye with the duty. Perhaps you can think about life while you're hauling muck."

We were standing in a traverse when Blackhall gave me the order. Pickering was sitting on a whale oil crate behind me, and when he heard, he broke into that whinny of his.

"Shut your mouf, Pickering," Blackhall said.

"All due respect, sir." I snorted, too, just to show him I meant it sarcastic-like. "You're talking here to two originals. You know that, don't you? We joined this company back when. And we're a dwindling bunch, sir, seeing as how Foy's in hospital blues right now. We're goddamned valuable to this battalion. *I'm* valuable," I said. "You don't have nobody to bring up the company kill totals like I do."

He lit his pipe, sucked a few times on the stem, and blew the smoke in my face.

"Easy on," Pickering called in warning, for he knew I was about to take Blackhall down, lieutenant or not.

"You've a bad attitude, Stanhope, and I mean to cure it or kill yer."

"You run this shit wallah idea of yours by Captain Miller?"

He laughed. "You'll still have time to play the sharpshooter. Oh, yes. I'll see to that. And if you don't, no matter. You're not as bleeding important to this company as you think." Then he walked away.

I went on down to talk some sense into Riddell, but when I saw the look on his face, I knew I'd have to take my complaint higher.

"Was that, or field punishment," he said. "Best take the duty, lad."

Nye reminds me of an old coon hound who's lost his tracking scent and has retired to sentry the yard. He keeps saying I'll get used to it. "Ain't so bad," he told me. "You holds your breath, that's the trick. And keep your head down when you takes the kerosene tin up the communication trench. Supposed to bury the muck, but I got me a special dumping spot, I does."

When I opened my first biscuit box latrine, I nearly threw up in the hole. It's different going at it ass-first. The rope handles were slimy. The tin was a lot heavier than I thought. I can tell you firsthand, Bobby: This army's plumb full of shit.

When I finally wrestled the tin out, I had to bend over so my face was real close to the places asses and peckers had overshot their aim. I had to fish around the hole for the cover. I found it, coated with dried yellow scum.

"Goddamn!" I spat. "Jesus! Fuck it! Shit!"

Nye got to laughing at me so hard that he nearly tumped his kerosene tin. "An' that's the truf of it, Yank."

"Son-of-a-bitching duty," I said. Shit was all over my hands and just then my nose decided to itch. I rubbed it hard against my shoulder. "I *hate* this! That ignorant SOB, Blackhall!"

From down the trench I could hear Pickering's merry loud laugh, Marrs's manic cackle.

I screamed. "You better shut the hell up! I'm coming up there, Pickering! You hear me? I'm coming to dump this crap on you."

Nye was laughing so hard that he could hardly walk. We must have awakened the Boche, for a couple of Maxim rounds slapped the dirt mound of the parados behind me. It startled me, and my hand twitched. Piss sloshed in the can, spilled, and soaked my puttees.

"Christ!" I shouted toward the German gunner, "You shit-for-brains kraut!" More bullets whined over my head.

I followed Nye from the firebay into a traverse where Pickering, Marrs, and Foy were sitting, convulsed with laughter. When they saw my expression, they got up quick and retreated down the trench. Above me, bullets punched the parados like small hard fists, sent dirt flying.

I shouted back, "You cock-sucking squarehead! If you know what's good for you, you bastard, you'll stop that right now!"

"Here!" Nye called.

He wasn't in front of me anymore. I turned to see him standing in the mouth of a communications trench. He was red-faced and watery-eyed from merriment.

"Come on, now, Stanhope, an' let's do our dump wif our heads and arses down. You've called our Fritz bad names, see? And now he's mad at us, ain't he."

We shouldered our way down the communications trench past a stray dugout, a small one, where two lost-looking men were sleeping. Just before reaching the support trench, Nye climbed the revetment and jumped the sandbags. I stood, holding onto my bucket while way across No Man's Land a Maxim played a slow and deadly rataplan.

"Come on," Nye called.

Tighter quarters here than the communications trench

where I saw LeBlanc's Boche. This was just a cramped, careless, zigzag gouge in the earth. The sweet-sickly smell of death—either human or rat—was so strong that it drove out the stink of offal.

Nye peered over a sandbag. "Got to do it, chum. That, or carry the tin three kilos down. Would'ye rather?"

Holding onto the tin's handles tightly, I climbed up after him. The land between the front trench and the support was clinging desperately to life. Not far from my splayed hand was one of those yellow flowers I'd seen when I'd gone skinny-dipping with O'Shaughnessy. By that was a tuft of grass, wonderfully, miraculously green.

"Come on, then, Stanhope. No time for sightseeing. Dump it here."

He'd found a shell hole, a big one; and he'd clearly been using it for a while. The crater was half full of sewage. I wormed forward, popped the cover, and let my load of sludge join the rest.

"Not so bad now, is it? Me, well, they made me shit wallah when I joined the company, an' I never knew any different. I figure it's a stinky duty, but better than some. Rather carry shit than carry up the ammo, meself. Something hit one of these kerosene tins, an' all it needs is a quick bath to set you right. Come on, now. Give us a smile. Don't know what you did to get the assignment, Yank, but . . ."

"Nothing, okay? I didn't do nothing."

"All right. No need to get in a bristle. Besides, this is just jankers duty, and not no field punishment or the clink." Nye said. "Trick is to keep your head down, though. Lost Partridge that way."

Lucky Partridge. I carted shit all day, working down the company platoon by platoon, getting to know the men better and more up-close than I'd ever wanted to.

"There's a tale to shit," Nye, the philosopher, said. "Take this lot. One's family sent him raisins. You can see how they all plumped up. Bad digestion'll do that: sends things through whole. Corn, mostly."

The Maxim had gone quiet. I wished it would start up again.

"Does worse when men has a scare in them. Plum jam'll turn you red, organ meats turn you green. All colors to shit, really. You ever notice, Yank?"

"No." Shelling. I longed for the clean sound of a whistling william, the low croon of a minnie.

Nye took a break for a cigarette, a cheap gasper. He didn't bother to wash his hands. When we ate lunch, he didn't bother washing them then, either. I don't know. Shit wallah. Some ends may be worse than death.

That night I went back to my dugout covered in sour brown sludge. My shoulders ached. Even in the stink of the trench, soldiers stepped out of my way.

Blackhall was in the door of his dugout, waiting. "Best thing for a mean dog—work him into minding. Think I'll work you for a bit, Stanhope."

Pickering was standing a few feet away, smiling already, waiting for my comeback; but I was too tired to reply.

I crawled into my cubbyhole and closed my eyes. I must have gone to sleep as soon as they shut. When I woke up the next morning, Pickering and Marrs had moved. I was the only one left in my dugout.

Exhaustedly yours, Travis Lee

AUGUST 3, THE REST AREA
ONE TO GIVE YOU FACE TO FACE

Dear Bobby,

They kept us too damned long at the front. Command knew that, I guess, because by the time they ordered us back, they ordered us all the way into the rest area and gave us an extended leave. Some of the boys had been getting pretty twitchy and trench-bound. Before we were even settled into the huts, the boys were running around organizing a football game. I lingered over my first shower in days, gloried in my clean uniform. But I could still smell shit on me.

Miller would straighten Blackhall out. I hadn't shot a Boche in weeks. Miller's totals were probably slumping. To be honest, Bobby, I've known for a long time that Miller's pecker stands at attention when I'm around. Hell, women flirt to get what they want, don't they? I wasn't too proud to wiggle my ass for the captain. God, I hate shit wallah duty.

So I made sure my uniform looked good enough for muster. I combed what hair the army left me into that forehead curl all the girls like. I shaved my face titty-soft; I slapped a little Bay Rum on. I made myself pretty, like I was stepping out with a lady.

Had to be a clandestine meeting, though. And I thought a powerful lot about how I'd approach him. Get him alone. Real secluded kind of alone. And I'd start slow and subtle, like you do with the girls. Get up close to him—not touching, but near to. I'd look him right in the eye and keep my voice low. Old Martha Jane Van der Hooven says she nearly wets her drawers when I make my voice husky.

I'd say something ambiguous like, "You know, Captain Miller? I can't help noticing you."

Let me stop right here and give you a lesson in seduction, Bobby. You don't have to tell a woman you love her. Just say something ambiguous and they'll ponder it. They'll turn your words this way and that. They'll look at them upside down and sideways. They'll think about those words so much that, with you not doing a thing, they'll build their own romance.

Not that I was considering any activity with Miller, you understand. No, sir. I never had nothing like that in mind. Just a flirtation, that's all. Why, if life throws a pry bar your way, seems that God means for you to use it.

I caught sight of him leaving the officers' hut. He was walking by himself. He looked kind of sad, really—just him and the road. I trailed him, keeping out of sight.

I hoped he wouldn't up and kiss me. God almighty. I'd have to make awful damned sure that things never got that far. No laying on of hands, nothing like that.

But the deeper we got into the countryside, the more scared I got. He was easy to track, no turning around to look, no eyeing the scenery. Where the hell was he going?

He turned, strolling over a fieldstone bridge. I hid in a hedgerow until he was out of sight, then double-timed it after him.

"Oh, it's you, Captain Miller!" I'd say, like I was surprised.

Would he ask me why I wasn't back at the hut getting ready for that afternoon's inspection? Maybe not. Not if I gave him the eye first.

But flirting with him could prove dangerous. I mean, hell, the boy was lonely.

So I'd treat him gentle, the way I would a starry-eyed piece of jailbait with aspirations. "If things were different," I'd say. Or "If I ever decided to do it with a man . . ." Something like that.

Ahead was a woody copse. The canopied, shady lane through it was empty. Damn. Where had Miller gone? I kept close to the roadside weeds and saw signs ahead: broken fern stalks and snapped branches where someone had left the trail. The forest was too quiet. Too dark. Had he figured out that I was behind him? He could be waiting up ahead to ambush me.

It was an idiot idea in the first place. What was I thinking? I'd gone AWL from the barracks. Miller would have me up on charges. He'd catch me here all alone and force me to, well, you know. Damnation, Bobby. I didn't know how I could put up with that. I'd knock the fire out of him first. But then it would be my word against his. What was the punishment for striking an officer?

Voices started up a few yards ahead, and laughter. I hunkered down by a nearby evergreen bush and listened. Two men, keeping their voices low. I crept around the bush to take a peek. Miller and Dunston-Smith. They were just standing there talking, casual as any two fellows, when all of a sudden Dunston-Smith up and kissed Miller. It wasn't just a peck, either, but one of those sloppy tongue-down-the-throat types. Miller wasn't exactly backing away.

Made me want to puke. I mean, I knew he was a light-stepper and all, but still. Dunston-Smith? He let Dunston-Smith poke his tongue in his mouth? Jesus God. Didn't Miller remember that Dunston-Smith was at the stables that time I rode his big sorrel gelding? Well, if he didn't remember that peckerwood drinking cheap wine and gossiping about him, why, I do. And I remember real clear what he said as Miller walked away: ". . . right schools, but how could they have taken a sheeny?"

Dunston-Smith has a prissy laugh, Bobby, and a way of looking down his nose at you. And, well, I may not be any judge, but don't seem to me that he's anything to look at. Still, there Miller stood, letting him tongue his tonsils and feel him up. When Miller stepped back, I thought, *Boy's finally come to his senses*, but he took Dunston-Smith's hand and led him away to a tumbledown hut.

I should have gone back then. I didn't. I don't know why I stayed. There was nothing to see but the hut's blank wall. There was nothing to hear but the birds. I thought about how the two of them had seemed so comfortable with each other, like they'd been loving long enough to clear away the silliness.

The spot they'd chosen was pathetic. The roof's thatch had a case of mange. It would leak when it rained. And they must have been there in the rain sometimes. In the heat of an afternoon. In the chill of a twilight. Miller. So familiar with that hand. So sure of where he led him. How Dunston-Smith trustingly followed.

There'd be a blanket inside to wrap themselves up in. Straw, and an oilskin to keep it fresh. The place would smell of hay and mildew, forest and mushrooms and sweated bodies. I waited. All I saw was the mute wall where moss spread in gentle feathery blooms across rain-stained planks. Late flowers blossomed nearby: pale, secretive, fleshy things. So hushed was that tree-dark that the birds' cries seemed piercing. Still I sat, breathing in the scent of evergreen, until the sun sank under the horizon and my head had cleared and I figured I could stand.

I got back late—late for dinner, late for inspection. In the lamp-lit dark, I ran into a pair of red caps. They arrested me, of course. Then they marched me down to Blackhall, who shook his head and told me, "Stanhope, you're a lazy bastard.

Is there nothing you won't do to shirk duty?" and ordered me clapped in the glasshouse.

Jail. Better than shoveling shit.

Travis Lee

AUGUST 4, THE GLASSHOUSE

Dear Bobby,

I can't sleep here. Something about the place. I toss and turn. I listen to the click of heels as the sentries make their rounds. Nights, I watch crosshatched moonlight climb the wall; and when the moon sets, I get up and pace the three short steps from iron-barred door to meshed window. I stop there sometimes, my palms flat against the wood wall. A damp, grass-scented breeze comes through the mesh, nose-high.

Funny. I didn't think being jailed would make me jumpy, but it's the knowing I can't leave, Bobby. It's the having to sit here that drives me crazy. I jiggle my foot to bleed off the nerves. I work my hands together so tight that my nails turn blue.

When I lie down it seems like spiders are crawling my skin, and I picture the daddy longlegs in the root cellar and how Ma used to hold you tight; how I'd hold you when Ma was too sick and the storms were coming. Do you remember that, Bobby? Do you remember how I used to wrap my arms around you when spiders threatened and the wind howled upstairs? I haven't been such a bad brother, have I?

Time travels slow here. Marrs and Pickering came to see me today. Pickering studied me this way and that. "Don't look half so handsome in clink as you do mucking out latrines."

"Hear they gives you bread and water," Marrs said. "That all?"

"Otherwise wouldn't be much of a punishment, Marrs." Pickering lit up a Woodbine, offered me one. "We're going into town to prang whores, Stanhope. Wish you could come."

Marrs, shy and nervous as a mouse. "Don't be telling nobody I'm going to visit a tart, now. Don't want the folks at home to hear, me dad friends with our parish priest and all."

"I say, you all right, Stanhope?" Pickering asked. "You sure? Well, you're the talk of the company again. Good old Stanhope, the font of bloody conversation. Here. Let me light that gasper for you. You sure you're all right, now? Why'nt give us a smile, then? A fart?"

"Something," Marrs said.

The cigarette tasted stale, but I kept on smoking. "Do me a favor, Pickering. Prang your whore once for me."

He put his hand through the bars. "Be five shillings."

Marrs gave out with one of his high, insane cackles. "Pickering's talking you up to the whole company, about you being a red Indian and all, and how you can come and go without being seen, like. He's goes on about you forever. Got them all believers."

Pickering's face went serious. He took a pensive drag of his cigarette, let the smoke trail out his nostrils: a droll, horse-faced dragon. "So where were you off to, then? I mean, really?"

I paced the room, trying to outdistance Pickering's stare. "I can't sleep no more. Ain't that funny? No Maxims, no shells, and I can't sleep worth shit."

"Too bad," Marrs said.

Blank gray sky in the window, the smell of rain. "You boys bring me back something from town?"

"Whores're too heavy to carry, Stanhope," Pickering told me. "Especially that fat ox you favor. Besides, you'd have to stick your bird through the bars. Think it would go, Marrs? Think our Stanhope's that gifted?"

I turned in time to see bashful Marrs duck his head. "Dunno. Ain't like I ever looked."

"Ain't you, then?" Pickering can do a dead-on parody of Marrs. He's a mockingbird like that—mimics everyone. He's a hurtful kind of funny, Bobby, if you know what I mean.

Marrs takes the joshing a lot better than I would. "Hey," I said. "Hey, Pickering. No kidding. You bring me something from town?"

Pickering does Texan with less success. He stuck his thumbs in his belt. "Whut'chu be wantin', son?"

"Bottle of that French brandy. I'll pay you for it."

Pickering lost his smile. His arms dropped. Marrs said, "Wish I could, Stanhope. But it's plain against regs."

"Then just bring me a swallow of your rum ration, okay? Okay, Pickering? Huh, Marrs? You can put it in a pozzy pot. Hide it in your shirt. No one'll have to know."

Pickering was shaking his head real slow. It drove me nuts the way he did that. If the bars hadn't been there, I would have slapped him ugly.

Marrs looked miserable. "You can see how it is, can't you, Stanhope? What if we was caught?"

"Your priest might find out. You fucking piece of shit." I spanked my palm against the door so hard that my hand went numb. I hit it again. The iron bolt rattled crazily.

A red cap poked his head around the corner. "What's it?"

"No problem, sir." Pickering sounded so calm, so sure of himself, that the red cap nodded curtly and left.

I said, "The hell with you. It's not like I'm asking for something hard."

Marrs backed away, shrinking in on himself. Pickering said, "No use getting yourself bothered, Stanhope. Wasn't us who put you in there."

"I'm not goddamned bothered. Look. I thought we were friends, you know? All I'm asking for is one swallow from your ration. Hey, Marrs? Can't you spare one shitting little bitty swallow of your ration?"

I begged and begged them, but they wouldn't pay me no mind. They threatened to go, and I pleaded with them not to leave me. Those yellow-belly, worthless shits. Those goddamned peckerwood bastards. I thought they were pals, but they made me cry, and that shamed me. I'll never forgive them for that.

The red cap came and hit the bars with his nightstick, a bare inch from my fingers. Iron rang. The vibration tingled in my bones. "Next time your head," he told me.

I went back to my cot and tried to sleep. I tried to pray,

and that didn't work out, either. I couldn't remember any goddamned words but the last ones I had shouted. *Please don't leave me.* Too late. Pickering, Marrs, you, Ma. All gone.

Travis Lee

AUGUST 6, THE GLASSHOUSE

Dear Bobby,

Worse today. I feel sick to my stomach. My body aches like I got a fever. I got the shakes so bad, I can't light a cigarette. I broke down and boo-hooed this morning for no good reason. I want to forget, that's all. One little swallow. Is that too much to ask for? One little swallow for company. Just something to hold me when nobody else will.

I close my eyes and memory comes crowding: you and Ma. Pa in one of his beating moods. Trantham on the wire. Smoot in his glass-topped grave. I try shoving them back, but my arms aren't strong enough. Faces come. They stare at me close. Shit, Bobby. They're driving me crazy.

Travis Lee

AUGUST 8, THE GLASSHOUSE

Dear Bobby,

LeBlanc came to visit. "You look like warmed-over crap," he said. "What's your sentence, anyway?"

"Dunno."

I paced. He watched me. He was smoking one of his French manure fags.

"They're moving us up tomorrow."

They were all going to leave me. Every damned one of them. Jesus. I wanted a swallow of rum so bad. I wanted it the way you feel when you want to come with a woman, but you can't: a huge, limitless Almost.

"Bring you something before I go?"

"Drink," I said.

"Huh? Speak louder, Stanhope. You're mush-mouthed."

I went to the bars and faced him, lunatic eye to lunatic eye. I whispered, "Drink."

He cupped his ear. "You want a drink? That what you're saying?"

"I'd suck your pecker if you'd bring me a swallow of rum."

LeBlanc has a smile like a knife. Without a word, he turned and left. How long would my company be gone? Nearly a month the last tour. Miller. *He* wouldn't be alone. Not hand-in-hand with Dunston-Smith. Not sharing secrets in a cramped dark place, not breathing in the smell of straw. I sat on the floor, holding tight to the bars.

LeBlanc was back a few minutes later. He sat cross-legged on the floor across from me. "All right," he said. "But you can skip the blow job." He took a pozzy pot out of his uniform blouse. I snatched it away from him. Not cheap watered rum. Pure French brandy.

"Easy," he said. "Easy. Don't drink it all, eh?"

I couldn't help myself. He tore the pozzy pot out of my hands. "Not yet. Don't. Don't. Get off me, Stanhope. Settle in for a minute. Let it work on you. Take a breather."

The brandy felt good all the way down. My fingers itched to hold the jam tin again, my throat ached from wanting.

"Had an uncle who was a boozer, eh? So I know how it is."

"I ain't a boozer."

His laugh cut the quiet. "He saw things sometimes. You seeing purple gnomes yet?"

A dead Boche. A calico girl. "I ain't a boozer."

"Uh-huh." He gave the pozzy pot back and watched me drink. "Better cap it off now. Hide the rest. They toss your room every other day, but not if you're sick. Pretend you're running a fever, eh? Act like you're about to get the shits. Otherwise they'll start feeding you Number Nines, and that'll make sure you're loose-boweled and regular."

I capped the pozzy pot and put it under my mattress. When I got back, LeBlanc was holding two new packs of Woodbines through the bars.

"I figured you didn't like my French fags, so here's some Brit gaspers for you."

I sat down and stuck the cigarettes in my pockets. "Hey. Thanks." When I looked up, I saw him watching me.

"Hey," he said. The sun must have broken through the clouds right then, for a silvery rectangle on the wall behind him suddenly and gloriously blazed. "I missed you. No hard feelings." He stuck his hand through the bars.

I took it, remembered the Boche boy's blood, the childlike bewilderment in the ghost's brown eyes. LeBlanc's palm was dry and cool. "No hard feelings," I said.

Travis Lee

AUGUST 10, THE RESERVE TRENCHES
A LETTER FOR THE KEEPING

Dear Bobby,

In the dead of night before the company left, Blackhall came to visit. The lieutenant and the red caps woke me. Blackhall jerked me out of bed. "Where was you off to the other day, Stanhope?"

They'd woke me up too quick. The shadowy room, the question, made no sense at all.

Blackhall's arm whipped high, came down fast. Pain in my shoulder drove me to my knees. It hurt so bad, it stunned me. When my eyes could work again I saw that Lieutenant was holding a truncheon. The red caps were looking on, expressionless.

"Where is it you went, Stanhope?"

I caught his wrist just as the truncheon came down. The red caps cuffed my hands behind me, and when I was pinned and couldn't fight Blackhall punched me between my shoulder blades. Air exploded out of my lungs in a kind of gagging bark.

"Where?"

"I don't know what you're talking about. Goddamn it. Don't hit me again. You can't treat me like this. I'll report—"

He rammed the toe of his boot into my crotch. The pain

was bigger than sight or thought or hearing. My ears roared with it. My spine went weak. I fell curled, wanting like blazes to hold myself, working my wrists against the cuffs.

"Where?"

I couldn't breathe.

He kicked me in the kidneys so hard that it brought tears to my eyes.

"Where?"

I tried to explain, Bobby. I said I'd felt twitchy that day. Said I'd walked out of camp just so I could be by myself for a little while. He didn't listen. A metal-tipped toe slammed into my ass, too goddamned near my balls.

"Where?"

"In the country. In the country. In the country."

"What'd you do there?"

I started talking fast. I swore before God that I hadn't done nothing. A kick to my stomach doubled me up again.

"Liar," Blackhall said, and the way he said it sent a shiver up me. "Who'd you see?"

Christ. I couldn't tell. Not for Dunston-Smith's sake. God help me. I couldn't do that to Miller.

A kick to my thigh. Not so bad. I knew I wouldn't walk without limping, but all in all, not so bad. "Nobody. Please. Didn't see nobody."

"I'll beat you senseless, you bastard."

The whisper of the truncheon through air, breathtaking agony in my kidneys. Another soft whistle, something rammed into the pit of my belly.

"Best stand back, Lieutenant," one of the red caps said.

My stomach contracted, felt like it folded in on itself. Bile erupted up my throat. It gushed, stinging, out my nose. It pooled, hot and sour, under my cheek. I couldn't raise my head, but Blackhall grabbed me by the hair and raised it for me.

"I got my eye on you, Stanhope. I been hearing how you sneaks out and about. But you never met the likes of me. I ain't no wristwatch officer. Ain't gone to the right schools. Don't drink me tea with me little finger lifted. I was a copper, and my beat was the East End streets. So I knows me tarts. I knows me lifters. I knows me soaks and me sods." He let me go. I fell back into the puddle of vomit. "And I know you," he said.

He stepped back. "Get off your arse, Stanhope. I'm sending you up tomorrow with the rest of the company. And best you don't tell nobody about our talk tonight, else I'll have you doing a stunt a week. See how long you last."

It took some doing to get to my feet. I stood there swaying.

"Mind you don't go sneaking again," Blackhall said.

The next day we marched and my back hurt from the pack, my balls felt sore and pulpy. The bone-deep bruise on my thigh made me limp.

Marrs told me it was good to see me. He asked me what the matter was, and I didn't dare tell him.

When we stopped for lunch, LeBlanc sat down next to me. "Worked you over, eh? The bastards. Brought you a present."

A spare canteen, full of brandy.

"Don't drink it all at once, for Christ's sake. You get too happy around here, they'll knock the smile off you every time. Hide it."

Hide it. Hide the happiness. The comfort. Hide the truth about Miller. The army is after us, Bobby, Miller and me.

Travis Lee

AUGUST 14, THE RESERVE TRENCHES
TOO SAD TO SEND

Dear Bobby,

Time's all out of whack. We're off schedule. How long have we been in reserve? I forget, and I'm scared to ask anybody. Still hauling shit. I stopped pissing blood three days ago. Or was it four?

Nye doesn't tell me funny stories now. Nobody sleeps in my dugout anymore. Maybe there's too much stink. Pickering and Marrs come to visit sometimes. They bring me candy that their families sent them. Toffee, brown as the shit on my hands. They don't stay long. LeBlanc comes to visit, too, and he brings me comfort. He brings me forgetfulness. Not a bad boy.

Ma always called me her bad boy. You remember that? No. Too many years between us. You and me, Bobby. The good boy and the bad.

Every night the Boche have been giving us drumfire. One big gun, then the next. All along the horizon, a fast drum-roll flourish; above us, the high piping squeals of shells falling. I sleep, anyway. That's the magic that LeBlanc brings.

Some shells fall with a soft whuffle. They burst with the bakery-shop smell of mustard gas. Foy came back from the hospital in time to catch the whiff of bonbons. He got his mask on in time, but his arms broke out in yellow blisters. They sent him away again. Poor Foy. Poor life.

Travis Lee

AUGUST 18, THE FRONT LINE
A LETTER TO KEEP WITH ME

Dear Bobby,

Today O'Shaughnessy found me. "Travis. The lieutenant will be wanting to see you."

I started to shake. I trembled so bad I had to put the shit-can down.

"Come wash yourself."

Nye watched in bewildered jealousy as O'Shaughnessy took my arm and led me away. We went down the trench to his cozy little dugout. When we were safe inside, he pulled the blanket across the doorway. He poured me a basinful of water. He handed me a bar of soap and watched as I scrubbed.

"Travis? I hear that you haven't been eating, lad."

The water felt clean. The soap smelled astringent, like that lavender stalk I'd had for a while and then lost. I remembered the curl of the letter's Gothic script. The fondness in it. "I had a stalk of lavender once."

His quiet, "Did you now?" Then, "Ah. But things leave us."

"There was a place I used to dream about," I told him. "A graveyard and a pretty woman. Smoot and Thweat and Charlie Furbush were there. I haven't been back since Dunleavy left. So goddamned peaceful. And the girl's so sweet. I don't know why he would want to leave that place. Nobody would."

The air was close with the blanket pulled to. The dugout smelled of damp and incense; a shit smell that was me. I stripped off my uniform blouse, plunged it into the basin.

"Tell me about the woman," he said.

"I miss her. I miss going there. Lord, but it was a pretty graveyard. The platoon was resting, and she promised she'd take care of them for me."

"And do you believe her?"

From down the trench, muffled laughter. My hands knotted on my shirt.

"I think I got to." Around that makeshift curtain, sun drew a halo of sublime light. "Listen. The lieutenant's going to send me on a stunt. He wants the alleyman to get me. He wants to see if I can dodge Emma Gee."

"Are you afraid, Travis?"

"No," I said. Funny dreamlike names for bare bone realities. All these months being afraid of the Boche, the Frenchie's dread *Allemagne*. I'd been terrified of shells and ghosties and machine guns. Now that there wasn't anything but death left, I wasn't afraid at all. "I think I'm ready to see the lieutenant now."

"You can't die, lad."

The flat, hard tone made me turn.

His eyes were flat and hard, too. Stripes of sunlight lay docile as wings against his cheek. "You daren't die yet. Fear will keep you from the place you're wanting to go. And anger. And drink will keep you from it, too. You'd roam, Travis. And you such a fine lad, really. A good lad."

Like I was already dead. Pity. Always such a good boy.

I took my shirt out of the basin, wrung it as dry as I could. I put it on. "I want to see Blackhall."

Lieutenant was waiting in a support-line dugout, like he had been made a real officer or something. When I came in, he threw a report across the room. Papers fluttered to the dirt floor, a fall of pale leaves.

Blackhall glared at O'Shaughnessy. He glared at me. "Stanhope?" he said. "Report to the med officer right away. None of your lounging about, mind. 'E wants to 'ave a look at you."

But I had been so ready, Bobby. I was prepared like Trantham was prepared just before he ran to the wire. All the war to go, and I don't know if I will ever be that ready again.

"Damn yer eyes! You deaf or sommit, Stanhope?"

"No, sir."

"Best get him out of here, padre, 'fore I sticks me boot up his arse."

A hand on my arm. I turned. O'Shaughnessy guiding me again. We walked down the trench to the medical dugout, where an orderly had me take off my clammy uniform blouse. He told me to sit on a cot. He checked my eyes and temperature and heart, then called for the med officer.

The doctor took himself away from lavaging a soldier's arm wound. It was a small angry cut the doctor was occupied with, one too ragged for bullet or shrapnel. Rat bite, probably.

The officer bent to peer at me closely. "Well, you're right, padre. He's looking decidedly infirm. Shooting pains up your shins, soldier?"

"No, but my legs hurt."

"Specifically up your shins?"

"No."

He clucked over me and asked how else, then, was I feeling?

I told him I was just so damned tired.

"Breathe deeply." He touched the cold toe of a stethoscope to my back. "Again."

He stepped back. "Well! A spot of good luck, padre. No trench fever; but a bit of congestion, and he's definitely warmish. The leg pain worries me, and I don't care for the bronchial sounds." The doctor turned to the orderly, who pursed his lips in disapproval. "Coming down with some ague is my guess. Best send him back before he infects the whole battalion." He took up a clipboard and marked on a page. "Soldier, I'm ordering you back to the reserve trench and the regimental aid post there. Report to Major Landis. Major Landis. Can you remember that? Good show. Tell him that Captain Fielding has sent you there for observation. Think you can make it on your own? Good. Excellent. Blake? Give the boy here an aspirin and send him on his way. Well, ta-ta, padre," he said brightly, and went back to his basin and gauze and oozing wound.

O'Shaughnessy escorted me to the communications trench. "Do you think you can make it from here, lad?"

I thought of the canteen in my dugout, but the comfort was too far away. The world was stretched to the point of exhaustion. "Yes," I told him. I left without saying thank you. He saved my life, I think.

It was a long tiring shuffle to the reserve trenches and the aid post there.

"Feverish? Nauseated? Leg pain, you say?" Major Landis asked. When I nodded, he did, too. We were in complete agreement. "Yes, quite. And faint, I shouldn't imagine. I'll wager you're dehydrated. Take that cot there." He pointed. "Clear fluids and salt. Jennings! Get the private here a measuring bottle to piss in. Soldier? I expect one hundred cc's every four hours."

I took my measuring bottle to bed with me. Every hour the orderly filled a pint glass with water and told me to drink. He made me nibble on salted crackers. Then he'd take a look at my measuring bottle and make a note of how much I'd pissed. He didn't smile. There was a private with an abscessed tooth in the cot across from me. He didn't smile, either. My piss was measured with the gravity of a court martial. Direct orders: one hundred cc's. But the piss came out rust colored and muddy looking, and there wasn't nearly enough.

The aid post was quiet. It smelled of carbolic and packed damp earth. The walls were wood paneled and sturdy. I closed my eyes and listened to the birds sing. Shells fell, harmless and far away.

It wasn't the graveyard I dreamed of, but the creek that runs through the ranch. It was just like I was there, Bobby: the glassy water, the murmur and gurgle of the spring. Cedar trees crowded around like they were gathered to the most wondrous thing in the world. And I was so thirsty. And the air was cedar-sharp and clean. I knelt on the bank and plunged my face in. The water was cold, the way it always is. I drank, and the cold spring water numbed me. It tasted like it had flowed through summer: all mown hay and lemonade. I filled myself to bursting, so that in the dream I knew that I'd never have to be thirsty again.

I lifted my head, water dripping. On a limestone boulder in the dark grotto of cedar, the calico girl sat dunking her feet. By her hand was a stand of maidenhair fern, clumped leaves like lime-green bubbles.

So quiet there. I could have stayed, if O'Shaughnessy hadn't cheated me.

She looked up, too. Her laugh came, bright as specks of sun. "You can't stay here. That's an order." She kicked water at me. It sprayed up rainbows. It fell in icy droplets on my cheek. "You're to piss one hundred cc's."

I woke up with a violent shiver. The aid post was dark except for a single lamp. The open doorway was murky with night, and I had to piss real bad.

I filled the bottle that time. The color looked better. I drank my liter of water and asked the orderly to bring me more. I've been pissing ever since.

Travis Lee

AUGUST 19

A POSTCARD FROM THE AID POST

Dear Bobby,

Don't worry. Got me a little cold is all. I'm ordered to three days of bed rest, and it's the first chance I've had to write in near a month. They're keeping me busy, but everything's fine. Tell Ma I send her my love. Give my mare some sugar cubes and pet her some. Kick Pa's worthless ass for me.

Travis Lee

AUGUST 19, THE RESERVE TRENCHES
ONE FOR LATER

Dear Bobby,

Blackhall came to the aid post today to release me for duty. "You're back to sharpshooter, Stanhope. Them's the orders."

I smiled. Things were looking up. Miller. Maybe O'Shaughnessy. Someone was watching out for me.

"Captain wants to see you. Best you go right away." He stood there, not able to meet my gaze at times, at times staring holes through me. Blackhall was scared I'd tell Miller on him. "*Now*, Private."

"Sir." I walked on down the trench to Miller's dugout. The day was overcast, the sky pearly. I lifted my head just in time to see a flock of birds vault toward a pale biscuit-cut of sun. It was funny, Bobby. The desire to fly was so strong that my arms ached. My body felt heavy and unnatural. I nearly called out for the flock to wait, wait up, that I was coming as fast as I could. When they vanished from my trench-bound strip of sky, I felt abandoned, the way I felt when Marrs and Pickering left me in the jail.

I knocked at Miller's dugout, my thoughts on the birds. My head felt light, my feet not earthbound anymore.

Miller sent his batman away and ordered me to sit down. "Well, Stanhope. A spot of grippe, I hear. Are you quite recovered?"

"Yes. Thank you, sir."

"You look . . ." His brows knitted, searching for a word. From the shadows at the wall, his sad-eyed lady watched, mute. "Are you *sure*?"

Should I tell him about Blackhall? Carrying tales has never proved an easy burden for me. I stared at the single candle. The silence stretched longer than it should have. "I'm sure, sir. Thank you."

"Well." There wasn't a pencil handy for him to play with. His fingers drummed the tabletop. "It seems there have been rumors floating about the battalion, and so I am forced to ask: The night you were arrested for going AWL, where on earth had you been?"

There was that awkward silence again. Miller's fingers stopped drumming. His small smile faded. He looked stricken. Oh, shit. He knew. Like that time in the poppy field. We've never needed words between us.

"For a walk."

He frowned. "Whom did you see?"

"Nobody."

"You're lying to me, Stanhope. I won't have you lying to me."

"No, sir."

"Were you so drunk that you couldn't remember?"

The tension in my back gave way. I slumped with relief. "Yes, sir. Could have been real drunk, sir. Yes. Come to think of it, that was it."

He didn't look any happier. "A girl is dead, and you cannot remember."

Miller was speaking a foreign language. I should have understood, but taken together, the words made no sense. Girl. Dead. What I pictured was birds leaping up into a pearly morning.

He rubbed his chin. Rubbed it. All traces of his wry humor were gone. "You were drunk. And you cannot remember."

"Sir, I just went for a walk. There wasn't any girl."

"You have just told me that you cannot remember. Which is it?"

"I would have remembered a girl, sir."

"Would you? Would you recall forcing yourself on her?" His voice rose. "Would you recall impaling her with a tree branch? Would you remember that, damn you? Or were you just too bloody drunk?"

The ground under my feet opened, Bobby. I was alone and falling, without anything to hold onto. How could anyone have thought that I'd do that? God help me. And my own damned fault.

"Oh, Jesus." The words came out weak: neither oath nor prayer. "Not me, sir. You know I'd never—"

"You got drunk and soundly drubbed a tart. Do you recall that? Or did she not make an impression on you, either?"

Who told him? Pickering had been there that night. No. He wouldn't have said anything. O'Shaughnessy? But he was honor bound by promises. "Sir, that was just—"

"A tart?"

Miller's voice was a splash of acid. It made my eyes sting, my cheeks burn.

"You know I wouldn't ever do that."

"No. I do not know anything about you. You are a sot, Stanhope. You shirk duty, you are insubordinate and insolent. You thrashed a whore. And you are lying to me again."

"Sir, please. I just went walking."

"Get up! Get up! Didn't you hear me, you cheeky bastard! Get on your feet! I'll hand you to the red caps myself."

I couldn't obey. My knees wouldn't hold me. "I watched you and Dunston-Smith."

Miller fell back into his chair like he'd been shot.

"I didn't see nothing. Not really. Look. It was just . . . All that time in the trenches and the boys were getting ready to play football and I don't see the goddamned point to that game. I just wanted . . . No. God's honest truth, sir. This flat embarrasses me to say it, but I was following you to see if I could talk my way out of shit wallah duty. I wanted to catch you alone, sir. I didn't want Blackhall to know I was going over his head. Didn't think *that* would be smart. And so once you left the road, sir, it surprised me, but I just kept going, too. Didn't mean nothing by it. But all of a sudden there you were, and there was Captain Dunston-Smith, and there was that hut and—Is that an old stable, sir? I'd been wondering about that." I ran out of excuses and breath all at the same time.

His cheeks had gone pasty. "Good God," he said.

"I'm not going to tell, sir."

Abruptly he was on his feet, pacing. He grabbed his swagger stick and started whacking the wall with it. That close, hot, airless gloom; the old food and moldy mud smell of the dugout. That slapping—like something made by a tiny, furious hand.

"Sir. It's your business and all. I'm not spreading that around."

I saw in the light of the candle that his face had turned a bright, embarrassed red. "How long were you bloody there?"

"Just for a while. Well. Just till dark."

"Till dark?" I knew he was counting off the hours. He'd gone in the hut about five. Had I really waited outside so long? If he asked me why, I wouldn't have any answer. "Well, Stanhope. You've cocked it up again, haven't you? I'm your only blasted alibi."

"No, sir! You don't have to come forward, sir. Not until somebody arrests me."

He stopped pacing.

Girl. Dead. The repercussions were too terrible to think on. "Are they planning to arrest me, sir?"

"No. There are no proofs, only surmise. The army is bound by good English law, after all." His eyes had a faraway look. He was thinking hard on something.

"How old a girl, sir?" I asked quietly.

I tore him out of reverie. "Oh. The dead girl? Twelve, I believe."

Twelve. Reason enough for Blackhall to have gone after me like he did.

"Seems she was murdered late afternoon. Mother was a washerwoman; the poor child was making a delivery. Someone dragged her off the road and into a copse at least an hour and a half's walk from the hut where you saw me. The police put the death at five or perhaps six o'clock at the very latest. So. It seems my testimony could clear you quickly enough." He shot me a look. "Should you need it."

That was my cue. I got to my feet. "I'll try not to need it, sir."

He nodded and kept nodding, like he was working up the spit to say something else. I knew it would be a thank you.

I waved the words away and he gave me a feeble acknowledging smile. We understand each other like that, me and the captain.

His words caught me at the door. "Stanhope? You might have a chat with your platoon. I have the feeling they natter on about wild Indian adventures. Bad idea, that."

"Yes, sir." I felt the door's rough pine beneath my fingers. I wanted to sit down in the comfortable shadows, have a cuppa, and talk ideas with him. I wanted to get into a pissing contest over poetry. Nobody in this place knew me as well as Miller. But how could he have imagined, drunk or not, I'd do something so goddamned ugly?

I let my hand fall from the latch and turned.

"No, no, Stanhope. It's quite all right. No need to thank me. You'd enough of shit wallah duty, I think. Simply keep your head down from now on. Keep your hands clean. No running off again."

Maybe we didn't know each other well at all. "Can I speak frankly, sir?"

He chuckled, waved an indulgent hand: our private unspoken language.

"Sir? You just accused me of murder and rape and God knows what, and with a twelve-year-old kid, to boot. Well, I don't care what you think of me, but I got something I want to say, and you can take it for what it's worth."

The knowing smile went quizzical, his eyes went guarded.

"Some women take advantage. Tell you straight to your face how much they love you, and laugh behind your back. They'll leave you crying. I think sometimes that's what they're after. Got to be careful of women like that, sir."

No smile at all now, only the caution, like he thought I was about to confess.

"Well, look. I guess it works the same, sir. The same types. The cock-teasers, the gold diggers. Hell, I don't know why they do it. But in love, you got to keep your wits about you. And when your pecker's pointing hard at something, well . . ."

Softly, "Is there a point?"

"My frank opinion, sir? That Dunston-Smith's not near good enough for you."

He frowned, his eyebrows bunched. I knew for sure that he was about to chew ass; but he burst out laughing. "Oh, my dear Stanhope," he kept saying over and over, wiping his eyes.

"With all due respect, fuck you, sir. I was just trying to help."

He came over, clapped me on the shoulder. He was still smiling when he said, "My dear, dear Stanhope. You've no idea how you've touched me." But the sentence ended as a whisper, and he wasn't smiling anymore. His hand felt hot. We were face-to-face, and his eyes seemed far too bright. The candlelight glinted there, as if it had struck water.

He was going to tell me he was sorry. Then I'd tell him that it was all right.

But all of a sudden he was way too close for comfort. His lips came down on mine.

"Oh, shit!" I blundered backward.

Instantly, he let me go. "Sorry."

I scrubbed my mouth hard.

"Do forgive." Then, with awkward and comical concern, "Are you all right?"

"It's okay." I backed up another step.

"Unbelievably boorish of me."

"It's okay. Forget it."

"Yes, best done, what?" The too-bright glint returned to his eyes again. He ducked his head quickly. "Never happen again."

I know that it won't. That kiss laid something to rest between us. I know for sure now that what I feel for him isn't romance. There's love there, though. I felt it from him, strong as I've felt from any woman.

I stuck my hand out. "No hard feelings."

Unlike LeBlanc, Miller's hands were clean. He held on a shade too long. "Thank you."

He pulled away a careful distance and stood watching me. I could see it in him, plain as day. I guess when I looked at him from now on, I'd see how he wanted me.

"Needn't worry about this unpleasantness, Stanhope. Seems you were indeed on a country stroll. In fact, I found you'd caught sight of me where I'd gone windmill viewing. Would have accosted me at the time, too, had you not been AWL. At any rate, seems you've verified the places I stopped, what I looked at, that sort of thing. We'll be vague with our stories, shall we? Windmills. Canals. Picturesque country, that sort of thing."

"Makes sense to me, sir."

I think he meant to clap me on the shoulder again, but thought better of it. "Do keep yourself safe, Stanhope."

Awkward, standing there, that kiss rift between us. I wanted to say something, but like all pathetic should-haves in life, I didn't. When I left, I left us both unfinished.

I can't help but wonder how I would feel if he got killed tonight; so I just wanted to tell you that I love you, Bobby. I wanted you to know that you take up all the half-pint places in my childhood. I think about myself and always remember you: how you trotted after me wherever I went, that diaper of yours drooping. When I'd pick you up, you'd go to kissing on me. Embarrassed me down to the floor sometimes. And your kisses were always sticky. I don't know why. I'd tell you not to do it. Sometimes I'd spank you—never very hard. Even with the spanking, you'd kiss on me, anyway. Love comes out like that, I guess.

If it was me who died tonight, you'd get the things in my pack. You'd get my letters, so if there was ever any question about my loving you, you'd know. You'd get a "Sorry to inform you" letter from my captain, and you'll know that when I died, he cried over me in secret, like he got misty-eyed when I pushed him away.

I don't want him touching me, but I'd sooner tell him I loved him than I'd tell any woman. So if I die, write him for me. Enclose this letter. He should know that much, I think.

Travis Lee

SIX

AUGUST 23, THE FRONT LINES

Dear Bobby,

Sorry my letters were spotty for a while. And you're about to find out that there's a big gap between this one and the last. It doesn't mean anything, really. Kinder if it did. Home seems so faint and far, that's all.

Last week the heat was like a sledgehammer. Not a breath of wind. Flies covered No Man's Land like a black, restless snow. Swarms of flies filled the trenches; killing heat settled in the dugouts. We stripped down to our shorts and splashed each other with water.

The heat was so bad that when the Boche started coming up for air every once in a while, I didn't have the heart to shoot them. Their snipers didn't shoot our boys, either. That week on the front lines I watched bare-assed Germans taking sunbaths: bright pink shoulders, bright pink cheeks. I watched them hang up their laundry to dry.

"Best keep it quiet, now," Riddell warned us. "Last winter we cut the Boche a Christmas tree and took it over, didn't we. They came up out of their trenches. We sang carols together—"Silent Night" and "God Rest Ye Merry"—and we gave each other presents. Then someone 'as to go tattle, and orders come down: our artillery's to lay into the poor blighters worse. We bloody pounded them, we did. Right at Christmas. And for us, it was speech after blinking speech on the joys of killing till they figured we'd got back our stomach for battle."

Stomach for battle. I've had that, Bobby. So has Riddell. It's a bad belly, and when you got it, you do things that make you sick to puking.

For me, the worst was when I shot a Boche who had reached over the parapet to get something. I don't know what he was reaching for, or why it was so important. He was half over the sandbags when I hit him, and I didn't get him clean. Maybe in the throat, for that's where the blood seemed to come spraying and bubbling out. He thrashed real bad, Bobby. He flailed around so, he fell the rest of the way into No Man's Land.

I should have finished him off. You'd do that much for a deer. But I was too shaken, and pulling the trigger again was too hard. I'd popped all the other Boche without much thought, and they'd fallen fast out of my sight. This boy was suffering so, it made me heartsick.

Instead of doing what I needed to, I sat down on the fire-step. I guess I was hoping the whole thing—his mistake and mine—would just up and go away. But when I peeked through the trench periscope again, the boy was still twitching.

His buddies had thrown him a rope, but he evidently didn't see it. They started to shout, too. I thought they were yelling at him to grab hold; then I caught on that they were shouting in English. They were begging me to kill him.

You do what you have to. It took me two shots, for I was shaking pretty bad at the time. I didn't even bother to change my position. I was lucky, I guess, that their sniper didn't nail me.

The next morning I was relieved to see that he had vanished. His buddies had gathered him in.

When bad things happen you put them in a little box somewheres, Bobby. You wrap those memories up real neat and store them in a closet. When you least expect it, though, you'll turn a corner and find that damned package sitting out. Riddell's back to his normal self after bayoneting that Boche boy who was trying his best to surrender. Sergeant must have boxed the memory up. Still, I bet sometimes he opens a piece of mental mail and finds out too late that it contained the boy's death throes and how the rifle stock felt, twitching in his hands.

I hadn't had a drink until the day the Boche begged me to kill their friend. Hadn't wanted one, really. But LeBlanc found me, made me sit down with him on some old empty ammo boxes. As the sun set, we had us some brandy.

"Tell me about your mare," he said.

LeBlanc's a strange sort. I don't know where he sleeps night to night. I suspect nobody does. Sometimes when I'm lying in the dugout with Pickering and Marrs I get to thinking about LeBlanc and wondering if he's out in the dark, hunting No Man's Land. It sends shivers down me.

"She's a born cutting horse," I told him. "Hell, she wasn't but a year-old filly when she started watching cows. I think sometimes she figures it's a step-down for her to guard goats. She sees I got the Border collies for the chasing, so what the hell? What about yours?"

"Had to sell him when I joined up. So your mare figures you got her slumming, eh?"

It's like LeBlanc was raised up without any stories to tell, and so he wants to possess mine. I resent that in him. There's times I feel like he's thieving my memories in the casual, sneaky way he takes lives.

I asked him, "You're Catholic, right?"

Twilight was falling. The trench was murky, the sky above an unsettled color, not blue, not quite pink. I heard LeBlanc moving around, saw the flare of a match, smelled the nose-tickling, intoxicating smoke of a Woodbine cigarette.

"Want one?"

I reached out, fumbled for the pack. LeBlanc was just a dark hulking shape with a coal in its hand. We sat smoking and sipping for a while.

"Yeah," he said. "Raised in the Church, anyway. You had your nose up O'Shaughnessy's butt for a while. You turning Catholic there, Stanhope? Better watch yourself. Once the Church gets hold of your short hairs, they never let go."

"He saved my life once," I told LeBlanc.

"Who? That mick? That's what *you* say. You also promised to kiss my great big *bâton*."

I watched him take a drag on his cigarette. The coal at the tip went bright. Somewhere outside the sun must have been setting in a bonfire blaze. Pink and orange streaks gloried across the sky.

I said, "I'm puckered and waiting."

LeBlanc doesn't laugh a lot, leastways not happy ones; so his gut-loud guffaw surprised me.

"You're such an asshole, Stanhope."

The fondness in his tone surprised me, too.

I said, "I thought priests wasn't supposed to tell on you, I mean, your secrets and all."

"Can't trust a priest." Then he said, "They lie all the time, especially about Heaven and Hell, you know? All that shit." The cinder-tip of LeBlanc's Woodbine fell like a shooting star, then lay there, smoldering. "None of us goes anywhere, eh? When God's finished with us, He tosses us in a garbage can. That's all we get: darkness. Maybe the stink of old cabbage. Shoulder to shoulder with used rubbers. Goddamn cats rooting around you. Flies all over, and rats pissing on your head. That sort of thing."

I laughed. I took my last lungful of Woodbine and threw the butt down. Above, the gold and pink rays had faded. The first shy stars were peeking through.

"You think it's funny, eh? You've been in this crapper of an army, Stanhope. You chicken-shit sentimental cunt-headed bastard. You've seen what death looks like. You think after death'll be any better?"

"Well, okay, but you said 'God,' right? Seems to me that if you believe in God, you got some sort of pattern going. Come on, LeBlanc. See what I'm saying? Else why believe in God at all?"

"Goddamn Church never gave me any choice."

He sounded so sad when he said that, like the Church had stolen all his could-be's.

I don't know. The way that Boche boy of mine fought dying, you'd think he'd caught a peek of what was to come.

He whipped his arms around so, maybe he was battling LeBlanc's trash-can Purgatory.

Me, I've been dreaming about the cemetery again. The mausoleum's doors have been flung open. The marble niches are empty and waiting. A warm breeze blows through, and birds flutter around the domed glass ceiling. Fallen leaves gather in the quiet corners; they scrape along the floor.

The platoon's gone, but for some reason that's all right. Trantham doesn't call anymore, and that's all right, too. I walk the gravel path and look down into the glass-topped graves. There are other soldiers sleeping: Boche and Frenchies, Tommies and boot-black Algerians. I look for familiar faces, but all I see are strangers.

I see the calico girl sometimes. Coming across her is always a surprise. When I least expect it she'll be seated on a fallen tombstone or standing by a pensive angel. She has a thoughty look, as if she's concentrating hard on all her drowsy charges.

The graveyard's flowers have gone to seed, Bobby, the plants long bolted, life sucking them dry and woody. Fruit has gone so overripe, so sweet, that it's all windfalls now. Even in my dreams, autumn's coming.

Travis Lee

AUGUST 25, THE RESERVE TRENCHES

Dear Bobby,

This afternoon a shell hit one of Nye's secret dumping grounds. Shit went skyward. It came down over the enlisted trenches in brown, aromatic sprays. It pattered down in a heavy stinking rain all the way from HQ to the aid post. Hear tell Major Dunn got his fat-assed self a face full. Ain't war wonderful?

When we'd cleaned ourselves up, me and Marrs and Pickering and the new man, Calvert, were sitting around the dugout when the Boche began shelling for serious. Marrs looked up dubiously at the piece of elephant sheet over our heads. The strikes were close, but without punch, mostly all Jack

Johnsons. Still, the earth vibrated. The dust on our plank table erupted into clouds. Bits of dirt and pebbles danced the boards. Pickering and me exchanged looks. Calvert's first time in a barrage. He'd go to screaming or crying or shitting his pants.

Marrs lit the primus stove that we'd all chipped in to get. He put on a kettle for tea. A Jack Johnson exploding outside the door made our tin cups clatter, sent black smoke billowing over the parapet.

"Milk or lemon?" Marrs asked.

Only powdered milk. Just dried lemon rind, but still. Riddell's sister had sent him a box full of tea fixings and he shared it with all the platoon. Poor old Foy. Rumor had it he was due back about the same time we got those tea fixings. The fool sent us a message that said he was happy he didn't have a Blighty. Crazy, isn't it? Said coming back to the platoon would be just like being home. But I heard that three nights later he took a turn for the worse, his blisters oozing again.

A sharp crack, the blast so near that even Pickering ducked. Dirt rattled down the sheet metal of our elephant like hail.

"Bloody hell," Marrs said.

A startling cuss for him. He'd dropped the lemon rind, and now set about salvaging it from the floor's muck.

There was a vacancy where Foy should have been, a place where the too-silent Calvert sat now. I exchanged another glance with Pickering, the unspoken language that all originals know. My shrug was, *At least he's not crying.*

Pickering's ironic smile meant, *Not yet.*

A long, seemingly endless whistle, descending the scale. The whizzbang struck somewhere down the trench. Someone far away started screaming for the medics.

The kettle screamed, too. I flinched, then laughed at myself. You get used to it, Bobby. Folks die with the shelling, one and two at a time: a parsimony of war. I remember how scared I used to be of artillery, and I have to wonder if the barrage was really so bad the night MacPhearson got it. But seems like I can remember the dumb, inescapable blows of 8.5's coming as fast as windmilling fists, loud as freight trains.

Heavy shelling is like an act of God, Bobby. They call it "hate." And the real hate, the lunatic mad-God hate, kills in squads, in platoons, in companies. I remember the endless storms of 8.5's. I remember the Boche that we found huddled together in dugouts, stunned to death by our barrage. Compared to that kind of hate, what we were living through was heavenly dislike.

Calvert finally spoke up, and his voice sounded steady enough. "Likes me tea plain, thanks."

Marrs poured the water into an old biscuit tin, wrapped a field towel around it for a cozy. Another close strike. One of the sandbags on the south wall burst. Black dirt avalanched, burying Pickering's haversack.

Marrs caught our biscuit tin before it could topple. "Bought us a real teapot a month back," he said apologetically to Calvert. "But it broke, didn't it."

"Considerate old Boche." Pickering ignored his buried haversack. He lit up a Woodbine, offered the pack around. "They break our teapot, but give us time between shells to . . ."

A blast from a whizzbang left him mouthing his last word, left my ears ringing. I dug my fingertip in my ear and shook my head to clear it. The next sound I was able to hear was Pickering's laughter. "Talk," he said. "They give us time between shells to talk."

Three fast ones in succession that left me in a cold sweat. I licked my lips and listened, but the Boche settled down into their slow rhythm again.

"Teatime, gentlemen." Marrs unwrapped the tin with a flourish and poured.

Calvert took his first sip and spewed it. Marrs got a spray of tea full in the face. His eyes went as wide as eggs.

"Sod all!" Calvert shouted. "Bleeding sugar! There's bleeding sugar in 'ere!"

"Well, it comes together, now, doesn't it?" Marrs was saying. "The tea and the sugar. Comes packaged. Can't pick it apart."

But Calvert's polite façade had cracked; no explanation

would mend it. "Bleeding army! Effing, bleeding war! They puts the effing, bleeding sugar in our effing bloody tea? An' wifout asking? Them bastards! What if we don't likes it, then? They ever bleeding stop and think about that?"

Pickering and me nearly split a gut laughing. No doubt about it. Calvert's going to work out just fine.

Travis Lee

AUGUST 31, THE REST AREA

Dear Bobby,

Yesterday Riddell asked permission for all of us to visit Foy. There, just outside the mess tent, Blackhall looked from Riddell to Pickering, from Marrs to me. It was my eyes he lingered on. He owes me. He knows I never told anyone about that beating. But just so I remember that he has the upper hand, he keeps riding me and riding me about my drinking. The asshole. He knows as well as I do that if I ever had a problem, I sure don't have it now.

Still, he can't help but put a dig in once in a while. "Long as you sees Stanhope 'ere keeps his nose out of the bottle."

Then it was salute-the-shit and a chorus of Thank-you-sirs.

"Back on time, now. Won't have yer loitering."

A click of heels—my uncarved-on, uncomfortable boots. Peckerwood Blackhall wouldn't have it any other way. We got out of there quick as we could, left the rest of the boys to their forever football game.

The breeze was still warm, but walking the road I could see that summer was ending. Autumn comes on different here, Bobby. It's like life just thrives so hard in the hedgerows, on the canal banks, in the deep woods, that it wears itself out. I can see it happening around me: stalks gone thick and woody that used to be moist and translucent green. Flowers have used themselves up into seed. Nature's like an aging woman, sucked dry by childbearing, gone thick around the middle and knobby-fingered.

On the way, Pickering and Marrs pushed and slapped at

each other like a couple of kids. Riddell would stop every so often to collect one of his weeds. It was a fine afternoon, Bobby, with clouds towering like white marble fortresses and elfin sun rays slanting through the trees.

We scared ourselves up a lark by the side of the road. It flew toward the dark ceiling of branches. Frenzied, trapped, it made its wild and flapping way down the lane until it was free. Beyond the trees, the bird forgot its panic. Cheerful now, it launched itself toward the radiant clouds, singing.

" 'We look before and after,' " I quoted softly. " 'And pine for what is not.' "

The three of them stared.

"Shelley," I explained. "He said that no matter how contented humans are sometimes, bad memories hang around. The future's always worrying at us, too. We just can't ever be as happy as that damned lark."

They stood in the road, a trio of blank-faced sheep.

"Oh, fucking goddamn never mind," I said.

The moment, if it had ever been, was over. Pickering mock-punched Marrs. Marrs dodged and slapped back. Riddell stepped off the path to pick a weed. I wondered where Miller was and what he was doing.

We stopped at a little arched bridge over a canal and stared down into the dark water for a while. I thought of Coleridge, of Xanadu and its sunless sea. Then of Poe's morbid ghosties and how old Edgar Allan would have been drawn to my dreams' cypress-dark.

"Think I could thump meself up a fish?" Marrs let a pebble drop. It sank into the black water, leaving dark concentric ripples in its wake.

Pickering said, "Gas him. That'd be faster. Go ahead, Marrs. Give him one of your famous farts."

Pickering held his throat and pretended to choke. Marrs punched him lightly in the arm. They slapped each other for a while.

We walked on. The yellow flowers were gone from the meadows, but wild ducks floated a nearby canal. Spotted cows nosed under wire fences, in a search for the forbidden. I thought of the tumbledown hut, of Dunston-Smith and Miller. Did they talk poetry there? The Holsteins and me—pining for what is not.

Then Marrs started singing. His voice was as pure as a flute, so high that only the top branches could catch it. His voice dazed me. His Latin came so easy. How could something that extraordinary come out of such an unexceptional man? And the song, Bobby. God. That song. If there was ever an anthem for my graveyard, he was singing it.

"What on earth are you bawling about there, Marrs?" Pickering asked.

I could have knocked him down.

"Taverner's 'Magnificat.' I was a choir boy, wasn't I."

Pickering huffed. "No. I meant what were the words you were mouthing? I couldn't understand the bleeding words."

"Well, that's 'cause it's Latin, then." All in a flood, he said, " '*Magnificat anima mea Dominum. Et exsultavit spiritus meus in Deo salutari meo . . .* ' "

How could he do that? How could he remember the words so well, and say them so quick and so matter of fact? It was too fast for me to follow, still I knew the prayer was magic—an incantation for the lips of marble angels.

Pickering's "Ye-e-es" teetered on the edge of aggravation. "All very well and good, Marrs, but what does it *mean*?"

"Well, the fathers don't tell us *that*, now does they."

"Sing it again," I said.

Pickering rolled his eyes.

"Please," I said. "Sing it again."

Marrs opened his mouth. Song poured out of his small, ordinary body. I dropped back a few paces and walked behind them to hide the tears he brought to my eyes.

I should have saved them for the C.C.S. aid station, maybe. Easier to get choked up over beauty, though, than it is ugliness. And that hospital was an ugly place.

You could hear the wounded moaning long before we ever got there. They were lying in the grass around the portable buildings. Men, towels over their eyes, were sitting dumbfounded and gasping in the road. We picked our way around dead still on their stretchers, left where they were dropped when it was seen they were without hope.

And there wasn't much hope, Bobby. In the yard, the freshly wounded; inside, men were puffed grotesque with rot: fingers the size of pickles, arms and legs like blood-sausage balloons. God, it stank. The air was thick with the sweet-sick stench of spoiled meat. I wondered if those boys knew they were death-bound, or if they were still hoping.

Riddell stopped a doctor to ask directions. Marrs's face had gone pasty. Pickering kept looking at the ceiling. I tried the best I could to hold my breath, tried not to meet any of the bedridden's eyes. Then I saw a familiar figure in a corner. O'Shaughnessy was comforting the dying.

"This way," Riddell said.

We hurried after him, escaped past a canvas building and barrels piled high with bloody pus-stained gauze to another cheap canvas-and-wood barracks, one filled with the drowning-man sounds of the gas victims. That's where we found Foy.

He was sitting up on pillows. His arms were raw and oozing. He'd crusted his sheets, and in places they were stuck to him. His eyes were swollen nearly shut, dripping and thick with pus. It looked like he was crying amber.

" 'Ello there, Foy," Riddell said gently. He went up to the bed when none of the rest of us would.

Foy kind of tilted his head funny, squinting sideways at Riddell. He whispered something, I think. At least his cracked, swollen lips moved, and bleeding fissures opened. Jesus. He couldn't be hurt that bad. It was just a little sniff of gas. He'd got his mask on in time.

"You're right, Foy. 'Course I brought the others." How could Sergeant understand that dry-leaf whisper? How did he have the heart to smile? Riddell turned and pointed to where we stood in the safety of the aisle. "See, lad? Brought you Pickering and Marrs and old Stanhope, too."

I looked away. Toward the back wall, yellow-blistered men were strapped to their beds, trying their damnedest to scream. Nothing came out of the wide dark of their mouths but hisses.

"Brung you a comfrey poultice," Riddell was saying. He took a paper packet from his uniform blouse. "An' horehound and licorice for your cough."

I swallowed hard to force my unruly laughter down.

"No, no, it's all right, lad. Needn't try to speak. We'll do the speaking, won't we?" Riddell looked at us, warning in his eyes.

Pickering said in a wild, bright voice, "Got yourself a Blighty!"

The little joke went through me. Foy's grunting pain made me shiver. He was trying to smile. The effort cracked his skin apart again. *Don't*, I wanted to tell him. *Don't you dare. Don't you go smiling at Pickering's lousy jokes.*

Marrs's turn. The best he could manage was a nod and a wave.

"We miss you," I told Foy.

Pickering looked at me in surprise.

"We got us a new guy, name of Calvert. He's nice, I guess, but I miss you. I thought you should know that."

Pickering let out a high, insane giggle. "Long as he doesn't fart in the dugout, like Marrs."

Then Marrs asked the unintentionally cruel question: "When are you coming back, then?"

What was left of Foy's mouth moved. His throat must have been all blisters too. I couldn't hear what he was trying so hard to say.

Riddell didn't either. He bent down. "What is it, lad?"

It was a stupid question that Marrs had asked; and the answer cost too much. Foy's struggle made me look away. In the corner hissing men were lashed tight to their beds, their raw, blistered tongues protruding. I looked away quick, and that's when I saw them.

They were just standing there, Bobby. Not pale like you'd expect, but hazy all the same, like they didn't have as much stuffing as the living. God. There were so many. There must have been more than a company, shoulder to shoulder. A silent parade of dead men.

A shock wave of despair went through me. Not my despair,

but theirs. I felt their loneliness. Their confusion. Felt the combined fear of over two hundred strong. And through that attack of emotion came a barrage of other people's memories, too—hand-me-downs, all sepia and faded: snatches of nursery rhymes I'd never known, a fierce mother-bond at the sight of a woman I'd never seen. Dozens of little boys and little girls, pictures of my children, each and every one of them a stranger. Grimy English streets and smoke-filled pubs. Wide sleet-spattered moors. Trout fishing with a father who loved me.

I felt a tug at my sleeve. Heard Marr's concerned, "You all right, Stanhope? Need some fresh air, then?"

I shut my eyes quick. When I opened them, the ghosties were gone.

I left, too. Left Foy with his prolonged and hideous dying. In the fresh air of the yard I bent double, sucking air. A passing nurse eyed me. I started walking fast, past the surgical hut, toward the road.

O'Shaughnessy's call stopped me. "Travis!"

I watched him scurry over the grass. He had a purple stole over his shoulders. It flapped, its embossing scattering the light. He was holding a Bible in both his hands. When he reached me, he didn't speak. All around that meadow I could hear the low, sad song of the wounded.

" 'Magnificat,' " I said.

He cocked his head and squinted, a gesture so near to what Foy had done that ice balled up in my belly: O'Shaughnessy trying to see me through the crust the both of us had built.

"Tell me what it says."

He smiled. "Ah. 'My soul doth magnify the Lord,' lad. 'And my spirit hath rejoiced.' Was that what you were seeking?"

"Yeah. Thanks." Nearby were piles of garbage from surgery: red mountains of gauze; a blue-white arm, its graceful fingers splayed.

"Will you not sit down and have a chat with me, Travis?"

I took in a deep breath. Rotting flesh, but under that, the sweet smell of damp earth, the perfume of crushed grass.

"You've been to see Foy I take it?"

I nodded.

"Good that you did, lad. He'll be appreciating that."

Foy's slow march of the hours. None of us could go with him, not even those poor bastards whose screams had been stolen; not the ghosts who had already passed through these painful billets and were awaiting orders.

"A hard death," O'Shaughnessy said. "And hard to look at. Don't go blaming yourself for turning away."

Wide of the mark. Like Miller had been that time. Misunderstandings from men who should have known me better. "It makes me mad, sir. That's all."

"Don't be mad at God, lad. Wasn't Him sent Abner Foy to war. It was the British Army. And still, Travis, you see the horror of it surely, but you're a thinking man, and so I know you see the glory, too. Suffering the more to appreciate Heaven. Suffering as Christ himself did. Seen that way, why, pain becomes a blessed thing."

"Should tell Foy. He'd like to know that."

"I have told him. I tell them all. Come now. I can see how distressed this has made you. Come. Sit down and let's have a chat."

Misunderstandings. He put his hand on my arm. I pushed it away. "You talked about things I told you private-like. I thought priests weren't supposed to do that."

"And what would that be?"

"About the whore. You told Miller, didn't you?"

O'Shaughnessy's attention wandered from canvas hut to dying soldiers to a far line of trees. "I could tell you that what we had was nothing that near to confession, neither the form nor the fact that you're not of the Faith. You're an apostate, lad. And there are ten bishops at home who would pass over what I did without a squeak about my breaking the seal. Well, truth is, there would be ten bishops as well who would tell you that I'm a poor excuse for a priest. But it was just that Captain told me what the police had found, you see. Then he told me you had scarpered off somewhere that night. He was horrified by the implications, I can tell you, and frightened what the rest of the officers were gossiping. He asked if I thought you could do something so terrible."

I felt the first strong emotion since the ghosties' hand-me-down despair. It was rage.

He said, "I told him no."

Coming out of a door into the cleansing sunlight were Riddell, Pickering, and Marrs. Foy would still be inside, his leaking body on its stained bed.

"But I had to tell the captain the rest, Travis, for you're a puzzle whose pieces don't quite fit. And if it meant breaking a vow and taking on the sin of it, I intended to save your soul."

"The army would have give a ten-minute court-martial, then took me out and shot me. What about trying to save my life a little before you went off blabbing about me, sir?"

"Ah, lad. If it was lives I wanted to save, I'd be telling all these boyos to go home."

Marrs, Pickering, and Riddell were waiting. By them, an officer. I ached to confess to someone, anyone, about seeing the ghosties, but it was too late.

I had started away when I heard O'Shaughnessy's quiet, "Sorry, lad."

Said serious enough, but he was grinning. In the middle of screaming and dying men, talking about suffering and glory. Smiling forgiveness for his own sins. In his purple stole, magnifying the Lord.

I trotted across the grass to Riddell. The officer with him turned to watch my approach.

". . . a week, I shouldn't guess." The officer was a major, one with medical corps insignia. "A bit of bad luck, that."

Foy's body weeping into his sheets. Bad luck. A blessing.

From Marrs a shockingly irate "But I thought he was getting better."

The major didn't take offense. Get used to gassing victims, I suppose, you can get used to disrespect. "Um. Yes. Looked better for a while. Thought he'd turned the corner, what? But it had worked its way into the lungs. No way to know until the lesions started suppurating. Still, a kind word, a familiar face. Cheering them up does wonders, I always say."

"It's possible, then? He could get better?" Marrs asked.

The major cleared his throat. "Well! I'm sure that he enjoyed his little visit. There's that."

I left Pickering shaking his head at Marrs's question. I went back into the ward and closed the door behind me. No one, not the patients trapped in their grotesque bodies, not the overworked nurses, paid any attention to my entrance. No ghosties came to lend me memories. I walked over to Foy's bed.

He was either dead or asleep. I stood and watched until I saw the slight rise and fall of his chest. Too bad. Poor Foy, brimming over with blessings.

I reached down and took his swollen, scaly hand. "There's this graveyard, Foy. Look for it, will you? You'll know when you get there, because there's no other peace like it. There's marble angels and a mausoleum with a glass ceiling, glass so thick that light from it shimmers down on the tiles a pure water blue."

I couldn't tell if he was hearing me. The tip of his dry tongue came out, licked his lips. The inside of his mouth, I saw, was bleeding.

"There's a woman," I said. "You'll like her. Tell her I sent you. Tell her she needs to take care of you special. She'll do that for me. This is the truth, Foy. I'm sure of it now."

I started to leave, but he held onto my fingers for a heartbeat, so light and brief a holding that it might have been reflex.

I squeezed back, careful not to hurt him. "That graveyard. It's a goddamned beautiful blessing."

The four of us didn't talk much on the walk back. It was coming on twilight. We passed under a line of poplars, disturbing a roosting flock of pigeons, sending them flying, rustling softly through branches, fluttering and cooing above our heads, tree to tree. We walked like potentates, the birds announcing our coming. Rabbits in a nearby meadow lifted their heads to watch us pass.

When we hit the rest area, Riddell had a long private conversation with Blackhall. He came back grinning. "Got us a few hours more leave. That inn? Frenchie cook has learned 'imself fry-ups. Does a fair fish and chips. Anyone want to go?"

The fish was soggy, the fries cut too big. I had a few glasses of wine and tried to explain to the cook about cornmeal and buttermilk, about the need for bacon drippings.

Pickering just had to visit the whores, and even Riddell took a turn. I got the skinny one this time. Her hair was all done up in dark curls. Ringlets framed her cheek. We lay side by side, not talking, not fucking. She had the most amazing milk white skin, Bobby, and rosy little nipples. I ran my hand all over her slow. A miracle how whole her body was, what a blessing. She kept trying to kiss me. She played with my pecker. But after a while she stopped trying to earn her five shillings so hard. She stared at the ceiling, and she was smiling a little. I stroked her. I smelled her skin, Bobby. I buried my face in her ringlets and smelled her hair.

When my nose and hands knew her, I rolled on top and nudged her legs apart. Being in her felt safe. I rested there for a while. My head was against her chest. I could hear her heart beating, a sound to sleep to.

I took hold of her hand and put it to my cheek. Whores are good at understanding what a man needs; and so she caressed my face, my shoulders until I felt real again. She moved against me slow, and we rocked together into loving. She showed me a nice time, and I left her a pound note for her trouble. When I started to go out the door, she grabbed my hand to stay me. She ran her fingers over my forehead, my cheek. She kissed me real light on the corner of my mouth.

"All right," she said in her broken English. "All right," she promised, stroking me. "Is all right."

It *is* all right, I think. When I got downstairs, Riddell was beaming, so proud of himself he was near to bursting.

"A fine night, d'ye think so, Stanhope?" As if a good fuck

had turned him into Pickering, he punched me in the arm. "Fine night."

And so it was.

Travis Lee

SEPTEMBER 2,
A POSTCARD FROM THE FRONT LINES

Dear Bobby,

They got me sharpshooting the way Blackhall says it should be done. No more acting on my own, either. Got me a partner. Gives me somebody to talk to, I guess. Heatwave's broken; the weather's fine. The nights are downright chilly.

Travis Lee

SEPTEMBER 2
ONE YOU DON'T NEED TO SEE YET

Dear Bobby,

Blackhall called me into his dugout today. "I'm putting an end to your little game, Stanhope. Starting tomorrow, you sharpshoots from No Man's Land, the way the other sharpshooters does."

My knees started to buckle. I would have sat down then and there if I'd had a place to sit. Instead, I took a quick step back so I could brace myself against the sandbags. From his perch on an ammo box, Blackhall looked up at me. He knew how scared I was. That's why he was smiling.

"Lacks the belly for it?"

I tried to keep my voice from shaking. I wouldn't give him the damned pleasure. "Sir. Aren't my totals good enough, sir?"

Blackhall's dugout, like most, was open to the trench. A breeze found its way to me down the traverse, but it wasn't enough of one. I was sweating. Farther down, men argued as they repaired the walls. Over the ceaseless barrage of grumbling came Pickering's braying laugh.

"Ain't your totals. Don't like your attitude is what." Blackhall scratched furiously at his belly. He's a hairy man, with bunches of black curls climbing the front of his collar and springy tufts growing out his ears. The lice get to him bad. "You don't get your head shaved like the rest of us. Got to stay pretty, don't you, nits or no. Lifts extra rum. Or won't tell me who gives it. Don't sharpshoot like the others. Can't bear to do sod all the way anybody else does."

Despite the sluggish cool breeze, it stank in Blackhall's dugout: the lieutenant's rank animal odor, my own sharp fear.

"Nights, you reads your bloody poetry. Waste of candles, my opinion. Schoolgirl notions. Takes the fire out of your belly. Won't have it." He leaned back, took out his pipe, packed and lit it. He took his time, maybe hoping I'd leave. I didn't.

"Sir? When I started sharpshooting, they gave me a choice. I proved I could get me enough kills without moving any closer. Point is, aren't my totals good enough? If they're not up to snuff, just send me out there. Do whatever you goddamned please. But seems to me that if something ain't broke, you don't go trying to fix it."

"I'm tired of your insubordinate, degenerate ways." He made an O of his lips and blew a smoke ring my way. It rose toward me like a gray halo before dissolving into ghosties. "I won't have nobody bucking my orders or stealing rum or scarpering off. I wants real soldiers in this platoon, not prissy little sods who go giving others ideas."

"What the hell kind of ideas you talking about, sir?" I knew what the bastard meant, Bobby, and my knuckles itched to knock him down.

He smiled. There was a dark gap where three of Blackhall's front teeth were missing. The Tommies have bad teeth, damned near all of them. Maybe Blackhall resented my teeth, too.

"I knows Captain give you an alibi, Stanhope, but I takes that for what it's worth. I figure you done that girl in. Figure 'e knows it, too. But you're a pretty boy, vain as a cock and a bit of a pet, I figures. Too, you got them bleeding sharpshooting totals. For whatever reason, 'e thinks you're a valuable piece of muck. But for now, I owns you. So tomorrow before sunup, Stanhope, I want your arse out through the wire, and you're to take a spotter along."

"A spotter? I've done without till now."

"You'll sharpshoot by the book. Besides, I don't trust you out there alone."

"I'll take Pickering." Then I changed my mind. "No, sir. I'll take Marrs. We work good together."

"LeBlanc."

The eerie cold that possesses LeBlanc found its way down the traverse and entered me. I swallowed hard. "Sir," I began, but he didn't let me finish.

"Should like that—partnering with LeBlanc—seeing as how he's a sneaky devil just like you."

I tried to protest again, but he wouldn't listen.

"Wouldn't give you who you chose, any case. Might get out there and start your mischief. Slap and tickle. Dropping your bloody pants. Maybe you already 'as, you sharing a dugout with Marrs and all. Is that it? Is that why you wants Marrs out there with you?"

My face went hot. My fists clenched. "Goddamn it."

He moved fast, Bobby. One heartbeat he was sitting, sneering at me, the next he was on his feet. There was a trenching tool in his hand.

I took a deep breath, counted real slow to ten. "I ain't no goddamned queer, sir."

He was clutching the trenching tool so tight that his knuckles were pale. Not from fear of me, neither. From absolute killing hate.

"That girl had a tree branch rammed up inside 'er. I figures only a poof would go buggering a woman with sommit other than what 'e was born with. It's unnatural. Well, degenerates can't 'elps themselves, I suppose. See? I knows you, Stanhope. Didn't I tell you once? Now go find LeBlanc. Tell 'im to get his arse 'ere on the double." When I hesitated, he took a step forward. I didn't back up. For a disturbing time we were too close.

His breath bathed my face; and it was so heavy with rot that it made me sick. He growled, "Get out of me sight."

LeBlanc took the news the way he does everything: a few cusses, then sulky resignation. But I saw something else in him, too. A deadly joy. Part of him wants to go under the wire, Bobby, and that scares me bad.

Travis Lee

SEPTEMBER 4, THE FRONT LINES
ONE TO HANG ONTO FOR A WHILE

Dear Bobby,

The night before LeBlanc and me crawled out to No Man's Land, Marrs and me and Calvert had ourselves a little good-bye party. Marrs made tea. We put some of my rum stash and some of Pickering's jam in it. It tasted like chlorinated puke; but even Calvert, who likes his tea and rum plain, drank it down. In war, you do what you got to, I guess.

Marrs tried to make me feel better. He kept patting me on the back. And every damned time he did, I thought about what Blackhall had imagined us doing.

"Yeah, okay," I said, and shrugged him off.

But he kept hovering. "It'll be all right, Stanhope. Won't be so bad. You'll see."

Always patting on me. "Yeah, Marrs. Okay. Fine."

"Lucky it's not Marrs who's going," Pickering said. "Lie down out there, and his bum would rise to the breeze. Only soldier I know who ever got shot in the arse, our Marrs. Did you know that, Calvert? Poor Fritz. Considering the size of his target, he couldn't bloody miss."

Get enough of Pickering's shit, anyone would sour. "Fuck you, Pickering. Can't you leave him the hell alone for once?" The sun was already low in the sky. Soon night would come. And sleep, if I could manage any. Then waking up before the sun came up and crawling into the dark with LeBlanc. I took another drink. "Needs lemon peel," I said.

"And fuck you back." Pleasant old Pickering. Not a feather ruffled.

"Don't like them eff words like you uses." This from Calvert. "Wif the bof of you, it's effing this and effing that. You talk like that wif ladies about?"

"With the ladies? I've never had complaint." Pickering clapped his hand down on Marrs's knee, stared deeply into his eyes, pursed him a kiss. "Isn't that true, my sweet?"

Marrs snorted so with laughter that tea ran out his nose.

I don't know whether it was Pickering's bad joke or the helplessness of Marr's laughter, but right then, Bobby, right that very minute, I loved those boys so much. They were my chums. The originals. They were all I had.

After we had climbed into our cubbyholes that night and the candle had burned down to nothing, long after the others had started to snore, I reached down and prodded Pickering.

In the cubbyhole below me, he stirred. The sky was clear, the dugout cavern-dark. Across the way, moonlight flowed down the sandbags like cascades of milky water.

His throat sounded clogged; his voice was sleepy. "What?"

Outside, misty light coated everything—even a pozzy pot left illegally on the firestep. The night was fragile, like you could take a deep breath and blow the dusty moonlight away.

"What?" Pickering was irritated.

"You see anything funny about me?"

Cloth rustled. There were sounds of a heavy body moving. Pickering had evidently turned over on his back and pulled the sleeping bag aright. "Har-har. I'd like to laugh more at you, Stanhope, but it's so bloody late. Also, not to put too fine a point on it, it's so effing *dark*, you see."

"No. Really. You ever see anything different about me?"

"Yes." Very sober now. "It comes as a surprise, Stanhope, but I must tell you in all honesty—and in this light it's quite plain—you're black as the ace of spades."

"Blackhall thinks I'm . . ." I couldn't just jump in and tell him, Bobby. I mean, our cubbyholes were on top of each other; well within groping distance. "You know."

More shifting sounds. The noise of Pickering clearing his throat. "I know what?"

"How some fellows are. Funny."

"I've never thought you particularly funny, Stanhope."

Pickering was the clown of the platoon. He didn't care much for competition.

"Blackhall doesn't think I like the ladies."

I could hear him breathing.

I filled my lungs with the dank trench air and then just let all my worries go. "Hell, he accused me of being a poof, is what he did. I don't think I am."

I thought of the way I loved the platoon. How I loved Miller. But that's different, Bobby, isn't it? Pickering was awful damned quiet, so I went on. "I used to think you could tell, like you can tell a high yellow by looking at the palms of their hands. I mean, queers'd walk a certain way or stand kind of funny. Something in the way they said things, maybe. Not a lisp, particularly, but somehow, someway, you could pick 'em out. Then I come here and there's two men who figure I light-step; and now I got to thinking—what if I really am queer, and I just can't see it yet? You been around, right? You're married and all. Hell, Pickering. You think I'm like that?"

Cloth rustled. His voice came muffled. He'd turned toward the wall again. "Go to sleep."

Outside, moonlight sat atop sandbags like a pale dusting of snow.

"Oh, and Stanhope?"

A rat, cloaked in magic, crawled along the firestep.

"Don't play with my bum," he said.

I shut my eyes and went from peace into peace: the sun-drenched, peeling steps; angels with downturned, shadowed faces. I kept walking, past the mausoleum, past glass-topped graves with soldiers sleeping under. Through a landscape still green with the remains of summer.

A cool wind struck my cheek. Autumn coming.

I turned and saw that I was dangerously near the cypress, so close that I could fall in. The cold breeze came at me from the dark. It ruffled my hair. It teased my collar. It sucked me to it.

Faster now. Racing toward my already written future. Past the last grave, an angel desperately but uselessly reaching. Past the birdsong and sunlight and into humming silence. I stopped, teetering, at the edge. In the pitch black beyond, someone called—not man, not woman. Not eager, but not indifferent, either. A cool wind and a tepid sort of voice.

And then it was LeBlanc calling from the trench's shadows. The moon had set. The air was damp and chill, the world quiet in the way it can only be when night has made its slow swing toward morning. I crawled out of my cubbyhole and jumped to the ground.

"Come on. I got our breakfast and lunch in my haversack," LeBlanc whispered. "Your turn tomorrow."

A surprise. He sounded sleepy, and because of it, vulnerable.

In a firebay of the early morning trench a candle was burning, the sentry, Harold Martin, beside it. He had set a ladder up, and he was waiting for us on the firestep, half-asleep.

"Luck," he mumbled as we started our way up the parapet. I looked down and caught one final glimpse: Martin weary and nodding in the warm light of his candle.

I crawled through the hole LeBlanc made in the wire. I wormed after him into the raw, churned earth of No Man's Land. We found us a shell hole and waited for the sun to rise.

LeBlanc must have picked up on my mood. "It won't be so bad, Stanhope. You needed out of that crappy trench, anyway. Needed some air."

The sun came up in pastel shades of pink, our briar patch of wire black sutures on the tender cheek of dawn. In the faint rosy light, rats slunk back toward the trenches and home. Birds stirred. Across the way, the Boche army stretched and yawned.

LeBlanc popped up, quick as a squirrel, and down again. He grinned at me. "Clear. I make it one hundred and thirty yards."

"I don't need anybody computing distance for me."

"Sure. There's a break in the parapet about thirty yards to the left."

"I don't need anybody wiping my ass for me, neither."

I popped up for a look-see. A little slower than LeBlanc, but still plenty safe. Nothing was happening.

"Don't get mad at me, Stanhope," LeBlanc said. "It's that cocksucker Blackhall who's your problem. You know what he wants, eh? Eh? He sends us out here hoping both our asses'll get blown to hell, that's what. Bang, Stanhope. Bang, LeBlanc. Two less headaches."

That scared me. "We'll snap a few quick ones and then change position," I said. "I don't want no mortar rounds tossed my way."

"Sitting fucking ducks." LeBlanc's scope was hooded with brown paper, so as not to reflect the light. He fiddled with it. I thought he was about to go spotting, but he sighed and twisted belly-up to watch the sunrise.

After the pink light came the gold, like a visitation from God. Grandeur shone through LeBlanc's lifted fingers and striped my sleeves with grace. It wasn't a morning to go killing.

"Or," I said, "we could just pretend to shoot and not really do it."

LeBlanc balled up the camouflage tarp. Out of rage, I thought at first. His voice, though, was calm. "We could."

Abruptly he threw the tarp upward. It left the blue shadows of our hole and for a magic instant caught the dawn. Two quick snaps across No Man's Land, no louder than the pop of a finger. The tarp jerked twice as it billowed down—the Boche sniper had shot it. The Maxim went off then, too. Bullets started smacking the dirt.

LeBlanc held his sides and laughed. "Hey. You mad enough now, Stanhope? Ready to shoot some Boche?"

"You crazy damned peckerwood."

LeBlanc started screaming.

The helpless, stunned agony in his voice made me go cold. Despite memories of Smoot, I reached out to help him. LeBlanc was rolling around in the shell hole. For the life of me, I couldn't see where he was shot.

He twitched out of my one-handed grasp and slid down

the incline, right into the mud. His screams were weaker now, more grunts of pain.

I slid down after him. "Where's it, LeBlanc? Where you hurt?"

When I got closer, I saw that he was grinning. Above us, the bullets stopped. "They think they got us," he said, and winked.

"You crazy bastard." Said with such venom that he stopped smiling. My hand tightened on my gun.

He didn't apologize. I didn't bother to warn him not to pull a stunt like that again. We stayed where we were for a while, and when the sun had risen high and the day was warming, we crawled out of that shell hole and found us a spot where the turf had been lifted up by an explosion. We had us some breakfast. Eventually, we both forgot our mad and got to joking around again. I watched the spot where the Boche parapet was falling down and weak; and when the crew showed up to resandbag it, I got me a kill. After that, LeBlanc and me, under cover of that gouge, moved on.

We ate lunch. The Boche never did get a fix on us—the Maxim was shooting way right of the mark. When the day got hot, we hunkered down in a hole and took us a little nap. I didn't dream. I don't know, Bobby. Maybe dreams come harder here.

Late afternoon, we moved around a little more. I snapped myself off a few more shots, didn't hit anything. When night started to come on, LeBlanc and me risked the moonlight to get ourselves home.

We crawled over the parapet and jumped down from the bags. Marrs and Pickering were waiting for us, wide-eyed.

"Who was shot, then?" Marrs asked. "We heard a terrible screaming, and we thought someone was shot."

Poor, solicitous Marrs. LeBlanc and me laughed ourselves silly. I threw the camouflage tarp over Marr's head and stuck my finger into one of the bullet holes. I tickled his ribs. He tried to whip the tarp off, but I wouldn't let him. We wrestled around in the twilight-filled trench. He crashed into the sandbags. Maybe he hurt himself, I don't know. Anyway, he got to whining, the way Marrs does sometimes. I let him go.

"Not fair," Marrs pouted when I lifted the tarp off him. He started touching his nose ginger-like, as if it hurt him. "I thought you was dead, Stanhope. First Foy, then you. Felt all blue, I did."

"Blue? For me?" I laughed, but he still looked woeful. "That was just LeBlanc throwing off the Boche. Got 'em to stop firing. It was just a joke."

Then I saw Pickering standing in the wash of light from the dugout door, his droll face solemn. "Not funny, Stanhope," he said.

How would he know? He has to be the comedian; nobody else has the right. And that Brit humor, Bobby. Their goddamned puns and all. Shaggy dog stories without any point. Maybe it's better that I didn't get one of them out in No Man's Land with me. They'd fall apart out there. One thing I can be sure of: LeBlanc never will.

Travis Lee

SEPTEMBER 6,
A POSTCARD FROM THE FRONT LINE

Dear Bobby,

It rained yesterday. LeBlanc and me found a little bit of shelter under the lip of an odd shell hole. Just when I get comfortable, LeBlanc drops his pants and squats to take a shit. Bastard's laughing, too. Shit stank like something'd crawled up his ass and died. Well—bullets and rain or no—we had to move on. Goddamned Canuck's got a weird sense of humor.

Travis Lee

SEPTEMBER 9, THE RESERVE TRENCHES

Dear Bobby,

The rotation's slow now. They keep us too long at the front. Still playing cards with Gordon, the rum wallah, and

I'm still winning. I take a full canteen to No Man's Land now, just to while away the hours. Not that there's much free time. Damned LeBlanc was born with a fierce need to go stirring things up.

I try to get him distracted by conversation—not the easiest thing to do.

"You ever notice how the army's kind of like high school, except with bullets. You ever notice that, LeBlanc, huh? I mean you got the same asshole teachers, the same brat kids. You got your friends. Everybody's got a group they belong to. Folks got a tendency to herd, you know?"

All but for LeBlanc. The herd and the predator.

"Like goddamned sheep." He has a nasty kind of laugh that makes me want to wash my hands after. He flopped belly-down and lifted his scope. "Twelve yards left, by that gap in the bags."

By the time I took aim, the gap between the bags was empty. I lay back down and took me a drink. "I liked school," I said.

"I hated it. Hated every Jesus and Joseph fucking thing about it." He'd gone pale at the corners of his lips. "Nuns all the time after you. 'Settle down, boy, settle down.' Things don't go their way, and they knock your knuckles bloody. You're not doing anything, eh? Maybe just sneaking a little smoke. And all of a sudden you look around and there she is: one of them waddling bitch penguins, with a ruler in her hand."

I laughed so loud that the Boche popped a couple of shots our way. "Your sister's a nun, right?"

He took my canteen away, treated himself to a drink.

"Aw, hell, LeBlanc. My teacher had her a bois d'arc plank paddle with holes in it. You sneak a smoke at my school, and you'd have to drop your pants and bend over. Strong damned woman, too. Arms big around as your thigh. Raised big old welts." I took back the canteen.

He peered at the sky as if he was looking for a sign. The day was cool, with gray cotton roller clouds to the horizon. "It was always 'Yes, Sister' and 'no, Sister' and 'thank you so much, Sister.' Made me want to puke. The whole building smelled like dust and Church and women. There were crosses plastered on the walls, saints waiting around every goddamned corner. And everybody moved so *slow*. Have patience, Pierre. Don't go so fast, Pierre. Wait for Johnny. Wait for George. And that old mick priest sided with the nuns all the time. He had a metal ruler, too, only he'd heat it up in the grate, and he'd slap me on the arm to show me what perdition was like. When I got home, Papa beat me more, eh? Said Father wouldn't have burned me if I hadn't needed a lesson. When I was a kid I was scared I was going to Hell."

"Baptists worry some over Hell, too, LeBlanc."

He wasn't even listening. "I thought I was going crazy, eh? Every week I'd go into confession hoping that old mick'd help me. But all he'd say was, 'Stop having those thoughts. Just stop it,' he'd say. Sure. Like it was easy as turning off a spigot. I figured there was something wrong with me, eh? I was possessed by a devil or something. Then, when I was in eighth grade, a kid moved to our school from Montreal. He said he knew boys who had got felt up by their priest. Altar boys. And right there in the rectory, too. That's when I saw that priests were no goddamned better than we are, and I stopped worrying so much about Hell. Still, you know? My mama always said I acted like Satan was nipping at my heels. But I think that's only because I liked to go fast. Ran everyplace I went. Ran my horse, too. Hey. You like that, Stanhope? Climbing on the back of a horse—just jumping up, no saddle or bridle—and kicking him into a run?"

"Sure."

"Yeah. Yeah. I knew you did. That's what I like best—going fast, climbing high and diving off into the river. Stepping right on the train tracks while the train's coming, eh?"

I knew I was looking inside him for the first time, like I'd found a key that unlocked a vacant house. The furniture there surprised me.

"There's plenty of time to slow down when you're dead," he said.

A fine drizzle started falling. He covered himself with the tarp. I rolled around in the hole until I was comfortable and closed my eyes for a little nap. When I woke up, the clouds had lowered, the day was darker. All I could see of LeBlanc was the glint of his eyes—a snake under a rock. It scared me so bad, I sat up fast. A Boche sniper took a wild, fast shot at me. I hugged the ground, my heart hammering.

He didn't say anything. Didn't ask what had startled me into sitting up, nothing like that. I didn't speak, either. I took a steadying sip from my canteen.

I don't know. It doesn't seem to me like LeBlanc lives fast, Bobby. That stillness, like a scorpion's. Like a spider's. The glint of his eyes under the shadow of that tarp. But when he moves, he moves so quick you can hardly see him. I don't have to watch him kill to know that.

He was ready to move again. "Come on, Stanhope," he said. "Get up. Let's go shoot some Boche. Don't be so goddamned slow."

Does he kill the stragglers? Was murder part of those thoughts that used to scare him? When he moved to the next shell hole I moved too, not daring to stay behind. A hundred or so yards from me, Emma Gee played her deadly rataplan.

I swear, Bobby, nobody loves adventure like LeBlanc.

Travis Lee

SEPTEMBER 12, THE RESERVE TRENCHES
ONE FOR ME

Dear Bobby,

Life narrows in the trenches. You spend your time nearsighted. The sky's small. The horizon's the next wall of sandbags. Worse, your world of people shrinks till it seems like there aren't any folks outside your own platoon. Sometimes when it's quiet you wonder if the rest of the trench is empty, and the war got over, and everybody went home.

I saw Miller today. It was a foggy, dim afternoon, the

clouds hanging low. He was moving down a communications trench to visit the troops, I guess. I was headed up to the med dugout for an aspirin. I made the next zigzag and there he was, taking up my horizon. We both stopped dead. His eyes went darting away from mine.

"Afternoon, sir," I said.

His face was already turning pink. "Good to see you again, Stanhope."

"Good to see you, too, sir." And I meant it.

He must have heard the welcome in my tone, for his gaze snapped to mine.

"Sorry, sir. You can't pass without the password."

His eyebrows rose. Cautious now, like a horse the first time in snow, not sure which way to step. "Ah?"

It was cool. Right in that spot, the air smelled fresh, like there hadn't been any death around to spoil it. "Yes, sir. Sorry about that, sir. New regs and everything."

So damned serious. It broke my heart. He'd caught the upper-class stuffiness of Dunston-Smith.

I said, "I'll start it for you, sir. 'Thou, that to human thought art nourishment.' "

He frowned.

I prodded him with another line. " 'Like darkness to a dying flame.' " Daylight was dying, too. And my smile along with it. He had to know *Hymn to Intellectual Beauty*. Hell, it was one of Shelley's better-known works, not like *The Masque of Anarchy* or something. To be truthful, I always thought of it as Miller's and my private anthem. I went on slow. " 'Depart not . . .' "

A smile broke out all over him. It was like, for that instant, that the sun had pierced the clouds. " 'As thy shadow came!' "

"Doing good, sir. Just the couplet to go. " 'Depart not, lest the grave should be . . .' "

"Password's too bloody easy, Stanhope. 'Like life and fear, a dark reality.' "

We stood in the mist grinning like a pair of fools. "Good to see you, Stanhope," he said again, and this time he meant it. "You're well, I take it?"

"You bet, sir."

"And the sharpshooting from No Man's Land suits you? Lieutenant Blackhall and I had quite a discussion about that. He's a stickler for rules, you know. Sometimes it's best to let subalterns have their head, if they don't abuse the privilege."

"I understand, sir. Everything's fine."

"Well." He cleared his throat. His eyes went wandering the gray afternoon again. "Excellent totals, at any rate. Must buy you a dinner when we're on leave. Perhaps a run at one of your tarts." He was smiling when he said that, too; but there was a hint of condescension, too.

It put me in my place. And it hurt, too, Bobby, if you want to know the truth. I've seen coloreds get that smile to them when they're together and a white boy like me's around—it's like they share all kinds of secrets, or like suffering makes them better. Maybe it does.

About then Fritz decided to lob a few shells our way. A Jack Johnson landed toward the rear. Black smoke rose into the cool pewter day.

"Take you up sometime on that dinner, sir."

We shook hands on it.

A whizzbang landed next—so close that we both ducked, and then we laughed. "Best find shelter, what?" He sounded sorry to be leaving.

We had an awkward time of it, squeezing past each other. The trench was tight. We went chest to chest, but he kept his hips best he could away from me. He's a gentleman like that.

And when we were past each other and I had started away, I heard him call my name. I looked over my shoulder to see him smiling, there in the misty gloom, in the constriction of that trench.

" 'While yet a boy I sought for ghosts,' isn't it?"

The next line of verse. I'd forgotten. Jesus. How could I have? It sent a shudder through me. "Yes, sir. You're right, sir."

He nodded, tapped his cap with his stick. "Must have us a real challenge some day. A witness each to mark our shots and wipe our brows when we're sweated. The English Romantic poets and fifty paces. Well. Ta-ta, Stanhope."

"Goodbye, sir."

I watched him leave, then I went on my way, too—through the gloom of the narrow trench.

That night Foy was in the graveyard. His yellow blisters were healed. His round baby-face was peaceful. He was in his grave, and there were blood-red flowers and ferns tucked all around him. He was smiling a little, even though his eyes were closed.

I kneeled down at the edge of the grave and put the flat of my hand on the glass. I called to him, but he didn't stir. The glass was cool to the touch, the roses around him pimpled and wet with dew. I rested my palm over where I thought his heart would be.

"When you wake up, why don't you stick around for a while, Foy?"

The rest of the platoon had all left. I couldn't bear to lose Foy, too.

I got up and started away, but stopped when something told me his eyes had opened. I went back. He was still sleeping. I didn't see the calico girl around, but I left him, anyway. When I woke up this morning I thought of him lying down there, hands crossed over his chest, his eyes blank and open. What's he seeing, do you think?

Travis Lee

AUTUMN 1916

Seven

September 14
A postcard from the road

Dear Bobby,

They've moved us out. We're heading north, I hear. Maybe I'll get to see the ocean.

Thank Ma for the angora underwear. I'm the envy of the platoon. Tell her next time, though, she don't have to dye the wool. Believe me, up here with this bunch, plain goat-tan's best.

Travis Lee

September 14, on the march

Dear Bobby,

They pulled us back and sent us north, away from the best trenches we'd ever had. Nobody wanted to go. That place had been home for a while—a little damp, maybe. Certainly stinky. Still, there was elbow room in all the dugouts and most of the walls were strong—decent Boche digs. Then one morning, as the Brits would say, Bob's your uncle. Another battalion was coming to take our place. We don't know why. They tell us to go, and we march. They tell us to fight, and for some unknown reason we do.

The land here is even flatter. We march past black dirt farmland plowed by combat. Plants grow—mustard and turnips and kale—but everything's growing in the fallow. Here, war shoulders up to the road. It encroaches on the towns, Bobby. You can see it in the roadside trash, in the odd shell holes, in the forsaken, dismal little villages. This afternoon, we passed our only hints of life: a woman poling along in a flat bottom boat and an old man scavenging through a weedy garden.

Teatime, we stopped by the burned trunk of what had been an enormous tree. It must have lived centuries, that tree. Must have spread its branches near fifty feet across. Around the bare trunk was piled trash: rusting tins with labels in English, in French; a broken Boche belt buckle.

Pickering leaned his back against the charred bole. He lit up a smoke. I asked him if I could have one, but he flat-out ignored me.

Marrs caught on pretty quick to the reason for his mood. "New place won't be so bad, maybe," he said.

Without a glance in Marrs's direction, Pickering muttered, "Sod off."

Pickering's scared, Bobby. He'd had to leave his cross on the sandbag, that sun-faded T that he took as some sort of sign. I remember the day we got to our old place, he'd seen it. He just had to have that cubbyhole, always had to sleep with his head toward that particular sandbag. Marrs's private salvation is the letter from his sweetheart promising she'd marry him, the one he keeps over his heart. With me, it's nothing I can touch particularly, but Emily Dickinson's poem of grief my mind can't help playing with: *This is the Hour of Lead—/Remembered, if outlived,/As Freezing persons, recollect the Snow.*

Thinking on that, I went quiet, too. I was disoriented. I'd packed up that morning and left home. Pickering had walked away without his sun-bleached cross and now he watched the sky, afraid a shell would kill him.

Marrs kept trying to get Pickering to talk, but I knew how heavy those lead hours could be, so I didn't bother anymore. Across the way I saw O'Shaughnessy praying with a soldier, LeBlanc staring at them both. Having those bad thoughts again? Was he wanting O'Shaughnessy to help him? Wish he *could* help us. It'll be a new No Man's Land I'll be facing. I'll have to find new shooting spots, new resting spots, new places to snipe from. War's so goddamned tiring.

At sunset we bivouacked in a fieldstone farmhouse with shattered walls. Rain started falling faster. Our charcoal fires went out, and we drank lukewarm tea with our cold dinner. When we were finished eating, we settled into our sleeping bags and watched the world fill up with night.

From the dark next to me came Pickering's quiet voice. "Bleeding luck."

"What?"

He was no more than two feet away. We've slept beside each other so long, I knew his smell. Out of all the snorers, I could pick out his breathing. "Should have cut it out with my penknife, Stanhope, that cross of mine. Would have too, if they'd warned us ahead of time that we were leaving."

Pickering leaving his cross. Riddell, his gramophone and Elgar. Miller and Dunston-Smith their straw-warm hut. There wasn't anything I wanted to go back for. I took a deep breath. The air was perfumed with rain.

"Might have carried it, you know. Just the T part. The rest of the sandbag might have stayed."

"Yeah," I whispered back. "It's a shame."

"Bleeding British luck," he said, a man resigned to fate.

I couldn't sleep. Every time I closed my eyes it felt like I was tumbling into the graveyard's dark. Before dawn I got up and crawled around the sleepers. I went outside. In the yard of the farmhouse I found an old lean-to. There, I lit a candle and read a little Shelley. I wrote you a postcard, then I wrote you this letter.

When I get to the new trenches, Blackhall will send me into the No Man's Land there. I have the strange feeling that I'll recognize it, every nook and hole and cranny. What's worse is, I understand why: When it comes right down to it, Bobby, all darkness is the same.

Travis Lee

SEPTEMBER 19, NEW RESERVE TRENCHES

Dear Bobby,

The trenches here are crumbling. The mud's ankle-deep. Dig a hole anywheres, it fills up with water. The soil is full of stinking bodies and white, knobby bones. The earth spews up death. It's built into the walls. Down the trench a Frenchie, last season's casualty, is sticking halfway out the bags: one horizon-blue leg; a bloated arm with two fingers off, another rotted to bone. The boys who were here before us said they'd miss him.

Hearing that, Riddell did a double take. "Whyn't take 'im with you?"

They didn't, but before they left every damned boy in both platoons shook that Frenchie's gray hand. They bid him adieu. Then they marched away, leaving us with their piss-poor trenches and their dead Frenchman.

The dugouts here stink of piss and rot. They're dripping wet. They're so small that the four of us have to take turns sleeping with our feet stuck in the aisle. Goddamned sentry's always tripping over us.

When the Boche shell, we huddle up real tight together, shoulder to shoulder, knee to knee, and wait for the walls to fall on us. We hunker shivering under the elephant sheet. There's not even the comfort of hot tea. We light up the brazier, but the charcoal stinks so bad it chases even the rats out.

I woke up the other night to hear Marrs crying. He went on for hours, sobbing quiet so as not to wake us. I don't know if the others knew. Nobody spoke. Thinking on it, I should have said something, but I was too afraid of embarrassing him. Besides, what could I say? Everything'll be all right? Jesus. Even Marrs is smart enough not to believe that.

And Pickering's in a funk. It's that goddamned cross of his. He's convinced himself that he's going to die here. The second night, when everyone else was asleep, he punched me. "Stanhope? Do me a favor."

"Yeah?" The dugout was dark and too close, with the four

of us crowded together. Calvert was snoring; Marrs was so quiet that he might have been dead. Even the rats had settled down for the evening.

"When I die, bury me proper, will you?"

"Better not die on me, Pickering. Else I'll have to go to London, look up your wife, and fuck her."

"No," he said. "Truly. You must promise me, Stanhope. I'm not joking."

I rolled away from him, disturbing a rat, sending it scampering over my legs.

"Please." The whispered plea behind me, nothing of Pickering's banter in it. "You must bury me, Stanhope. There's only you to ask. I'm afraid Marrs might muck it up. He has a soft enough heart, but he's always a bit muddled, isn't he. Like a fart in a colander. I know you'd see it through."

I squeezed my eyes shut and wished he'd go to sleep. "Yeah, okay. I'll bury you."

Just like Pickering to get an agreement, then glue caveats on. "Not in the parados, mind. I'd bloody fall out into the trench eventually."

"Not in the parados," I promised.

"And I wouldn't care to be sticking out of a wall someplace. You must promise me *that*. Bloody awful to be rotting where everyone can see. Good God. And I know it would be my luck to be hanging out the bags with my trousers about my ankles."

I started laughing. Calvert stirred in his sleep. I bunched my sleeping bag up to my mouth to stifle the noise.

"Not funny, Stanhope. I have a horror of being left out with the flies and the maggots. I have nightmares about it, if you must know. Don't you?"

The conversation was macabre, considering the darkness, the reek. I wanted to tell him about the graveyard, but I knew he'd either make a joke or he'd tell me to prove it. Pickering's a rock solid boy, the sort who doesn't hold to visions.

"Best you don't go thinking about things like that, Pickering. You go crazy that way."

"Well, we're here, aren't we? Proof we're bleeding bonkers. Also, if you don't mind, Stanhope, I'd rather not be left someplace where rats could eat me." His last sentence ended in a tired whisper.

He must have been exhausted. We all were. "Yeah. Okay. I'll see what I can do."

Something fell on me. I flinched and nearly cried out. Only Pickering's hand. He squeezed my shoulder tight, tried to speak, but choked up instead.

We were originals. I knew what he meant to say. "Oh, shit, Pickering. You're welcome."

I couldn't sleep, not when he was crying. I hated the sound of that. I was so damned tired, Bobby—too tired to even try giving him any ghostie and graveyard hope. He was too tired to hear it. Maybe that's why he boo-hooed, why Marrs did. Life here beats you down. It's exhausting, being helpless. Every day we rebuild walls and put up revetments. It doesn't matter. At night, the sandbags fail. If whizzbangs don't burst them, damp does. Walls tumble. They bury people. The trenches. What great goddamned shelter.

Yesterday O'Shaughnessy came on me where I was taking a breather from filling sandbags. My arms were trembling, my back ached. I'd been thinking longingly of Dickinson's description of freezing: *Chill—then Stupor—then the letting go.* I started thinking how death and grief must be the kinfolk of exhaustion.

"I've had word from hospital, lad," he told me. "Foy passed on a week back."

I nodded, thought about letting myself go into tiredness—just lying down where I was, closing my eyes, and giving myself so completely to sleep that my resting heart would stop.

He sat down beside me and lit two smokes. He handed me one. "Have you been seeing his ghostie, then?"

God, that cigarette tasted good. It woke me up, made me feel alive. I took a deep, steadying drag and blew smoke into the monochrome afternoon. It's the ugliness that beats me down the worst. Everything the hue of dirt—it's like being struck colorblind.

"I reckon so. When I dream about the graveyard now, Foy's always there," I said. "He's down in a grave with glass over him and pretty flowers tucked around. His eyes are open, mostly, and that worries me. But the calico girl says he's just dreaming. What do you think he could be dreaming about, sir? Down in that grave like that?"

"Heaven," O'Shaughnessy said.

All this time I'd been thinking that the graveyard is Heaven, but maybe I've been wrong. After all, if the graveyard's Heaven, why did Dunleavy and the platoon leave? If it's Heaven, would the flowers fade like they do?

"Keep watch over Foy, Travis. Don't be letting him wander."

The idea chilled me: Foy sleepwalking through the brightly hued cemetery. Foy wandering past the cypress and stumbling accidentally into the dark.

That night I went back to the graveyard to look down into Foy's blank blue eyes.

"Don't you be getting up and walking off, now," I told him.

The calico girl was standing by a fancy marble urn, laughing.

"But I got to watch over him," I said.

Autumn sunlight tilted through the trees, threw long shadows of blue. Behind her, maples and hickories were already starting to turn. Winter would come soon. The last of the green would dry to brown. Color would leave the graveyard. Snow would gradually, quietly cover the glass. I wondered what Foy would dream then.

She was still snickering at me.

"I got to take care of him. It's my job, ain't it?"

The wind rattled through the cottonwood, sent a handful of leaves scattering. Watery sun silver-plated her hair. "He's never out of my sight."

It was said as a promise. And right then, right in the middle of that dream, in the silence of the night, I woke up smiling. The trench stank. Pickering's elbow was gouging me, Marrs's butt was in my face; but in the damp of that dugout I felt so damned lucky, protected and coddled down to the bone. Never out of her sight. You see what that means, Bobby? Not just Foy, but you and me, Pickering and Marrs. Every single one. Nobody can ever be lost. Even if we wandered, she'd find us.

Travis Lee

SEPTEMBER 19
A NOTE FROM THE RESERVE TRENCHES

Dear Bobby,

This goddamned toy's supposed to make me feel better? Shit. Tell Pa if he wanted forgiveness so damned bad, he should have asked sooner. If he couldn't help what he was doing, he should have left when I was a kid. Now's no time to be carving me animals.

You're wrong, Bobby. It's a selfish thing he did, not a kindness. He's asking too much payment for this wood horse. So don't go begging me to forgive him. And don't you dare tell me where to find peace. You say Pa and me are staring death in the face. That may well be, but Pa needs to find his pardon somewheres else.

Travis Lee

SEPTEMBER 20, THE RESERVE TRENCHES

Dear Bobby,

This time I went looking for O'Shaughnessy. I asked if I could talk to him alone. We sat on a couple of jam crates in the weak afternoon sun. He treated me to some French chocolates one of the nun nurses had given him. We ate the candy like kids—picking around the box for our favorite. They were great chocolates, Bobby: hearts and leaves and some painted up like gift boxes. They went down smooth as cream.

He asked how I was, and I told him I was doing okay, considering. I asked how he was doing, and he looked surprised.

"It's kind of you to ask, lad. I'm well as can be expected, I suppose. But you've come to tell me of your troubles, and not be hearing of mine. What brings you, Travis?"

I could have told him "chocolates." I rummaged around in the tissue paper and picked out a dark square with a pink stripe around it. It was bittersweet with an aftertaste of cognac; and it made me think of Pa and the wooden horse he'd carved me.

I must have been quiet for too long, for O'Shaughnessy said, "What is it, lad?"

"Wish you'd talk to Marrs, sir. He keeps crying at night and everything."

"Does he?" O'Shaughnessy picked out one I'd had my eye on: a spiky ball that looked like it had coconut in it.

"Yeah. He cries when the boys are all asleep and he thinks nobody can hear him. He keeps it down, so as not to wake us. I reckon he's kind of ashamed. Pickering cries some, too. Well, Marrs is Catholic, so you got yourself a leg in; but Pickering's not much of anything religious. Still, a word or two from you might not hurt. Hell, I don't know what to tell them."

He looked pensively down into the chocolate box. "Don't you?" He plucked out a white lozenge with a red marzipan heart and rolled it around in his fingers.

"Hey. Don't tell them I said nothing, about them crying and all, okay?"

It seemed he was sad to be eating the candy. He finally popped it into his mouth and sucked a while. "Well. I've seen this sort of thing before: men breaking down when they're moved out. I'm sure they'll be settling down soon enough. And you, Travis? How would you be?"

Marrs's and Pickering's despair dismissed so carelessly. "I'm fine, okay? This ain't about me. See, Pickering left his cross behind in the old digs. It was just a faded mark on a sandbag. I never did see much in it, but he took a shine. Always thought it protected him from the shelling. Now he's scared. Guess he feels like he don't have nothing to hold onto anymore."

"A cross, is it?" O'Shaughnessy shrugged. "Well. Seems he has something after all. He's not entirely a nonbeliever, lad."

"No, sir. That's not the way it is. What he's hanging onto is superstition."

"Who's to say that religion and superstition are not sometimes one and the same?"

That threw me. Before I could recover, he changed the subject. "You were well for a while, Travis. I saw your joy come back, and your gentleness with it. What causes you to drink again?"

"I'm not drinking."

He set the top on the chocolate box, put the box away. "Would my eyes be lying?"

"Look. I come to ask help for Marrs and Pickering, sir. Not to talk about me."

"Ah, and what a grand altruistic gesture."

The contempt in his voice got me to my feet. "What the hell's the matter with you? I come to talk about problems, and you go riding me again. Damn your ass, anyway."

He seized my wrist. "You've no right." His grip was so tight, it hurt. "Listen to me, Travis. If God gives you a gift, you've no right to be throwing it away. You've been sent to us because we need you. When you drink, souls can be lost."

Sent? Shit. I didn't like the implications of that. "All due respect for your beliefs and such, sir, but I don't see this ghostie stuff as no goddamned gift. It scares me sometimes, thinking I'm going to turn around and come face-to-face with a dead man. Now, that graveyard's all well and good. Hell, the truth of it is, I like being there. But don't you go looking to me for answers. I don't know nothing. Besides, that girl in the graveyard, why, it's her job to keep an eye on things."

"And well it might be; but we need you, anyway. Her keeping an eye on us doesn't mean we can't be blinded."

He confused the hell out of me. Troubled me, too. I jerked free and stumbled back. "Sorry, sir, but you don't want to go counting on me handling things. I'm really kind of worthless, you want to know the truth."

"Worthless or no, promise me, lad. Will you promise me one thing? If you ever see me in your graveyard, promise that you'll stay with me. Will you do that? Will you keep me company a while?"

In his voice was such an ache that I broke out in goose flesh.

"Travis?"

I walked away fast. He might have called me again, but if he did, he called soft-voiced, and I didn't hear.

No matter. O'Shaughnessy begging my help to get to Heaven? Because begging was what he was doing, Bobby. There was something frightened in his eyes.

If Heaven lies beyond the graveyard, a priest of all people should go. Oh, I could see God leaving Pastor Lon wandering. If war's taught me one thing, it's that the Church we grew up in is shallow, all fellowship and "Shall We Gather at the River"s and dinners on the ground. Preachers fretting about dancing and vaudeville shows. They'd never recognize an ancient, murky dark like the one that's hiding in LeBlanc. When LeBlanc was a boy, that Catholic priest must have recognized it. I figure that's why he beat him with a hot ruler. Baptists are sunshiny folks. They don't know how to exorcise a demon. Hell, they're too inconsequential to even bury somebody right.

I couldn't ask O'Shaughnessy about what was really worrying me, so I caught Marrs alone. He explained last rites and why O'Shaughnessy goes out into the field even when Emma Gee's firing. His job, no matter what, is to save the souls of the dying.

"Well, what if O'Shaughnessy himself dies out there?"

"A priest?" It must have been the first Marrs had considered it. "Without extreme unction? Unconfessed and all?" He looked worried, and I didn't care for that. "Well, if he'd a mortal sin, he'd have Hell, wouldn't he. Venials, a bit of Purgatory."

The whole notion's crazy: Heaven depending on the timing of your death and who's around and all. It's just not fair.

O'Shaughnessy's been so damned faithful, Bobby. God owes him Heaven. He shouldn't have to count on me.

Travis Lee

SEPTEMBER 22, THE FRONT LINES

Dear Bobby,

Early yesterday before the sun came up, LeBlanc and me went out to the new No Man's Land. The sky was overcast, not as much as a star to guide us. I might have been a blinded soul wandering. The world was reduced to touch: sharp things that startled me; mush things that made me sick. We crawled through shell holes that stank of dead fish, and I wasn't sure if were smelling old carcasses or phosgene gas.

Black finally lightened to gray. A colorless sun came up over mud fields. We ate breakfast in a watery shell hole where two swollen rats floated.

LeBlanc was too chipper; but after all, it was his sort of weather, his landscape.

"You find yourself a dugout?" I asked him.

"Yeah. Hey. I been working on something. You ever blow up a toad?"

"Nope. So who you rooming with?"

"You never blew up a toad? Holy shit, Stanhope. What kind of childhood didya have? I'm thinking of making firecrackers out of bullets. Stick 'em up rats asses."

More about killing things. I rolled over on my stomach and lifted the periscope to see if I could spy some Boche. In the other trenches, nothing much was happening.

"Ka-blooey," LeBlanc said. "Get enough powder up 'em, there'll be guts and brains flying, you know?"

I looked around. He'd lit up a cigarette. I slapped it out of his hand. "You asshole. Get us killed that way."

He didn't yell or nothing. He stared, and that was worse.

"Come on, LeBlanc. They'll pinpoint our position. Smoking like that is dangerous."

"And your drinking's safe?"

I took another peek through the periscope.

He said, "Rum slows you down, Stanhope. It makes you do crazy things. Maybe you're crazy, Mama's boy. You ever think of that?"

"Could be."

Something hard slammed my back. Air exploded out of my lungs. For a terrifying minute I couldn't breathe.

He relaxed his fist, spread his fingers. The sympathetic heat of his hand pressed the spot between my shoulder blades. He whispered into my ear, warm and soft and close, "You think you're better than me. You're no better than me. Nobody is. You shit like I do, eh? You piss like I do. Only I don't get scared. Do you ever get scared, Stanhope?"

He jumped to his feet, waved toward the Boche trenches, shouting, "Hey! Hey, assholes!"

I caught him around the knee, bowled him over backward. He fell, and we rolled down the slope into the water. Bullets buzzed in a fury over our heads.

He thrashed and spat. The dead rats bobbed wildly. I grabbed his bandolier and pulled him out.

"You think you're something special, Stanhope. You and your Harvard. Your mother sending those blue angora socks. Your goddamned dun mare. You're nothing but shit."

"Stop it."

"You think you're smart, don't you? Mr. College. Kissing up to that kike Miller."

I shook him hard. "Shut up."

"You a kike, too, huh, Stanhope? You a sheeny? Wait! Maybe you're a poof. That's it! You and Miller've been butt-fucking, eh?"

Rage made me careless. I raised my fist up high. Something stung my upper arm. A bee, I thought, until I saw the blood pouring out. I'd been goddamned shot. And by the Boche sniper.

Just a scratch. Not much of a wound. Still, I forgot all about hitting LeBlanc. I hugged the ground. He started laughing like nothing at all had happened. He clapped me on the back, on the place his fist had bruised me. "Jesus and Mary, Stanhope, but you're fun."

Right then, Bobby, I felt the future roll away, this never-ending war, the years whirling out of control, always beyond the reach of my fingers. Days of mud and bullets and lunacy. Seasons passing, ugly and colorless. At my feet dead rats rode the waves of our struggle.

When LeBlanc said that we ought to have lunch, I told him hell, why not. I drank from my canteen until the future didn't hurt no more.

Travis Lee

SEPTEMBER 24, THE FORWARD TRENCHES
A QUICK NOTE JUST IN CASE.

Dear Bobby,

Riddell came by during supper tonight. Seems Major Dunn's got a bug up his butt again. A few hours from now, our company's due to go on a stunt—me and LeBlanc included. Even my scratch of a bullet wound—aching as it does once in a while—wasn't enough to keep me back.

So if anything happens, I want you to have my mare. Only sell her if you have to, and then go to Sharon Jewel Whitehead first. Sharon Jewel's always had an eye for that horse, and she's got a gentle hand. I can sleep easier knowing no one'll take whip nor spur to her. Sell my books in Austin. They might bring a penny or two. There. I reckon that's about all of me that's worth messing with.

Make it a short funeral and a cheap one. If it was me choosing, I'd have that Taverner's "Magnificat," but I doubt anybody back home knows the words. If it was up to me, I'd have O'Shaughnessy in his black dress and linen petticoat, and I'd have everyone speaking Latin, too; so nobody'd have to listen to Pastor Lon droning on and on about folks being called home too soon and all the God-works-in-mysterious-ways excuses. But you and Ma do what you have to. Y'all the ones has to sit through it, not me.

Pickering's depressed. Ever since Riddell told us the bad news, he's been sitting around moping. Marrs went on down to see O'Shaughnessy. There wasn't nothing better to do; I went on down, too.

Remember going to the fair and seeing the gypsy? How she stayed in the trailer, and there was a line of folks waiting? Then you went in one by one and she shut the door, remember? Just you and her and your secrets. And there was that candle on the table and all. Well, confession was just like that.

When Marrs lifted the blanket and came out, crossing himself, I went into the dugout. O'Shaughnessy saw me and smiled a satisfied kind of smile. "Ah! Turning Catholic now, are you, Travis?"

"Thought we might pretend."

His new dugout was cramped. Still, there was a table set up along the back wall, a big white candle and a cross and a painted statue of Mary on it. She had on a dark blue cloak with stars, and she was looking down, mild and indulgent. There was a book resting in her hand, but she wasn't reading. She was smiling at the tame yearling bull at her feet.

"My Mary. I felt I must bring her. In war we too easily forget the gentleness of women," O'Shaughnessy said.

There was a Bible on the table, too. A fancy one. It was open, a red ribbon trailing down the page like a narrow stream of blood. I scanned the Latin: *Dum transisset Sabbatum Maria Magdalena et Maria Jacobi et Salome emerunt aromata ut venientes ungerent Jesum.*

Easier to translate seeing the Latin than hearing it. " 'Then' . . . no, *when*. 'When gone over Sabbath,' well, 'When the Sabbath was done,' I guess. 'Mary Magdalene and Mary of Jacob'?" I turned. He was eyeing me.

He didn't need to know which page, which line. "Mary the mother of James."

I ran my finger along the words. " 'Mary the mother of James and Salome brought,' what?" I looked at him again. "Perfume?"

"Spices."

" 'And to go . . . ' " I stopped reading then, for I knew the next two words, and what part of the Bible I was reading.

" 'Anoint Jesus,' " O'Shaughnessy said softly.

He was sitting in his black wool, his purple stole. His hands were laced together on the table. Near him was a bottle I knew was the wine, a little box that must have held the bread. And a tiny glass vial.

"Did Marrs get the oil and everything?"

"I give the extreme unction for those who want it. Will you be wanting it, Travis? For you're not baptized in the Faith, and it would be a sin for me to give it."

Bad as he worried about Purgatory, I wouldn't ask that. "Just thought it might feel good to confess."

"It'll be face-to-face, lad. No grille between us."

"I know."

"Then sit down. You needn't look at me."

It was him who turned his face away. He propped his elbow on the table and rested his head in the fingers of one hand.

I looked at Mary.

"Bless me, Father," he said.

"What?"

He didn't raise his head, but he grinned. "It's what you say before confessing, lad: Bless me, Father, for I have sinned."

"Bless me—" My throat closed up on the next word, Bobby. It was too hard to say. And the three words taken together started me shaking. The quiet in that dugout, like the magnificent stillness of churches. My eyes burned from the pressure of childhood. By the candle, Mary's gold leaf halo caught the light.

I tried to say it. I tried, but my throat, my lips, wouldn't go on. O'Shaughnessy, waiting so patient. I started thinking about that damned wood horse Pa carved me—painted dun with a blaze, its face as intelligent and sweet as my mare's—that carefully carved toy that I had hidden down in my haversack, as much of an icon as anything else.

"Bless—" I had to stop again. Something came pushing from way deep inside. It bottled up in my chest, tight and huge and aching—too big for me to swallow anymore.

I thought of Ma, and memory swelled even bigger. It pushed a sob out. I clapped my hand over my face. Through the confines of my fingers, I said, "Bless me, Father."

I cried. Just like Pickering and Marrs. Just like we all do when we're tired or war's made us heartsick. Shit, Bobby. Crying doesn't matter.

O'Shaughnessy put his hand over mine. "Are you frightened, lad?"

I shook my head.

"Well." All he needed to say. I guess he knew everything then; knew what was haunting me as sure as I knew those last two words of Latin. He saw in an instant the tragedy that my crying implied. "For your penance, I'll be having you write a few words to your father, lad. You needn't send them, but you must put them down." A whispered incantation. I looked up in time to see him finishing the sign of the cross.

He told me to go in peace and sin no more, and so I went out and got pen and paper. I figured I'd best put the words down so they won't be lost.

I don't forgive Pa. You tell him that. Hell, that's not important. I doubt we're really expected to try and live happy-ever-afters. Tell him that when I come home—if I come home—I'm not going to go hugging on him or nothing. I did all the crying for him I'm going to do.

But hating's no good either, so tell him I'm shut of that. I'm not sorry I tried to kill him, and if I had it to do over, I'd aim better. Still, I'm sorry. I'm damned sorry he couldn't enjoy what life gave him. He had a wife who loved him. A pretty little ranch. Two children. I'm so sorry that instead of being content with that, he spent all his energy fighting his own mind's monsters. It's just damned sad, is all.

Odd, but I'm thinking now that he probably suffered much as Ma and I did. After all, there's a pecking order to things. Whether he imagined it or not, life beat on him. He just passed the sorrow down.

So tell him I understand. That's better than forgiveness, anyway. Forgiving and forgetting's only for them dim-witted folks, the ones with the short memories. And I don't expect Pa to forgive me, neither. I just want him to understand his legacy: my nightmares, why I hide in dark, small places. Why, no matter where I am, I never feel safe.

If I die tonight, kiss Ma for me. Lie and tell her I was happy. Tell her I forgave Pa for everything. Tell her the war wasn't so bad.

Travis Lee

SEPTEMBER 29, THE RESERVE TRENCHES

Dear Bobby,

Five nights ago we blacked our faces. We took off all metal. We left our packs and our helmets and gear. We pulled stocking caps over our heads.

Strange to be leaving all that I owned behind. Strange to see Marrs and Pickering in blackface. Miller passed down the dark of the trench and caught sight of me. His smile was blinding, so bright in that black world that color didn't matter.

"You fit, Stanhope?" he asked.

"Ready to go, sir."

He nodded as if he had expected nothing else.

Riddell blew out his lantern and the trench subsided into the quiet pool of night. A soft rain was falling. The air was heavy and quiet. Men jostled each other, cursed softly. I heard the sucking sounds of boots in the trench floor mud, the thump of heels on duckboard.

Then the squeak of a burdened ladder, a whisper down the trench, "Up and over." Another whisper of, "Luck."

I went, Bobby, up the ladder, over the bags, down the incline of our raised parapet. I moved by touch, by sound. A man's grunt to my right. Not a yard away, the twang of a uniform catching the wire. Right by me, a splash. A whispered, annoyed, "Have a care."

Men stumbling, their noise so loud I knew it'd awaken all of Germany. Coughs and sneezes. The soft thump of colliding bodies, a hissed "Bloody flaming tramp-about."

I took a step and the ground dropped. My feet went out from under me, and I slid down the incline of a shell hole, splashed into water that was reeking and greasy with corpse-rot. I held my rifle up into the dry as best I could. From above, came a furious chorus of warning hisses.

I waded to the other side and clawed my way through the mud to the top. Then I was walking again, trying to keep quiet, never quite sure how close the Boche were.

There was a sort of lethargy to the night, a feeling of being outside my body. I was so disconnected, in fact, that when Emma Gee started barking, it confused me. The next instant, I realized I'd been waiting all evening for that sound. I dropped to the mud and watched the fast blink-blink of orange from the barrels. A pair of machine gunners were down in a forward emplacement—two men, covering both perimeters.

I felt along the ground for cover, didn't find any, got sprayed with mud by a near miss. A Boche flare went up, turned the night a sour-apple green. I looked around quick for a crater, found a piss-poor one, crawled to it.

Keeping as low as I could, I snapped three or four shots toward the emplacement; but the machine gunners were dug in deep. We were done for, Bobby, just like Pickering had feared. Not ten yards from me was the tangle of Boche wire. Twenty yards beyond, the hill of the Boche parapet; at its top, a line of sandbags like loaves of buttermilk bread. Flashes were coming from up there, too: the front line Boche picking us off one by one.

I slid back down into the crater. No use fighting back. We were pinned down. We'd never had a chance but surprise. Now the attack had stalled there in the mud, under the merciless green glow of the flares.

Left of me the night hissed and blazed orange. The smell of kerosene dirtied the breeze. In the blinding, mad crackle of the flamethrower, soldiers shrieked. Jesus God, Bobby. It was a dragon kind of terror. In awe of it, I nearly dropped my rifle and ran. Instead, I squinted through the glare, looking for movement in the dark behind.

From the howling chorus of burning men came one familiar high, keening voice: Pickering's. I searched for my target. One shot, that's all I had time for, then the barrel flash would give my position away. By the time I caught a glimpse of a coal shuttle helmet, I was panting too hard to aim right. My hands shook. I sucked in a breath, let it out slow, counted to eight. Christ almighty. How Pickering shrieked.

I squeezed the trigger slow. Recoil pushed the rifle butt solidly into my shoulder. It was a sweet shot. The dragon died, hemorrhaging flame. Its blood spilled over the sandbags in a dazzling waterfall. It splashed high, and rained brilliance over the trench. Wails drifted down from above, like a disaster had occurred in Heaven.

I ducked and reloaded. Miller's shout brought my head up again. Emma Gee had gone quiet, too. Tommies were already sprinting upward to the bags, lobbing grenades as they ran. The barbed wire was torn, its edges gaped. I readied my gun and ran with them.

Ahead, the pop of rifles, the deafening crack of Battye bombs, of jam-pots, the boom of cricket ball grenades. Shouts of alarm in English, in guttural German. I slipped in the mud, caught my uniform on the crossbar of the German wire, pulled free, and clambered high, higher until the ground ended.

I was looking down into the trench, a Boche looking up. I shot him in the face, killed another coming out of a dugout, killed a poor wounded bastard before I could stop myself. Not fury, Bobby. Not hate. What I felt had gone beyond fear, too. It was a bleak need, like something that would make you step across the border at the cypress.

I jumped over the bags into the Boche trench and stumbled. The walls were rough and too close. Down the way, British grenades thumped like drums. They beat like a heart in my ears. The flares were dying, but a Very light went up. I saw Jerry Winters beside me, grinning like a maniac. Harvey Bowes was there, too; and Calvert.

Winters said, "Bastards 've gone phut now. Went out like an Asquith."

I wasn't detached anymore. I was edgy and excited. "I shot that damned flamethrower. Fire and shit went everywhere. You see that? Huh? One shot. You see that?"

"Where's the others?" Calvert asked. "Where are they?"

He wandered, stepping on duckboard, treading on dead Boche.

I heard Miller far down the trench to my right, calling for a charge. I ran, the others at my heels, around the corner and into a deserted traverse. Then farther, past dark mouths of communication trenches, past rude ditches to the forward saps, wondering if a shot from one of those side paths would kill me. I ran through the artery of that trench until a clot of fallen sandbags and corpses slowed me down.

Then clawing over broken bodies and into the next traverse, through the sharp smell of cordite, the sick-sweet smell of blood. A Boche popped out of a dugout, firing. Ahead, Winters grunted and went down. Calvert tossed a Battye bomb. It went off in our faces—blinding light, deafening sound, a spray of mud and meat. It stunned me so, I believed for a minute I'd been killed. And it wasn't a bad death, considering. All in all, quick and without pain. Still, the pretty graveyard and the calico girl weren't there. The dim, stinking trench was. And the sandbags where the Boche had been standing were avalanched down.

"Go!" Calvert shouted. "Go!"

We left Winters behind and climbed the hill of mud. In the next traverse Riddell stood with his Very pistol. Beyond, Miller and a group of men were furiously shoring up a cave-in.

"Shot the flamethrower, sir!"

Miller turned. "Stanhope! That you? Bloody hell! Secure our flank, man! Lead them, Sergeant! Sergeant Riddell!" Riddell snapped to attention as if he'd been torn from a dream. "Are you deaf? I said, go secure our blasted flank!"

Riddell told us to fix bayonets. We charged back down the muddy, corpse-littered trench and climbed the mud hill that Calvert had made. On the other side Winters was sitting, bleeding from the thigh.

He waved cheerfully as we passed. "Got me a Blighty!"

We stumbled along in the gloom of the trench, coming across nervous, confused knots of Tommies. We went, bayonets pointed, past Boche bodies chewed by grenades and burned by flaming kerosene, past the blackened, roast-pork and burned-rubber-smelling mess that had been the flamethrower. Just beyond the firebay a fallen wall stopped us.

Pickering was there, sitting in a wide spot of the traverse. LeBlanc was there, too. And Tommy Deighton and Eugene Humphreys.

Pickering. For a minute I was sure that we had advanced until we'd reached Heaven. Only Heaven should have been a wider, prettier place. And the air should have been sweet.

Pickering was sitting on the German firestep. He looked up at me. His face was stark and hopeless; still blackened from the burnt cork but for pink stripes down his cheeks. "Marrs," he said.

"Hey, Stanhope." LeBlanc was laughing. "You just crawl up from some funk hole? Welcome to the battle, Mama's boy."

"I got the flamethrower," I said loud, my voice twitchy. I wanted everyone to hear what I had done. I was ready to run some more. To shoot. To watch Boche fall. "One shot. That's all. Burning fucking kerosene went every which-a way."

Tommy Deighton rocked back and forth, his head cradled in his hands. "God have mercy, Christ have mercy," he kept saying.

Humphreys, agitated, told us, "Brought more grenades? I'm out, and the Boche has been tossing potato mashers."

As if he had called for one, a potato masher came sailing up from the other side, black against the green sky. It landed with a bright, sudden crack, wide of the trench, between us and the wire.

"Not that they have any aim, mind." Humphreys shrugged.

We pitched a couple of Battye bombs over the fallen wall of bags. They went off with twin thuds, leaving silence in their wake.

Truce settled. We waited, but the Boche lobbed no more grenades. We didn't throw any more either. Without a word said, without another shot, the battle was over.

We looked at each other. Deighton rocked. Pickering sat

rigid with grief. *Marrs*, he'd said. Not Pickering, but Marrs. Marrs lying out there in No Man's Land.

I sat down beside him. He smelled like kerosene and smoke. "I need to go help Marrs?"

"No." His body was stiff. If I touched him—if I said another word—he'd break.

Calvert asked, "What's to do now?"

Bowes, fidgeting and nervous, kept looking up at the cave-in, the one between us and the Boche.

Calvert said, "Well, the effing Boche is on bof sides of us, ain't they. An' us sandwiched in between like a bleeding slice of 'am. You gentlemen thought of 'ow we're effing supposed to get out of 'ere?"

The flares were faint now. In the dying light, Riddell looked about, blinking slowly. "Best find shovels."

Well, we shoveled ourselves out, Bobby, digging shell hole to shell hole. Before the sun came up, Miller sent James Hickey across with a message to Dunn. Our ditches and Dunston-Smith's met someplace in the middle.

I don't know how the Boche feel about us being here, rubbing shoulders and asses with them. I don't know if they can sleep at night. We have a problem with it. No more grenades, though. They were probably as relieved as we were to stop that part. They plink a few haphazard shots our way. We fire their own Emma Gee back.

For we found the two Boche machine gunners, Bobby. Them and their reloaders were dead. It was LeBlanc, not sneaking up on them with his knife this time, but running full tilt with jam-pots in both hands. LeBlanc's been mentioned in Miller's field reports. He'll be decorated again.

I hear the other men talk about him, men who don't know what LeBlanc's made of. "Should get Dunn to pin him on a medal." And "Needs Dunn's bloody job, ask me." And "Deserves at least a V.C. for that one."

Me, I just shot behind cover, and not soon enough to be a hero. Not even soon enough for Marrs.

Despite potshots from our Boche neighbors, I crawled out to find him. Marrs and the six others in the shell hole had shriveled to the size of little kids. Their heads were charred skulls. Their eyes had melted, the sockets emptied; jaws were stretched wide in a last grinning bony scream. Their legs were drawn up and their arms were cocked like they had been fighting the dragon, but lost.

I sorted through identity disks until I found him. Marrs's body wasn't peaceful like the things you see lying in caskets. It wasn't even sad, like when you see a boy with his head cracked open or one with his guts hanging out, like Smoot. Marrs was disgusting. Maybe the worst thing was the smell. Sure, there was the stink of burned rubber in that shell hole, and kerosene, too; but it was the odor of cooked meat that got me.

I held my breath as best I could. I left Marrs the green disk for a time when someone could rebury him right. I took the red disk so Miller and the army could inform the family. Then Pickering and Calvert crawled out and helped me bury him. It was our job, you know. It was us who had slept with him, ate with him, put up with his whining; us who made him the butt of our jokes. And all the time I was keeping my head down, digging his grave, I thought of Sunday pork roasts and crusty barbecued brisket. Such a goddamned pitiful shame. For all of Marrs's sweet-natured kindness, what I'll remember most about his death is my hunger.

O'Shaughnessy and the rain got there just as we were finishing up. On his knees, O'Shaughnessy sprinkled holy water and said some words. We put up a field cross and crawled back to the trench.

The next day we marched off and left Marrs in the company of strangers. I poked my head above the trench to tell him goodbye, and saw that rain had knocked his grave marker down.

I want to tell you I saw Marrs in the graveyard right after, but I didn't. I thought about him a lot. The night after we were relieved, I closed my eyes and, while I was still awake, imagined myself walking out across No Man's Land. I thought hard, pictured the new ditch we'd made and the place where the Boche wire had been breached. Nearby I found Marrs and another soldier sitting on the edge of a shell hole, waiting.

He looked happy to see me.

"Need to come with me, Marrs," I told him, and put a hand down to help.

He was grinning that muddle-headed grin of his. "Can't, Stanhope. Lost me letter."

I said, "It's bad out here. You need to come on."

I tried hard, but I couldn't make him get up. You'd think you could control daydreams, right? I must have fallen asleep about then, for the next thing I knew, I woke up to a gray dawn. Pickering had set our kettle on for tea, and he was looking out the door into the rain.

I didn't talk to him. We had revetment duty that day, and worked side by side. He didn't talk to me, either.

Travis Lee

EIGHT

OCTOBER 1, THE RESERVE TRENCHES

Dear Bobby,

Well, it's a disappointment. The weather went from hot to cold with not much in between, just like it does in Texas. Spring was long and pretty, but fall doesn't have much to show for itself but rain.

They issued us goatskin vests. Warm and cheap. For good reason, we call them "stinkies." The hair's still on them, lumpy, raggedy hair, nothing like our goats at home. I got a black-and-tan one. We fought over the white-hair vests. Pickering won.

The other day the wall where the Frenchie was sticking out collapsed, and we had to build it up again. Still, we lost our mascot. Just as well. We scraped up what was left of him with our shovels and buried him farther on. O'Shaughnessy sprinkled water, said a little Latin. We all went back to the dugouts for a wake.

It's like Marrs's death has changed things for the better somehow. Jesus. I hate to think that. Maybe it was that damned raid that woke everybody up; or maybe we've all got used to this slimy hole we're living in. Whatever happened, Pickering's out of his sulk.

A few days after Marrs's death we were sitting around in the dugout just enjoying a smoke, and out of the blue, he said, "It was me who was supposed to drop off the hooks, Stanhope. I mean, all the signs pointed to me, didn't they. And when your time has come, no getting out of it. That's for dead cert. You're phut, and that's that. I think whatever powers might be—God or what—cocked it up, didn't He. Took Marrs in error."

I told him I wasn't sure. "You're basing your theological doctrine on your sandbag cross, right? What sort of foundation is that?"

"Sod all, Stanhope! You talk like a schooled wog. Most useless bit of muck on the planet." Well, he was a little put out; but that might have been because it was raining and Calvert was sleeping, and me and Calvert and the tea fixings were taking up most of the dugout. Pickering was hunkered in the doorway, half damp, half soaking wet, trying to keep his cigarette dry. "Do you know what I can't help but think? I saw the flames hit Marrs's shell hole, you know. Well, it was a bloody inferno is what it was; and it hit them straight on. They thrashed about quite a lot, actually."

His tone was nonchalant. It most always is. But Marrs's terrible death was reflected in his eyes, in the knotting of his jaw. God, Bobby. He must have watched every twitch. I wondered if he knew he had been screaming.

"Well, so," he said. "I'd been with Marrs only seconds before. A bit of rum luck, that. On Marrs's part, that is. But there you are. Marrs dies; I'm still stuck in the trenches drinking bloody awful tea. I've decided that this God thing is a balls. If He doesn't figure out His cockup, I could bloody live forever."

Then, just like the old Pickering, he cackled.

Live forever? Not me. The worst thing I can think of, Bobby, the very worst, is living like a ground squirrel in this shithouse, never getting a clean breath of air. Fact is, I know what ground squirrels must feel like now, watching for death from the skies. One red-tailed hawk, one accidental misplaced hoof'll kill them. It's not the dying, but the fear that wears you down.

I spent some money, but was able to finagle several more fine canteens of rum. Like the Tommies say, it's good for what ails you. But I'm not going heavy on it like I did that once.

The time I spent in the glasshouse taught me a lesson. Need's not worth a damn. I never got the point of loving nothing—not even a woman—so bad that you couldn't live without. Still, a man should have a little enjoyment once in a while: a willing woman, a good smoke, a sip of whiskey.

I hide the canteens, for I'm worried one of the new boys will be getting into my stash. It's hard to keep track of things, moving from place to place. I lost that wood horse Pa carved me, and a pair of blue socks. Life drops off you here; you shed it slow: manners and memories. I don't know that I'll ever be able to sit with a lady and make polite conversation. After this, I don't know that you and me will ever truly understand each other again.

Anyway, LeBlanc got his decoration. Got a week off from sandbag duty, too. He's Major Dunn's fair-haired boy. Not that it makes any difference to LeBlanc, mind. And not that he charged Emma Gee out of bravery, either.

"I knew I wasn't going to die," he said.

Around here, everybody's got a death theory.

"It wasn't my time, eh? When your time's up, your time's up. No use hiding. Death'll come get you, anyway. So why be scared, Stanhope? See what I mean? Like I keep telling you, you need to look death in the eye and say, 'Fuck you.' Then you too can get your nipple pricked by some asshole ranking officer. You too can have majors and colonels kissing your round pink butt. That's all it takes. So can you do that for me? Huh? Next time we go into No Man's Land? Can you look over to the Boche trench and say that?"

I laughed. "Sure. Fuck you, LeBlanc."

My own death theory is that Marrs needs to get to the damned graveyard. I lie at night with my eyes closed and try to push all the distractions out—the clatter of the sentry up the duckboard, the chitters and squeals of the rats—and I go out into No Man's Land. There are other folks there besides Marrs, and that kind of surprises me—puzzled, dim people. Some are familiar: folks I know by sight if not by name. There are Boche and Frenchies, too. Sometimes I see Scots wandering around in those damned kilts. You wouldn't think that would happen, would you, Bobby? You wouldn't think that your waking mind could go strange.

I can't control my own daydreams. If it was up to me, I'd have the ghosties speak. Lord knows, I fantasize that I'm speaking to them. But most of the time they just wander on, not paying no mind, not to me, not to each other.

I feel and see things, though, and that's hard—the cool inky shadows of a fir tree woods; the happy noise of beer and pretzel camaraderie—alien impressions as brief and hazy as the ghosties.

It scares me sometimes, and I open my eyes quick. I don't know if I've really traveled No Man's Land or not, Bobby, but I feel damned guilty when I leave.

It eats on me that Marrs won't come. And when I dream of the graveyard, Foy's still down under his glass, asleep. When I talk to Marrs about going to visit Foy, he's always looking for that damned letter. It got burned up by the flamethrower, Bobby, is what it did.

I told Marrs that. I explain to him that he's dead, but he just goes on about his business, whatever pointless business that is.

It's useless. All useless. Ghosties milling around, time and hunger never pushing at them. They act like they got an eternity to waste.

Travis Lee

OCTOBER 1, POSTCARD FROM THE RESERVE TRENCHES

Dear Bobby,

Do me a favor. Kill me that old billy, the crochety one who can't get it up no more. Have Ma make me a vest out of him, all that long hair of his still on it. Tell her I appreciate the kindness. This goatskin vest they gave me stinks to holy hell.

Tell her I'm sorry I don't write more often. Tell her I'll try to do better.

Travis Lee

OCTOBER 3, THE REST AREA

Dear Bobby,

They finally pulled us back and I found out that there's still green in the world, here way back of the line. I saw grass and just sat myself down in the middle of it. Blackhall kept telling me to get up and go into the YMCA pavilion and have lemonade like everybody else. But that wasn't no kind of military order. I spread my arms and let myself go, fell down flat on my back, and looked up at the sky.

Blackhall finally walked away, his steps squishing across the damp meadow. It was misting rain. Water gathered on my face, ran down either side of my forehead. Drops hung like crystal beads on my lashes. Every time I blinked, I blinked prisms. I dug my fingers into the soil. Instead of bones and war trash I felt damp loam, good strong roots, hidden grubs. I felt life, Bobby. I felt of it careful. And it was intimate—like holding the earth gently, so gently, by the snatch.

I could hear them in the pavilion. A gramophone was playing some idiot march by Sousa. Pickering, probably wanting company, called from the door, "Yank music, Stanhope!"

A smile spread slow across my face. Elgar and John Phillip Sousa, music for building empires.

He called a few more times and then Pickering, too, left me alone. I snuck away from the company and started walking. The air smelled of passing summer green and leafy autumn decay. LeBlanc was down by the stables, grooming a horse, a turbaned Indian stablehand standing by. I watched for a while, the slow firm press of the brush, the ripple of the horse's withers like a breeze across a chestnut pond.

I left before LeBlanc could turn around and see me. The back paddock smelled of strong, earthy horse shit. I took a deep breath, caught sight of Wilson's gray standing, head down. Miller's huge sorrel, casual and sprung-hipped, was looking over the meadow as if measuring it for planting.

I left, took an arched bridge across a stagnant canal to the officers' huts. In a pavilion, the brass had gathered to practice some sort of show. Dunston-Smith was banging away at an out-of-tune piano. Wilson, McCarthy, and to my surprise, Miller, were dancing a chorus line and belting out a song.

He looked so happy, Bobby. The four officers, acting silly as a bunch of girls. Their flat-footed dancing, arms across each other's shoulders, red-faced with laughter, that asinine little song.

I stood hidden and sheltered by overhanging branches. I watched them until the rain stopped and the sun came out. The officers were drinking beer, but they weren't drunk on that. They were drunk on silliness. Falling-down drunk with it.

I heard Dunston-Smith's voice come faint but cheery, "Once more into the breach!"

Major Dunn's aide stepped forward to strike a pose. "Oh, nurse!" he cried.

That was the chorus line's cue. Their song was so out of tune, so out of rhythm, that I only caught every two or three words, but it had something to do with a fatal dose of the clap. "Done for, done for," the three of them sang to the beginning chords of "Rule, Britannia." Then they sang about some mixup in the nickname for First Aid Nursing Yeomanry and female parts. The chorus was a screaming repetition of "So lend me your FANY!"

Well, their show didn't have much plot, Bobby. But it made up for it in pecker-talk and pussy-talk and general all around dirt. I guess for the show itself, the chorus line's going to be wearing dresses, for at intervals they would whirl around, bend over, and point butts at the audience. On that cue, Major Dunn's aide would give a resounding fart.

That's the thing about rich people, Bobby. I saw it in Harvard, and I've noticed it here. I don't know whether it's that they don't have the time for it, but poor folks never act that stupid.

What saddened me is how Miller fit right in.

I slunk away, walked past parked lorries, past idle field ambulances, down a lane with trees to one side and a marshy canal to the other. There was a castle, Bobby. A small castle, but a real one, with a turret and all. A mile or so later was a town with houses like gingerbread, all spiked roofs and geegaws. It was wonderful. The best town yet. They had a square with flower sellers and a bar that made a brandy that tasted like heaven. And there was a bakery shop with a girl shaped like a dumpling. She had flour up to her elbows and a tiny slip of an apron that didn't begin to fit her. Still, she had soft-looking titties, big as rounds of potato bread. She smelled of cinnamon and yeast, and she had the prettiest smile.

I told her so. 'Course I told her in English. The man in the bar spoke it, but she shook her head. She smiled and blushed. Those plump cheeks of hers went so pink. Oh, hell, Bobby. Girls are girls. She knew what I was saying.

We talked in shrugs and pointing and laughter. We had us a good chat. I picked out a sweet roll shaped something like a cow patty and an almond something or other. I handed her all my money. She plucked out a few coins and gave me back the rest. I was so happy right then, I nearly reached over the counter to kiss her. I could have lifted up that blouse, shoved my face between those doughy titties, and loved on her till morning. I started wondering what the whores in town were like.

But the sun was slipping down the sky. Free time would be ending, and they'd find out I was gone. I started back.

God, Bobby. I got to see wonderful things. How the afternoon sun gilded the castle. I watched fallen leaves sail the canal like boats. I looked into the dark of that little patch of woods and heard an owl hoot, waking early.

By the time I reached the officers' quarters, the sun had dropped below the horizon. In the blue twilight of the bridge, in the overhang of a huge willow, in the song of the frogs, I came upon Miller.

He was with Dunston-Smith, not touching, but standing close. When I walked up I startled them. I must have disturbed one of those tender moments.

My thought was to pass by without speaking, but Dunston-Smith stopped me with a happy, "I say, Stanhope! Heard about your bagging the flamethrower chappie. One bullet. Good shooting, what?"

They hadn't stepped away from each other, but Dunston-Smith had lifted his hand in a salute. There was a beer bottle in it.

Miller, I saw, was drinking, too. "Seems I owe Stanhope here two dinners, one for bringing up my totals."

"Oh, Richard. Your bloody totals." Dunston-Smith's tone was terribly upper class, terribly bored. "I'll nick him from you, shall I? Arrange him a transfer. Would you like that, Stanhope, old sport? Get you in a white man's company."

It was like a slap in the face. I think I might have knocked him down if Miller hadn't laughed. It was a whore kind of laugh. A suck-up, scared-to-be-left-out kind of laugh.

The air was heavy with silt-smell and malt. "Envious, is it, Colin? I suppose I should have Private LeBlanc for a dinner, too, as he saved the day."

LeBlanc? But the dinner was with me. Just me. Talking poetry over a white linen-covered table.

Dunston-Smith took a swig of beer. Down the canal a fish splashed. Ripples widened, caught the last blue glimmers of dusk. "Wouldn't mind having either of the two," he said.

"Can't have them," Miller said brightly. "Besides, Stanhope here is quite an obliging chap." He dropped the bantering tone. "A dear chap." His voice went low. His gaze was level and private. "Couldn't make do without him."

There. Damn. The admission hung in the twilight.

"Isn't that right, Stanhope?"

The purr in Miller's voice. God. It went right through me. I didn't know whether to bolt or laugh. Then I noticed that Dunston-Smith sure looked bothered.

So I told Miller, "I'd hope so, sir."

Dunston-Smith upended the bottle, chug-a-lugged the rest of his beer, then hurled the empty into the gathering night. I heard the splash as it came down. The frogs, taken aback, went quiet.

"Mustn't keep you, Stanhope," Miller said. "Needn't be going in late, having Blackhall angry."

"Sir." I saluted. "You two have a nice night, now." I started away, but turned. They were just darker spots in the gloom. I called back, "No orders for me later tonight, sir?"

The dark spots moved, separated a bit. Then Miller's voice, sparkling with glee. "Shouldn't think so, Stanhope. Some other evening, perhaps."

The willow's overhang and the darkness swallowed them. "Looking forward to it, sir!"

That Miller and his courting games. Sly with it as I am sometimes with the girls. I made sure that I was out of earshot when I burst out laughing.

Travis Lee

OCTOBER 6, THE RESERVE TRENCHES

Dear Bobby,

Toward the end of our time in the rest area, I left the others with their drills and found me a rock-and-earth wall. I put some cans along the foot of it, and set about fine-tuning my sights. I'd shot about fifty practice rounds when Riddell came, looked over my shoulder a while, and asked me if I wanted to take a bit of a tramp.

It was a nice day for it: autumn-crisp air, the sun filtering down through low, amassing clouds, an on-and-off mist falling. I shouldered my rifle and we walked deep into the countryside.

We followed a canal seeping its slow way toward the ocean. We went by manure-rich pastures dotted with milk cows. At the next turn of the road, Riddell waded into the roadside weeds and picked a double armful of stalks out of a hedgerow. Grinning, he brought them back, offered me some.

The weeds stank, but he pushed his nose into his own bouquet. "Wormwood. Put it in your clothes. Nothing like it for the lice. Strew it around your dugout."

I thought not, but I thanked him kindly, anyway.

" 'Eard from me sister," he said when we walked on. "Buying 'erself a cottage with a bit of land, she is. Growing 'er some 'erbs. Thinking to make a business, like. Asked me if I'd care to come along with 'er."

If after-war stories can have happy endings, that would be Riddell's. Just a short walk into the country and he was already bursting at the seams. Get him in the green, he grows, Bobby. He gets taller and sturdier, somehow.

"Likes me gardening," he said, "bringing them seeds along. To me, it's like raising up crowds of green spindly children. Sounds silly, but there it is. Can't change. But the medicines? Well, nobody's better at decoctions and salves than me sister. Her and Mum would go tinkering on recipes. Me, I barely boils water for tea wifout burning meself. Give me spade over pan any day."

I nodded. "Herb gardening with your sister. I think it's what you should do."

"Knew you'd understand, Stanhope. Seen you out and about, looking at nature. Knew you 'ad the 'eart of a gardener."

"Goat herder," I said.

"Goat 'erding? That's what you'll do when you gets back?"

"I don't know." For the first time I really didn't know, and that scared me, Bobby. It was like I was looking ahead, but not seeing any more road. There was this gray place where the future was supposed to be.

I told him, "Getting late. We better get a move on."

We turned around and started walking back. "I sees me mum sometimes," Riddell said. "Feels 'er about."

So that's what he'd wanted to say all along. The walk wasn't about gardening. It was about ghosties.

He avoided my gaze. "Bit of nonsense, actually."

"Maybe not," I said.

"Still, it's as if she's right there wif me sometimes. And you want to know the truf of it, she was there at that last stunt. Boche was firing right down on top of us, wasn't they. Could see me plain as day. Wasn't no shell hole about for me to duck into, but I wasn't scared. I didn't see 'er, mind. Ain't like I'm bonkers. But this calm came over me, Stanhope. It's like . . . When you was a boy, you ever wake up in the sickbed and your mum was just putting 'er 'and to your face? Well, there you 'ave it. No matter that the Boche was shooting at us. Knew somehow that I'd make it through."

I remembered cool fingers against my lips, a hushed and private peace; not Ma's hand, but the calico girl's.

My road stretched: war, more war, and then the grayness.

"Nice to tell somebody," he said. "Good to be finally saying it aloud."

But him. I could see his future so clear: Riddell walking down a shady lane toward a cottage at the turn of the road. There would be a white fence with climbing roses, dizzy with blossoms and bees. His sister would be on the stoop, waving.

I said without much heart, "It's going to be great for you, getting home."

I could go back to school, but that didn't feel right. Home, maybe? God, how I wanted to. If wishes were power, I'd have walked right though that onionskin page of memory, past the corral with the horses gazing over, up the wooden porch to the fieldstone house. I'd knock, and Ma'd answer the door, beaming.

But I couldn't make it real, Bobby; not like the way it felt walking No Man's Land, not as real as the graveyard.

When I got back to billets, I found Pickering and Calvert waiting for me. They wanted to poke some whores.

I thought I'd gotten over missing Marrs, but the walk to town seemed incomplete, and by the time we got there, I was morose.

The three of us went to the estaminet first, ate mussels and hard bread, drank rough red wine, listened to the loud complaints and the louder jokes of the soldiers.

"If you're going to drink that way, eat bread, Stanhope; else you'll get up to prang your whore and land on your arse instead, the way you did that time," Pickering told me.

I told him to shut up.

Calvert said to Pickering, " 'E's an old soak, ain't 'e? 'Iding them canteens, like we don't know what's in 'em. 'E knocks down the wine like it's bloody water."

I told him to mind his own goddamned business. They thought I was funny.

About that time somebody ran into the back of my chair, pushed me belly-first into the table, and made me spill my wine.

I jumped to my feet and spun.

There was a British private behind me, a kid from our company, 6th Platoon, I think. Dinkens or Blinkens or something. His eyes were wide and startled, and he was trying his best to apologize.

Pickering pulled at my fist, my arm. "Easy on," he was saying. "Easy on there, Stanhope."

I coldcocked him, Bobby, sent Pickering stumbling back into another table, sent carafes of cheap wine flying, sent mussels on a last wild ride. When Calvert grabbed me by the shoulders, I knocked him down, too. And when I heard the red caps' whistles shrieking, I pushed my way through folks who were trying to stay me. I vaulted over the bar and bolted through the kitchen, through a little apartment where surprised kids looked up from their meal. In the next room, I squeezed through a window and landed in an alley that smelled of cat piss.

I must have gone wandering then. There's a vague impression of throwing up in a canal, of taking a piss against a shed.

The red caps found me just before morning where I was lying passed out in the road. Blackhall marched me in to see Captain Miller, who raised his eyebrows and asked Blackhall what punishment he thought I deserved. The crucifixion this time, field punishment number one, not the glasshouse. Blackhall said they'd be needing me.

So I spent the last rest day lashed to a fence at billets, bound by my neck and ankles. I threw up all over myself. Pissed myself, too. Nye was ordered to give me water when I needed it. There was old shit and piss caked under his nails.

I was hungry, but thank God Nye didn't feed me. My pecker was sore. A great fuck, and I couldn't remember a bit of it.

They left me hanging on the fence all night. My feet hurt.

My legs went numb. Every time I fell asleep, my head lolled and I started to strangle.

The next morning Blackhall ordered me cut down. He gave me my pack and told me I was moving out. I made it all the way to the reserve trenches, throwing up when I had to, dropping off to sleep when we took our breaks. But I got there. You do what you have to.

Pickering and Calvert filled in the blanks my drinking left in the bar fight. Come to find out I didn't pay my tab, but I didn't hurt that Dinkens boy, thank God. And Pickering's over his mad now; his black eye's healing.

It was after I'd had myself a swallow or two of rum that I remembered, later that night, a narrow street. I was alone. Light was pouring out of a second-story window, a soft light, maybe a candle. A three-quarters moon was up. Something was happening there in the tight canyon between the houses. I could hear the quiet echoes of meat slapping meat. Somebody beating on someone I thought, until I rubbed my eyes and stared harder. No. Two people fucking.

She was a big woman, and she was leaned over a wheelbarrow. Her skirt was pulled up to her waist. He was going at her from behind. Her pillowy ass was lifted. The man—the soldier—hadn't bothered to pull his pants down. He was ramming it in her, Bobby. It was an assault of a fuck. In the dead-white light of the moon I could see her big thighs quiver.

They were close—no more than ten yards from where I hid in a cranny between houses—so I could tell there wasn't any moaning going on. No little female cries of pleasure. The man was as passionate as a damned piston.

Thinking on it now, I don't know why the scene did me like it did. It wasn't no more than dogs going at it. Utilitarian was what comes to mind. But despite the wine, despite everything, I got me a hard-on so needy that I had to shove my hand into my pants and hold myself tight.

It was me looking on and them not knowing. It was him fucking her, still dressed. It was her with her bare compliant butt in the air. It was her just spreading her legs the way she did, and letting him.

I like it when girls talk soft to me and croon in my ear. I like it when they groan. Still. That dumb animal contentment. Imagine fucking someone and never seeing her face.

When I couldn't stand it no more, I pulled that chicken neck of mine out of my pants. Right there in that shallow nook, I choked the hell out of it.

I'm not sure when I noticed the blood. But after a while I started looking at her arm where it was hanging out over the edge of the wheelbarrow. There was a black, glistening stripe down it, and a puddle on the cobbles below.

I'd like to tell you I got my pants buttoned real quick. That I ran over there and pulled that boy off her. That I asked if she was all right. But the real bad wanting had settled in and I couldn't stop. I pulled on myself, harder, faster. Down the alley, the boy gave it a few last toe-curling pumps and pulled out. In the dim light of the candle, I saw her pussy spread and waiting, saw the slick glimmer of their shared wet. I came so hard I nearly fell down.

That's when I noticed the boy had turned and was staring right at me, his face dark in the shadows.

"Stanhope?" LeBlanc called.

I buttoned up my pants and ran.

You know, I could have just dreamed the figures in the dark of the alley: the shadow with LeBlanc's voice and the woman spread and waiting. The memory bothers me. Still, I have dreams sometimes, Bobby. Doesn't mean every damned one of them makes sense.

Travis Lee

OCTOBER 8, THE RESERVE TRENCHES

Dear Bobby,

I must have wanted to go home last night, for I was there. The dream was more real than these stinking trenches. I was walking down the hall from the kitchen. Sun was hitting the eastern rooms, casting silver stripes across the hardwood floor, throwing rectangles up the wall.

At the door to Ma's room, I stopped. Her windows were

open, the lace curtains blowing. The morning beyond was overcast; the breeze quiet with autumn, scented with cedar and sour pecan decay.

Light bathed Ma's iron bed, the double-ring quilt, the one she had when I was a kid, the pastel-colored one whose pattern I used to follow round and round until I was dizzy.

Pa was there. He was sitting on the side of the bed, in that fall of light, his white hair radiant. His head was down, his gentled hands resting in his lap. In his cupped palm lay that carved wooden horse.

Pa had come and took his gift back. I didn't love enough for him. I wasn't a good enough son. He knew I was there. He was waiting for me to come in. The house smelled of floor wax and age. It was so quiet I could hear the clock in the living room ticking. I stood at the door a while longer, but he never looked up. In the end, I went away.

I woke up then. Outside my dugout, the sky was clear and so deep a black that you felt you could fall up and just keep falling. The stars were dazzling and close and clean. The confines of the trench, that vaulted, sparkling ceiling; it all gave me a dizzy sense of rushing upward, like the way you feel standing in a Gothic cathedral. I let myself go, drifted down the misty river of the Milky Way, hung for a while onto the North Star, opened my arms wide to catch the Big Dipper's glittering handle.

But the earthbound part of me remembered how light fell like a shawl across Pa's bent shoulders, remembered the curled fingers, those gentle-looking hands. God, Bobby. I've never loved Pa as much as I loved him in that dream. But then, he'd never been so perfect.

Travis Lee

OCTOBER 9, A POSTCARD FROM THE RESERVE TRENCHES

Dear Bobby,

Sorry I can't write more often. The army keeps me busy. Anyway, I'm glad Ma likes her lace tablecloth. Tell her I'm saving up to get her some napkins to match. Now, you wear that beret I sent you tipped to the side, little brother. The French shopkeeper gal who sold it to me said it's sexy that way. Shit. Them goats'll swoon all over you.

Love, Travis Lee

OCTOBER 9, THE RESERVE TRENCHES

Dear Bobby,

It hurts when you write about how Ma waits for my letters, how she pours over them line by line with her piss-poor eyesight, wanting so bad to read. I can picture her in that wing chair, those damned lace doilies pinned on the arms, the lamp lit on the table. Thank God you're there to read them to her aloud.

Don't be nagging at me, Bobby. And don't accuse me of not caring. I think about you all the time. I think of Ma, of barn dances and fried chicken Sundays. My arms remember wrestling with you; my forehead remembers the tickle of Ma's kisses. But it's too late, and I'm too changed. If I wrote more than a postcard, the death stink and the mud would come out.

Y'all don't need that. Plenty of time later to find out how things were, if you want to. There's some things folks at home are better off not knowing. Go ahead and think of war as something with honor. Something grand. That way if I die, you can believe I died for something.

So if the British Army has sent you these letters, I want you to think real hard before reading any further. Decide first if myths like duty and honor soften mourning.

It started this way: I was ordered to report to Miller's dugout this morning. He wasn't there. While I waited, I got to studying that picture on his wall.

The woman was younger than I'd thought—just a year or two off my age. Her face wasn't pretty in a comfortable way—nothing soft nor oval there. She was exotic: high cheekboned and sloe-eyed. Her mouth was too ripe for Baptist comfort.

There was a whalebone stiffness to her, too, that I doubted any man was going to break; a curl to her mouth that told me she'd kick the traces—go off and start a career or something. Become a suffragist.

I fell in love, if you want to know the truth—a strong, pretty woman, one raised in the same household with Miller. They'd have argued growing up. Miller was a man who liked to lead, and she didn't have a follower's face. This wasn't a woman who'd make her way around soft-footed nor manipulative, either. Those sad, steady eyes: they'd meet things head-on.

I started wondering how she'd be in bed. I figured her for the type who heated quick to a simmer, turned all tongue and thrusting. Her nipples would get hard as little pebbles. And when she came, she'd heave her hips up, take you deep inside her, pecker and soul.

I wondered if she was spoke for. I wondered what her family would think of me. Hell, I could fit in if I tried hard enough. Go back to school. Be a doctor if I had to.

Christmases with Miller, poetry over the turkey and dressing. After-dinner brandies before the fire, remembering the war, snug in a safe place. Holidays and high holy days, or whatever it was they celebrated. I'd never have to lose him.

I'd become a Jew, if they let you train for that. We'd live in England if she wanted. For a woman like that one, I'd make my life over, burnish it till it was clean and shiny.

When Miller came in, he found me standing, still mooning over that picture.

"That girl there's got a good face."

He put his helmet on the table, shot me a cautious look. "Thank you."

"I don't mean especially that she's pretty, even though she is. Pretty, I mean. But she looks smart, too, you know? Like she could hold up her end of a conversation."

That got a smile out of him. He struck a match, lit the lamp, pulled the door to. "Quite true, actually."

"She fond of poetry?"

The quiet was filled with the smell of burned match, the hot-metal reek of the lamp. "An opera lover. But she enjoys renaissance works: Shakespeare, Milton, John Donne. She has a mind for trivia. Can recite, like you do, great stretches of things. Only her recitations are of opera lyrics and bloody *Paradise Lost*. A waste of talent, if you must know. A crashing bore."

Like me. She was like me. I looked at the photo again. "I bet I could get her to recite Shelley."

"You'd have a fight on your hands, Stanhope. Sarah's one of those debaters who knows chapter and verse, and doesn't mind rubbing your nose into your errors. She has quite a wicked sense of humor. Puts most suitors off, actually."

"If I'm ever in England, you introduce me?"

His surprise set, became brittle.

I said right quick, "I don't mean to be forward here or nothing, sir. I know what you think of me, but I clean up pretty good. Hell, I graduated Harvard, remember? Wasn't top man in my class, but they accepted me into med school. All it needs is me going back and taking up my studies again."

He picked up a pencil from his desk, toyed with it.

"Sir, I'm just saying she seems like an interesting woman is all. I know I visit whores, but if I had me a decent girl I wouldn't. And strong women don't scare me none. Hell, I'd be a better bet for her than some old English boy who keeps her homebound all the time. I like a woman with some fire to her. Oh. But, look, sir. I wouldn't be trying to sweet-talk her into bed or nothing. Don't get me wrong. I know how to treat a lady. Besides, I wouldn't ever take no liberties with Sarah, not seeing as how she's your sister and all."

He put the pencil down. He said, "She is my fiancée."

He must have got tired of me standing there with my limp dick in my hand. He sat down at his desk. "Do take a seat, Stanhope."

I fell down into it. Fiancée. Maybe when the war was over he planned to put away his light-stepping, like boys will put away their late nights and their whores.

"There has been some unpleasantness." He laced his fingers. "Another village girl was attacked and violated."

Strange how you can get used to anything: living in shit holes, being shot at, being accused of rape. "When, sir?"

"October third."

The night I'd got so drunk. I sat back. I knew the answer before I even asked the question. "Who did it?"

"We're not sure. Your name has been bandied about."

"I didn't do it."

"I didn't think so."

I wiped my hands over my face. Cool in the dugout, but I was sweating bad. I asked the questions I should have all along. "The girl all right?"

"Alive. And more's the pity. She was beaten badly about the head. Beaten silly, in fact. Can't testify. Doesn't remember. Don't know that she'll ever be right. Cut about the face as well. Terribly disfigured. The man cut her in—shall we call it a private place'? At any rate, there's no marriage in her future, certainly. Can't even work in her blasted little bakeshop for fear of terrifying the customers. A bloody disgrace."

It came over me hot and fast, the way Marrs must have felt under the thrall of the flamethrower. The white floury skin, the shop's yeasty cinnamon smells, the girl's sweet smile. I got up so fast that I knocked the chair over. I wrenched the door open and stumbled into the rain before I threw up. Vomit splattered duckboard, pattered across the mud. A passing sentry stepped carefully out of the way.

Miller's calm voice behind me. "I'll need your boots."

Damn LeBlanc. Shoving it in her while she was battered and bleeding. Cutting her up, so he'd be her first lover and her last—because she had been a virgin, Bobby. I could tell by those blushes.

Damn me for standing there and watching him do it. For giving myself a hand job while he did. I remembered her spread, submissive butt and how hard I came. Lust inserted itself into my disgust—a bad mix, like the hunger I felt at Marrs's death. I bent over, threw up again.

"Your boots, if you don't mind, Stanhope. Have you been drinking?"

I straightened, wiped my mouth. My gullet burned, my throat tasted sour. The trench stank of death and bile. The air was heavy. No matter how much I breathed, seemed like my lungs wouldn't fill.

"I regret to make this an order, Stanhope, but I haven't the time to lounge about watching the results of your pub crawl—however entertaining that might be. Your boots, please."

Seeing the blood. Watching him fuck her, anyway. I pushed past Miller, went back into the dugout and sat down. I pulled at my laces, but they were tied too tight, my hands were too clumsy.

"No need to be rattled, Stanhope. I'm sure this will prove your innocence. The bastard left a bruise on her back, a clear boot print. Here. Here." He knelt at my feet, said gently, "I'll have those off for you." He took out his pocket knife and cut the laces. "No sense taking such care. They won't be given back, I imagine. I've another pair here for you somewhere. I've arranged, in fact, an oversized boot. Your feet are wider than the norm. Comes from walking barefooted, I suspect. Which is why I should think the proof of your innocence definitive. I have it on quite good report that the boot which caused the bruise was a small one."

He slipped my right boot off, checked the bottom of it. "Yes. Just as I thought. Your sole is intact. The marks on the girl's back show an odd-shaped mark—a broken nail, I do believe—plus two nails which are either worn or missing. Yes, indeed, Stanhope. This should clear you straightaway." He looked up at me then, and his expression fell into woebegone lines of concern. "What is it?"

"Ask LeBlanc."

"Pardon?"

"LeBlanc done it, sir. I saw him." Cold in the dugout, and I was wet. I couldn't stop shivering.

"Are you certain?"

"We were close as from here to the turn of the next traverse, sir. Saw him clear as day." Didn't see him, really. But felt his presence. Heard his voice.

Miller dipped his head, slipped my left boot off.

"Sir, listen to me: I saw him do it. Well, the rape part, anyway. It shames me to say it. I should have stopped him but, hell, I was drunk. Couldn't even figure out what was going on there for a while. But go ahead and get his boots. They'll match."

He set both my boots carefully aside.

"I should have put a stop to it at once, sir. Arrested him right then and there. Called for the police or something. She was a sweet girl. She waited on me once at her bakery shop." Then lamely, for there wasn't no other way but lame to say it: "I should have stopped him."

Miller rose, refused to meet my eye. He found my new pair of boots under his batman's haversack and brought them over. I thanked him and put them on. "If you want me to testify before a court-martial board, just ask, sir. I'll be willing."

"Need to change your socks more often, Stanhope. Wouldn't want trench foot. Be your own fault."

The new boots were almost comfortable. I tied the laces. "Yes, sir."

"No excuse, you know."

Our eyes met. I got up, saluted and left.

Mark this day, this time. It was the first I ever thought about suicide. And it wasn't that I wanted to rest in the graveyard. No, I wanted to lose myself in the dark.

That girl's rape. The shame of what I'd done was like swallowing a knife. Every which way I'd turn, it'd poke at me. It was tearing my guts out.

In the end, I went down to O'Shaughnessy's dugout. I waited until he was finished talking to a soldier, and then I went inside. It was quiet and cool and dim. He was sitting, a candle beside him on the table. I knelt in front of his chair and crossed myself the way I seen Marrs do.

"Bless me, Father," I said, surprised that it came easy; and then I told him the rest. When I was done, he asked me what penance I thought my sin deserved.

I said what I'd done had no forgiving.

"You make too harsh a god, Travis."

I told him I'd burn myself alive, then, the way Marrs got it. Told him I'd go running off toward No Man's Land the way Trantham did, leave myself hanging on the wire.

He said, "An unforgivable sort of sin: despair."

I told him the shame hurt too bad to abide, asked him how I could stop it. He told me he didn't know. Then he asked me to get up off my knees and sit in the chair. He lit a cigarette, handed it to me.

"Why didn't I stop him?" I asked.

And he said, "Lust."

A one-syllable explanation for my shiftless nature and even for my drinking; for it was lust I felt for the bottle, too. I took a deep drag, let it out, watched smoke curl toward the board ceiling.

"I need to quit drinking," I told him.

"Pray," he said. "Ask after Sergeant Riddell's herb cure."

I promised I would. I promised, too, I'd quit.

He said, "Don't do your promising to me, lad."

"They put LeBlanc in front of a firing squad?"

He checked his pocket watch. Did it so sneaky that I barely caught what he was doing.

"It's what he deserves, Father."

O'Shaughnessy stared into the corner for a while, then asked if I wanted tea. Whatever appointment he had was going to be broken.

I said I'd be appreciative of some tea, and he put water on the primus. He opened a tin of butter cookies with currants and put it on the table.

"Should imagine it will go hard for Captain."

My cookie stopped a few inches from my mouth. "Why?"

"Because he's a Jew, and that lad's the most decorated soldier in the battalion. Don't be altogether surprised, Travis, if nothing comes of it. When word gets to Command, they'll be blaming it on the girl herself, on the natural lusts of a soldier, on Captain not keeping a watch when he knew the boy had a history."

I put the cookie back in its stiff paper cup. So hurting women was the trouble Miller tried to tell me about.

The water started steaming. O'Shaughnessy went to tend the tea. "Well, Pierre's a hard and bitter lad. A troublemaker as well, which is why the Canadians wanted rid of him. It was Major Dunn who took a liking to the lad's combat record and asked after the transfer; but it won't be the major taking the blame. No, it will fall on Captain, and him only having pity for the boy."

"LeBlanc murdered that little girl, and Miller knows it. He knew it all the time. Goddamn him, anyway." I can tell you how betrayal tastes, Bobby. It's gall-bitter, with an aftertaste of tarnished-penny rage.

"The worst shame of it is that she's been forgotten already. One death among thousands now. Let it go," he said quietly and firmly. "Let it go."

"I'll kill LeBlanc, Father. Or he'll kill me out there. He's bug-eyed crazy."

"He's lonely, Travis."

"Lonely, shit."

"Comes from being raised without a family, and the Sisters of Charity no replacement. Comes from running the Toronto streets. He'll be looking for belonging, yet pushing friendship away. One has to feel pity for a boy like that."

"I don't have to feel a goddamned thing. That's your job, Father. I'm shut of him."

I left. We never drank that tea. I never ate the cookie. It's night. Hours have passed. I haven't told Pickering, even though he keeps asking what's wrong. I don't dare tell him. LeBlanc hasn't been arrested yet. Maybe he won't ever be.

Anyway, tomorrow we march to the front lines. There, I'll be crawling out into No Man's Land with a murdering boy. Tonight LeBlanc's curled in his covers, wrapped in his lies, safe. Maybe he's dreaming of his fantasy horses, his imaginary family. Maybe he's dreaming about fucking that mangled girl.

Travis Lee

OCTOBER 12, THE FRONT LINES
Dear Bobby,

Still not arrested. And LeBlanc knows I know. The first day out in No Man's Land with him was a day of terrible silence. I plinked away at Boche. It was all I could do not to blow LeBlanc's brains out.

That night I dreamed red dreams, and when I woke up, my jaws ached from chewing on fury.

I ate some breakfast before dawn, careful not to wake Pickering and Calvert. By the time I was done, LeBlanc was waiting for me outside the dugout. I didn't speak a word to him. We climbed up the ladder and snuck out into the dark.

It was about noon that I got started thinking about that girl. I probed the memory like a mouth ulcer, wondering how many other women LeBlanc had hurt. God knows I wasn't blameless. I wondered what I would have done if I'd seen him with that twelve-year-old girl.

"Three yards to the right of that white post." He was peering intently through the field telescope.

"Fuck you."

Rain was beating on us in that halfhearted way it does here.

He looked around, said, "Take the shot. Don't be an asshole."

I snapped one left instead, scared the bejesus out of a Boche officer, dinged the prong off the top of his helmet, sent him diving for cover.

I was ready for LeBlanc, too. When he reached out to slap me like he does when he thinks we're playing, I struck back, left-handed but knuckle-first. I slammed him hard on the side of the mouth, Bobby. Knocked his helmet off, split his lip for him, made blood run. It felt good. I hit him again, right-handed this time—clubbed my fist down on his ear.

My hand hurt. Christ. Hurt all the way to the elbow.

The blow stunned him. I saw it in his grimace, the way he cupped the side of his head.

"You lying chicken shit bastard," I said. "You want to ride

a horse? Let's put you on Miller's damned sorrel. You'd crap your pants, city boy. See, I know all about you, about the orphanage, about how you go fucking women. Is that the only way a girl'll have you?"

A blow from an unexpected direction. He kicked, bruised the hell out of my thigh, missed my balls by an inch. My rifle, his telescope, went sliding down the mud incline and into the water. He grabbed me. We went slipping down the mud, too, and hit the water, still pummeling each other.

There were dead things down there. The water wore a greasy film of putrefaction. It was greenish-yellow and saturated with gas. I pushed him face-down into it, tried to hold his head under. I was bigger, but he was desperate. He pushed me off, came up sputtering.

"Holy shit, Stanhope!" he yelled.

He rolled out from under me. I hit him again—a glancing blow off the side of his jaw. He gave me one back, but he wasn't nearly fast enough. I ducked under, grabbed him one-handed by the throat. I saw terror come all over him. He pulled away, started crawling fast up the incline.

I grabbed at his tunic, got a handful of mud for my trouble. He kicked, caught me, sharp and painful, on the side of the neck. I snatched at his trouser leg. He squirmed free.

I climbed the hill after, caught him in the flat, rolled him belly-up. He tore at my face, at my eyes. A bullet smacked a hillock of mud near us, splashed my face. A quick, violent tug at my leg. Not LeBlanc. The Boche sniper had shot my boot heel off.

That surprised me, made me relax my grip. LeBlanc skittered away, fast as a crab. I went after, caught him on the downside of another hole, flipped him over. His eyes were wide. His mouth was bleeding.

"You're crazy!" he said.

I hit him again.

"They're shooting at us, Stanhope! Jesus. Don'tcha see? The Boche sniper's shooting at us!"

"Who's scared now?" I asked him.

He kept begging me to stop, kept trying to fight back; but I beat him, Bobby. I pulled him down into a shell hole and beat him stupid. I pounded on him till my hand couldn't take no more. By the time I was finished, I was too exhausted to move. It took me hours to pry my fingers open.

Both his eyes were swollen nearly shut. There was a star hemorrhage in his right. His nose was broken, squashed flat. His mouth looked like one of those ugly cartoons they draw when they're making fun of coloreds. He really didn't look human anymore.

I crawled off, found the telescope and my rifle. When dark fell, I let him make his own way back. I could hear him, though, tagging along behind like a kicked dog.

Jesus, Bobby. What does he want from me, anyway? The horses? My family? Well, shit. He can have all my memories of Pa.

Back in the trenches, Blackhall held up a lantern. He checked LeBlanc's face, looked at my knuckles.

"A dust-up, is it? Daft, having a row out there. How'd it start?"

I didn't answer. Maybe LeBlanc's mouth didn't work well enough to speak.

"Me, I'd shoot the bof of you, and save the Boche the trouble." He called for Riddell, who came and blinked sleepily at LeBlanc, looked crestfallen at me.

"Take 'em down to Captain," Blackhall said. "Let 'im see how 'is two pets is getting along."

Miller didn't seem surprised. Unlike Riddell, he didn't even seem disappointed. He gestured toward LeBlanc. "Sergeant? Accompany this man to the medic. See that both are fined a week's pay. No free time for a month."

Riddell said his "Yes, sir"s and "right away, sir"s.

I told Miller, "Think I broke my hand, sir."

He waited until the dugout door had closed. "Best that you have. That should give you a few weeks apart. Because I shall expect the both of you out sharpshooting when the rotation comes round again."

"You can't mean that, sir."

He sat down, crossed his legs that prissy way the Brit public school boys do. He lit a cigarette, didn't offer me one. "Indeed I do."

"I'll kill him, sir. He'll kill me."

He reached into a haversack, threw me a towel. "Clean your face, Stanhope. You're an utter wog."

I wiped mud with my good hand.

"What occurred out there?" he asked.

"What occurred in here?"

"Pardon?"

"You never told Major Dunn that LeBlanc raped that woman, did you? You're scared he'll accuse you of knowing LeBlanc's tendencies and not watching him careful enough. Shit, sir. Didn't killing that little girl like he did teach you any kind of lesson?"

He leaned back in the chair, blew a cloud of smoke my way. "Dismissed, Stanhope. Report to the medical dugout."

I stayed where I was, the towel wadded in my hand. "Where's the goddamned justice in this, sir? Jesus. Somebody has to do something."

Miller contemplated the end of his cigarette.

"Well? Don't they?"

He pursed his lips, tapped ash.

"You forced me into teaching him a thing or two, sir. Just 'cause somebody had to. Now he'll be hunting for me. I know him. I know how crazy he is. You'll find me laid out somewheres, stabbed in the back."

Miller stubbed his butt out on the side of the table. A shower of sparks fell. "Now that you have trounced him, Private LeBlanc will respect you. He is a dog of sorts. Had you beaten him in public, he would have been forced to revenge himself. But do take care not to lose his esteem, Stanhope. Tarnish yourself, and he will feel betrayed. Dismissed. Discuss this matter with no one."

"You're just going to forget about those girls? He'll do it again, sir. Can't break him of the habit."

"Dismissed, Stanhope."

"Goddamn you to hell, sir."

He looked away, said in a tone of utter boredom, "Dismissed."

Come to find that I only sprained my hand, Bobby. Bruised it pretty bad, too. The doctor wrapped it, gave me aspirin powders. When I got back to my dugout, Riddell came by. He unwrapped what the doctor did and tied me up in a poultice. It feels a sight better, but it still aches something fierce when I try to write.

Well, enough about my wounds. Hear tell, though, I cracked LeBlanc's cheekbone for him. Uh-huh. Ain't that too damned bad. Bet a broken cheekbone don't hurt near as much as guilt.

Travis Lee

NINE

OCTOBER 14, THE RESERVE TRENCHES

Dear Bobby,

A couple of nights ago I finally took another trip to the graveyard. It had been too long. The gathered angels, the headstones, were just like coming home. I was glad to see it was still green, that there was a place in the world where it wasn't raining.

It was a simple dream, and a short one. The calico girl sat beside me on a carved bench. She took my bruised hand in both her own, and held it.

She didn't say a word, but I woke up feeling healed. My hand still aches, but there's a drawing pain—a mending pain—in my chest, where shame cut me.

I haven't told anyone what happened between me and LeBlanc. Pickering wants his gossip and so he's in a pout. No one knows about that bakery shop girl, either. It's best that the rest of the boys don't know. Some would be making fun of her getting fucked that way, some would be laughing and calling her a cow. I don't think I could take that.

Blackhall gave me a new boot heel. I had to nail it on myself. Still, my hand's not well enough for sandbag duty. The boys leave me in the morning; they come back a couple of hours before dark. I sit and read, play a little solitaire. I've tried some of the penny dreadful novels Pickering's wife sends him.

By the way, Calvert's wife sent him sugar. Do you believe

that? A three-kilogram package of sugar. The next day we were due to move back to the reserve area, so we set about eating that sugar so Calvert didn't have to cart it. We made syrup of our tea, ate the stuff in spoonfuls out of the package. We passed it down the trench. By the time he got the sugar back, the package was wet and the last of the sugar was melting. He was relieved, I think.

Rain has made the trenches into shallow, narrow creeks; the dugouts are inlets. The water's up to our ankles. We sleep on top of crates, surrounded by the flotsam of drowned rats and the jetsam of maggots.

Every Thursday, Riddell holds trench-foot inspection. Pickering jokes that he's hoping for a case, waiting for a Blighty; but I've seen men's flesh soften like boiled chicken, seen pale, bloated meat fall off the bone. We've lost three out of our company already from it, and the rains have just started.

Riddell packs weeds into our whale oil when Blackhall's not looking. It turns green and stinks like a compost heap—worse than the drinking cure he made me—still, I'm not drinking, and our platoon's free of the rot.

The enemy's changed, Bobby. We fight mud. We battle lice. We hold entire campaigns against trench foot. Miller lectures about nits and the importance of changing socks. When he comes by for his dugout visits, he'll give offenders a gaze that'd make your balls wither.

But I'm disappointed in him, Bobby. I'd thought Miller was a brave man. For those girls' sake, I reckon he's just not brave enough. I think about his fiancée sometimes, when I dare. When I let myself. I wonder if she stares at him from that wall. It's a haunting face she's got. An unforgettable one. He must have to turn away.

Last night was the first time I walked No Man's Land in my sleep. The afternoon reveries were one thing, but God, that dream was real. A three-quarters moon was up. I felt the chill of the rain on my back, smelled the stink of that death-saturated earth. The light was spectral and full of deceit, the way moonlight always is. And walking through that lacerated place—a land frozen into upheaval—I came upon Marrs. He was sitting bowed, his shoulders, his head splashed with moonlight. I sat on the lip of the shell hole with him.

"Need to come with me, Marrs."

He'd finally got tired of his wandering, I guess. He wasn't grinning anymore. His elbows were propped on his knees, his hands clasped. His head was down.

"Can't catch me breath, Stanhope."

"You're dead," I told him, gentle as I could. "Don't you remember?"

"Can't catch me breath."

It must have been the fierceness of the blast that stayed with him: the oxygen burning, and not himself.

"Come on. Come with me."

He looked up, not at me, but at the sky. His face sagged into an expression of vague woe. "They firing?"

"Not anymore."

"Seen me letter?"

"It's waiting for you in the graveyard."

He looked down at his hands. "They firing?"

I told him the firing had stopped. That the battle was won. That he could go on.

"Stanhope?"

"Yeah, Marrs?"

"Sometimes," he said in hushed confusion, "I just can't catch me breath."

I finally had to leave. I don't think he ever noticed my going. Marrs carries with him such a foggy sadness. All of the wandering spirits do. There's nothing keen about ghosts, Bobby. A shame that death takes all our passion.

Travis Lee

OCTOBER 16, THE RESERVE TRENCHES

Dear Bobby,

Today I was alone, sitting in the dugout reading, when a shadow fell over the page. I looked up to see LeBlanc blocking the dugout doorway. What I'd done to him was awful, Bobby.

Green and purple bruises bloomed across his cheeks. His nose was grotesque with swelling. His lip was torn. His eyeball was full of blood.

"Hey." Looked like it hurt him to speak.

I'd tensed so, my hand throbbed. "Hey."

Standing at the door, he looked up the trench and then down. Calvert and Pickering were gone, the sentry not due. LeBlanc'd take out his knife. He'd gut me the way you would a deer.

"You won't tell anybody?"

I swallowed hard. Tell what? About the rapes? About besting him? I couldn't best him now, not with my hand the way it was, not if he had a knife.

"Promise?"

He was such a murdering, lying shit, how could I promise him anything?

He shifted his weight, cleared his throat. "Hey, Stanhope? I don't want anybody to know I was a born a bastard."

How can something as fragile as childhood hide such lasting things? Pa's beatings; LeBlanc's orphanage. Fungus secrets that thrive without light, without air.

"You bet," I told him.

He shouldered his way further inside the dugout, stood looking down at me with his blood-filled eye.

He shoved his hand toward me. "No hard feelings."

I shook it, left-handed. "No hard feelings." And I knew that I was the only one lying.

"So. We're going back out there in a couple of weeks, eh?"

"Seems like it."

He put his hands in his pockets, looked around.

"Want some tea?" I asked him.

"Nah."

I'd known he'd refuse. LeBlanc wasn't one to stay put long. "Want to set a spell?"

"Gotta go."

Sure he'd have to go. He had to run fast. Had to jump off those high places. Always had to be on the move. Only he wasn't leaving.

He wasn't looking at me, either. "Hey, Stanhope? You teach me how to ride a horse sometime?"

Such dignified pleading in his voice. It caught me unaware. Tore at me, too, like when a strong woman busts into tears. "Yeah. Sometime."

He nodded and left. I tried to finish my chapter of Pickering's penny dreadful, but simple as it was, as much as I kept rereading, I couldn't hold onto the words. Finally I put the book down, found Blackhall, and asked permission to see Miller.

Blackhall was sour about it, and suspicious. Still, he agreed. Must be strange, standing on the outside, watching Miller and me. Hell. I don't understand it. Nothing, not even hatred, is simple.

In the rear trenches, someone had put elephant sheets up over the top of the sandbags to make little shelters from the rain. In the shade of one of those elephants I found Miller standing with one of the other subalterns. I stood in the pelting rain and waited.

At last he looked up. He didn't seem real happy to see me.

"Sir? We'll be marching up to the rest area tomorrow," I said.

"You're confined to billets. You're aware of that." He started talking to the lieutenant again.

I stood quietly, there in the downpour. The lieutenant was trying to listen to Miller, but he kept looking at me, too. Finally Miller whirled. "Blast. What is it?"

"Permission to speak to you in private, sir."

"Permission denied." He turned away.

Cool rain pounded my forehead, dripped into my eyes. My greatcoat was heavy with it.

Miller spun. "What? What is it, Stanhope? You're a bloody nuisance."

"Permission to borrow your horse, sir."

His face screwed itself up into the most amazing expression of confusion. "You what? Want to borrow my horse? Good God, Stanhope. What do you plan to do with him?"

"Ride him, sir. Just around the billet area. Need another one, too. A gentle mount. Private LeBlanc has asked."

His expression smoothed. He'd read my face and understood it better than I had understood that penny dreadful. "During your free time, then. I'll see to it. Request Captain Dunston-Smith's bay mare. She'll give him no trouble."

"Thank you, sir."

He tapped swagger stick to cap, then went back to his conversation.

For pity. O'Shaughnessy had said that's why Miller took LeBlanc in, took him even knowing what he had done. He was forgiving him even now. How could he do that? Like Christ forgiving the Pharisees. Was self-destructive pardon like that ever worthwhile?

I could never forgive Pa for hitting me, even though if I live long enough I might learn to forget. It's not the sins against me that matter. It was him hitting Ma and drawing blood. It was hearing Ma cry the way she did. It was watching the way he made her grovel. Not even Jesus could forgive that.

Miller didn't see how LeBlanc used that girl. He never saw her pretty smile or the way she blushed. Pity came easy for him. He never got caught up in the same incriminating passion and hated himself for it.

Travis Lee

OCTOBER 17, THE RESERVE TRENCHES

Dear Bobby,

I walked through home again in my dreams. It was quiet. The air in the hall smelled of camphor and rosewater and dust. The boards were waxed to satin in the shadows, buffed to a high gleam in the pewter light. Ma's door was open.

Pa was sitting on the side of the bed, still waiting for me. That wood horse was lying in his cupped hands. I stopped just long enough to feel the dragging undertow of duty, then pulled myself free and walked on.

Is he dead, Bobby? Is that why he keeps coming back?

Wish you could tell him to stop bothering me. Visiting doesn't do no good. Shit, I haven't been able to save Marrs yet. I don't know if Foy's still around. It's them I need to dream about, not Pa. What the hell kind of gift is this, anyway? Now I'm supposed to feel guilty for hating him? I got me enough good people to feel guilty about.

Travis Lee

OCTOBER 18, THE REST AREA

Dear Bobby,

Blackhall had been told we were going riding, but it was hard for him to believe. He walked us down to the stables himself.

"Just around the billets, mind," he warned before he left.

The sorrel and the little bay were saddled and waiting in the aisle of the army's cheap clapboard stable. Blackhall checked the stalls as if he was looking for women or liquor. When he finally left, I told LeBlanc to take off his boots.

He kept staring starry-eyed at Dunston-Smith's mare. "Hey, you worthless peckerwood," I said. "You hear me? Can't get those hobnails through the stirrups."

He sat down where he was and unlaced them. I caught a glimpse of the right sole as he put the boot away. One hobnail was broken. There were holes where two nails were missing.

"Only a chicken shit has to lie about where he came from," I told him.

Easy to say. I knew about my dugout mates' families, but they had an incomplete picture of mine. Not even Miller knew about Pa.

LeBlanc hadn't heard me. He kept looking at those horses as if he was seeing glory.

When he got up, I saw he'd kept his socks on like a city boy. Odd how gentle he touched the horses. His hands were tender, like yours are around puppies, Bobby.

I always envied you your hands. I wonder if my fingers ever caress anything that way: women or horses or kittens. I wonder if my face ever goes as merciful, if I ever look at anything with such beautiful longing.

I gave him a leg up, mounted Miller's sorrel from a block, and we walked the horses into the paddock. LeBlanc rode about the way I thought. He sawed at the reins. When we trotted, his ass bounced. He hung tight as he could onto a lock of that poor mare's mane.

She was good-natured with him, and patient—a beginner's mount. Me and LeBlanc rode all that afternoon through the misting rain. We rode around the officers' quarters, around the enlisted barracks. I showed him how to keep his hands down, how to tuck his elbows in. I showed him posting, but he only tried it once. He came down and that mare came up. LeBlanc's nuts and the pommel met in the middle with a God-awful slam. Knocked the wind out of him, made his face go sickly. Thought he'd quit then, but he didn't. LeBlanc kept trying his best. I've been riding so many years that I forget how it first happens; but at some point I think you have to surrender. You have to stop trying so hard.

Too bad, Bobby. He doesn't have enough time to learn. I don't think it matters. As we cantered past the barracks for the tenth or twelfth time, I looked back. I've never seen a grin that wide on any grown man.

When the light turned blue and the mist thickened, we dismounted and led the horses into the stables. We lit lamps while hazy twilight gathered at the windows. The air inside was warm with horses, the straw golden in the lamplight.

LeBlanc was so sore from riding that he walked bow-legged. He couldn't sit without groaning. Still, I didn't want to laugh at him. He'd stayed the course.

I showed him how to strip off a saddle, how to hang it, how to rub a horse down. He currycombed with the clumsy diligence of a little kid. "What's her name?" he asked me.

"Don't know."

"What's Miller's horse called, then?"

"Never asked."

"If you ride a horse, you should know its name."

"Yeah? You know the name of everything you ride? Huh?"

I asked, my voice sharp. "Do you, you shithead? You as gentle with everything as you are with that goddamned horse?"

He looked surprised.

"You should know people's goddamned names."

I jerked the sorrel's reins, was mortified when I saw the horse flinch. I rubbed him behind the ears and led him into his stall. Calf-deep in the dry straw, I slipped his bridle off, hung it aside. When I looked around again, I saw LeBlanc eyeing me.

"You like him?" he asked.

"Who? The horse?" I scratched the gelding on his blaze, sweet-talked him a bit. "You're okay for a worthless, stilt-legged thoroughbred, aren't you, son?"

He nuzzled my arm, whuffled. Miller must have made sugar cubes or carrots a habit. I held up my hands, fingers flat, to show him I wasn't carrying. Damned if that horse didn't rub his nose up and down my shoulder, a gesture that won me.

"Old horse," I murmured. I scratched up a storm on his ears and forehead. "You old horse."

It's amazing what animal affection can give you: no demands in return. We had us a mutt one time. I know you don't remember. Died when you were just a baby. Every time Pa'd whop on me, that old dog would come looking; and he'd find where I'd be hiding. He'd put his head in my lap and let me hug on him. Made it easier, the beatings. That horse of Miller's, the smells of that stable, the foggy blue twilight at the door—they eased the war.

The two of us tended to the little things. We soaped Miller's and Dunston-Smith's saddles. I showed him how to check the bridle leather for cracks. When we were done and he had started away, I grabbed LeBlanc's arm. The bruises on his face were fading like sallow sunsets.

"Only say it once," I told him.

He was attentive, like I was going to tell him something about horses.

"You do it again—you know what I mean—and I'll blow

your brains out. No discussion. No nothing. You understand?"

He nodded and I let him go.

Nearly a perfect day, Bobby, the horses, the misty cool. But when we got to where we'd left our boots, I saw that somebody had moved them from the spot where we'd set them down. My belly wobbled. I remembered clear: My boots had been nearest the door.

LeBlanc didn't notice. He was still smiling horses. He sat down and pulled his boots on.

Someone had checked our soles, Bobby. And whoever did it had known we were at the stables. Miller? Dunston-Smith?

LeBlanc looked up at me. "Hey, asshole. You going to go barefoot to dinner? Those damned limeys won't like that."

No. Blackhall.

"Come on, Stanhope, for Christ's sake."

I nodded. "Sure." I shoved my boots on and we walked down to the enlisted mess.

When we were finished eating we wandered back toward the barracks. Blackhall was standing outside tamping his pipe bowl under the light of a hanging lantern. Beyond him the night was foggy and close. A pale dusting of rain blew through the circle of lamplight. When we passed, he returned our salute with barely a look. Five or six steps later I turned around and saw that he was eyeing us hard.

I give LeBlanc four days at the most, Bobby. Takes gossip that long to spread. Then they'll haul him before the court-martial board. I'll testify to what I know. They'll bring up the other charges: the blinded old lady, the dead little girl. They'll put LeBlanc before a firing squad.

It's best that way. He'll go quick, and I can remember him well: bouncing up and down on that bay mare, grinning.

Good to go happy, I think. No matter what you've done, you should have one of your dreams come true. LeBlanc's will be a death that won't haunt me. It was me who gave him an afternoon of horses.

Travis Lee

OCTOBER 19, THE REST AREA

Dear Bobby,

Well, it's back to drills, back to marching. We get a few days off, and the army can't leave us alone. About four o'clock when the drills are done and the boys get their free time, LeBlanc and me scrub the barracks floor. We peel potatoes and carrots down at the mess hall. We scrub pans. We lime the latrines.

It's nice to have tasks with limits, ones that you can tell when you're done. LeBlanc and me scrub the floors on our hands and knees. It's a prayerful sort of thing. I like the rasping sound the brush makes. I like the memories it brings, too: Ma and me in the kitchen, splashing buckets and flicking water at each other. You never was no good at it, Bobby. Have you learned the chore better? If you do learn it, you'll find there's a calm, soapy goodness to floor scrubbing. Don't you never tell Ma I said that.

They haven't come for LeBlanc yet. It'll pain me some when they do, for he sticks to me like slick on grease. He does things like me. Walks like I do. Eats like I do. LeBlanc's private game of Simon Says. It scares me sometimes, like there ain't enough stuffing in him to make a person, so he has to go borrowing from someone else. How will it be, I wonder, to watch my own shadow die?

Travis Lee

OCTOBER 20, THE REST AREA

Dear Bobby,

Last night while I was walking the graveyard alone, I heard someone singing. The clear tenor voice wound like a lustrous thread around granite markers, between praying angels. Marrs. And not Latin this time, but Scots-tinged English.

". . . the broom, the broom, the bonnie, bonnie broom . . ."

Marrs had made it out of No Man'sLand. I hurried into

the mausoleum, calling his name. The place was empty but for stray autumn leaves and the plaintive echo of his voice.

"... all maids that ever deceived ..."

I stood in the puddle of light from the glassy ceiling and listened. Where was he? And who was he serenading? I left, twined my way through mounds of bright paper flowers, past graves of sleeping strangers. I turned a corner and there he was, seated below me on the steps. He looked wrong somehow.

I stopped behind him. At his feet was a glass-topped grave. There, comforted by flowers, a little girl was sleeping. She was dressed all in white, and in her hands was a bouquet of violets.

The song stopped. He turned, tapping his finger to his lips.

It wasn't Marrs. It was Foy. "Poor mite. Too young to be married," he said.

I sat on the steps beside him. The breeze was chill. It smelled clean and astringent, like lavender.

He sang, "... the bonnie, bonnie broom ..."

Marrs's same high, piercing register; Marrs's clarion tone.

"He gave me his voice when I dreamed," Foy told me. He was grinning, hugging his knees like a kid.

I looked down at the girl: the blinding white lace, the childish innocence of her hands.

"You're holding me here," Foy said. Accusing words, but there was nothing but concern in his voice.

He wanted to leave me. Panicked, I stood. Down the steps and beyond a cluster of gravestones, the calico girl waited by the mausoleum's iron gates.

"Please, Stanhope," Foy said. "Don't need me so bad."

But who would be left to understand when all the old gang went away?

He stood, too. "She's been though a hard spot, the girl."

LeBlanc's smallest victim. I knew it sure as the world. "Seems to me you need to stay with her, then."

"I'll stay if you want."

But he wanted so damned bad to leave. "Please," I said. "Can't you, please?"

I knew he couldn't; and so I watched him go—up the stairs and down the gravel path. I caught glimpses of him making his way among the tombs. His leaving knocked the stuffing out of me so that I had to sit down.

I sat there for a while with the girl. Her face was sweet. Her lids were closed, but underneath them her eyes slid, restless with visions. I kept watch while the sun lowered and the light turned brassy, until foxglove blooms blazed like indigo candles in the last of the light.

I woke up feeling sad. The sad stayed with me, and so that morning, cleaning up the officers' mess, I didn't have much to say.

LeBlanc was a blabbermouth. "Hey. When this shit's over, I'm gonna save up my money and raise a buncha horses. You want to be partners with me?"

Three days left for him to live, I figured. Three days, time enough for aspirations. "Sure," I told him. I plunged the brush into the bucket, sent water sloshing.

"Yeah, yeah," he said. "That's what we'll do. I won't even mind cleaning out the stables or anything. We'll get us some land in Alberta, eh? Right near Calgary. It's terrific there. I saw it once—went through Alberta on the train. I won this spelling bee, see, and the Sisters sent us on a trip. Christ, Stanhope, the mountains. Jesus and Joseph, you wouldn't believe the mountains. And a yellow plain that comes right up. The whole damned place is yellow and purple. That's Alberta."

He was whistling as he scrubbed. Even if I went looking for LeBlanc after the firing squad was done, I wouldn't find him. He'd be traveling so fast, I'd never catch up. He'd be running over the golden plains. He'd be climbing purple mountains. And all the time he'd be grinning. I just knew he would.

He said, "We'll have us paint horses, those white ones with the big brown spots. And palomino horses, and solid black ones, too. Shit, Stanhope. We'll have us all colors of horses."

He got up, took our buckets out to the tank to get more water. I kept on scrubbing. He'd gotten me to picturing it too:

t-colored land, a purple petticoat of mountains. All colors of horses. A sound startled me out of my fantasies. O'Shaughnessy was standing in the door of the kitchen, a case of officers'-issue tea in his arms.

He was smiling a cheerful little smile. " 'Tis very domesticated you're looking, Travis. It strikes me that you've a natural way with the brush."

"Back home, floor cleaning was one of my chores, Father."

"Ah, and your mother had you doing the rough for her, was it? Me own mother spoiled me. I'm useless for housework. Can't wash a kettle."

It was comfortable there in the kitchen. The air smelled of pine soap and damp and hardwood ash. By O'Shaughnessy's shoulder hung a braid of yellow onions, their chubby bellies taut and translucent. Sun cascaded through the windows, poured in a broad glowing stripe down the wall.

"Does it make a penance, lad?"

I scrubbed the boards around the table leg, startled myself up a bug. "Not suffering enough, Father. If you want to know the truth, it's kind of fun."

A shocked, "Dear God, but you're a hard case, Travis! Well, since you're expert at penance, choose one for me, for you've caught me stealing tea from out the storeroom." He didn't look particularly ashamed of himself. In fact, he looked button-popping proud.

"Well, good on you, Father, as they'd say around here. Your penance is to steal yourself some currant and cinnamon loaf while you're at it."

He laughed. "Needn't tempt me. For the family I'm visiting, bread's a plethora. It will be the tea that's dear."

I stopped scouring. Another bug crept out from a baseboard, hurried its way past me. I let it go. "I'd like to give that poor girl something," I said.

I stared at the top of his boots. Near him, in the light from the doorway, sun winked on a puddle, turned a froth of bubbles into pearls.

"Just some little something. I saved up some money to buy Ma another present, but the lace napkins can wait."

The floor shook. It was LeBlanc walking heavy-footed—burdened by water pails—on the stair. The door banged open.

"You?" LeBlanc said when he caught sight of O'Shaughnessy. "You'll get our goddamned floor dirty."

"Well, lad. But the red caps will have their evidence, won't they? And with the boyo here to give his testimony."

LeBlanc's cheeks went a hot, furious red. He stared down at me.

O'Shaughnessy tipped his hat—a common man's gesture. "Good day. I'll be taking my plunder. 'Tis an excellent job you're doing, Travis. Me compliments to your mother."

When he left, LeBlanc dropped my bucket down next to me with a thud. Water crested, splattered my already clean bit of floor.

"What'd the mick mean by that?" His voice was shaking.

Too painful to watch. Maybe when they came for him, it would be best if I wasn't around. "I don't know. He was making jokes about stealing tea."

"Up your ass, Stanhope. Come on. Tell me the goddamned truth. What was he doing here? What were you two talking about?"

"Nothing," I told him.

He took his own water pail and went to his corner of the room. Officers' morning teatime came and went. Cooks tracked mud from pantry to stove and back. LeBlanc and me refilled our buckets, set about scrubbing again.

It was near lunch when Harry Barstow came bursting in. "Stanhope!" He was out of breath. "Captain wants to see you straightaway, and he's having himself a royal blinking paddy. He says to me, 'Barstow, sees you brings Private Stanhope here on the double,' and all the time him slapping that stick of his into his palm. Best go on."

God almighty. Blackhall had taken the boots to him, dropped the problem of LeBlanc right into his lap. He'd think I'd been loose-lipped about it. I left brush and bucket and ran fast as I could to the officers' barracks.

It wasn't raining, but the clouds were considering it. Miller was standing outside the portable building having a chat with

Dunston-Smith. They looked public-school elegant, upper-class composed.

When I saluted, my hands were shaking. I was so out of breath, I could barely speak. "Private Stanhope reporting, sir."

Miller sketched a return salute. "Ah, Stanhope. I've been told that you've volunteered to help Father O'Shaughnessy with a bit of an errand. Is that so?"

It took me a few whooping gasps to sort through theories about LeBlanc and the firing squad, through charges of rape and a battered girl. Then I understood I'd been put smack in the middle of a game. But who was playing, O'Shaughnessy or Miller? "Yes, sir. He wanted me for an errand, sir."

"You do realize that you are under discipline."

I wondered what Dunston-Smith was making of the scene. There was an arch little grin playing around his lips.

"Yes, sir. Sorry, sir. Shouldn't have offered."

Miller turned to Dunston-Smith, shook his head. "I don't know quite what to do with him at times, Colin. The boy is so damnably energetic."

In turning away he missed his reward: Dunston-Smith's defensive sulk.

I said, "I'll just tell him I can't, sir."

"No, no, Stanhope. I'll not have you disappoint him. He'll have you for one of his bloody good deeds, I expect."

"Yes, sir. I expect so, sir."

"I suppose there's not much enjoyment to be had. Charity and all that. You may go, but not for long, mind. And do your best to stay within O'Shaughnessy's sight, what? No chasing off on your own. Oh, Stanhope?" he called as I turned away. "I've a donation you might add to your coffers."

He dug in his pocket, came up with a fistful of money, handed it to me.

"Good God, Richard," Dunston-Smith said in fiscal shock. "You've given the boy over twenty pounds."

"Yes, quite. One of my favorite charities. See that you use it well, Stanhope. Won't have it wasted. Least I can do. Twenty pounds or so. Not much, actually. It's the very least I can do."

His eyes so level. His mouth rueful. I knew then. The red caps weren't coming for LeBlanc, not ever. Twenty pounds as a blood payment. LeBlanc would get away with it all.

I left Miller, walked fast across the yard, and found O'Shaughnessy. He'd been standing around the church building, waiting. When he saw me, he started to chuckle. "Ah, the poor lad! I see you've been ordered to help my efforts."

"I need to stop by a place so I can buy a present."

He nodded.

I carted the tea for him. "Those bastards. They're going to let him go," I said.

No need explaining who. "That's likely."

"Just 'cause Miller's scared." He was letting them win. Well, there was no way for me to judge the effects prejudice has on courage. I was raised around them, and I can't hope to understand what coloreds go through. Still, I bet his fiancée would have given those Oxford assholes what for.

"Ah, lad. It's that everyone's tired, is all. And it's not Miller's fear you're dealing with, but the fright of the British Army. For Pierre's a hero, and you can't be tarnishing nor punishing that. After all, what—other than stories of valor—makes soldiers follow a charge? No, Travis. For an army to win, heroes must shine like suns. They must be rewarded. Heroes are why other men go on."

For war's sake, men die, women are beaten. "There's no damned justice."

He shook his head, amused. "Ah, lad. If you're expecting justice, you'll be disappointed. It's only death that's fair."

We walked in silence for a while, then he asked me for news of the graveyard. I told him that Foy had gone on, that LeBlanc's youngest victim was staying a spell.

"Does she look happy, lad?"

I thought about it. Hard not to be happy there. "I know she's dreaming."

He liked that.

"But death being equal still don't make everything right," I said.

"Don't you think so?" I've never seen such contentment

on a person as I saw in O'Shaughnessy right at that moment. Oh, LeBlanc had been happy on his horse, but this was different. It was like O'Shaughnessy was savoring something, even knowing it was bound to end; and somehow loving the ending, too. It was a deep, peculiar satisfaction that O'Shaughnessy had. I wondered if he loved death too much.

We arrived at town, pausing to pass the time of day with the town's priest. From his armload of food, I figured the old man'd been on his way home from shopping. The two blathered away in French. The old priest offered us an early apple each. Mine was still sour.

It was odd watching the two talk, casual as workers on a break. I wondered if this was the man O'Shaughnessy confessed to, tried to imagine what sins he wanted rid of.

Then they were saying their adieus and nodding and waving. O'Shaughnessy took me a few blocks down and showed me a place to shop. I sorted through pearl brooches and sapphire rings, garnet earrings and onyx necklaces. It was a cross on a chain I finally bought, for it was pretty and I thought it might give the girl's heart some ease.

It was an expensive, frilly gold cross; to buy it, it took all my money and Miller's, too. The shopkeeper wrapped it pretty. When he was tying the red ribbon, he winked.

"He thinks you've a lass you're stepping out with," O'Shaughnessy explained. "And like all jewelers, he's blathering on about what a fine selection you've made and complimenting your good taste. Say *merci*."

"*Merci*."

The shopkeeper's head bobbed. He handed the wrapped gift over and we left. Once in the street, O'Shaughnessy laughed. Like Miller, he must have found me amusing.

"Do you know what the shopkeep said to me, Travis? That he'd not have served you had you come in alone. A British soldier, and buying a piece of jewelry? Why, he'd have imagined you set on seducing a town girl. Ah, but you came in with a priest, didn't you? And to make matters even safer, you purchased a cross. Well, now he knows your intentions are honorable. He asked if you'd set a marriage date as yet." O'Shaughnessy went to cackling again.

I thought about the girl, about how Miller said she'd been ruined. The gift made me a little sad. "What'd you tell him?"

"That you were American, and not British; and that America is a long way away. Ah, but the man was a romantic. He told me that the only thing better for a man's soul than overcoming obstacles of affection is pining over unrequited love."

Right then I recognized what I saw in O'Shaughnessy. It wasn't happiness, but security. He'd never had reason to doubt that he was cherished.

"You know where the girl lives?" I asked, for it seemed like he was making a beeline for someplace.

"Just ahead here. Ah. We'll have a lovely time. She always enjoys her visits."

I shifted the tea crate, slowed my steps. The cobblestone streets were close, the row houses—some white plaster, some red brick—standing shoulder to shoulder in short blocks. The houses were two- and three-storied, with high pitched roofs and gables. One wooden front door each: painted green or white.

The street was deserted but for a wandering cat. War had emptied some of the houses. The whole town looked as if it was waiting.

O'Shaughnessy stopped at a house on the corner. Before he could knock, I shoved the tea into his arms. "Listen. You give the necklace to her for me?"

"Her family's here, lad. They're lovely people. You'll not be wanting to give the gift to her yourself?"

If I looked into her face, I'd remember her spread, submissive ass. I'd hate myself if that happened. "It's not like no penance or nothing, is it?"

"No. You needn't see them if you'd rather not." Still, he looked disappointed. "Will you knock them up for me, then?"

I perched the gift on top of the tea crate, gave the green-painted door a couple of raps. Then I started away fast. Behind me I heard voices in French, a man's, a woman's, heard O'Shaughnessy reply. When I turned, I saw the man eyeing me. I shoved my hands into my pockets and rounded the corner.

Just out of sight, I stopped. Near me was a window, its lace curtains worn at the hem and yellowed with age. A fine rain started falling, not heavy enough to seek for shelter. The wind gusted. The curtains heaved. I hunched against the cold, my back to the street.

It was the turning toward the house like I did, it was the wind parting the curtains that made me see her. She was asleep. The bed covers were rumpled, her pudgy hands clutching the feather comforter as if terrified it would leave.

Lots of things would. The ruin of that face would make people scatter. Jesus, Bobby. Her top lip still curved in that perfect, rosebud way I remembered; but her lower lip had been cut off.

And God, how LeBlanc had beaten her. The pink cheeks I remembered were yellow and misshapen with swelling. It was her clutching the bedclothes in her sleep that tore at me—that vigilant, never-trusting hand.

When O'Shaughnessy came back around the corner, I ducked my head and walked away from him fast. Rain fell harder. I heard his splashing steps behind me.

"Travis!"

The blank faces of the row houses, the blind eyes of their windows. A sudden gust sent fallen leaves tumbling down the cobbles, made scavenging pigeons plump their feathers.

"Travis."

He caught up with me, grabbed my arm, and spun me around.

"He hurt her," I said.

"You knew that."

Didn't know. Didn't. Not about the lip cut off, not about the teeth exposed. She wouldn't eat right again, talk right again. Never smile. From that night on, no one would look her full in the face. I jerked my arm free and kept walking.

"Travis. You knew that. Should have been no surprise, lad."

"Shit!" I yelled, startling pigeons, sending birds and echoes scattering. "That makes it all right? Jesus!"

He touched my arm, but I couldn't stand it. "I'll kill him," I said.

The serenity in O'Shaughnessy vanished. He looked frantic. "No, lad. No. Don't be taking that sin on yourself."

"You don't know shit about sin. I lived with it. It slept in the room next to me. I tried to kill it once. Hell, you probably tell that girl in there she's supposed to be happy because God loves her, ain't that right, Father? Well, if God loved her so goddamned much, why'd he let Pierre LeBlanc do that to her face?"

"Travis," he said real soothing, like he was quieting a spooked horse.

"Why'd he do that?" I meant God as much as LeBlanc. O'Shaughnessy kept reaching for me. I kept knocking his hand away.

I started walking fast toward the billets. Behind me, O'Shaughnessy shouted something. His voice was drowned out by the soft chuckles and contented-baby gurgles of the rain.

It was a long walk back to billets. On the way I thought about LeBlanc's hands, how kindly they were on the horses, about Pa's hands lying gentle in his lap the way they did in my dream. I looked at my own, the knuckles red from scrubbing, the fingers scarred from rough work.

Jesus God, Bobby. For all of us it's only one short step to Pa's savagery, another step to LeBlanc's. Kill him? Take the sin of it? How many had I killed already, anyway, and O'Shaughnessy forgiven me? God had to be stuffed to the gills with the fruit of heroes.

I turned a corner and there he was. I would have struck him down right then if he hadn't been standing at the door of the stables, grinning. He waved me over, "I traded chores, eh? Grab a pitchfork!"

The afternoon smelled of wet manure and rain. It stank of ammoniac horse piss.

LeBlanc, grinning the way the bakery shop girl never

would. "There was a captain by here, Stanhope. He said we could go riding, after."

I walked into the shelter of the stables, out of the gray afternoon and the drizzle. "They know," I said.

The smile fell off his face.

"Miller told me. The red caps know everything. They got hold of your boots yesterday. You stepped on the girl's back and left a bruise. On your left boot you got one broken hobnail. Two are missing. Ask me how I know."

He leaned on the pitchfork and lifted his boot, studied the bottom. His cheeks went sallow.

"They're gonna get you," I told him. "Just a matter of time. If it was me, I'd run for it. Head for that last farmhouse where we billeted. You remember where it was?" They'd shoot him when they found him. And I'd tell the red caps where he'd gone.

Outside the stable door, rain fell faster. It trickled from the roof, pattered on wet straw. To the back of the dim, shadowy building a horse whuffled and stamped.

"You were there that night, Stanhope. I saw you. You had your peter in your hand. I'll tell them you fucked her, too."

"I'll deny it."

"They won't care. They'll get you. Hey. It's almost true. You enjoyed it. Looked that way to me."

I grabbed a pitchfork. He held his ground, brought up his own pitchfork up the way you do in bayonet training. A strange sort of eagerness went all through me, keen as Marrs's singing. I tightened my grip on the handle so hard that a stray splinter in the wood bit.

LeBlanc knew I was going to kill him, just like Pa'd known that time. Like Pa, he gave up; and that was his salvation. The tines of his pitchfork lowered a fraction of an inch. His stare wavered.

I lunged forward, stabbed the tines hard as I could into straw. I started shoveling horse shit fast and furious. He joined me. It wasn't long after that when I saw O'Shaughessy pass by. I pretended I didn't see him. LeBlanc and me shoveled manure until the sun set and Riddell came to call us to dinner.

Why didn't I kill him? I was taller, stronger. I knew my way around pitchforks. I couldn't use Miller's excuse of pity, either. Shit, if I'd been good at pity, I wouldn't never have killed no one.

It's just that when I was facing him, I got to thinking how tired I was. LeBlanc was tired, too. Flanders' air is thick with the stink of rotted soldiers. The soil is root-bound with bones. In that charnel house, one girl's pain just didn't seem to matter.

Travis Lee

OCTOBER 24, THE FRONT LINES

Dear Bobby,

It feels good being back in war. A couple of hours' march, and life gets real again. I need edges now, Bobby: shells and bullets. I need big noises. That green, quiet world behind the lines is just a fantasy.

I buddied up with the new rum wallah, and last night was the best sleep I've had for days. While I slept I walked out through No Man's Land. I went looking for Marrs.

"There's not much time left," I said when I found him. I wasn't sure why I knew. "You got to come with me."

He'd gone beyond looking for his letter, beyond laboring to breathe. He was more tired than I was. Still, I kept pestering him, the way Ma'd do me sometimes.

"Please," I begged him finally. "Please. I can't let you stay here."

I did anyway, Bobby. I walked away and left all of them, the Boche, the Frenchies, and Marrs.

That morning when LeBlanc and me crossed the wire, my hand touched something smooth and round like a marble; barbed, too, like an old arrowhead. It was an interesting-feeling thing—my fingers liked the comfort of its roundness, were fascinated by those edges. It was only when the sun came up that I saw what I'd been holding.

It was a spine bone, the small one at the base of the skull.

I slipped it in my pocket and every once in a while I'd go to rubbing on it. You know, Bobby, that bone had been the prop of thoughts once, a buttress to love and fear. My thumb slides over it, polishing it more. Sometimes I think I can hear thoughts from it. Is that crazy?

Best talk to that bone. Lord knows LeBlanc and me, we don't speak much anymore. He'll peer through the field telescope and say, "Three and a half meters left of the coffee tin," and I'll snap a shot off.

We lunch in silence. We bear the wet in silence. When I get back to the dugout, I take the silence with me. It's like I've forgotten how to talk.

I lie in my damp cubbyhole, ignoring Pickering's and Calvert's gossip. I slip my hand into my pocket and rub that bone. It tells me about Alpine meadows: a hoop of mountains, an embroidery of wildflowers. It brings me the smells and lowing of milk cows. It sends me to sleep.

I dream of Pa, sometimes twice a night now. I'm always walking down that same hall, seeing Ma's door ahead and knowing what's waiting. I want real bad to turn and go the other way; but I don't. I can't. I just keep walking that same steady pace.

The light still falls across the hardwoods. The hall smells of floor wax and camphor the way it always does. And like I always do, I stop at the door.

I'm supposed to go in. It's not just Pa waiting for me to make my move; it's forgiveness.

Pa sits on the bed in that benevolent wash of sun. Light from the window crowns him, throws a radiant stole across his shoulders. He's always the same: head lowered and pensive, hands cupped. While I stand there, some powerful force pulls at me. I have to grab the doorjamb to keep from being drawn in.

Still, I walk on despite the soul-deep tug. It's my choice and I take it, no matter what God expects.

Travis Lee

NOVEMBER 1, THE RESERVE TRENCHES

Dear Bobby,

Today was the day I got your news. Riddell came down to the place we were working to find me. Pickering and Calvert and me were working on sump holes, and we were head to foot with mud. Pickering had been telling jokes all morning. Calvert—who'll surprise you sometimes—was relating a story about a fishmonger philandering uncle of his who pranged a whore in an alley once, then hid his used rubber in his pile of herring.

Calvert told it good, too, making his voice high and squeaky when he was imitating his aunt. Got me to laughing so hard I couldn't catch my breath. Pickering was wiping away tears.

Calvert was saying, "But when me auntie leaves, 'e goes to find it, doesn't 'e, and it's *gone*! Bleeding thing's *gone*! And 'e wonders if it were in the kilogram 'e sold to the last old lady customer. Crikey! 'e thinks. Old biddy might fry it up."

All of a sudden Calvert stopped talking. Pickering stopped laughing. I turned around. Riddell was standing there looking at me, his face full of bad news.

"Stanhope?" He's a considerate man, but I'd never heard his voice as kindly. "Captain wants you."

I thought of Ma. Then for a dizzy, terrible moment I thought of you. I ran pell-mell down the duckboards, pushing soldiers out of my way. I slogged my way through the mud in the communications trench, then down the twenty or so yards to Miller's.

I knocked. He called for me to come in. I opened the door, breathless, and found him sitting, looking down at a paper in his hand. The lamp was lit behind him and the warm glow had settled across his shoulders. The man and the room were wrong, but something in the way he was sitting, Bobby. Something in the way the light fell. For that brief instant I stepped into my dream. I felt a pull, the tug so strong that I had to clutch the door to keep from falling in.

Miller looked up, broke the spell. "Stanhope." His eyes

were full of secondhand sorrow. "Do come in. Sit down. There is something I need to tell you."

"My pa's dead," I said.

"Dear God. How did you know?"

As I came into the dugout, I staggered. He bolted up as if he was going to catch me. I found the chair, sat down in it hard.

"The Red Cross delivered the news as soon as they possibly could. Your brother thought the tidings too grievous to telegraph. It happened a few weeks past, actually. Dreadfully sorry."

"It's okay, sir. I think I've known for a while."

"There's a letter." He handed it over.

Funny. It wasn't that I loved Pa, but my vision couldn't focus. Your clear, carefully written words swam.

"Shall I read it to you?"

I wiped my eyes. "No."

"Well. I'll leave you alone for a bit, shall I?"

"I didn't love him," I said.

My words must have caught him at the door. Behind me, I heard him clear his throat. "Perhaps you'd like a chat with Father O'Shaughnessy."

I froze, staring straight ahead. I couldn't look at the girl he was going to marry, couldn't turn to look at him. He'd left his pencil on his tabletop. What the hell would he do with his hands? It was a cheerful yellow pencil. There was a red eraser beside it. Some things are made so they're easy to change.

"I been thinking," I said. On a wall peg, the lantern flickered erratically. Something was wrong. The wick was bad. Maybe the oil low.

"Yes?"

"You're stuck with your fathers, you know? No choice or nothing. I reckon your fathers are stuck with you." My eyes were tired, my lids heavy. The room went hazy, all the edges blurred. "You love yours?"

Miller cleared his throat again. The door squeaked as it opened. Light and air rushed in, rattled papers on his desk. He must have stood there for a while, half-in and half-out of the rain. When he left, he shut the door so quiet that I knew only by the darkness.

O'Shaughnessy arrived to find me staring at the lantern, your letter crumpled, still unread, in my hand. I heard him walk up behind me.

"I'm all right," I said.

He put his hand on my shoulder.

"He didn't mean nothing."

It struck me that I'd been sitting there too long. Miller would want his dugout back. They'd be needing me at the digging. I thought of that damned story about the rubber in the herring and how I'd been laughing only a little while ago. I thought about the way Pa'd hug on me sometimes, right at the start of his drunks, when he must have been feeling bad about how things had turned out between us. I thought about that little horse Pa'd carved me. Dun. He'd known to paint that mare dun.

I got up. "I better go."

"If you need me," he started to say.

"I won't."

I shoved your letter in my pocket and left. Back at the sump holes Pickering and Calvert were still cussing. I told them my pa had died, and then I picked up a shovel. They were respectful for a time. Then Pickering told a joke about a man who'd trained his pecker to sing. Calvert dumped a load of mud on Pickering's foot. I shoved my hand in my pocket and rubbed that spine bone.

That night I got a little drunk. I went to pushing Pickering around. He pushed back, and I would have hit him if Calvert hadn't pulled me off. I went out walking along the trench until Billings, the sentry, stopped me.

He lifted his lantern. "It's past lights-out, Stanhope. Best get your arse back to the dugout. Can't let Blackhall see you drunk. He'll have you in field punishment soon enough."

I said, "Fuck Blackhall."

He laughed. "You're a caution." Then his face fell. "Oh! I heard about your father, chum. Me condolences."

I jumped him. If he hadn't dropped the lantern quick as he

did, if he hadn't ducked, I'd have broken his nose. Calvert and Pickering, knowing I was up to no good, had followed me. They arrived in time to wrestle me off. Lucky Billings.

"Why'd he want to hit me? You see that? He hit me for nothing. Why'd he hit me?" Billings said.

Calvert had me pinned in a hammerlock. " 'E's in mourning."

They hauled me back to the dugout, kicking and fighting. Pickering scrounged up some rope. The two of them hogtied me, threw blankets over my legs, and told me to go to sleep.

I said they had to let me go. I said I had to piss. I said that come morning, I'd get them.

They said I'd better shut up. That if I kept yelling, Blackhall would come. He'd find out I was drunk.

I told them I hated my father.

Calvert got a Woodbine from his pack. "Mine's all right." He struck a match. "I suppose 'e's all right." The cigarette was damp, and he had to suck on it hard to get the fire started. "For an ill-tempered sodding little blighter."

Pickering said, "Mine hates my house. Thinks my wife's a tart. And when I was at the bank, he was forever asking when I planned to get a decent job. Silly me. All the while I'd imagined I had one."

"I gets wif me da, I ends up wif me peter shriveled. Stubborn old sot. Never can win an argument wif 'im."

"Mine's always in a paddy about something," Pickering said. "The government's cocked up. The newspapers print trash. Nothing's ever right."

"That's me da," Calvert agreed.

I'd stopped struggling long ago. No use. I was too tired. You can't ever win the war with your father. I closed my eyes and heard Calvert saying, "Pickering? You write a note to me da for me? Just a little note, maybe just asking 'ow 'e's getting on."

I slept. I didn't dream. Now that I've been told, maybe Pa'll finally leave me alone.

Travis Lee

NOVEMBER 1, A POSTCARD FROM THE RESERVE TRENCHES

Dear Bobby,

Captain called me in today to tell me that Pa's sucking flames. Go ahead and do your crying, but don't bother telling me any more about how he suffered. I see better suffering here most any day.

Kiss Ma for me. Tell her all the old lies about him being in a better place.

Thanks for the goatskin vest.

Travis Lee

Ten

November 4, the reserve trenches
Dear Bobby,

LeBlanc'd been watching me all that day. That should have set me wondering. He never said nothing to me. Well, neither of us talked. We ate lunch hunkered down in a shell hole. The Boche had thrown some mortars, and we kept having to move. It was cold and it was raining. The mud dragged at my legs, sucked at my feet. My whole body was weighted down with wet. I guess we were both tired.

And I was drinking heavy. It pains me to admit it, Bobby, but I'd been drinking hard again—ever since I'd seen what LeBlanc did to that girl. Drinking makes time go fast; and there's something nice and uncomplicated about speed, Bobby. It's got a dimwit kind of happy to it. No thinking. God. No thinking. Thinking slows you down. LeBlanc knows that.

Still, he was watching me; and I knew he was up to something. I drank anyway. My own damned fault. Drink does that to you, too: blunts importance. Muddles things.

I don't remember going to sleep that afternoon, but I remember waking up.

I was blind.

"LeBlanc?"

It was so damned quiet. But for the cold and the wet, the whole world was missing. I wondered if I'd died without knowing it and fallen into that cloying dark beyond the cypress. I stuck my dirty fingers in my mouth just to taste something. I shouted just to fill up my ears with noise.

"Hello!" I called, hoping the calico girl would hear me. "Anybody?"

She wouldn't come. My mouth was gritty from the mud I'd tasted, my throat raw from yelling. The air was too cold and clammy to be Hell. I was lying with my head higher than my feet. No Man's Land, then; and probably a shell hole. But where were our lines? Where were the Boche?

It was one of those nights when the air's nearly too thick to breathe. No rain, but damp condensed on my face, tickled down my forehead. I took a breath and thought I could smell the sea.

Something splashed through a nearby puddle. I jumped, hissed "Shit, shit, shit," groped through the darkness for my rifle, couldn't find it. My heart beat so fast that the insides of my chest quivered.

"LeBlanc!" I called. "Hey! Hey! Anybody!"

No answer—not a tracer bullet, not a flare. I wanted for shelling, longed for the brilliance, for the clamor of it. I scrabbled out of my shell hole, my eyes desperate, my body frantic. I got to my feet, mud sucking and pulling at me. I nearly toppled, nothing but black to hold onto.

"Hey!" I called.

I took a step into nothingness, went tumbling into the dark, splashed into frigid water, smelled dead fish, thought, *Gas. Phosgene gas.* Stale water made me sputter. My eyes stung. I thrashed my way to my feet. I was waist-deep in that stinking water and, God, I couldn't see.

I clawed my way upslope. At the top I hugged ground, my mind as empty as a panicked animal's.

The air was icy, there in that blackness. I lay for a long time, my teeth chattering. A sly and terrible way that LeBlanc had of killing me—leaving me drunk and sleeping. For I was bound to perish there in No Man's Land. I didn't know which direction to head for safety; if I tried to stay where I was until dawn, I'd freeze to death.

When I saw the blue glow I first thought I was seeing one

of those visions you get when it's so dark that your eyes play make-believe. Still, I crept through the blackness, over jagged trash, over things slimy and wet. My uniform caught, snagged. I was terrified that the blue would evaporate like a mirage when I got closer, but it lingered: a small, contained patch of color. The ethereal sort of blue the sky turns at twilight.

It was a corpse. A Boche. His skull was cerulean. The tatters of skin left him were the complex hue of the ocean. A god of a creature, Bobby. His hands were open. Maggots shone like golden suns in his palm.

I raised my head and I could see, Bobby. Sweet Jesus, it was beautiful. Across the torn field, bodies gleamed a calm, tender indigo. Rats raced among them, brilliant earthbound meteors. Even the soil teemed and sparkled with life. My own muddy hand burgeoned with it.

I watched a sentry peer over the Boche sandbags—glowing like a yellow petal backlit by sun.

I stood up, but the sentry didn't raise his rifle. When I looked back at my own trenches, I witnessed a golden angel on the parados take a fiery piss.

So I started home, slogging through the glittering mud, past shell craters where brilliant existence twinkled on the water. Past last season's bones shining gas-flame blue. Beyond the British sandbags, our sentry was a beacon. Goodson, I saw as I got closer. He didn't hear me until I was nearly on him.

He raised his rifle quick.

"No," I said. "Don't shoot."

He peered so hard, Bobby. Confused and frightened. Awed by me, maybe.

"It's just me, Goodson."

"Gorblimey! Stanhope? That you, Stanhope?"

I climbed over the sandbags and into the sizzling incandescence of his candle. He was so bright, I had to shield my eyes.

Then Goodson was yelling. "Sergeant! It's Stanhope! Thought he was a ghost! But it's bleeding Stanhope, Sergeant, standing right in front of me!"

Riddell came sparkling down the trench. He grabbed me

by the arms. "You all right, lad? Stanhope, you 'ear me? The boy's freezing! Get 'im a blanket! Sod all! Get 'im some tea!"

Riddell took me to his dugout. A universe away, he was shouting orders. "Nash? Best get Lieutenant. Bring 'im 'ere. Go tell Captain that Private Stanhope's been found alive."

Blackhall came. Then Miller. They asked me questions and I answered. When Miller and Blackhall left, Pickering and Calvert came in. They shook my hand. They clapped me on the back. Filthy as I was, Pickering hugged me. On Riddell's order, they accompanied me to the medical dugout. The doctor's assistant gave me a cot, a bucket of warm water, a couple of towels, and a change of clothes.

When everyone left, I scrubbed down, dried myself in the warmth of the brazier. Alone, I watched the mud wall gleam. The intensity of it, Bobby. Life, every place I looked. I slept cradled in it. When I woke, the vision had faded. Just as well.

They kept me a day. When I was released I was told that Miller wanted to see me. I found him in his dugout, reading field reports.

"Now that Blackhall is not about, you should have no fear to tell me: What actually happened out there?"

"Like I said, sir: LeBlanc and me just got separated."

"I have not discussed my suspicions with Blackhall, but it would not surprise me to find that you were drinking, and that LeBlanc was annoyed enough to leave you where you had passed out." His doubting eyes searching, still searching.

"You're right, sir." His fiancée smiled at me from her perch on the wall. A girl with fire in her. A golden, blazing girl.

He nodded. "Well, I should think your night out has been punishment enough. Still. Intolerable of LeBlanc to report you dead. Despite how Command feels about him, something will be done about it, I can assure you."

"I know I been a worthless shit, sir. That's going to change."

He looked at the picture, then at me. Was it jealousy I saw, or caution? I could never steal her from him. Didn't have the elegance, the breeding. Wouldn't embarrass him like that.

"I say, Stanhope! Would you care to see the letter I had

started to your family? Worked bloody hours on it. Brilliant piece of prose, actually. Someone should get the good."

I took the paper. Address neat in the upper left corner.

Mrs. Leon Stanhope
Box 56
Harper, Texas

My dear Mrs. Stanhope:

I regret to inform you that

Then nothing.

"Worked literally hours. Stared at the paper. Nibbled on the pen. Hadn't the least idea what to say. Hate to write them, you know. One more of your adventures, and I'll force you to write your own."

"Please, sir. If it happens, write to my brother. Tell him I died of a hard-on."

He laughed, shook his head. "Dismissed, Stanhope. Report to Lieutenant Blackhall."

"I'm not going to be drinking anymore, sir. I learned my lesson." Truth was, Bobby, I'd seen something that made me scared to drink, for fear I'd be throwing something magnificent away.

"Yes, yes." He waved his hand. "Whatever you wish."

Blackhall was waiting in his dugout for me. "Poof squabbles," he said. "Won't 'ave you and LeBlanc working together no more. Nothing bloodier than two fairies fighting it out. Besides, I figures you and LeBlanc got something to 'ide, ain't you?"

"He beat and raped that bakery shop girl, sir."

"I knows that. Knows you was there, too. Confronted 'im wif it. 'E as much as told me."

I shook my head. It didn't matter.

"When you takes up sharpshooting duty again, you'll be going out wif another gentleman, name of 'Arold Crumb, a bloke I knows from the old days. 'E'll keep you on the straight and narrow, 'Arold will."

I saluted.

"Didn't dismiss you as yet, Stanhope."

"Sir."

"Seen this before, two blokes as got a secret between them. One always ends up murdered, seems to me. If LeBlanc ends up wif a shiv in 'im, I'll know 'oo did it."

I didn't go looking for LeBlanc this time. He didn't go looking for me. Whatever tie we once had had been severed. Through the grapevine I heard that he'd come back from No Man's Land with my rifle. Said he'd seen with his own eyes that I caught a mortar round. The bastard. Still, look what he gave me, Bobby. For an hour or two I was surrounded by splendor.

Travis Lee

NOVEMBER 4, A POSTCARD FROM THE RESERVE TRENCHES

Dear Bobby,

Well, LeBlanc pulled one of his crazy stunts and they made him shit wallah for it. Hear tell he hates the duty, ha ha. Nye's not all that enraptured with him, either.

I was a couple of days off duty. When we're back at the front, I'll be plinking Boche in No Man's Land with some hardass named Harold Crumb.

Travis Lee

NOVEMBER 6, THE RESERVE TRENCHES

Dear Bobby,

The shelling's picked up. The rain has, too. The communications trenches have collapsed, but there's no sense digging them out again. The earth doesn't have any hold to it anymore. Flanders is tired, Bobby. Rain and shells have beat it down. Corpses have softened it. Walk to the rear now, and you go overland, dodging whizzbangs and daisy-cutters, slogging around craters and their pools of sludge-yellow water.

Pickering isn't taking things well. "Should just bloody give it up, shouldn't they? Not sportsmanlike to go on bashing us."

We were huddled in the dugout waiting for the sump pumps to start working so we could finish revetment duty. Calvert and me laughed. Pickering wasn't in the mood.

"Unenlightened sods, the pair of you. Like the bloody British Army, can't look at things reasonably. We're down and out. Only an idiot would advance in this sort of weather. Since both armies are mired, why can't we simply postpone the war until the weather improves? Done it before. Remember that time we took up residence in part of the Boch trenches?"

Calvert said, "It's effing Command that's the problem, ain't it? Leave it in my 'ands, we'd pack it in and go home."

Pickering brightened. "Yes! Let's!"

Calvert and me slapped each other and howled. Outside the cramped misery of our dugout, a waterfall of rain splashed down the revetments. Even the birdsong had drowned.

No way the pumps would work today. I lit the primus. Calvert picked ants out of the tea. Still, when the tea was brewed and poured, a few were left floating. I pinched mine out with my fingertips, wiped the bodies on my pants. Calvert, who once liked his tea plain, drank it down, sugar, bugs, and all.

Conversation was too heavy to lift. I listened to rain drum the sandbags. Pickering wiped an ant off his tongue, sat there looking at it. "Bloody surrounded by death. Depressing, if you ask me."

It *was* depressing, and I wanted a drink. Riddell's weed cure only blunts the need a little. I beat the craving twice already. I'm near as tired as Flanders now. The calico girl made quitting so easy that I had taken it as cheap. Damned if I didn't throw the gift she gave me away.

Listen to me, Bobby. Never drink. For to give up whiskey, you have to be strong every single minute of your life. Pa knew he wasn't sturdy enough. I think it pissed him off. Made him beat on me, maybe—knowing there was something in this world more by-God stubborn than he was. It took control of him; and Pa couldn't abide weakness, not mine, not Ma's, not his own.

I watched the bloated corpse of a rat sail the trench, bumping its nose on floating duckboard, on sandbags, until it beached on the rise of our dugout. The current nudged it around until it was facing me. Its black eyes were fixed and intent.

"I keep dreaming the same damned dream about my pa," I said. "After I heard for sure he was dead, I thought they'd stop. Bastard won't leave me alone."

Calvert opened a pack of Woodbines, passed them around. A fresh pack, but the cigarettes were stale.

I took a deep drag, sent smoke streaming out into the gray day. "Ain't that a pile of shit?"

Pickering's jaw was tight. "Sometimes I dream about Marrs."

"Don't dream, meself," Calvert said.

I asked, "What kind of dreams?"

The two looked at me. A whistle, falling down the scale. The whizzbang struck not far away. I waited for the screams. None came.

"Pickering? Tell me. What do you dream about Marrs?"

A whuffling noise above us. Calvert raised his head. Not a gas shell. A good solid crack that made the three of us jump. Black smoke trickled down the sandbags.

"So. What about Marrs?"

Pickering said, "Just a dream is all."

"It's real important."

"It's a bloody, piddling dream!"

Only a dream. Marrs stuck out in No Man's Land. Pickering holding him there.

"Stop dreaming about him."

Pickering's droll face twisted. A nightmare, then. "Blast, Stanhope! I don't *want* to bloody dream about him. Do you want to dream about your sodding father?"

"Don't dream, meself," Calvert said. "Blinking waste of time, seems to me."

I leaned toward Pickering. His gaze kept sliding away. "Got to tell me what he's doing in your dream, Pickering. Please. It's real important. You got to tell me."

His knee kept going up and down, a crazy never ending toe-tapping, like there was some ditty playing. "I see him die, is what it is."

That wasn't the answer I needed. "He died bad," I said.

"No bleeding use to dreams, far as I can see." Calvert, near the door, blowing smoke rings. "No use in remembering the sad, either. Wallowing in it. Me mum always made us look on the cheery side. Should try that, the pair of you, 'stead of nattering on about death and the like."

There was more to the Marrs story. The tension hadn't left Pickering's jaw. "Tell me the rest," I said. "He was your best friend. Tell me."

"He's all in flames the way he was. Fire up and down his arms, even in his bleeding hair. He reaches a hand out to me, and his hand's burning, too. 'Pickering,' he says. 'Do you see me, Pickering?' Of course I can ruddy well see him, clear as I saw him that night. He's on bloody fire, isn't he. Well. So. There it is. Totally useless dream."

"Grab him."

Pickering barked a shocked kind of laugh. "Will you leave off?"

"He's scared. Next time grab his hand."

"It's a *dream*! A sodding *dream*!"

"Grab his hand!"

"Bugger off!"

Calvert flicked his cigarette butt into the stream, watched it float away. "Don't 'old wif dreams and the like. Gypsy fortuneteller sort of muck."

"Marrs won't listen to me," I said. "I keep trying to tell him he's dead. He's still stuck out in No Man's Land. You got to help him."

An incredulous and betrayed look from Pickering. He shot to his feet. A sharp whistle in the air nearby, the loud crack of a whizzbang, much too close. "Off to give LeBlanc some duty," he muttered, and set off by himself in the rain.

"Like reading them books," Calvert said. "The bof of you should be out and about, instead. Fresh air and all. Bit of exercise. Books gives you notions. Bad for the 'ealth, seems to me." He lit another cigarette.

I sat watching water cascade down the sandbags. When Pickering came back, we didn't talk about dreams anymore.

Travis Lee

NOVEMBER 8, THE REST AREA

Dear Bobby,

There's not much green left. The grass sank into the mud. The trees are losing their leaves, but without fanfare. They turn a sickly yellow and fall like they're just tuckered out. I stand at the barracks window and watch them dropping. Still, there's an enchantment to it, that slow rain of leaves, the hushed gray blanket of sky, like the world is settling down for a nap.

Nothing much else to do but watch the leaves fall. It was LeBlanc's fault there was no free time this rotation. He must have known that. They couldn't single him and me out to stay behind. They didn't dare let him go to town.

I drilled with LeBlanc and the others today. We didn't look at each other. We didn't talk. After lunch, when the skies cleared a little, we watched the Maconochies beat the fire out of the Jam-Pots. I was holding the bets for Calvert. LeBlanc was standing near the goal, alone.

Pickering watched the game beside me, bemoaning the lack of whores. "My cock is wanting for a tight little cubbyhole, Stanhope," he said. A Maconochie kicked the ball across the sidelines. An agile half-step, and Pickering kicked it back. The player foot-dribbled away.

Across the muddy field, Miller was passing the time of day with Dunston-Smith and Wilson. He must have told a joke, for the other two officers burst out laughing.

"Hate to admit it, Stanhope old chum," Pickering said. "But you're looking better and better." He missed seeing a

Jam-Pot goal attempt and my brief, wild confusion, because just then Stewart Fowler sidled up.

"Well, Fowler. You're looking lovelyish, too," Pickering told him.

I picked up the conversational thread in time to explain. "He's missing his whores."

"Oh." Fowler's puzzlement cleared. He stepped back, eyed Pickering head to toe. "Ain't you a charmer? Got *pinard*, if you've a mind."

Pickering grabbed for the canteen. "Fair stolen my heart. Must wed you. Do remind me." He put the canteen to his lips, upended it. Cheap red wine dribbled out the sides of his mouth.

"You're spoken for, I hears." Fowler took the canteen back, handed it to me. "Stanhope here's available."

"No, thanks." I waved it away.

"Me heart's broken." He shoved the canteen back.

I could smell it—a raw, harsh wine. A wine with a bite to it. The need came on me so strong that it near tore my guts out. "Quit! I don't want nothing to drink!"

Pickering turned, beaming. "Oh, right-o! Good on you, Stanhope! Deserves a kiss."

Before I could escape, he threw his arm around my neck, pulled me close, and planted a big wet one on me. I shoved him away, scrubbed my cheek with my sleeve. "Shit! God-damn it, Pickering! Stop that!"

Across the field, Miller seemed taken aback. Dunston-Smith was smirking. Blackhall's eyes had narrowed. The enlisted won't believe it, but the officers sure will. Old Travis Lee Stanhope done got himself a new boyfriend. As many girls as have delighted in this pecker of mine—ain't that a pisser?

Travis Lee

NOVEMBER 8, A NOTE FROM THE RESERVE AREA

Dear Bobby,

I'm sorry for that next-to-last postcard. Didn't mean to make light. Tell Ma I'm glad he had a nice funeral. Tell her it doesn't matter that not a lot of people showed up.

Leastways I know all them old church ladies were in attendance, the biddies who go to weddings or funerals just so they can be stepping out. And whether or not Pa's conversion took, it's good to have them Baptist hymns for planting: "Shall We Gather" and "I Walk Through the Garden Alone." They're good solid songs you can lean on.

Your letter was nice, and I'm sorry I rode you hard for it. I don't hold forgiving Pa against you, Bobby. Fact is, it makes me happy that he never overburdened you with mad. Maybe you can be more content with what life brings you. Maybe sense will come easier, too.

Travis Lee

NOVEMBER 10, THE REST AREA

Dear Bobby,

The boys' last day for playing football this rotation, and it rained buckets. It was so muddy that we didn't even drill. The officers went back to their barracks; we went to ours. Every rifle is clean. Lord knows we made enough jam-pots and Battye-bombs. Now the platoon's lounging around playing cards. A few are reading. Those that have to are mending socks.

I've been thinking about you. It was past time for that apology, but Pa's death just caught me sideways for a while. You talk about how you wish I was there. Well, I wish I was, too. Still, you're wrong to think you need me. You've done just fine so far. Don't let nobody, not Ma, not the preacher, tell you different. While we were growing up I know that Ma always treated me as the clever son, you as just the good; but if I was smart, I wouldn't be here. I wouldn't have thrown that scholarship away. Goddamn it, Bobby. There won't be another chance for me, no matter what I promised Ma. No matter what the deans at Harvard said.

It's not a choice of wanting to. Something—the shelling or the bullets—have ruined me. It's hard to sit still. My eyes lose their focus. My mind's dulled to everything except survival. I can hardly make the lines of Keats and Wordsworth make sense.

Pickering said he joined the army to please his father. Calvert said he thought he owed something to his country. I just wanted out—out of the ties of family, out of the damn Yankee East. What a worthy reason to die.

Seems like lately I been treating you the way Pa treated me, only without the fists. That kind of bullying is handed down. Please, Bobby. Let the family tradition end here with me apologizing and you letting it go.

We just now had mail call, the only bright spot in the day. I was left empty-handed again. It's okay, Bobby. I know you're busy; know you don't hear much from me anymore. I'm hoping that when the war's done and you see the letters I didn't send, you'll realize I never once forgot.

Letter or not, though, mail call's a happy time. Pickering got saltwater taffy from his wife. I ate so much I nearly got sick.

After lights out I heard sniffling. It happens sometimes: bad news at mail call. I knew Willie Whittington's sister had been sick. I was hoping the crying I heard wasn't his, but I didn't dare ask.

I was surprised to hear Goodson's whisper in the dark, "What's it?"

Damn. If the weeper had wanted us to know, he'd have told us. We're pecker to cheeks here, Bobby, but a man's allowed his own bubble of privacy.

The soft sniveling sounds went on. Above my head, a slow rain pattered on the canvas roof.

Goodson's disembodied voice again, insistent. "Come on, then. Tell us. What's your name?"

"Blandish, sir." The new boy. Hadn't been issued his privacy yet. Blandish sounded so damned young.

Through the dusky shadows of the barracks came Pickering's snort. "Not 'sir.' Henceforth, Blandish, please address Goodson as 'sod.' "

A creak of wood as someone shifted their weight. "Go on. What is it?" Goodson again.

"I'm homesick," the boy said.

Quiet, except for the hollow tapping of the rain.

Then the boy, sobbing again. "You just don't know how it is, being homesick."

Wind rattled the door softly, made its icy way around the ill-fitting jamb. The air smelled of coming frost. The room was warm with the heat from the coal stove, the body warmth of the resting men. I pulled my blanket tighter.

"No," Pickering said into the darkness. "Don't know balls about it. Love it here. Particularly like the shelling."

Calvert. "Fond of them gas ones, meself."

Hutchins. "Me? It's all that flaming mud."

From his corner, Riddell said, "Leave it be."

A polite wind. The door shook gently on its hinges. The weather drummed delicate fingers on the canvas. Then Orley said, "Can't get enough of that Maconochie."

Chuckles splattered around the room. "Settle it down," Riddell said.

We slept, lullabied by the drizzle and the new boy's muffled weeping. I woke before dawn. It had stopped raining. I got my coat and went outside. Under the glow of the lamps, the ground sparkled with frost. I huddled by the barracks wall in the placid yellow light of the lantern, and I finished this letter to you.

Love you, Bobby. Don't say it near enough. We'd all of us cry for home if we could.

Travis Lee

NOVEMBER 11, THE RESERVE TRENCHES

Dear Bobby,

We marched to the reserve trenches today. Tomorrow, we'll head to the front lines. Not much marching to it, really. It's staggering, it's sliding, the mud working every step against you. The rain weighs down your pack so that you can hardly stand upright. Takes a whole day to travel what used to take half a morning. Fighting the mud steals your wind. It leaves your legs quivering and weak. They give us breaks every hour. Every time I sit down I wonder if I'll have the strength to get up again.

That afternoon I found myself slogging next to the new boy. Blandish and me struck up a conversation. I'd forgotten his voice. It was only his weeping that I remembered.

He had a delicate-featured, earnest face and no hint of a beard. "God almighty. How the hell old are you, anyway?"

"Sir?"

The new boys and me—always a problem in translation. "You. How old?"

"Oh. Eighteen, sir."

He was lying by two years, if not more. He slipped on a rough patch and went down. I watched him struggle to get up, finally gave him a hand.

"You're the Yank," he said.

"I'm the American."

Ahead of us, Pickering slogged beside Calvert. They were taking turns cussing.

"Lieutenant told me to stay away from you."

"He did, did he?" Blackhall was gone to some sort of meeting, leaving us to slog it out in the mud with Riddell. I suspected that him and the other subalterns would catch themselves a wagon ride to the trenches.

Blandish was staring at me. I started wondering what else Blackhall had said. A strange feeling, knowing you got a reputation. Right then a Jack Johnson came humming down, exploded with a sullen bang fifty or so yards away.

"Crikey!" Blandish yelled. He hunched his shoulders, looked skyward.

Pickering and Calvert turned. "What's it?" Calvert said.

I rolled my eyes. "The Jack Johnson."

They laughed, shook their heads, and fought onward through the muck.

Another low thrumming made Blandish peer anxiously about.

"Settle down. It won't hit us," I told him.

It hit a good seventy yards to the right, sent a gush of dark mud and smoke upward.

"Gor." He sounded awed.

It struck me that the boy wasn't acting strange. We were. Shells were falling. The only sane reaction was fear. We were a whole company of lunatics.

"You're brave," Blandish told me.

I laughed.

"No. All of you. Wish I could be brave like that."

It wasn't courage. It was adaptation. It was damned lethargy. Another Jack Johnson came down. Pickering slipped. Calvert caught him.

The shell hit, closer this time. Calvert said, "Gor lumme!"

To our backs, McWhorter's irate "Stanhope! Will ye nae go shoot that fooking muggins oov a gunner?"

A low pitched drone set my head bones to buzzing. "Pickering!" I barked. I grabbed Blandish's arm and pulled him fast and hard to the right. By the time the shell hit, we were clear.

"Buggering Boche mug!" McWhorter shouted. I looked back at him. He was pockmarked with mud.

The boy had halted. His face was ghastly and waxen. First I thought shrapnel had got him, and then I realized what had wounded him was fear.

I grabbed his bandolier and dragged him along with me.

"I can't." He was trying his best to get away. "Please, sir. I can't no more." I don't know where the hell he thought he'd run to. He was leaking tears.

I kept hauling him along. It started to rain, and a while later the shelling stopped. Under a feathery overcast sky, Riddell gave the order for a break. My legs went out. I sat down hard, nearly pulled the kid down with me. My fingers had cramped around his bandolier.

The boy sat down beside me, still leaking those fat, pathetic tears. I loosed my straps, let my pack fall off my shoulders. I got a piece of Pickering's saltwater taffy out of my pocket and handed it to him.

"Wipe your nose, willya? You got snot and stuff."

Blandish popped the candy into his mouth, rubbed his face with his sleeve. "He said I was to keep me eye on you, Blackhall did. Said you was a drunkard and rotter of a K.B.B. Said you'd make trouble."

"Well, shit on Blackhall, too." I got myself out a Woodbine, lit up.

"You seems a regular enough gent, though, for a Yank. A bit of all right, really. You brassed him off or sommit, sir?"

Miller was coming down the row, riding that sorrel of his. "Brassed him off," I agreed.

The gelding was slipping every few steps. Fear of the mud had made the horse go lathered and wild-eyed. Every time he lost his footing, he'd jerk his head. Miller had a rain slicker on. The wind was flapping it. The gelding didn't like that, either.

When he was abreast of me, Miller reined in. "Stanhope? Where is Sergeant Riddell?"

"Up ahead." I pointed. He knew where Riddell was. But he saw the new boy, saw me sitting by him. Miller was keeping an eye on things. "Best take that martingale off that sorrel, sir. He needs his head in this mud."

"Haven't the time."

"I'll do it." I flicked my cigarette way and got up, bitching and groaning.

"I'd prefer you not get under him," Miller said. "You'll get yourself trampled."

I stroked the gelding's withers. He was blowing and trembling. He looked around at me, as far as the martingale would allow. I scratched his nose. He rubbed his velvet muzzle into my hand.

Miller laughed. "I do believe he remembers you."

The horse watched as I got under his belly, watched me unbuckle the strap from the cinch. Strap in hand, I reached around Miller's leg, my head pressing against his thigh.

At my touch, Miller tensed. The gelding started.

"Easy, easy," I said, as much to the horse as to Miller. I moved on slow and gentle, gathering leather, till I got to the chest strap. "Give me your reins," I told Miller quietly. He did. I pulled the reins through, handed them back. "There," I said. "He'll like that some better."

"I should suppose you'll take that with you," Miller said, "as I myself have no place to carry it."

I put the martingale over my shoulders.

"You're welcome, sir."

"You are thanked, Private."

We saluted each other, and he rode away.

I went back to Blandish, collapsed down in the mud next to him. He was watching me, round-eyed. "Captain spoke to you like you was a mate or sommit."

"No, he didn't."

"Strange thing, innit? You two so chummy and all."

"We're not chummy." He made me uncomfortable. I lit up another cigarette.

"Go on. All the men here, and he stops and talks to you. All that cheeky 'you're welcome, sir' of yours. As much as ignoring his orders. Don't see him talking like that to nobody else."

I took a drag off my Woodbine, sucked it in until the smoke hit bottom. It felt good, but not as good as a drink.

Blandish laughed. "Chums with the captain. Thinks I know now how you brassed Lieutenant off, sir."

Smart kid. Guess he's figured out a little part of the answer, at that.

Travis Lee

NOVEMBER 14, THE FRONT LINES

Dear Bobby,

The day before we jumped the bags together, I met Harold Crumb. Riddell introduced us, and we shook hands. He was older than standard Emma Gee fodder, forty or so. Old enough to know better. And he was so green that the new hadn't worn off his uniform yet.

I asked him if he was okay with the duty, and he said he was. I told him to meet me in that same firebay the next morning, that we'd go out into No Man's Land a hundred yards or so. He didn't blink.

When Harold came yawning down the trench the next morning in the dark and the drizzle, I asked if he was planning on taking that haversack he was wearing.

He set his lantern on the firestep. "Needs a 'aversack."

"Them Boche boys'll just shoot it off you. Stuff your food in the gas mask pouch there. Take your canteen and your field scope. Follow me. I reconnoitered us a good trail yesterday."

I watched until he'd stripped down some of his gear, then I climbed the ladder and set off into the dark. I'd gone a ways when I realized I didn't hear him behind me. "Harold?" I called. He didn't answer. I turned around and headed back. About six or paces later, I stepped on him.

He yelped.

"What you doing down there, Harold?" I asked.

" 'Ands and knees is what we're told."

"It's dark." The world was black the way it can only be at three o'clock in the morning. "Them Boche ain't gonna see you."

I heard squishing. Then he was on his feet beside me. "But best to crawl, ain't it? No telling what's out there. Can't see me 'and in front of me bleeding face."

"I reconnoitered us a trail, like I told you."

I sang so that he could follow. Not as good a voice as Marrs, not as pretty a song, either. " 'Shall we gather at the ri-i-iver,' " I thought of Pa decked out in his finest, pale hands folded, surrounded by flowers.

Behind me Harold said, "Can't put a bung in it? They'll blinking 'ear us."

I imagined the funeral Pastor Lon had given, a long sermon, one from "no one knows the hour" to "washed in the blood of the lamb." All Pastor Lon's funerals were altar calls. " 'The beau-ti-ful, the beau-ti-ful ri-i-iver.' "

Old Harold must have been scared to stay close. He wandered off the trail a few yards. I heard a thud as he fell. Heard a splash. Heard a resigned "Blast." Must have found a shell hole.

" 'Gather with the sa-aints at the ri-iver.' "

Behind me. " 'Old on! 'Old on a tick, Private Stanhope!"

I listened to him wade toward me through the mud. Too old for this kind of war. He was puffing and blowing.

"Sing along with me, Harold. 'That flows by the throne of God.' "

He didn't sing, but after his little dip, Harold stayed close. I found us a nice bit of shelter, one that wasn't flooded. I spread the tarp and settled down.

Day was coming on. The sky was turning pearly. Birds started to chirp. I looked up at him. "You need to get your head down now."

He seemed more afraid of me than he was of the Boche.

"I ain't no poof, Harold. I'm not going to go sticking my hands in your pants. Promise."

It was what he wanted to hear, I guess. He plopped himself down, not as close as a spotter should, but still.

That morning I snapped a couple of shots off—not any good targets, but I dinged some helmets. The day stretched, long and boring. Harold didn't want to talk at first, but by noon I got him jawing. Seems he'd been a flatfoot back home. Blackhall had been his sergeant.

"Beat cop, huh. Why'd you join up?"

He tipped back his helmet. His face was all dry washes and gullies. "Me wife left, didn't she."

Was it suicide he wanted, or lost-youth adventure? He shouldn't have come. He was a pitiful excuse for a soldier. I had to show him everything: how to move from defilade to defilade, how to hold the spotter scope so it didn't reflect the light. He would have ended up with an array of head holes if I hadn't kept pushing him down.

But he was a good cop. At lunch, he said he'd left his canteen behind and asked for a sip from mine. Took a real cautious first sip, too.

"I don't drink no more, Harold," I told him.

He pretended he didn't hear me. He handed the canteen back, wiped his lips. "Can't abide the bleeding chlorine."

While we ate, he fished around conversation-wise, found out in a sneaky way what I thought about women.

"I fuck 'em nice, Harold. I don't rape 'em, if that's what you're asking. It was Pierre LeBlanc who beat that girl. Now, I know Blackhall looked at our boots. I know he told you what he found. I figure he wants to nail somebody for the rape, and since he can't get LeBlanc, he's out to get me. Doesn't like me worth a good goddamn, the lieutenant doesn't."

At this point Harold was looking a little scared. Well, shit, Bobby. I was the one with the gun.

"Head down!" I snapped.

He ducked, but he was still kind of pop-eyed.

"Harold? I'm just going to tell you once. I'm not a poof. More than anything else on God's green earth, I like to fuck women. I never raped one. I used to be a rummy, but I don't drink no more. Won't bother me if you want to check my canteen every once in a while, but I wish the hell you'd bring your own. Now. We're gonna have us a day out here of sharpshooting, Harold. We'll have us the rest of our lunch and a little dinner, and when the sun sets, we're going back. That okay with you?"

He nodded.

And that's exactly what we did.

Travis Lee

NOVEMBER 16, A POSTCARD FROM THE FRONT LINES

Dear Bobby,

Harold Crumb's not the hardass I thought he'd be. It took us a couple of days to settle in, but now we get along fine. He's a good, solid spotter. Doesn't get spooked when they toss mortars our way. Doesn't go horsing around like LeBlanc did, either. His only drawback is a predilection for puns.

Travis Lee

NOVEMBER 17, THE FRONT LINES

Dear Bobby,

For a long time now the graveyard's been with me in fits and starts: a glimpse of whitewashed steps leading down, leaves settling across the gray shoulders of an angel. But last night I went and stayed a while.

The sun was going down; the light had turned the mausoleum's dome the delicate hue of a shell. Leaves were falling—from that close sky of branches, a gradual rose-gold snow. I wondered how the nights were here. Had to be a quiet sort of majesty: The marble angels would glow, the flowers glitter.

In the pink twilight by the mausoleum's iron gates Dunleavy was waiting.

"I came back," he said, "to tell you something."

I searched the peach-colored twilight for the calico girl. The steps, the terraces, were empty.

"Something very important," Dunleavy said.

Leaves were strewn across the mausoleum's floor, had gathered in piles of tarnished brass in the corners. Across the tile, watery blue light shone.

"Something in here." Dunleavy pressed the flat of his hand to my chest. Power surged through me; it tingled down my arms. The force of it rooted my feet to the spot. When he dropped his hand I felt abandoned, like Blandish had the night he cried.

"It will be all right, Travis," he said.

It would. Dunleavy had put all that power inside me somehow. I could feel it churning.

When I woke up, I got my rifle, my satchel. I met Harold at the firebay. We set out across No Man's Land.

When Harold got to the wire he made some pun about playing a concertina. Then he said he'd been looking slanty-eyed through the scope and spied a Chink in the Boche defense.

I just didn't feel like talking.

The sun rose in shades of drear. Harold said he'd gotten

to hugging on his housewife bag in his sleep and pricked his cock right fair on one of his pins.

I thought about the tender hue of light in the graveyard, remembered Dunleavy's hand coming down on my chest, that stunning rush of power.

"Quick, Stanhope! Two meters left of the forward sap."

A Boche was there, peering through field glasses. An officer, by the looks of the shoulder patches. I raised my rifle, found my target, but I couldn't pull the trigger. That clear target: a Boche officer, his face as bright as a candle flame.

"Shoot!" Harold hissed.

Beautiful, the living. Fragile as a match in a wind.

"Stanhope?"

I turned. Harold Crumb shone. The mud behind him twinkled. I put my rifle down. "I'm sorry."

"You all right?"

I handed him the rifle. "You take him." I wouldn't watch, couldn't bear to see that flame wink out.

"Couldn't 'it me Aunt Tilly's broad bum. 'Ere. 'Ere." Gentle-voiced as Dunleavy was in my dream. "Wrap the tarp over. Bloody cold. 'Ave yourself a bit of a lie-in. Nobody's to report."

I closed my eyes and smiled. Old Harold. How quick he'd made the change from cop to soldier. That day I didn't fire a single shot, and when dark came we slogged back to the trenches.

Harold caught my arm before I walked away. "No need to tell 'im."

"Got to. Ain't going to get no better. I can feel it." And I went to see Blackhall anyway.

"Lost my nerve, sir," I said.

His dugout was as cramped as an enlisted's. He was perched on a crate of whale oil, and he didn't bother to ask me to sit down.

"Never knew you 'ad any."

"Lost my belly for killing, sir, is what I mean. Me and Crumb were out there all day, and I couldn't snap off a single shot. Ask him. He'll tell you."

Blackhall plucked his pipe out of his pocket, blew through the stem. He took out his tobacco and started packing the bowl. God, I was tired. I stood there, dull-headed, and watched him.

He lit the pipe, gave it a few long pulls. "You'll shoot soon as they starts shooting at you."

"Don't think I will, sir. Don't think I can kill anyone again, is what it is."

"Too late to be painting yourself a bleeding conchie."

"Permission to see Captain Miller."

"Denied."

"Permission, sir."

He sucked furiously on his pipe. The dugout was blue with tobacco smoke. "Bleeding cheeky soak," he muttered.

"Haven't been drinking. I figure Harold Crumb's told you that."

"Go on. Get out. Go where you wants."

And so I went. Miller was friendly like he usually is. He asked me to sit down and listened patiently to my story. I told him everything, about LeBlanc leaving me in No Man's Land, about me waking up drunk. I talked about how the mud sparkled, about how the Boche officer glowed like a candle. When I was finished, he frowned and offered me a cup of tea. I took it, saw that my hands were steady. No wonder. There was all that power in me.

"Had you been struck on the head recently, Stanhope? No? A fever perhaps? You certain? Well, best to sleep on it, what? I'm sure everything will seem less formidable to you in the morning."

"No, sir." I looked up at his girl. "Don't think it will."

"Not to be tiresome about it, but you *did* realize when you were sharpshooting before that the Boche were alive?"

Said that way, it was funny. I laughed.

"Quite. You see my point."

"Yes, sir. But it was like *Adonais*, sir. You know where he talks about life staining the white radiance of eternity? And how death tramples it to fragments? I know it sounds silly, sir, but that's the way it was."

Earl Grey tea. No sugar. It tasted elegant, I thought.

He said, "Shelley would have made an abominable soldier."

I laughed. He didn't.

"Can't win a war without killing people."

"I understand, sir."

He sighed, sat back, and studied his fiancée's picture. I wondered if he loved her; if he put the photo up as reminder or camouflage. "Cushy duty, sharpshooting."

The vision had faded hours ago, but it had left a deep calm in me, like the calm you feel after exhaustion. Even if they were shelling, I could have put my head down on my arms and gone to sleep.

"I feel I must ask: Have you considered, Stanhope, that you might be insane?"

"Every day since I been here, sir."

That got a smile out of him, but it was quick to die. "If you will not fight, you do realize that I must assign you to litter carrier duty."

He looked pained. He was holding his cup in both his hands as if he was cold, and he was watching me over the steam.

"Yes, sir. I know that, sir."

"Terrible job, that."

I grinned. "Not as bad as shit wallah."

"Do not make light of this. You will force the issue."

"Have to, sir. I'm no use to you out there anymore."

He put his cup down, picked up his pencil, toyed with it. "Tomorrow we are to pull back to the reserve trenches. I will make this a temporary assignment only, Stanhope. Do you understand? It will not be permanent until you request it for a second time."

I finished my tea, stood up. "Yes, sir. Thank you, sir."

"Stanhope?" He cleared his throat, contemplated his cup. "My concern is not with my totals."

"I know that, sir."

But I saw it in his eyes, Bobby. The resentment. I have forced him to give an order he thinks will kill me.

Travis Lee

NOVEMBER 19, A POSTCARD FROM THE RESERVE TRENCHES AID POST

Dear Bobby,

I've been assigned to noncombatant duty. Notice the new address. I'll have the same company, but a different platoon.

Do me a favor. Buy me a mess of that pecan brittle Jewel Liddy Washington makes. Wrap it up good in waxed paper. Send me enough for my old chums. I want to leave them something to remember me by.

Travis Lee

NOVEMBER 19, THE RESERVE TRENCHES AID POST

Dear Bobby,

Two nights ago I sat on a Fray Bentos crate in our dugout while the boys gave me a going-away party. Everyone came. Blackhall said he'd close his eyes to the rum as long as no one got sloppy. The Boche cooperated by not shelling. We had us a grand time.

Pickering and Calvert lit all our candles, so our nook was bright and warm. They put the primus on for tea. Hutchins and Orley and Goodson came by, shook my hand. They told me they wanted Blighties, as if I could order them up one. Riddell stopped for a minute to solemnly wish me luck.

Little Blandish stayed a while, had one drink too many. His smooth-cheeked face was flushed and he was giggling. He was a happy drunk, careless as a puppy. Not like Pa, not like me. He kept hovering. I pushed him away nice as I could.

"Come on. Come on, sir. Drink up." Blandish shoved a cup at me so hard that rum splattered my coat, my pants. The fumes rose, made me dizzy with wanting.

Then Harold Crumb was shoving him aside. "Sergeant!" he called. Riddell came wading back down the trench. "The boy 'ere might need a walk in the weather."

Riddell agreed. He snatched Blandish up by the coat collar and led him away.

Harold leaned down, whispered, "Come out, Stanhope. Needs a talk wif you."

I got up. Outside the overhang of the dugout, the rain had stopped, the air was sodden and stank of piss. I followed Harold down the trench to the traverse, wading through the ankle-deep water. At the corner, in the light of a lamp, Harold stopped. He was shivering a little.

"Talked to Lieutenant about you," he said.

I was cold, too. I hunched, clapped my gloved hands.

"You're a bit of a peacock, and a cheeky, insulting blighter. Must be Yank 'abit. Sometimes I wonder if you even knows 'ow brazen you are. Looks people straight in the eye and tells them what you thinks. By the by, don't appreciate you calling me 'Arold."

"Sorry." I felt ashamed, Bobby. He was right. I wouldn't ever have taken that liberty at home.

"Still, you knows what you're about out there. While we was working together, you took care not to get me shot. Appreciate it. Lieutenant sent me out wifout any training. Shouldn't 'ave done that."

"He just wasn't thinking."

"No excuse."

Right again: no excuse. Not for an officer. Not in war.

" 'E was thinking like a copper, Stanhope."

I blew on my cupped hands, caught the clean, devastating scent of liquor, drank the smell in.

"Well, you're out from under the duty. They put me on revetments, and so I'm out, too. Still, no matter 'oo your new lieutenant is, Blackhall'll be keeping a watch. No, no. Don't be glum. Chin up. Just keep your arse clean."

"But I didn't rape her."

"If Blackhall decides you're guilty, well, that's all that matters, isn't it. Seen 'im bludgeon more than one. There's a pickpocket in London 'oo'll never 'ave full use of his fingers. A burglar 'oo'll never be right in the 'ead. 'E's not a bad sort, but 'e lacks patience. Best mind yourself." He shoved his hand at me. I shook it. "Did me best, lad. Told 'im you wasn't drinking no more. Still, best watch that. You're a soak. One drink and you'll cock it all up again."

He put his hands in his pockets, regarded me close. "Wanted to tell you: This is whiskey craving you're fighting. That's all it is. Maybe you seen a few strange things. All drunks do. But whatever it was made you lose your nerve out there, want you to know there's nothing shameful in it. Still, be a while before you're back to center. You were one man before. Now you're another."

He nodded and left.

One man and now another—drunk with revelation, converted by God's own D.T.'s. I took a deep breath. The air stank and was heavy with damp. I stood, hoping the walls would sparkle. They didn't, so I waded back to my party.

It's leaving Pickering that's the hardest. At lights out, I packed my things; and he tried to give me money for my share of the primus. I refused to take it.

He'd had a couple of drinks too many. He started tossing gear around the dugout until Calvert told him to stop. When the sentry passed, we crawled into our sleeping bags. Calvert blew out the candle. In the silence I heard the patter of rain.

"If you planned to duck duty," Pickering said, "you might have done it smart."

"Wasn't planning for this to happen, Pickering."

"That's balls!" he said so loud that Calvert went to shushing him.

Mean-voiced, Pickering went on. "No one in the battalion believes you lost your nerve. They say you wanted out and are simply pretending to be bonkers. Goodson as much as said, 'Surprised Stanhope didn't go shouting that he seen the three bloody blue lights, and peace was here, and it was no more use dawdling about in the trenches.' Me, I think you cocked up for the final time. We go through litter carriers like tea packets. You're a derby duck now, Stanhope. I hope you realize."

Maybe I was crazy. I looked around at the darkness. Nothing shone. It made me lonely, that dark. Tomorrow there would be a new dugout. Deadly duty. Unfamiliar faces.

"A derby duck," Pickering said.

The next day he had a bad head from drinking, but Pickering walked me down the trench to the place where I'd climb the bags. He hugged me, then shoved me arm's length away. We stood there in the trench, under the glowering sky.

"You do not have my permission to die, Stanhope. I hope you realize."

Down the traverse I could hear the curses of men, the gritty scrapes of shovels. "Hey. I'm still part of the company. We'll be seeing each other around."

"Not on a bloody litter," he said. "Have no intentions of that."

I promised. "Not on a bloody litter." He started to wade away. I grabbed his arm. "Need to ask you something. You won't be mad?"

He went serious, the way you don't often see Pickering look.

"Did you ever grab Marrs's hand?"

That still face. The hurt in him. Then he snorted, pulled my helmet down over my eyes. "Bonkers," he said.

I guess it's the last I'll see of him for a while.

Travis Lee

ELEVEN

NOVEMBER 23, THE RESERVE TRENCHES AID POST
Dear Bobby,

Under the barrage of artillery, the barrage of the rain, the earth goes slope-shouldered and surrenders in exhaustion. When shells fall, me and the three other carriers take up the litter and go looking for the wounded. We follow the shrieks and the moans. We find men with arms yanked off them, with bellies erupting intestines. We watch while the buried are exhumed. If the boys come up alive, we take them and slog up the trench, bumping the litter around the narrow bends. We lug them through the gluey mud to the aid post; and we don't have the strength to be gentle. Broken bones gnash. Stumps spurt. Life spills out of field dressings. The wounded scream every time the litter jolts.

Four litter bearers for two hundred and forty men. A stern taskmaster, that vision. Easier to sharpshoot No Man's Land. Still, the thought of extinguishing that fire numbs me. It makes me break out in a sweat clammier than the sight of the dying. Strange how murder wasn't a sin until I knew.

The new boys and me haven't visited much. While we're working we're too busy to talk; we're too tired for conversation when we're not. Turnhill. A boy they call Mugs. One they call Uncle Tim. The things we see.

Yesterday we carried one of the corporals up from behind the parados. The field telegraph had gone dis, and he'd been running a message from Command when a daisy-cutter got him. His only luck was that the concussion had knocked him out cold. He'd been hit in the side, too. Not much blood, but his belly had started to swell.

"Won't make it," Uncle Tim said. He was all for putting down the litter. It was pouring rain. Mud was to our thighs. Hard enough to get out of that muck without dragging that dying corporal. Daisy-cutters kept dropping on us, too. I didn't bother turning to look back, but I could hear the sharp cracks as they hit.

"Put a bung in it," Turnhill said. "I knows the lad."

Mugs said, "Know him or not, he's done for. Filling up with blood like a flaming balloon."

"If he's going to die," I said, "somebody grab that message."

Mugs pried it out of his rigid fingers, handed it to me. I opened the paper. It was addressed to Miller and was signed by Major Dunn.

Your field telegraph is out, the message read. *Please attend to it.* I stuffed the message in my pocket, and we picked up the litter and floundered on.

It was a long way to the aid station. Once in a while Turnhill or Mugs or Uncle Tim would call out to "Let up for a tick. Can't let up?" and we'd put the corporal down. In the thigh-deep embrace of the mud, my eyes would close. Gradually, relentlessly, the wet earth would start dragging me under like a slow current of the sea. Then somebody would call, "Ready!" and we'd cuss, lift the litter, and struggle on.

By the time we climbed over the sandbags that day, we were so covered in mud that we looked like rough clay statues, and the corporal was dead.

Turnhill stared down at the litter, his face moronic with exhaustion. The corporal's belly wasn't swollen anymore. A crimson trickle ran down his side, had congealed in a black jelly around him.

"Oh, well," Turnhill said. "Bugger it."

We try the best we can, Bobby, but the battle's lost. It's been lost for nearly forever. When the earth falls around us, it vomits out corpses: black-faced Boche, skin loose and scummy with rot, their bright hair falling out in patches, rats nesting in their bellies. At night I roll that spine bone in my hand, round as the world, prickly as danger.

It's still sunset in the graveyard. Dunleavy's gone again, and except for me and the sleepers, the twilight most of the time is empty. But even though it's lonely, I relish being there. The air's so sweet for the breathing. I suck it down deep—all cool crystal. It's the way that I remember air used to be.

Two nights ago I saw someone skipping beyond the monuments and the trees—the little girl that LeBlanc had murdered. She was laughing. Her white wedding dress swirled. I walked toward her, but she dashed away giggling, grave to grave. Her laughter danced with her up the steps and fell down on me like confetti.

I'm so tired and the graveyard's so peaceful that I ache to stretch out on one of the marble slabs. I wonder if I would die there, sleeping. I wonder if I'd dream of Heaven.

Travis Lee

NOVEMBER 24, THE RESERVE TRENCHES AID POST

Dear Bobby,

Just when I thought I couldn't take no more, the shelling let up. The nights are quiet now. I go to sleep hearing the fading calls of "Lights out!" down the trench.

Last night long after lights-out I was curled in my tiny cubbyhole near the aid station. Feet woke me, splashing and thumping up the duckboards.

"Bloody idiot," Miller said under his breath.

For a minute I thought he was talking to me. The footsteps halted. Outside my narrow door a match flared yellow. I caught the smell of cigarette smoke.

Then I heard a *tsk* and a "Really" from Dunston-Smith. "Mustn't let on, Richard. Best not to stir things up."

A mutter of "but it's murder" from Miller, and then the clear bright words, "keep silent any longer."

A hissed "Shut up."

Somewhere out there in the dark the two were discussing LeBlanc.

They walked closer. Dunston-Smith spoke again, his tone reasonable. "Look. One does what one is ordered, Richard. Good God. You can't afford to be awkward about it."

Miller said, "Don't touch me."

"Sorry." Dunston-Smith was breezy-toned.

My shoulder was cramping. I wanted to turn over, but I was afraid they'd hear me.

"You're much too careless with your affections, Colin. Someone might see."

"And it's not careless of you to go carrying tales?"

"But Dunn refuses to do anything."

"You're bang on, Richard. And you mustn't speak up either. You haven't the bloody pull."

The two of them smoked for a while, there in the concealing dark. Then Miller said, "You know why he's chosen me again."

Not really a question. There was no answer, either.

"It's my success. It irks him. He feels he cannot afford to have me in the army, Colin. He especially cannot have me outperforming his other officers. The bastard will kill half my company simply because I am a Jew."

So this wasn't about one man and a handful of battered girls. It was a bigger and uglier crime than that.

Another *tsk* from Dunston-Smith. "You see anti-Semitism under every rock, Richard. It's becoming tiresome."

A cigarette butt hit the water with a hiss. Another match blazed. Miller said, "He speaks of bloody surprise. Does anyone believe we can surprise the Boche in this weather? The colonel should visit the trenches. He should see the state of these men. He should try to walk in this blasted mud."

Dunston-Smith let his breath out in a sigh. "Will you lead them?"

"Otherwise it's mutiny, isn't it?"

"But will you lead them?"

Miller was quiet for so long that I was sure he wasn't going to answer. Then a mutter, "Of course I'll bloody lead them."

Pray for us, Bobby. Pray that Turnhill and Uncle Tim and Mugs and me have the strength to carry all the wounded.

Travis Lee

NOVEMBER 25, THE RESERVE TRENCHES

Dear Bobby,

I thought they'd move us forward, but we stayed. Around us, shells fall thicker. We catch sleep when we can; eat when we have the time. Did Miller win us this reprieve? I'm tired of it, the slow endless shelling. I'm ready to push onward. Sometimes I think that if we go forward far enough, we'll push through the Boche trenches and on the other side the graveyard will be waiting. I'll see Dunleavy again and the calico girl. I can lie down on that marble slab I've had my eye on. God, Bobby. I'll sleep through Judgment Day.

Today we fought our way down the trench, water to our knees, and saw a soldier brought up from his mud tomb, cussing. Cries for help sent us clawing our way over the bags. There, in the pockmarked waste between the trenches, a threesome had been filling sandbags. The daisy-cutter hit them bang on as the Brits would say. Bang on. There was a kid whose head had exploded: brains dripping down his chin like oatmeal, cherry jam splatters on his lips. Another, his thick-walled heart neatly sliced open and lying atop his chest like a medical illustration. There the aorta. There the ventricles. There the empty chamber that had once held his family. I remembered a spring afternoon and Miller quoting: *Mother, whose heart hung humble as a button.* We left the dead to rot.

One boy had been left alive, and he was the worse for it. A piece of shrapnel had struck between his legs. There was only a small rip in his pants. He kept reaching down, reaching down, his palm smeared with blood. His pecker and balls were gone.

Mugs saw. He went to shaking so bad that he had to drop the litter. Turnhill looked away.

"I still there?" the boy asked.

"Yeah," I told him. Then I told him to stay quiet so we could get him on the stretcher. He kept touching himself, his hands coming away empty. "Can't feel nothing. I still there?"

We got him on the litter and started wading toward the trench, when I heard a low thrum. A shell was coming, and it was close. I could feel its vibration in the bones of my forehead, in my teeth. Mud trapped me, kept me from running. I remember looking up.

The wind pushed and I went flying. There was no pain. No sound either, but my ears would ring for hours after. I hit the mud face-first, struggled to my feet, surprised to be alive, saw Turnhill rising, saw Uncle Tim sitting up. Mugs was standing gape-mouthed, his fingers curled as if he still carried the litter.

The blast had torn the wounded boy apart. Mugs was painted scarlet with him. The mud for yards around glistened like garnet.

Uncle Tim looked down at the ruins. "All for the best," he said.

We wholeheartedly agreed.

I kept touching myself the rest of the day. That night I went to sleep with my hand between my legs, wondering how it would be to reach down and touch emptiness.

Travis Lee

NOVEMBER 28, THE REST AREA

Dear Bobby,

Just when I thought the world would end, just when I wanted it to, they pulled us back. We marched, and by the time we reached billets, the mud had left us exhausted. There were showers and fresh uniforms waiting, and our first decent meal in weeks. I slept deep and didn't dream, and the next day after inspection Riddell and Blackhall asked me to dinner.

"Captain's order," Blackhall said, not sounding happy.

Riddell seemed shy, like he was going on a date. "We'll go

to the place that makes the fish and chips, Stanhope, if you've a taste for that."

And so that's how I came to be the only enlisted man in the company to go to town that rest period.

It was almost a splendid walk, nearly like I remembered. There was the castle, there the quiet canal. But war had passed by, too. Trash lined the roadside: rusted food tins, discarded wrapping papers, burst and leaking casks. I peered hard into the grove of trees, wondering if the owl was still alive.

The town was barren but untouched—still a gingerbread confection. The bakery shop was open, an old man and woman behind the counter now. The sidewalk in front of the bakeshop smelled of cinnamon, and rounds of potato bread were piled in the window, soft as pillows. I slowed my steps so, Blackhall barked at me to "Come along wif you, Private! Come along!"

The restaurant was empty except for a handful of officers. We ordered Riddell's fish and chips, and since Miller was paying, the two of them shared a bottle of good French wine. For dessert they ordered expensive cheeses. We enjoyed a couple of rounds each of thick, sweet coffee.

When we were finally finished, Blackhall pushed his chair back, belched. He called for a brandy, asked if I wanted one. I said no. He told the waiter to pour me one, anyway. I looked down into the brandy's topaz depths, said I thought we ought to be getting back.

Blackhall sent Riddell back to billets. I pushed the brandy glass a safe distance away. After three more drinks, the lieutenant finally got to his feet and told me to come with him. Together, we walked into the gathering dark.

He didn't look drunk. Didn't walk drunk, either. Still, I remembered what Crumb had said about Blackhall's kind of justice. I'd felt it once, and was too tired to take it again. I'd die first. I'd just let my spirit go walking out of my body, and I'd wander No Man's Land until I found that graveyard.

We headed back to camp, not speaking. I heard the owl hoot, then saw the bird's lumbering flight, enormous wings beating slow through the dusk.

The last of the twilight slipped away. Near the billets, on an isolated bend in the corduroy road, Blackhall paused to light his pipe. It was misting rain. Faint and far in the distance I could hear shelling—a low, mean rumble, like a growl deep in the throat of a dog.

" 'E doesn't think you done it," Blackhall said.

I knew who he meant. "Harold Crumb's a good cop."

"You knows more than you're telling, though, Stanhope." His pipe went out. He struck a match to light it again.

"Yes, sir, I do."

The flare of the match caught his surprise.

"I'll never tell you all of it, either. It's just too goddamned shameful. But it has to do with not stopping him, even after I knew what he was doing. It has to do with me being drunk."

The tobacco in the bowl blazed red. He dropped the match. It hit the damp logs and hissed out. The night crowded about us.

"Men involved in something like that, best to keep 'em off the streets."

It was so dark on that bend of the corduroy road, the mist falling. I wondered when the sentry was due, if they'd find me dead on the logs in the morning.

"Funny thing: justice. Can't teach blokes like that. Get 'em about women, they'll do it again."

I didn't dare move, not even to step away.

He sucked on his pipe. The cinders in the bowl flamed. Through the dank air came the smell of pipe tobacco, in it a surprise hint of vanilla. "Thing of it is, Stanhope, soldiers die in raids, don't they? Most is shot by enemy, some by their own chums. Mistakes 'appen. Nothing to be done."

He knew about the coming raid. He was planning on killing me. Nothing to be done.

I thought he'd leave, but he only shifted his weight. We stood for a long time, me watching the plug of his tobacco wax and wane with the steady slow rhythm of his breath. "Sometimes men're left to die on the field," he said. "Can't carry them all, can you. Leave the badly wounded. Sometimes leave ones who can be saved. Like I says, mistakes 'appen. If it comes to it, that's the best way, Stanhope. Your 'ands is clean. Any way you decide, wants you to know I won't be going after you for it."

So Bobby, that night in the rest area, Blackhall gave me permission to murder, and then he walked away.

Travis Lee

NOVEMBER 29, THE REST AREA

Dear Bobby,

Yesterday I went to see Pickering. He looked the same, sounded the same, but there was a distance between us, like I was looking at him though glass. In the sprinkling rain, him and me and Calvert sat on crates. We smoked and talked about the old times.

"Always thought you were a bit of an arse," Pickering confessed to me.

"Always knew you was."

"Funny old you." He laughed. "Miss having you about," he said, and he wasn't laughing anymore.

I thought about the raid. There was no use telling them what was coming. "Miss you boys."

Calvert took a drag, studied the end of his Woodbine. "Ain't the same, Stanhope. Blandish moved in wif us, you know."

It hurt, knowing someone had taken my place.

"Bit of a stick, actually," Pickering said.

"Doesn't know 'is way around a kettle, and you the Yank. Shame on 'im, I says."

Pickering agreed. "You always made good tea. No idea why. Only talent. Can't tell a decent joke or make a jam and biscuit mash, handicapped by your Yankness as you are."

"Bloody 'andicapped."

They tried, but bad-mouthing Blandish didn't make me feel any better.

"Bit of an emptiness, if you want to know," Pickering admitted. "The way you feel when your bloody pet dies. All these months I've felt of you as my dog, Stanhope, I must tell you."

With my thumb and middle finger, I thunked him on his cropped head, hit him hard, caught him totally by surprise. He dropped his cigarette, tried to thunk me back. I dodged, shoved his shoulder. He slipped off his crate into the mud, caught my arm, and tried to pull me down with him. There in the cold and the rain we laughed until we were out of breath and everything was like it was again.

The three of us went together to the battalion show, heard Dunston-Smith play an ill-tuned upright piano while Miller and Wilson danced a heavy-footed chorus line. Colonel Caraway's aide stepped forward across the stage, chirped his cheery, "Oh, nurse!"

Rich folks' silliness. The audience of poor men laughed and sang along. I watched Miller close. There were circles under his eyes. Beneath his plastered-on smile lay fatigue. I watched LeBlanc, sitting near the door, on the edge of his seat, a man on the verge of escape.

When the show was over we ate dinner. Afterwards, Pickering wanted to find a card game, and I walked out alone into the drizzle. I kept to the corduroy road, went past a quiet knot of sentries gathered to their fire. I passed the officers' billets and the raucous noise, the party continuing. Miller would be inside in the warm bath of light beyond the windows, soaking up the last of camaraderie before they sent him to die.

I walked a while and pondered dying. I knew I was ready, Bobby. Miller was tired enough; and when the time came, he'd be ready, too. He'd be an inquisitive ghost, never satisfied with the "just because" answers. I pictured him standing in the mausoleum's watery light, and the image was so vivid that it was like he was dead already. This corduroy road I was traveling would be the gravel path after an autumn rain. I'd be walking up the trail to meet him, no rank between us, no wealth, no danger of scandal, no heritage. I'd just pass through the wrought-iron gates and he'd be waiting.

At the end of my log path, a paddock, a lamp hanging on the wall. The paddock was empty, the horses gathered, like their officer riders, inside the warm. Because nothing's better for loneliness than horses, I opened the stable door. There, in the scent of manure and sweated leather, an officer was sitting on a hay bale, his head in his hands, a bottle of brandy by him.

Miller looked up, swaying. "Stanhope? That you?"

"Sir."

"What time s'it?" His syllables were mushy with drink.

"Just past nine, sir."

He didn't believe me. A wristwatch officer, the sort of gentleman captain that Blackhall disliked. He shoved his sleeve up, stared stupidly at his bare wrist.

"It's a little past nine, sir. Coming on toward lights out."

He upended the bottle, took a drink of brandy. Then he must have remembered his mama's lessons. He tried his clumsy best to hand the bottle to me. "Stanhope. Private Travis . . . Travis," he managed before his tongue twisted. "Oh, bugger it. Too bloody difficult to say all at once. Still, have a go. Private. Travis Lee. Stanhope. Ah. Well done. Good show. Yes. Do join me in a drink."

"Not drinking anymore, sir."

"Ah." He sat blinking, the brandy bottle in his lap.

"Should get back to billets," I said.

Dunston-Smith's little bay mare lifted her head over her stall door and stood watching. Lamplight ran down her silken muzzle like fire.

"Sir?" I asked. "Need a hand?"

He was horror-struck. "Good God, no! Bloody hell!"

His reaction scared me. Bewildered me, too. *I didn't mean anything*, I started to say, but then he was muttering. "Damned severed hand right there in the trench. Loathe that. Can't simply vomit, can one? Not with other officers and enlisted about. Still. Must see it all the time now. Don't understand how you can manage. Forgot." He frowned for a while at his bottle.

"Forgot what, sir?"

Somewhere to the back of the stables, a horse whuffled.

Such a warm sound. A nice sound, like the cooing of pigeons, like the homey cluck of a nesting hen.

Miller waved in exasperation. "Don't know, for God's sake. If I bloody knew, I shouldn't have forgotten."

A funny drunk, but full of a strange tense melancholy, too. He squinted up at me again. His expression went cheery. "Of course! Stupid of me. Haven't asked."

"Asked?"

"Asked," he said. "Begged," he amended, stretching the word carefully over his brandy slur. "Begged me. Have you. Shan't allow it." He gave me an arch smile, waggled a finger. "Shan't, Private—bloody hell. Private Travis—and the blasted rest of it. Not if I don't want. I am your bloody commanding officer. Tell you to get your rifle, you shall. Keep your head down, that's the trick. Have you keeping your head down."

"I can't shoot, sir. The stuffing's all run out of me."

"You are shit, Stanhope." His *S*'s were muddy. He stabbed his index finger downward in awkward jabs, making his point. A spiteful tone, one that surprised me. "A complete and utter shit. Means nothing. No. Not to you. Have the power, and won't allow me to save you." He started crying. Not sobbing or nothing. Just leaking tears. He wiped them angrily away with the heel of his hand, then looked down at his damp wrist. "My," he said in quiet dismay. "Aren't I the pathetic old poof."

Damn. The admission was so embarrassing that it hurt all the way up and down my chest. I hoped he'd be drunk enough not to remember it in the morning. Down the aisle of horses, Dunston-Smith's bay mare let out a long, contented sigh.

"You know? One tries to be the best," he said.

Gently, I told him, "I know that, sir."

"Like bloody hell you do. Best one can be. Don't know how Christians can live with themselves, frankly." Troubled politeness swept him. "Oh! But one religion's every bit as good, and all that."

I studied the lamp flame: steady sturdy base, the top a thin and nervous waver.

"Every bit as good. Still, confession, what? Do over everyone, go be forgiven. Well, that's a lark. Everlasting flames of a stick. Streets of gold of a carrot. Balderdash of a theology. Complained to bloody O'Shaughnessy. Living honorably." He swung his arms wide, nearly fell backwards off his hay bale. "Is the thing. What God expects, you know. A just and moral life without any expectation of reward. Damned simplistic sort of belief: confession and Heaven and all that. My father."

"Your father," I said when it looked like he wasn't going to go on.

"My father?" He peered at me.

"You were talking about Heaven and confession and all, sir, and then you said your father."

He gazed into the shadows of the stall across the way. "Is a just and moral man. Do you understand, Stanhope?" He searched my face.

"Yes, sir. I understand, sir. We need to be getting on."

He scrubbed his mouth as if the drink had burned him. "A man came before Raba and said, 'The chief of my village has ordered me to kill someone.' Well. I muddle the story. On pain of death, you see." Miller's eyes started leaking. This time he let the tears go. I wasn't even sure he knew he was crying. "Pain of death. And so Raba answered and said, 'Let *yourself* be put to death before you kill another' or some such—but you see my point, Stanhope?—Raba reminded him, 'for it is unlawful to kill.' "

I took his arm.

He pulled away. "You do see."

"Yes, sir. It's time to go now."

A poignant entreaty. "But you do see?"

"Yes, sir. I do."

I pulled him up, but his knees didn't have any starch. He started sinking and I grabbed him. His eyes closed. His head buried itself in my shoulder.

"Sorry," he whispered.

Not just sorry for his drunk, but for the coming raid, for the way he felt about me. He knew we were too close. He tried to pull back. I wrapped both my arms around him. He was heavy. His breath tickled my cheek, lured me with the smell of brandy.

"Hold onto me, sir."

A heavy drunken arm. A needy hand clutching my coat. He opened his eyes, but our faces were so close it scared him. He squeezed them shut again. I saw the brandy bottle forgotten in the straw. Both of us, a half-step from temptation.

"Sorry," he said.

I grabbed his hand, pulled his arm around my shoulder. With my other hand, I grabbed his belt. "Come on. Let's walk a little. Get you sober."

He walked—well, at least he tried his best. Miller will always try. Weak-kneed, he shuffled, bumped against me. We walked back and forth down the aisle of the stables, the horses watching. We struggled, holding onto each other. When I knew that lights-out was near and that we couldn't afford to be away from barracks any longer, I took him out of the stables and into the rain.

Down the way at the officers' billets, the party had broken up. Three captains were sitting under a lean-to, gossiping. When we neared the light of their lamp, Dunston-Smith got to his feet.

"Dear God, Richard," he said, fussing over him like a mother.

Dunston-Smith took him from me. Miller fit perfectly in his arms. He was yawning, already half-asleep. The two other captains shook their heads and, amused, helped themselves to another tot of brandy.

Dunston-Smith, the drowsy Miller cradled against him. "Best have yourself in barracks before lights-out, Private." His voice was hushed, the way voices are around sleepers.

My voice was hushed, too. "Yes, sir. Thank you, sir."

I walked back to the barracks, but my shoulder missed Miller's weight. My nostrils still held the smell of his brandy. He was near me all night. Even now, early the next morning, I can feel him, smell him, clinging. It's not a bad sensation; not like I might have thought once. Him loving me just is. It's a small quiet thing, as without risk as the mew of a kitten. You know, Bobby, he never expected me to love him back.

Travis Lee

DECEMBER 1, THE RESERVE TRENCHES

Dear Bobby,

This morning we woke to ice. Frost bloomed in crystal fronds across elephant sheets, across canteens. The air was sharp as cut glass. Icicles hung from sandbags. Cold had stiffened everything. Voices rang in the brittle air. The walls had frozen too hard to collapse.

The Boche artillery was quiet. The morning broke chill and blue, the sun tiny and incredibly bright. The rime at the edges of the shell holes glared so intense that it made my eyes water. In that cold, hard, blinding world, Mugs and Uncle Tim made tea. About noon, high clouds rolled in and I watched the sun's dazzle filter and go hazy. By dinner, it had started to sleet—angry pellets that stung faces, that rattled against frozen ground.

We lit the brazier and set it in the door of the aid station. Turnhill piled more blankets on our only patient—a boy fighting trench-foot. I dozed sitting up, my angora vest, my greatcoat, and a couple of blankets around me.

The graveyard was empty and the sun was inching lower. In the cobalt shadows the edges of leaves were starting to sparkle. They winked slow and calm, the way lights shimmer far across the prairie or a long ways across the ocean. In the pink last of the sunlight, leaves dropped from the trees, slow as blossoms.

All up and down the steps, the graves were empty and waiting, the flowers in them piled soft and deep. At the end of the path, the calico girl was standing sentry. And right then I knew that nothing, not even the cold, would stop the coming raid. And I knew that the raid would kill us.

I regretted that I had pissed my life away. That I'd hurt

Ma, hurt you. That I'd been cruel to people. That I'd cheated and lied.

"It's love," she said, and she took my hand. Her power felt like velvet, as easy to fall into as those graves—drowsy and safe.

I woke when a medical officer bustled into the aid station, shaking the sleet from his coat. He asked if we were keeping warm enough. The question was just for polite's sake, for he didn't listen to our answers. He went to the boy's bed and flipped back the blankets.

"Needs amputating." He ignored the boy's appalled wail. "Yes. And quickly. Best take him along to hospital. There's the good chaps. Do get back as soon as you can. We'll have need of you."

The medical officer never explained why we would be needed. I didn't tell my litter chums, either. We put the boy on the litter, wrapped him in three goatskins, his greatcoat, and four blankets. We struggled through the sleet and the knee-deep muck to the rear hospital. The four of us were too cold and exhausted to talk to each other, too tired to comfort the soldier. The boy cried the whole way there.

Travis Lee

DECEMBER 1, POSTCARD FROM THE RESERVE TRENCHES

Dear Bobby,

This morning I was thinking of you and Ma and that Nativity scene she always puts up, the one where she made the straw dolls of Joseph and Mary, and Pa carved the camels. They were good camels. Too bad he never was no good at people.

Well, merry early Christmas. If anyone asks after me, tell them I'm happy enough. Whatever happens, Bobby, always remember this: I was happy enough.

Travis Lee

DECEMBER 4, THE RESERVE TRENCHES

Dear Bobby,

They shouldn't have ordered us forward in December. In England, families are getting ready for Christmas. They're buying presents, wrapping them, hiding them away. Mothers and wives will send gifts soon. No way to stop it. No way to get the word back quick enough. Gifts will arrive here to this desolate place, all wrapped in pretty paper.

Mugs and Turnhill and Uncle Tim and me made it back in time to move up with the company to the front lines. The sleet had ended. Granular drifts of it shone in the morning like snow. It nestled in the crannies of shell holes. It smoothed the angular scars of the soil.

Wading our way to the front, over our puttees in mud, a Boche Aviatik buzzed us. The bastard strafed us, too. It was more a scare and a nuisance, for the gunner had poor aim. But every time he came thundering along our line, a cry went up: "Have a bloody care!" and "Not cricket!" Finally, to the cheers of the company, a trio of BEs came flying out of the clouds and chased the Aviatik away.

We slogged on. At dusk we reached the front trenches. The Boche had put up an observation balloon, but the BEs returned to shoot it down. I saw them darting like bright wasps around a bulbous gray mushroom, saw the balloon shudder with the shots, watched it collapse in on itself and fall slow.

All the rest of that day the officers went up and down the trenches, ordering men to blacken their faces, ordering jangling metal to be taken off uniforms. Shocked complaint raced down the trench like water down a flash-flooded creek. "Raid, is it? Senseless command!" and "They'll bloody kill us!"

We were going, anyway. The British artillery started pounding the Boche around dinner time. Mugs and me loaded up with extra field dressings. When the medical officer wasn't looking, Turnhill packed a scalpel. Uncle Tim rounded up sutures just in case we'd need to leave part of the soldier behind.

The sleet had started again by the time our company went

over the top. The four of us watched them slip away. When we climbed the bags after them, we saw that the night was dark but for mortar flashes. They lit No Man's Land in pulses of light. Scenes were arrested in snap photographs: the tightness of Mug's jaw; Turnhill's slack exhaustion; a crowd of soldiers moving far ahead.

We went, the four of us sinking through the thin crust of ice and into the soft ground below. We slipped. We fell. Sleet blinded me. It rattled against my helmet. The dark horizon came alive in a sparkle of machine-gun fire—a loud and deadly chatter. Ahead of us, soldiers started to scream.

Near me, a loud grunt. The litter lurched. A mortar flashed, and I saw Turnhill on the ground.

"Take him!" Uncle Tim cried.

Mugs was already bending over. "Done for!" he shouted back.

I knelt. Shells ripped the air over our heads. The ground quaked. Flares burst, lit No Man's Land in lime-green light. I looked up, saw three bright stars above me illuminating the powdery fall of sleet. Below me, Turnhill was dying, his chest seeping darkness, his lips bubbling black.

"Bloody hell! Take him!" Uncle Tim shouted.

We had rolled him onto the litter and were carrying him away when the litter jerked fiercely. It nearly tore itself out of my grip.

Mugs said in a tight voice, "Fains I!" and I saw that he'd been shot in the leg.

Somewhere in the green night machine guns rattled. Uncle Tim grabbed Mugs by his coat and dragged him into a nearby shell hole. I took hold of Turnhill and pulled him down with me, too.

Mugs was cussing without rhyme nor reason. His foot was turned the wrong way and his face was rigid with pain. "Bastards," he was saying. "Bloody, flaming, ruddy alleymen. The lot of 'em can kiss me bum."

Uncle Tim crawled to me. "I needs to get him back." He nodded in the direction the assault had stalled. "A balls, innit."

"Yeah," I said, Turnhill motionless and bleeding in my arms.

Uncle Tim unbuttoned Turnhill's greatcoat. Below, his goatskin and shirt were soaked with blood. "Belly or liver," Uncle Tim said.

The hole in his belly was pumping, but slowly. Turnhill's eyes were closed, his face so restful that I hardly recognized him. He stank of bile. A froth of blood and vomit ran down his mouth to his chin. A dark bubble hung from one nostril.

"Can't carry both," Uncle Tim pointed out. Behind him, Mugs's cussing had wound down into tired groans. "Leave him here?"

"I'm afraid he'll wake up. Afraid he'll roll down into the water and drown. I don't think I could take worrying about that."

Uncle Tim shrugged, gazed dully out over No Man's Land, toward the crumps of mortar fire and the company's shouts for help. "No bloody use, is there?"

Not two men to carry over two hundred. "No goddamned use."

So Uncle Tim grabbed Mugs and dragged him over the lip of the shell hole. I could hear them for a while as they cussed their way though the green-cast dark.

I cradled Turnhill and rocked him while the sleet stung my face, while mortars pounded, while far over No Man's Land my company died. More flares went up. They were burning bright when Turnhill's back knotted.

"It's all right," I told him.

Head against my shoulder, he stared, gaze furious with terror. The tendons in his neck stood out. His jaw snapped shut, again, again, as if he was biting back at his pain. I pictured how the calico girl might soothe him, and I tried to do the same. Alone there in the shell hole, I took off his helmet. I wiped the blood and the muck from his face.

"They're coming for you," I told him. "I know it." I could feel the calm of their presence, all of them: Dunleavy and Smoot, McPhearson and Furbush.

"See them yet, Turnhill?"

A shudder ran though him, head to toe. His back arched, tense and rigid. Dark spume oozed from his open lips. With my thumb, I cleaned it away. "You go on now," I ordered, my voice quiet.

Amid the din of battle, the unearthly peace of that shell hole. A long, tired sigh came up from his depths. When he went, he went beautiful, Bobby—like he was falling to sleep in my arms.

Way over No Man's Land, soldiers were calling for help. I put Turnhill down and crawled, dodging the muddy spurts of the mortar rounds, skirting shell holes. I found a body with its head and shoulders blown off. Found one of the company's football players lying in two pieces, his chest still linked to his waist by the pale strings of his guts.

I came across five men retreating. We tumbled into a rank-smelling crater together.

"Order's to withdraw," Halcomb said. " 'Eard it meself. And the man what says no is a liar."

"You seen Miller?" I asked him.

They looked at me, wide-eyed as owls. "Seen an officer. 'E's what told us. Best get your arse back to trenches, too."

The Boche machine gun paused its hammering rhythm. The five were suddenly up over the lip of the shell hole and away. I kept going, came across Goodson and Hutchins dragging Kennebrew behind them. He was face-up and unconscious. Behind him trailed a heavy wake of mud. They'd taken his greatcoat off so that they could manage his sodden weight. Kennebrew was dying of cold, I figured. His belly wound wasn't bleeding much anymore.

The two waved me on, yelling, "Withdraw! Orders to withdraw!"

"Are there more wounded?"

"Raid's all phut! Done what we could, but san fairy ann!" They dragged the dying Kennebrew with them.

Driggers came running fast as he could through the muck. I grabbed the lieutenant by his gun belt as he tried to get past. "Are there wounded?"

He looked at me, incredulous. He tried to slap my hands away. "Idiot. Of course there's wounded."

"Where?" I shook him.

Emma Gee chattered. The two of us hit the ground, crawled to a nearby corpse for shelter. In the waning light of the flares, I checked, saw that the dead man was Sergeant Norwood.

"Blast this mud!" Driggers was shouting. "Can't go forward, can't bloody go back. Done for from the very beginning!" A few rounds slammed into Norwood's corpse, made it shiver as if he was feeling the cold.

"Where are they?"

He pointed left. "Three men down in a shell hole. One of our padres, too." The machine gun quieted, and Driggers was gone.

I left the shelter of Norwood's corpse, came across a boy whose name I didn't know. He was bleeding from the arm, but still moving fine. "You seen three men in a shell hole with a padre?" I asked.

He shook his head.

"Was it O'Shaughnessy?"

He waved me off with his good hand and kept going. I crawled on toward the Boche trenches. Some of our company had nearly made it there. They hung along the Boche wire where they had fallen, like coyote carcasses on a fence.

I came across a shell hole, saw Runyon lying at the edge of the stinking half-frozen water. Sleet coated his face but for the cross that had been stroked on his forehead. Further away, two heads stuck above the slime—Tower and Vining—their faces glassy, both wearing the intent blank stares of corpses. Not far from them, a reaching hand.

I inched down the slippery incline, down to where the mud had been plowed by clawing fingers. I took hold of the wrist and pulled. O'Shaughnessy surfaced, his face shattering the pool's varnish of ice. Rusty water spilled from his open mouth. His purple stole lay, stained and limp, over his shoulders.

I pulled him to me, closed his eyes, for that's what they say to do. I held him, whispered in his ear what the calico girl had taught me: "It's love."

Looking up, I saw that the sun was rising. Day was coming on, gray and chill. I heard the machine guns go quiet, the mortars fall silent, until the only noise left was the fragile moans of the wounded.

I closed my eyes and slept, O'Shaughnessy lying close at my side. Instead of walking the graveyard, I walked the corridor of home. Pa was sitting on Ma's bed, holding the toy in his hands. The silvery afternoon was so still, I could hear the tap of the sash against the window frame and the flap of the lace curtains blowing. I stood in the doorway and watched him a long time, forgiveness plucking at me. I didn't go in; and when I woke up I saw that the sun was high.

I left O'Shaughnessy, went out to find the wounded, darting shell hole to shell hole, the way I did when I was sharpshooting. I took the first wounded boy I found, a soldier I didn't know. His collarbone was splintered. One sleeve of his coat had been blasted off him. The bone and gristle of his shoulder joint was poking through.

I seized him by the lapels and pulled him along, ignoring his shrieks, pulled him past boys wounded and crawling, past dying friends begging. I left him only once, even though he pleaded for me not to. I went down in a shell hole and caught Lefleur and Morgan before they drowned.

Morgan was still conscious. He clung to my sleeve. "Crikey, Stanhope. Didn't think nobody would come."

Both his legs had been shattered by a shell, so pulverized that he wasn't even bleeding much. I tied two tourniquets around him, anyway, and settled him higher in the hole. I propped his haversack between him and the waiting water. Then I said, "Somebody'll be back."

"Can't leave me!"

I pried his fingers off, but he seized me again. "Somebody'll come real soon," I said.

He clung to me, crying. "Oh, oh, sweet Mother Mary, don't. You can't leave me here."

I tore myself free and left him sobbing. At the top of the

hole, I took hold of the boy with the broken collarbone. We went on. It was late afternoon by the time I rested. In the chorus of the wounded, I opened my iron rations and shared it with the soldier I'd chosen to save.

"You're new, aren't you? I've seen you around. What's your name?" I asked him.

"Oakes." Exhaustion had taken him beyond pain to dull-eyed lethargy. "You're that old soldier Yank. Everyone knows you."

He ate a little corned beef when I spooned it into his mouth, but he turned his head away when I offered more. There was a grayness to his lips that I hadn't noticed that morning. Internal bleeding. He'd never make it back.

"Do us a favor," he said. His voice was weak and seemed to come from a great distance, as if he was already going away. "You take a pinch of that tea and put it on my tongue?"

I did. He sucked the leaves, smiling into the glowering sky. "Sweet," he said, and I knew that he was dying.

"Sweet," I agreed.

His eyes were shut but he was still breathing when I had to leave him. The day darkened, and I couldn't tell if rain was coming or if the sun was going down. I passed Lieutenant Jonathan Call's body, barely a mark on it, horror in his eyes. I passed a knot of three men together, their splintered bones and mangled limbs joined. A few yards later, I came upon Fowler. He'd been dragging himself home. Something—either a bullet or shrapnel or a flying shard of bone—had struck one cheek and exited the other. Most of his teeth were gone. He tried to smile when he saw me.

"Stick your tongue out," I told him. When he did, I told him his tongue was torn to hell, but it was still attached. "You'll be all right. Got yourself a Blighty."

Cheerful, he nodded. Blood ran his jaw, trickled his neck. I helped him along until I came to Wren. A small boy; and he'd been sprayed by shrapnel. His back was soaked with blood. I told Fowler that he'd have to manage. I was about to grab Wren when I saw Pickering. He was lying in the open several yards away. His eyes were closed, his face blue-white.

I crawled in a panicked frenzy to him, touched his face. "Pickering!"

He looked up at me, blinked.

"It's me: Stanhope."

His voice was faint. "Made that part out."

Light was fading but we were exposed. Any minute the Boche sniper would start shooting. I grabbed him by the shoulders of his coat and started dragging him to safety. His first scream shocked me. His second scream went on and on.

When we were safe in a shell hole I shushed him. "It's okay. It's okay. I'm taking you home now."

He sighed, closed his eyes, and for a second I thought he was slipping. I wanted to grab him, hold him back. "Rather long walk," he whispered, "England."

I opened his coat, saw a plate-sized badge of frozen blood on the front of his hip. I poked my head above the lip of the shell hole, saw Wren sinking into the mud. Another few hours and he'd drown there. Fowler, in his snail's crawl, was hauling himself inexorably closer to the trenches. I looked down at Pickering. "You're freezing. We got to get back quick. I'm going to have to drag you."

His long, droll face twisted. "Stanhope?"

"What is it?"

"It hurts unreasonably, you know."

I took hold of his coat and pulled. He grunted with pain, squeezed his eyes shut. I told him, "Go ahead and yell, Pickering. Everybody does."

He was too proud right then, maybe too breathless. Still, by twilight he was openly sobbing. My arms and legs were so tired they trembled. When I came to a good hole, I fell to my knees. We drank from our canteens. I cut open his iron rations and offered him some corned beef.

He wiped his tears away with his sleeve. "That bloody monkey meat?"

"Have the biscuit, then." I held it to him.

"Attempting to kill me."

I sucked on an edge of the bread, working some moisture

into it. I flipped his coat open, checked his wound again. "Looks like a bullet," I told him. "Good that it's frozen."

"Oh, yes. So effing, flaming lucky."

"I think you got a Blighty." A Blighty. That was all.

I made him eat, and was encouraged when he didn't vomit. We sat in the shell hole and watched dark come on. After the sleet the air smelled fresh, but the mud didn't gleam. No corpses glowed. The voices in the field fell silent as the dying slipped, one by one, away. I felt liberated, Bobby. Strange, isn't it? Battle was over. So many dead. Too many wounded to carry. But Pickering and me were alive.

We drank some more from our canteens. He complained that I'd picked the wrong time to dry out. "Could do with a bit of rum, actually," he told me. "And I'm so dashed tired of the pain. Can't get the litter here?" His tone was pathetic; his voice faint.

I told him to put his arms around my neck. When I stood up, I staggered. I wasn't strong enough to carry him. I sank to my knees in the mud, thought for a minute that I'd never be able to pull my feet free, that I'd never again be able to take a step. Still, I struggled out of the shell hole and kept going, weaving like a drunk under the burden. I went, sliding, cussing, sensing our trenches so strong that it was like a searchlight in my face.

In my ear, I heard Pickering's plaintive "Hurts."

His grip weakened. I grabbed his hands before he could fall. His fingers were cold. "There once was a man from Texarkana." We'd dueled limericks from time to time. I waited for the next line, thought it was never coming, then:

"It's bloody cold."

I tripped over something, slid, nearly fell. Pickering's whimper tore at me.

"There once was a man from Texarkana. Come on, Pickering. Think of something."

"Kept his pecker in his bandanna."

"And when he was wed."

Much too soft-voiced. "Chased her from bed." Abruptly,

his head lolled, knocked against my neck. I felt the muscles in his arms, his hands, loosen.

"Pickering?" I kept going. His helmet bumped me. He would have slid from my shoulders if I hadn't clung to him tight.

"Aw, shit, no. Aw, goddamn." I kept walking across No Man's Land until I got tangled in our wire. I called down for a sapper to come cut me out.

Blackhall came running out to meet me. "Stanhope? That you, Stanhope?"

I couldn't answer. He cut me free, tried to take Pickering. I shoved him away.

"I had to bring somebody back," I told him.

"All right," he told me. "All right. Let's have him in the aid post."

I handed him down to Calvert, then jumped down myself. In the light of the lamp I saw how Pickering's head rolled on his shoulders. His once-droll face was slack and gray and strange.

"Dead, inn't 'e," Blackhall said, and I told him to shut up.

"Get the med officer, goddamn you," I said. "Wake up the fucking medical officer."

Calvert ran down the trench. I slung Pickering over my shoulder and waded through the half-frozen water. Worthy and Higgens and Dearden saw us coming and stepped out of my way. I'd bury him right, just like I'd promised. Bury him so the rats wouldn't get his body, so the walls wouldn't tumble out his bones. I'd make sure he got to the graveyard right enough, and if I didn't see him there, I'd go back out to No Man's Land and find him.

The aid station was full, a fetid place of whimpers and carbolic and vomit. I found a cot, laid Pickering down, heard the groaning sigh of his last air being pushed from his lungs.

The doctor took my arm, jerked me away. I stumbled back, yelling, "You bastards! Where's the goddamned justice?" all the while the medical aides were telling me to shut up.

I saw the doctor cut open Pickering's coat, slice the uniform away from the wound.

"You shitass! Hey, limey! You hear me?" I shouted at the doctor while his aides fell on me, tumbled me to the floor. "I'll kill you, you asshole! You and Dunn, too! You another goddamned public school boy? Huh? Sending poor folks out to die."

The doctor straightened. "Get that man out," he snapped. "The wounded need their rest."

They wrestled me to my feet. I was too tired to give them much of a fight. A few feet away, in the quiet glow of the lamp, the doctor was tucking a blanket to Pickering's chin, and Pickering was blinking sleepily.

"Let me stay," I gasped. "Please. Please. Just let me stay with him."

The medical officer evidently forgave my outburst on the spot. He told me Pickering had a shattered hip. A Blighty, just like I'd thought. Who knows? Maybe I'd have made a decent doctor, after all.

They let me sleep on the floor beside him. I held his hand until I heard him snoring, then I went back to No Man's Land in my dreams.

The place was full of wandering ghosties, bewildered folks without direction. I didn't see O'Shaughnessy, but Wren caught up with me. He was beaming.

"Leaving in a tick," he said, and he was as chipper as I'd ever seen him. "Won't be long now."

Far away, along the Boche trenches, I saw one solitary and desperate figure running, running; formless and dark as a piece torn out of the night.

LeBlanc didn't make it.

Travis Lee

December 5, the reserve trenches

Dear Bobby,

The next day dawned cold and brittle. That morning I said goodbye to Pickering before they carried him to the hospital; and that afternoon, the obstinate, indestructible Fowler finally made it back. I thought of the ones I had left in the field, frozen now, their cries silenced.

Riddell made it through. And Calvert, who along with Billings, had saved Rupert Littleton. And Harold Crumb, who had brought back George Day. Miller came in two hours before sunrise after the long night of the raid, exhausted and trembling and dragging Swarthout with him.

I remembered Morgan and wanted to go get him, but Riddell said to wait until nightfall. Sleep dragged me down. It weighted my shoulders, it pushed my body into the blankets. It pressed my eyelids closed. I dreamed of a gravel path in the apricot dusk. Marble angels knelt with their heads bowed, their graceful wings folded. O'Shaughnessy walked beside me, laughing. We passed Wren, happy-faced in his grave, then a comforting surprise: Marrs and Trantham tumbled together like napping children. I stopped to study the sleepers nesting there under the glass, among the flowers.

"Tired lads. I put them to bed," O'Shaughnessy told me. "Come to find, Travis, the gathering 'twas intended as my job, not yours."

That was all right. Everything was. I saw Morgan sleeping and knew he hadn't made it. I told O'Shaughnessy how I had come across Morgan where he was wounded, told how he had begged me to save him. I said it was nice to stop worrying.

He chided, "Ah, but didn't you know they'd all be cared for?"

The graveyard was quiet except for the birdsong, except for the breeze coursing through the trees with the sound of a far rushing river. I looked into the indigo shadows, saw pale lights glittering. They outlined a tombstone's carved rose, a cherub's calm brow.

We went to the mausoleum, where the calico girl was waiting. She smiled at me, contented and peaceful. O'Shaughnessy's merry conversation resounded along the mausoleum's curved walls, its glass roof. We went out again, following the echoes of our voices. We walked into the long twilight, into the tall blue shadows and the twinkling leaves.

I saw that he was heading toward the cypress. The dark

was close, its blackness solid as a wall. O'Shaughnessy chattered on, never noticing the danger. His hands soared like butterflies, fluttering some sort of story. Oh, Bobby, I can't remember what he said—I only recall the joy of it, the terror of watching the dark approach. Then we were at the cypress; and O'Shaughnessy had to see it coming. He had to. The dark took up all Here, all Now. I wanted to run, but with the helplessness of dreamers, I trailed O'Shaughnessy inside.

I don't remember closing my eyes as we passed through that shadow membrane, but I remember opening them. Around me lay the broken countryside of No Man's Land. That was all. Nothing frightening, just a place like a thousand others—a spot where ghosties wander, searching for the land of the found.

O'Shaughnessy stopped, offered his hand in a goodbye, no extraordinary power but that of affection in his touch. "Travis?" he said.

"Yes?"

He leaned close to whisper a secret. His breath was warm and smelled of chocolate. "It's love."

Travis Lee

WINTER 1916

TWELVE

DECEMBER 10, THE REST AREA

Dear Bobby,

They brought Pickering back from surgery yesterday. I stayed by his bed in the dull light of that rainy morning. The clinic's air was thick with the reek of gas gangrene, the nose-stinging smell of carbolic. Pickering's eyes were closed. As I patted his hand, as I called his name, his fingers closed over mine. I stood watching him sleep while all around me they served lunch: boiled beef and potatoes and turnips.

Bound by that lax-handed grip, I waited while the other patients ate, while the Sisters took the trays away. A medical aide, seeing how things stood, brought me a chair. Later, a Sister brought me a cup of tea. She told me I could go on, if I wanted. She promised she'd tell him I'd visited. I thanked her kindly, told her I'd stay awhile.

Early afternoon, Pickering roused, groaned, asked for a drink of water. I tried to slip my hand from his. He must have still been groggy from the anesthetic, for he didn't let me go.

"I'm peckish," he said.

I was getting pretty hungry, too. "Can't eat until tomorrow. That's what they tell me."

He closed his eyes, licked his lips. "Some little bastard is drilling away in my leg." He drifted away. The nurses served tea. One took pity, gave me a few stale vanilla cookies. While they were clearing the plates, Pickering opened his eyes.

"Hullo," he said, surprised.

I gave him a drink of water. I wasn't sure that he realized he was still holding onto me. My fingers were hot and cramped and sweaty.

"Nice of you to visit," he said.

"Had to. Long ways out here. You'll be going home soon. Afraid I wouldn't get the chance to say goodbye."

He looked up at the slat ceiling and smiled in a happy, muddled sort of way. "What's the date?"

"The ninth."

His brow furrowed, his gaze went distant, as if he was peering through the slats. "Goose."

"Goose?"

"The dinner we always have. And plum pudding. Loads and loads of gifts. For breakfast, my wife's lovely buttery scones, plump and soft as a girl's teat, all loaded down with treacle. She's a Highlander, you know." I sat silent, and let him relish his Christmas. Then his smile dropped and he said, "Will be strange, don't you think?"

"Yeah."

"Not only the lack of battle, Stanhope."

"I know."

His fingers tightened on mine. His lips pressed together and he winced.

"Pain bad?" I asked.

His voice was strained. "Do for starters." Then he gasped out, "Bangers. Christ. Coddled eggs. No one makes coddled eggs like my missus."

I matched his grip. It felt like the bones in my hand were breaking. "You can scream," I told him.

His breath came in hard fast spasms. "Say I'll limp. Still. Small payment."

I called the nurse, who gave him a shot.

"Sergeant Riddell could have whipped you up a weed," I told him.

He snorted. His fingers gradually relaxed. His breathing eased. His eyelids drooped. I didn't want him to leave me, so I said, "There once was a boy from Texarkana."

"Wrong bloody rhythm."

"Tell me about home."

I wanted him awake, so I bore the agony of it: his sleepy voice droning on and on about homey corner pubs and rich, dark beer until the longing for it ached. Then great family stories about a comical witch of a mother-in-law and an affectionate doll of a wife. "Should marry," he told me.

"Haven't met the right girl."

"Won't, if you insist on tarts."

"You never turned down a whore that I know of."

"Gor." He rolled his eyes. "Don't tell my missus. You'll come visit? When it's over, I mean."

"You bet."

"There's talk of America joining. Shouldn't last long then, what with that famous Yank savagery."

"Won't be a whore in France safe."

A bad joke, but Pickering chuckled. I remembered the bakery shop girl, recalled a child in a wedding dress, giggles falling like rain.

He stopped smiling, too. His fingers tightened. "Listen to me, Stanhope. You shall get out of this and be done. You shall visit."

"I need to go now, Pickering." Outside the windows, dusk was coming on.

He wouldn't free me. "I'll write."

"I'd appreciate that."

"Need a letter, Stanhope. Bloody angora vest, but your family's a balls. I stole glances at the rare mail you get. Brother a complaining little prick. Mother only worried about herself. Too blasted good for the lot of them."

His take on the family surprised me. "They're okay, I guess. I'm no prize myself."

Eyes closed, he tugged on my hand. "Most kindly soul." His voice trailed off. "Do make it through."

I don't think I can, Bobby. The mud will hold me back. And England is too exotic. All the polite people, all those safe streets. Imagine sitting in a house, not thinking of it as a bunker.

Home would be just as foreign. Old friends and cordial questions; answers that aren't meant for speaking aloud. My words would come out like bullets, no matter how soft I said them.

Damn him. Pickering made me remember Christmas—the cheerful, clean smell of the cedar tree, and candles all around. Here, holidays are predestined to be dreary. With no one around to remind me, Thanksgiving had come and gone without a thought. The third Thursday of November. I couldn't remember if there had been shelling, if there had been sleet.

When Pickering dozed off, I tugged my fingers from his and left him. I hitched a ride on a motorized ambulance, sat on the back, my legs dangling. We rode through the rainy countryside while light faded, while outlines blurred. It wasn't until I was walking the corduroy road near barracks that it hit me, and my legs went so weak that I had to sit down.

It isn't right for a man to have to rebuild his world over and over again, Bobby. It tires you out. Too many friends gone, the mud earth constantly changing. Things should stay put, stay solid, so you can hold on.

When the sentry passed by he asked what I was doing sitting there, and I told him I'd just visited a friend in the hospital.

"You was in that last suicide club," he said.

Twilight was blue and chill, the far barracks dark silhouettes. "Yeah."

"Your sergeant make it?"

"Yeah."

"He know where you are?"

"He knew where I went."

The sentry sniffed, wiped his gloved hand under his nose. "All the same to me, but best get back." He put a hand down, helped me to my feet. "Your chum going to make it?"

"Got a Blighty."

The sentry broke out in a glorious smile. "Good on 'im!"

"Yeah." Lord forgive me. Only part of me meant it. "Good on him."

Travis Lee

DECEMBER 11, THE REST AREA
Dear Bobby,

I was called to the YMCA pavilion today. Blackhall was waiting, a stained pack beside him on the table. He pushed it across to me.

"Canucks is asking for 'is things. You knew 'im best. Thought you could go through, see what's trash and what's not."

I unbuckled the flaps, opened the pack, and set LeBlanc's impoverished estate along the edge of the table: a grease tin; a worn and discolored towel; his paybook, its cover and page edges gray with mold; one shaving brush, stiff with soap and shedding bristles; a comb; a small Bible. I opened it up, read the inscription: "To Gerald, all my love, Mother." Then a housewife bag, thread and needles in a tangle. A picture of a soldier in Canadian uniform standing arm in arm with a woman. There were mountains in the background. The woman was beautiful and smiling. The soldier wasn't LeBlanc. Next, a holdall. One cheap razor, rusting at the handle, and a palm-sized wooden horse.

I held the horse the way Pa did in my dream, my hands cupped, my head down. Light spread across the tabletop like spilled quicksilver. The toy was tiny. I hadn't remembered how damned pretty it was, how well-carved. A mare the tender color of doeskin, with a clean white blaze.

The bench creaked as Blackhall got up. A while later the floorboards boomed as he came back. He set a glass of lemonade by me. "Sisters of Charity," he said, "Canucks says they 'as themselves a trophy chest right in the entry of the orphanage. Made it into a memorial, like, of their boys who was lost in the war. I already give the Canadians 'is decorations. Man was a rotter, but 'e 'ad decorations a plenty. Should make a nice little show for the nuns. Anyway, officers is leaving tomorrow. Anything else there worth sending with 'em?"

LeBlanc—a man who hoarded others' memories. I thought of him grinning wide, bouncing up and down on that bay mare. Nice and gentle, I set the toy horse on the table, shoved it toward Blackhall.

"Pretty little thing," he said.

I watched it being taken away.

"The photograph?"

I shook my head. "He was keeping it for someone."

"And the Bible?"

"Borrowed it. Guy died before he could give it back."

He gave me a flat, cop kind of a look. He knew I was lying.

"Any words you care to pass along? Something 'e told you? Something nice they can remember 'im by?"

I looked at the moldy paybook, the stiff, shedding shaving brush, and knew there would be no one back home to give the message to. I shook my head.

Blackhall slipped the toy horse in the pocket of his British Warm. "All over, then, lad. For the best, innit?"

Inside of me, a stiff wintery worry begin to thaw. I smiled a little. "It's over."

LeBlanc was dead. The guilt we carried was ended. We shook hands.

"Anything you want, Stanhope? 'Spite of it all, you was friends once. Might care for some bit of memory."

I took a sip of my lemonade. Watery. No substance to anything anymore. "Don't think so."

I set LeBlanc's things back into the pack, buckled the flaps, and handed it over. It was too damned light. My own was twice the weight, loaded down with letters and homemade socks and a fine straight razor, despite a complaining brother. Despite a mother who might have cared more. Blackhall walked away with the last of LeBlanc, the half-empty pack dangling in his hands.

I was finishing my lemonade when Calvert came, told me that Riddell was asking for me in barracks. When I arrived, I found Riddell inside, waiting. He was standing with an officer and a corporal who were battle-dressed and covered in mud. The three stopped talking when I walked in.

"This Stanhope?" the captain asked Riddell.

"Yes, sir."

The captain studied me. "Private Stanhope. Where is Private LeBlanc's pack?"

"Lieutenant Blackhall already took it." I noticed Riddell's expression. "What's going on?"

The captain turned to the boy by him. "Marchbanks. Find Lieutenant Blackhall at once. Seize that bag for evidence." The corporal saluted and ran out.

"What's going on here, sir?" I asked Riddell.

The captain said, "Sit down, Private. I'll need a statement. Sergeant, you are dismissed."

Riddell didn't even look at me when he left.

I started to sweat. "Sir?" I wiped my hands down my greatcoat.

The captain pulled up two chairs, sat down in one, propped a clipboard on his lap. He crossed his legs. Mud dropped off his boots and fell onto the scrubbed planks with a splatter.

"Sit," he told me. "I shall make this brief." He took out a fountain pen. "Have you any idea why someone has murdered Private LeBlanc?"

I nearly missed the chair. The question left my head empty, my chest hollow. "Sir?"

A shit of an officer. He made his words real slow and clear, like he thought I was deaf or stupid. "Have you any idea why Private LeBlanc was murdered?"

"Half my friends were murdered."

The captain sat back as if I'd slapped him. His gaze drilled through me. "I'll have none of that."

And then I understood what was happening. It scared me so bad, my stomach twisted. "Don't be thinking I did nothing to him."

"No one said you had."

I remembered the long lists of the dead, of Morgan and Lefleur, of O'Shaughnessy and Turnhill. So many corpses. Nothing made sense.

"Why should you think you'd be suspected?"

I swallowed hard. Sleet tapped gently at the window. "Just that I knew he deserved it."

"Deserved killing?"

"Best leave it alone, sir, is what I'm saying."

"The man had the M.C. and Bar. He had every decoration worth having."

I sighed hard, and broke the promise I had made to Miller. "Pierre LeBlanc hurt women."

The captain had gray eyes that didn't give anything away. He said calmly, "That has never been substantiated."

I went cold.

He started writing. I wanted to grab the pen out of his hand, wanted to tear the paper up and throw it away.

Damn them. "Sir?" They knew.

The captain looked up.

"A lot of folks died. It was a raid, sir."

Those gray eyes, the color of the low Flanders sky. "That will be all, Private."

I got up, saluted, and left, found Riddell lurking around the door, a hangdog look on his face. "Sir? What the hell?"

He grabbed my arm, led me to the other side of the building. We stood in the shelter of the eaves.

A cutting gust of wind. Riddell hiked his coat higher on his shoulders. "Was one of the medical aides what seen it."

I leaned against the wall, felt the barracks shake. The heavy-footed captain was leaving.

"LeBlanc 'ad made it back to trenches," Riddell said, "even wif 'is knee cocked up. 'Ad 'imself a pukka of a Blighty." Sleet rattled against the roof, a sound like faraway machine guns. "But the aid station was full. Them wif Blighties was set out in the trench."

I remembered that it had been wet then, too. LeBlanc, his knee shattered, lying in the water, in the pelting sleet.

"Was just before dawn, and it was a bedlam, Stanhope, what wif wounded screaming and shells still coming down. Dark as pitch, too. One of the aides was keeping an eye, time to time; and last 'e'd seen of LeBlanc, seen 'im talking wif an officer. Next time the man checks, 'e's been shot dead in the chest."

I took a breath. The air tasted chill and clean. Snow coming, maybe. "There's some things you never knew about

LeBlanc, Sergeant. Trust me: It's better for everybody that he never went home. You tell Blackhall that if he needs me to speak up for him, I will."

Riddell looked haggard. Sleet had melted on his balding head. His eyes were red-rimmed and watery from cold. "Not Blackhall, lad." His mouth twisted as if he'd tasted something bitter. "Was the captain."

I took one step away from him. Then another. By the end of the barracks, I was running. And by the time I got to the officers' quarters, the red caps were taking Miller away.

Travis Lee

DECEMBER 13, THE REST AREA

Dear Bobby,

The night after his arrest, Miller slept in the glasshouse. I asked to see him, but the red caps turned me away. I went back to barracks. I couldn't eat, but I wanted liquor the way I had wanted it when all I could think about was the next sip of rum, when I needed it as strong as I'd ever needed a woman. See, if I got drunk, Bobby, I could forget what was about to happen. If I got drunk enough, I could finally sleep.

I asked Calvert for rum. I begged Hutchins. I begged Goodson. Uncle Tim said, "Easy on. Don't have none, mate. Can't see that? Nobody 'as none."

I booted my pack, sent it sailing across the room. I slammed my cot into the wall again, again, until the wood turned to splinters. I fought that room until I was so tired that my muscles went to jerking. That's when I noticed the sixteen survivors of my two hundred and forty-strong company. They were sitting on their bunks, watching me.

Calvert got up, offered me some tea. Blandish asked if I wanted dinner, and I told him no. They left for the mess hall together. I sat in the ruins of that room, and when the boys came back an hour later we played a little cards. I laughed once or twice. That night I lay on a dead man's cot and didn't sleep; and the next morning I walked out to see if I could stop it.

The YMCA pavilion was already being prettied up for the court martial. The doors and windows were open. The long table where kindly women once served lemonade had been cleared, a straight-backed chair set to its front. Enlisted men bustled around the huge room, sweeping the floor, carting carafes of water, bringing in paper and pens. Soldiers I'd never seen were coming and going, sergeants I didn't know were barking orders. And in the middle of that commotion, that mute and lonely chair.

The boys wandered out of the mess hall and gathered around. Blackhall and Driggers walked up. Blackhall looked natty in his dress uniform.

Driggers cleared his throat. "Men? May I have your attention, please? Lieutenant Blackhall and I have spoken with Major Dunn. As of this moment, you are ordered confined to quarters."

Not a one of us moved.

Blackhall sidled up to me. "Me tie straight?"

"It's fine."

"Flaming ties. Never could get the knack." He fiddled with his collar. "Requested permission to address the board. Somebody needs to speak up for 'im."

Driggers asked loudly, "Well, men? What are your plans?"

Hell, I didn't know. I doubted any of us did. Stand there until Miller was tried and shot. Until the whole goddamned war was over.

Blackhall leaned toward me again. "Anything you want me to tell Dunn?"

"LeBlanc was guilty of those rapes."

The busy pavilion. Our motionless knot of men. A misty morning, and the horizon lost in fog.

Blackhall caught my elbow, led me out of earshot. "Listen, Stanhope. Know you and Miller 'ad something between you. Don't need to know what it was. But don't want you to get your hopes up. Others would follow you, and that could start a riot. Miller's own fault, anyways. 'E was a fool."

I pivoted, started back to the others. He grabbed my elbow.

Blackhall's grip hurt. His voice held no room for doubt or charity. " 'E was a fool." A voice so full of indignation that spittle sprayed my cheek. " 'Ad too many witnesses. Poor, damned bloody fool. If only 'e'd asked, I'd have done it for 'im." He let me go.

A captain came riding up and reined in by Driggers. His chestnut gelding was lathered. The horse crab-stepped away, danced. The captain grabbed mane, held his seat the best he could. "Lieutenant!" he called. "Order these men into barracks!"

Driggers said, "Won't go, sir."

The chestnut fought the reins, tossed his head, blew noisily. "Men!" the captain said. "As of this moment, you are confined to quarters!"

I left Blackhall, walked over to the group, and stood beside the somber-faced Blandish—a small boy who'd grown up in a hurry.

The captain's face flamed. "Sergeant!"

Riddell, sitting on the corduroy road, shook his head. "Sorry, sir."

With a look of disbelief, the captain whirled his chestnut and cantered away. Through the open windows of the YMCA pavilion, my eyes riveted on a splash of color: a Union Jack.

We stood there for a while in the sprinkling rain until Blackhall looked over his shoulder, snapped to attention and barked, "Steady on, men!"

From the mist came marching an armed squad. Without a word, they surrounded us. Their commanding lieutenant stepped forward, ordered us to surrender our weapons.

Riddell raised his hands so they could take his side arm, then sat back down. Blackhall handed his pistol over. After some frowning indecision, Driggers gave them his, too.

"You are ordered back to quarters," the lieutenant announced. A well-spoken boy, like Driggers. Too unseasoned for his rank. He held Driggers's pistol, the barrel pointed at the ground; and his fright was so strong I could smell it. "That is a direct order from Colonel Caraway. Well? Did you not hear me?" He looked us over. I looked us over, too, saw the hard faces, the long-cast stares. Dear God, Bobby. We looked like convicts.

The boy cleared his throat. "The colonel has instructed me to warn you that noncompliance with his order may be construed as mutiny." A kid. Not much starch to him. "Do you not hear what I am telling you?" His voice broke, rose out of his control. "You men are under arrest! Fall out! I said, fall out!" He whirled to his squad, ordered, "Fix your bayonets!"

They were a green squad—clean boys, just out of training, ones who were good at orders; boys full of piss and vinegar and patriotism. They instantly obeyed. I looked around that ring of bayonets, at those blank, earnest faces.

The lieutenant said to us, "I shall give you to the count of three."

Outside the ring, Blackhall and Driggers were standing, calm and attentive. At the edge of our silent group, Riddell sat, elbows on his knees, head in his hands.

"One!"

Riddell raised his head, looked straight at the boy who was holding a bayonet to him. The kid's face was full of a disturbing and simple-minded innocence.

"Two!"

So loud that Driggers flinched.

I watched the boy near me—his expression held in such tight check that his jaw was knotted. The tip of his bayonet trembled.

I lifted my face to the sky. The air smelled of damp and grass. Cool, light-fingered rain touched my forehead. I closed my eyes and thought how nice it would be to walk through the sunset of the graveyard and watch the angels shimmer, to talk to Dunleavy and Marrs again, to see the leaves falling slow.

The lieutenant screamed, "Surrender or I shall have them shoot you! I shall order them! I do not wish to do this! Dear God! What is the matter with you men? Are you insane?"

I opened my eyes. Beyond the circle of weapons, the lieutenant stood, his bottom lip quivering. "Do you not hear me? You must hear me!" And then he whirled to his men and shouted, "Blast! Damn! Stand down!"

The squad lowered their weapons. The lieutenant stalked away. A while later, the captain galloped back. "This will not do," he said. "Court is to convene, and the officers of the board are hesitant to appear. This simply will not do."

It was funny somehow: sixteen unarmed men. I knew I should have laughed. I glanced over at Calvert. There was a strange, baffled smile on his face.

Blackhall went up to the chestnut's side. Him and the captain talked in whispers, the captain bending down, frowning. Then the captain kicked his mount and trotted back toward the officers' quarters. Blackhall followed.

The rain fell harder. It drummed against the shoulders of my greatcoat. It splashed and tinged on the new boys' helmets. In a while, Blackhall returned. He stood at parade rest in front of us and said, "Bringing in the court now. Promised the colonel there wouldn't be trouble. Promised 'im you'd stay where you was." His eyes caught mine. "Promised 'im you wouldn't hoorah nor jeer." He said, "I promised 'im. Agreed?"

I nodded. Around me, I heard a smattering of quiet "yes, sir"s.

Across the yard the officers came: Colonel Caraway, Major Dunn, Captains Wilson and Dunston-Smith. I watched the two captains pass and thought I saw Dunston-Smith cast a furtive glance my way. Then, so very soon really, and without much ado, they were inside the pavilion. A batman and two aides went to the windows, shut them with heavy caliber bangs. Into that featureless and enigmatic building they brought Miller. I saw him cross the yard, nearly hidden by mist, a red cap to either side. I caught one clear-edged glimpse as he looked around at the sixteen of us. Dangerous men. All of us killers.

They went slowly up the three steps and entered. Blackhall

entered after them, shut the door. We stood, let the rain fall, and watched the day slip into afternoon.

Driggers came by, stopped at Goodson's side, stared out at the shut pavilion. He took stock of us, and said into Goodson's averted face, "Come into the warm, man. Have a cuppa. The cooks have made us lemon biscuits. Why stand out here in the rain? There is nothing you can accomplish by it. Why, there is not even anything here to watch. I simply don't see the point."

Goodson ignored him. Like he was tired of standing, Calvert sat down on the logs. Hutchins did, too. The rain pattered down, soaked our knit caps, rolled into our eyes. After a while, Driggers went away.

A long time later, the door of the pavilion opened. Blackhall came out alone and walked toward us across the soggy grass.

Hutchins called, "What happened?"

"Don't want yer crying out," Blackhall warned. "Don't want that."

Goodson stood up. "What'd they say?"

Blackhall nailed me with a warning look. "Captain's been found guilty. 'E's to be executed in the morning."

I sat down hard on the logs. I didn't cry out. Blandish sat down beside me.

" 'E was always nice to me," Blandish said. "A real gent, like."

I told him to shut up.

The door opened again and two red caps led Miller out. His chin was high, his gait loose and easy, his expression calm. He cast one look at us as he passed. The afternoon was dark, but I thought I saw him smile.

Next the colonel came, and Dunn. Then Wilson with Dunston-Smith. Wilson stopped in the meadow and let the others walk on. He stared at us a long time.

Blackhall sat down beside me. "Blandish? Dismissed."

"Want to stay, sir," he complained.

"Go get the men sommit. You and Goodson. Men 'as to eat."

The two walked away in the gathering dark.

"Was wounded around who seen it," Blackhall said, "but they was our company, and wouldn't speak against 'im. Was only that med aide what served as witness. Fool admitted to it, right in court. Didn't 'ave to, you know. Officer's word against an enlisted. Anyways, I stood up and showed all me evidence, but the women wasn't an issue, that's what the colonel said."

Rain pattered down, soaked Blackhall's British Warm. He took his dress cap off, shook it, wiped the wet from his balding, close-cropped head. "Tomorrow, when it 'appens, you're to keep your mouf shut, understand?"

I pictured the firing squad in that broad meadow. Puffs of smoke from the barrels. The weary Miller slumping.

"Promise me," Blackhall said.

I did.

"The men can stay 'ere or can go to barracks. Tomorrow, when it's done, they can watch; but they'll need to keep to the road. That was the agreement. I guaranteed it. Stanhope, don't make me out a liar."

I hugged my knees, let the rain wash my face.

Blackhall said, "I got a way you can visit."

There in the mud he drew a map, showed me where the sentries passed the glasshouse, what times I could expect them. When he was finished, he scratched over the lines he'd made, said he was going to get dinner, said he had plans to sleep in quarters.

Then he shook my hand. "Miller's the best man I ever worked for, copper or army. But 'e's the kind of fool tries to make life right for everybody. 'E fiddles at things. Breaks 'is back trying. That sort of goodness always comes back on you."

He got up, groaning, knees popping, and walked over to Riddell. He bent down and they whispered back and forth for a while. The rain let up. When smoky dusk rolled over the meadow, when warm, welcoming lights came on in the barracks windows, Riddell got up and left with him.

Calvert sat down beside me, jerked his chin toward our

guard. "Scared of us." The squad had dwindled to three cold-looking boys.

He lit up two Woodbines, passed me one. We smoked and watched the last of twilight leave the meadow. Night came on. Hutchins and Goodson left, returned with a lantern and tarps.

" 'Ow'll it be, you think," Calvert asked, "to stand 'ere and watch 'em kill 'im?"

The wind was brisk. The cold buried itself under my coat, dug under my vest, and lodged in a place near my heart. The chill hurt. It made me shiver.

I got to my feet.

Calvert looked up at me. "You all right, Stanhope?"

I walked away, down the corduroy road and past the paddocks. I went into the warm of the stables and stood, my hand on the door, staring into the glow of the lantern and the empty golden straw.

Memory got so big that it pushed me out. I left, went down past the officers' quarters. Everything there was contained, the doors and windows shuttered all except for one. Inside a room Wilson sat on a straight-backed wooden chair, arms hanging so limp in his lap that it looked like he was dead.

I broke into a trot, then into a run. Past the place where the officers had once practiced their show—Dunston-Smith on the ill-tuned piano, Miller laughing in his chorus line—past the weeping willow and the bridge—Dunston-Smith and Miller close, the smell of beer heavy in the air. I didn't stop until the sentry challenged me.

"Talk funny," he said. He was just a dark blot in the night—a shadow soldier, same as me.

"I'm an American." Funny how proud it made me. Right then, right there. It made me homesick, too. I thought of the limestone hills, the Perdenales. I pictured the pavilion and its red, white, and blue flag; the stripes turned the wrong way, all the stars extinguished.

"What'chur business?"

"I'm in Captain Miller's company."

I heard the clank of his gear as he moved. Too dark to see,

but I knew he'd aimed his rifle. "Best be getting on." The fright in his voice amazed me.

I turned around and walked away.

I followed the memory of Blackhall's map, squeezed between the wall of a storage building and the latrines. I came out on the far side of the glasshouse: a long dark rectangle, one square of meshed yellow.

"Sir!" I whispered. The window was high. I took off my gloves, reached my arm up far as I could, grabbed the sill. "Sir!"

Rustling within. Miller's voice, first a dull "What?" then a disbelieving "Stanhope?"

Fingers met mine through the mesh. I jerked my hand away, then realized what I'd done. I reached out for him this time. The warmth of his touch made my eyes well up. It sapped the strength out of my legs.

"Aw, goddamn you," I said. I leaned my head against my arm, hung onto the wire tight. "Why didn't you just bald-faced lie?"

I didn't expect the laugh. I didn't ever think that, from a dying man, it could go on as long or could grow so loud. Then a "Shhh" from Miller, and the boom of footsteps on hardwood boards. From somewhere in the building, mutters.

I took my hand down from the mesh, stuck it in my coat to warm it. Across the way, lanterns winked slow and lazy the way the lights in the graveyard do.

Then from the window, "Stanhope?"

"Yeah?" I put my hand back up. His hand was waiting. I remembered Pickering in the hospital, unconscious but still holding on.

"I had to stop him," Miller said.

"I know that, sir."

"And I was caught at the thing fair and square. Aide said he'd seen me. Now no one else can be blamed. At least there's some justice to it."

"Ain't no justice, sir. That's just goddamned bullshit. Wasn't no justice when my pa came looking for me with the belt. Never saw a lick of justice, 'cept for what came from you."

He sighed. "Well. There is justice. I wish you'd believe that. Wish you'd try to bring it about. Otherwise what I've done has no meaning, you see."

We stood for a while, just touching.

"You scared?" I asked him.

His fingertip rubbed lightly up and down my knuckle and I let him. I wouldn't move my hand away. Never again.

"There's this graveyard," I told him. "It's a place I go in my dreams. Dunleavy's there. And Marrs and O'Shaughnessy and the others. It's pretty. There's a girl who watches over. That's where we go when we die, I think. I think we sleep for a while."

He sniffed. "Thoughtful of you, but I don't need any hope of Heaven. Most kind of you to try. Still, one turns to religion at the end. Must be inevitable, I suppose. I have been sitting there considering what sort of Jew I have made."

Miller, tinkering at goodness.

"Tell you one thing, sir. The guys in your company respect the hell out of you. Looks like they're going to hang around outside the pavilion until it's all over with. Funny the way it happened. Nobody's said anything. Nobody's made no plans. Haven't talked about mutiny. They just stand there, like everybody's too tired to move."

"You must persuade them not to do anything foolish. Shouldn't want any of you hurt for my sake."

We had jumped the bags for him. We had faced shelling and not run away. We had walked head-on into machine-gun fire. "I'll tell 'em."

"Kind of you to come." His fingers went away.

"Sir!"

His voice was faint with distance. "Best get back to barracks. Do persuade the rest of the men to go with you. Tell them I am perfectly well."

"Sir!" I hissed, but he didn't answer.

I splashed back to the storage building, fumbled around in the dark until I found something to stand on. I dragged the crate to the window, stood up on one end. I could see the cot, his boots. He was lying down.

"Sir!"

No answer.

"Damn it, sir!"

The boots moved off the bed. A tired grunt, and he was back at the window again. "Do go on to barracks, Stanhope." From his voice I could tell he'd been crying.

"I'm not leaving you." When they brought him out, I'd stand in front of his body. I'd take the bullets for him.

He lifted his hand to the mesh. In the light of his candle I could see his fingertips—skin pale from the cold, the half moons of his nails. I caught him, held on. "Listen to me. Whatever you believe, there's this graveyard."

"We are born, and then we die. We do the best we can."

"All right, then. Tell me what you believe."

"Just that. Doing one's best. Good Lord, Stanhope. It is complex. One spends a lifetime studying the Torah."

"Give me something to hang onto. Shit. Don't you see? Tomorrow I got to stand there and watch them murder you."

A long and contemplative silence, then " 'What is hateful to you, do not do to your neighbor,' " he told me. "Shammai said that that is the whole of the Torah. The rest is merely commentary on it."

I held his hand. There's something to touching, Bobby. Even asleep, Pickering knew that.

"As they lead me out, I'll be saying the *Shema Ysrael*," he said. "It's what a Jew should do if he knows he's to die. Well. So. Not the first time. Whenever I jumped the bags, you know, I said the *Shema*."

"Say it."

He taught it to me, syllable by syllable. *Hear, O Israel, the Lord our God, the Lord is One.* I said it with him while moisture collected on the mesh, while it beaded on the sill. He asked if I'd be there when he was buried, if I'd say a Kaddish over him. And then he taught me that.

"There's this graveyard," I said when he was finished.

He shushed me. "Dear Stanhope," he said. "Your being here is enough."

A noise. Miller's fingers slipped away. I reached out, tried to hold on, but the mesh stood in between.

From a distance, Dunston-Smith's shy question, "Richard?"

And Miller's surprised and heartfelt, "Colin. So glad you came."

I left them, walked past the storage building, the paddocks, the mess hall. I shoved my hands in my pockets and strode fast through the muck. Damn him. Forgiveness without limits is stupidity. I don't know, Bobby. Does God really expect that? Miller forgiving Dunston-Smith. Probably forgiving the men who would shoot him. Forgiveness lurked like a flaw in Miller, the way Pa does in my dreams.

After a while I wandered back. Miller's candle was still burning. I stepped up on the crate and looked inside. The room was empty except for the edge of that cot, those boots.

"Captain Miller?"

He bolted up so fast that the cot thumped the wall. "Thought you'd gone."

He came back to the window, but didn't lift his hand to mine.

"Hate to ask, but would you do me a favor? It's my father." He was crying and trying his best to hide it. "Would you write him? Could you do that? Just a short note. Let him know that I did what I thought right."

"You bet I will, sir."

"I've asked Colin, but he's in an awkward position, you see. Can't be helped."

Bullshit, I thought. "I'll do it. Don't you worry, sir."

"Yes, well." He was fighting sobs. "Perhaps you'd best run on."

"I won't ever leave you."

I heard his footsteps as he walked away.

"There's this graveyard, sir."

The cot creaked as he lay down.

"Look for me there," I said.

I slipped away into the dark, stealthy as Turnhill had when he was dying. I wandered down through the storage buildings and past the mess hall. I walked the log road to the dark, huddled obstacle in its path. The men were still waiting, and I knew then that they hadn't been waiting for me. They'd been waiting for dawn.

I sat down beside Calvert. "We're going to bury 'im," he said. "Me and Sergeant and Goodson and Hutchins. Blackhall says 'e'll be there. And Blandish, too."

I stretched out my legs.

"They was about putting 'im wif the cowards and the criminals, but that won't 'appen. Lieutenant spoke to Dunn about it."

Blandish threw me a tarp. Halcomb passed me down a cheese sandwich. I couldn't remember the last time I'd eaten, the last time I'd slept.

We sat and watched the sky go from ebon to charcoal. Lights came on in the barracks and in the mess hall. Halcomb and Goodson brought us all back a dixie of tea, and we drank while the sky turned pearl.

Down the log road Blackhall and Riddell and Driggers came walking. They were in their dress uniforms and they looked fine.

"Soon now," Blackhall said.

I stood. The others stood up with me. In the glasshouse, they'd be offering him breakfast. He'd refuse.

A foggy morning. Over by the mess hall a crew was dumping the morning's trash. A flock of birds flew up from a treeline and I followed their flight, my neck craning. A squad of men marched up and surrounded us, their rifles cradled.

In the glasshouse, they'd be directing the chaplain in to him. Miller would send him away. The last fear would hit. Try as he might to keep his hand steady, the teacup would jitter in his hands.

Dunn and Caraway emerged from the glasshouse first. Small as toy soldiers, they walked across the wet field. Then a knot of other officers came: Wilson, Everett, Dunston-

Smith. I watched them approach Dunn and halt. Everyone waited.

Through the gauzy fog came the firing squad: new boys, smart in their clean coats. A lieutenant carried out a straight-backed chair and set it down. Dunn barked an order. The lieutenant moved the chair closer. Caraway bellowed and gestured. The lieutenant repositioned. The firing squad looked at each other. The chair was no more than five yards away.

Two red caps came out of the glasshouse, the handcuffed Miller between them. They'd sent him out without his coat, and it was a cold day. Still, he walked proud, Bobby. He kept his head up. He didn't stumble. Beside me, Calvert came to attention. We all stood, saluting rigid and right as we'd ever had in training.

Miller's mouth was moving.

Shema Yisrael.

I remembered the feel of his hand in mine, but then thought that the hand I remembered might have been Pickering's. I was tired. Memories bled into each other and edges blurred.

The lieutenant was young and inexperienced. He blindfolded Miller too soon. Handcuffed, unable to see, Miller staggered. The lieutenant caught his arm and tried to pull him to the chair. Miller slipped in the mud, nearly went down.

Goodson muttered angrily, "Blast them."

Adonai Eloheynu.

Miller slipped again, his lips still moving. Dunn came forward, took his other arm.

Adonai Echod.

Dunn and the lieutenant played an excruciating game of blindman's buff, pulling Miller, stumbling, with them. Once at the chair, they let him go. He fell awkwardly into it, his back bent, his head lowered and swiveling right to left, right to left, searching for the correct posture. Miller, needing to do things right.

They were so far away that the lieutenant's shout was like the final reverberation of an echo. "Ready."

My hand shook so, my forefinger tapped my eyebrow. My

back, so straight, tensed. But I didn't cry out. Miller was sitting sideways, shivering in the cold and the rain, his head moving side to side, not knowing which direction to face.

Softly over the still-green meadow: "Aim."

Miller's back snapped erect as if they had already fired. He sat rigid, facing east. Miller, trying his best. His mouth was moving.

Blandish said, "Need to set him about, don't they." Then he shouted, "Bugger it! Set him right! He's cold! Give him a blanket! You blind or sommit?"

Miller raised his head in our direction.

Calvert told Blandish to shut up.

So quiet the order to fire. So faint the pop of the guns. Beautiful, the white puffs from the barrels; and I didn't cry out. Miller shuddered: once, twice. He slid from his chair, kneeling. Slow, so slow, he tumbled the rest of the way. He twitched once, I think, but it was so easy, really. A better and surer thing than battle. The lieutenant took out his side arm, cocked it, walked to Miller's side, and shot him in the head.

They left him and walked away. The bunch of us came forward to where he was lying. Blackhall knelt and took the blindfold off. The bullet from the pistol had stolen Miller's face.

We tucked him into one of the tarps and carried him with us. Riddell had found us a pretty spot, right by a poplar sapling. I said the Kaddish over him, like he'd taught me. The grave Hutchins and Riddell dug had filled up with water; and we put him in gentle, watched the water take him. All of us took turns filling the grave. Goodson had made a wooden cross with flowers on it. I watched him hammer the cross at Miller's head and didn't have the heart to correct him. But what Goodson did was all right. The worst was over, and everything was all right.

When we were finished we said words over him. The boys remembered odd kindnesses here and there. Riddell burst into tears and bawled like a baby. We left Miller in the drizzle and the cold, and we went back to barracks. The brass didn't badger us. They didn't ask us any questions. They levied no fines, no punishments. I fell into my cot and slept, and didn't wake up until late the next day. I didn't dream about him.

Travis Lee

DECEMBER 14, THE REST AREA

Dear Bobby,

The day after we buried Miller I went looking for Dunston-Smith. I stopped a batman, who hadn't seen him; found Wilson, who had. Wilson looked dazed and puffy-eyed. Still, with that British upper-class courtesy, he drew my route in the air: Turn by the mess hall, go down the log road to the officers' billets, knock up the fourth barracks on the end.

"He was a wonderful officer," Wilson said. "Nothing we could do, you know."

I left him, walked by the mess hall, down the corduroy road, past the officers' billets. I went up the steps of the fourth building and saw that the door was ajar. I knocked on the jamb, heard Dunston-Smith say, "Come."

He straightened when he saw me. He had been packing. There was an open crate on the cot. He was holding a book. The room smelled of Earl Grey tea. On a small table beside the bed was a pencil, a length of gold chain with a Star of David, and beside it a photograph of a beautiful, sad-eyed girl. I felt Miller in that room so strong that I nearly called out his name.

Dunston-Smith held the book out: a small book with a blue cloth cover, a bloom of gray mold across it. I remembered Miller and Dunston-Smith and a bloom of moss on a straw-warm hut in the woods. "For you, I believe. Richard was quite the romantic."

The book smelled of mildew. The pages were swollen by damp, rain-stained. I opened it up, read the words: *He has outsoared the shadow of our night.*

"He was in love with you, you know."

I looked up, carrying the next line of verse with me: *Envy and calumny and hate and pain.*

"Ridiculously, deliriously in love. Silly about you as a schoolgirl." Dunston-Smith's eyes were clear and empty; nothing—neither guilt, nor jealousy—to cloud them. He took another book from a stack on the table, read the spine. "A Talmud, in Hebrew. Doubt you would want that." Then, surprisingly, a hip-sprung stance. A toss of his head. An arch, pouting smile. Clues he had never shown me. "You're not of the same persuasion." He met my eyes again.

The volume of Shelley open in my hands. Simple white page; lucid black letters. *And that unrest which men miscall delight.* "No."

I heard the Talmud drop into the crate with a dull thud.

"I came to get his father's address."

He picked up the framed photograph and stared at it a while. The glass caught the light from the window, winked.

"He asked me to write, sir."

The sad-eyed girl disappeared into the crate, put down so gently that I never heard the sound of her leaving.

"Sir?" I said softly. "It was the last thing he asked of me."

I knew why Miller loved him. Dunston-Smith was a weak man, and Miller was so damned good at forgiveness. His finger tapped the stack of books.

"Sir?"

Abrupt and furious movement. He yanked a journal out of the stack, ripped a page from it, grabbed the pencil, and started scribbling. Under his breath, he muttered angrily, "Yes. Best that someone do, what? Best that it's known."

Dunston-Smith was giving me the address, even though I knew the whole story, even though I could tell Miller's father the truth behind why the army had hunted him. Why they had killed him. That Dunston-Smith had been his lover. I could even tell the whole wide world that in the end, Dunston-Smith had betrayed him.

He stood straight, as if he had been ordered to attention. He whipped his hand out, the scrawled page in it. His expression gave nothing away—he'd trained himself to hide things. But there was too much pressure. A muscle twitched in his cheek. I closed my fingers over the paper, took a crisp step backward.

"Whatever your relationship—" he said. He looked away quickly, picked up another book. "I'm glad his affections were returned."

I stood for another heartbeat in that hushed room that still smelled of Miller. Then I left, closing the door quietly. I went back to the barracks, got out my paper, and wrote: *Dear Mr. and Mrs. Miller, I knew your son.*

Like Miller had that time he wrote the letter to Ma, I stopped and couldn't go on. Around me, the boys came and went. A few of the newer ones, Blandish and Hunter, had already forgotten yesterday and were laughing. Against regulations, I stoked up the primus and made myself a cup of tea.

Calvert came around and asked if I wanted dinner. I had been staring at the paper so long that it surprised me to see the lamps had been lit and the sun was already going down.

"Got to eat, chum," he said. "Won't do, this bloody 'unger strike. Go into the faints. Won't carry you about, can count on that."

I told him to bring me something back. He left with Goodson and Hutchins. I watched them walk into the muddy yard, past the intermittent glow of the lamps; watched them skirt the lustrous puddles.

I took up my pen and, while they were gone, I finished the letter. Here's what I wrote:

Dear Mr. and Mrs. Miller:

I knew your son. He was a brave man. I guess you would want to know that. But more, he was a good man; the best commander I ever served under. Maybe the best man I ever knew.

I regret that there was no Jew here for him; but I assure you that he said his Shema before he died. We buried him soon thereafter, in a pretty spot; and I said a Kaddish over him. We did the best we could.

Mr. Miller, I want you to know that he spoke of you fondly. I think that must be important, sir, for I have noticed that boys in battle most often call out for their mothers. It surprised me, frankly, the affectionate regard in which he held you. My own father and I were not as close.

Also, let his Sarah know that he always kept her picture with him. He spoke of her often, and with great admiration. She must be an extraordinary girl. She was such an integral part of our friendship that it seems at times that I knew her.

His was a quick death, and therefore easier than most. He faced it well, and did not shrink. All his men were there with him at the end. I must tell you, I find it odd that we became friends. He was a Jew, and I had never before known one. He was an officer, and I was not. He believed in justice.

Whatever you are told, sir, I wish you to know the truth of the matter: Captain Miller died trying to do what was right.

Sincerely yours,
Travis Lee Stanhope

I sealed the letter—figuring it was worded safe enough to make it through the censors. After a while the boys came back out of the wet. Calvert brought me a fried egg sandwich.

"Shit," I said in surprise. "When's the last time I saw something like this?"

"Best fall down and kiss me feet, is what I says. Bit of a trick, that egg." He sat down by me. "Eat, Stanhope. Go on, chum. 'E's dead," he said reasonably. "Nothing's to be done."

The bread was fresh, the egg white firm in the center, crisp on the edges. Butter and yolk ran down my arm. I licked every bit of it off me.

After lights-out, I heard Calvert shifting around in his bed, his cot creaking. "Wish Pickering was 'ere," he finally said.

In a week or so, the army would move Pickering out. First the train, then the choppy ride across the Channel, then the damp smoky streets of home. I'd never again see him.

"Funny old war, innit," Calvert said. " 'Ow men come and go."

Faint as ghosts, sometimes. Even with your hand out, you can't catch them. I went to sleep, there amid the smells of the men I knew, in the drowsy mutters and the familiar sounds of their snoring. I slept hard, and I didn't dream.

Travis Lee

THIRTEEN

DECEMBER 15, A POSTCARD FROM THE REST AREA
Dear Bobby,

Got your letter. If the Edelhauser place is up for sale, you need to go on ahead and buy it. Talk to old man Reichwald at the Fredricksberg bank. Doesn't matter to me that they're German. The war's not personal like that.

Tell Ma I'm sorry to hear she's down in her back; and y'all have a Merry Christmas, too.

Travis Lee

DECEMBER 15, THE REST AREA
Dear Bobby,

Our new captain is a highly uninformed public school tightass named Gilchrist. He ordered us out in the field today and we stood in the freezing wind while he told us that he would not stand for insubordination. He gave this long speech about how he had heard we were troublemakers and how our former captain had allowed slack soldiering. He said things would be different from now on.

The sixteen of us stood as still and attentive as we could. Goodson's old wound was bothering him, and he was leaning cattywampus. Halcomb's frostbitten toe was giving him trouble. Still, we stood straight enough. We listened to the green captain drone on in his plummy, upper-class voice about how no-account we were and how our negligence was the talk of the entire battalion.

When he was done, Blackhall bellowed, "Attention!"

We were tired, but we saluted real fine. The rain had let up for the day, but the wind had a bite. It came whipping down from the North Sea, carrying with it the salt smell of ocean. I remembered a ghostie who once showed me a fishermen story. It was a wonderful story, all about boats bobbing on gunmetal waves and dripping, heavy nets. Funny. I couldn't remember if the dead man had been Scots or French or German; and I didn't know why I had ever thought that was important. While we stood there waiting, I remembered lots of things. I remembered the taste of that fried egg sandwich: the thick yolk, the sweet greasy butter. I remembered the white puffs from the rifles, and Miller slumping in his straight-backed chair.

The new captain's eyes kept sliding away, as if we were sixteen radiant suns.

"Very well," he said, waving a hand. "I suppose that will be all." He turned and wandered back to his quarters.

Blackhall told us to fall out. We stood there in the field and looked at each other.

It's all changed, Bobby. After the new captain, the green troops came—an invasion of them, ignorant and happy, chatty as a flock of sparrows. Calvert and Halcomb and the rest of us sat there in the barracks and watched them stow their gear. When a boy put his pack down on a bunk near Goodson's, Goodson knocked it off.

"You a nutter or sommit? Eh? You! Porridge face! Talking to you! You a bleeding nutter? Can't see that's Fowler's?"

The boy picked up his pack and cradled it against him, slack-jawed. "Didn't mean nothing."

Riddell came over, asked what the problem was.

Angry arm-waving from Goodson, like the discourtesy went beyond explanation. "Wanted to put his bleeding pack down on Fowler's bed, is what."

Gently, Riddell said, "Fowler ain't coming back."

Goodson's flailing arms—his mute and violent grief.

Riddell told the boy, "Find yourself another cot. Go on."

"Why's 'e so mad? Didn't mean nothing."

"Go on." Riddell grabbed Goodson's elbow. "Look at you," he chided. " 'Aving yourself a blinking paddy." He held on until Goodson stopped fighting the air. "Fowler got himself a Blighty. You know that. 'E's on 'is way 'ome."

"That's his bunk there," Goodson said.

Riddell nodded. "All right."

Goodson said real loud, eyeing us all: "That's Fowler's bunk there."

I wish I had an empty bunk like Goodson does. There's nothing for me to hold onto. I can remember the taste of that egg sandwich better than I can remember home. The dreams don't come to me anymore. At lights-out I try, but hard as I look, I don't see anything sparkle. No ghosties visit. Lately I've wondered if it was all my imagination. If, for a brief and glorious while, I just went crazy.

Travis Lee

DECEMBER 17, THE RESERVE TRENCHES

Dear Bobby,

We marched back to the trenches in the sleet, in the knee-deep mud. A sparse rain of shells came down. Around us, Jack Johnsons flowered sudden and black and smoky; whizzbangs fell with thunderous cracks. One good thing about it: The shelling finally made the new boys shut up.

When we reached the trenches, we found they were flooded, the sumps not working. The place held the old familiar stink of piss and shit and decay. When Uncle Tim and me were stowing our gear in the aid station, we heard screaming. In the dugout next door one of the new boys had burst a sandbag. There'd been a dead Boche behind the wall, and when the bag ruptured, maggots spilled down over the boy like grain from a feedsack. He was standing in them ankle-deep.

Uncle Tim and me laughed. The other new boy was trying

to help, plucking maggots off his friend fast as he could. He got his dander up. "You blokes is 'round the bend!" he shouted.

To the rear, shells started falling. The air vibrated. Artillery heavier than Jack Johnsons. The boys went still and pale.

Behind the boys, maggots still dripped slow and wiggling from out the dead Boche's sleeve. Time had stripped his hand to the essentials: dun tendon, cream bone. I wanted so bad to see that German boy sparkle.

"Trick is, you drown maggots, just like you does lice. That's the way you kills 'em." Uncle Tim walked up to the boys, pulled his pecker out, and pissed on their feet. Urine splattered. Maggots flew. The two boys backed out of his reach.

Uncle Tim stowed his pecker and walked away. I followed. Once in the trench, he elbowed me. "Good chuckle, that."

I thought of the spray of urine, the way those maggots went spinning wild and free. I started to grin.

"Teach them others, you know."

They would. My grin widened.

" 'Ave all them boys pissing on each other."

We laughed all the way through lunch just thinking about it.

But that afternoon, Calvert came looking for me, said he wanted to talk. We sat on a couple of crates near his dugout. It was snowing—fat white flakes coming down slow.

"Can't go on." Calvert was so tired he looked stupefied. " 'Ad enough. Sat there last night listening to them bleeding shells coming in. Nearly ran for it. If I do, they'll shoot me. And wif less of a party than they made for Captain Miller."

A snowflake drifted down lazily, settled on Calvert's shoulder and perched there like an angel.

"Another thing: Don't want to go shell-shocked, Stanhope. Seen 'em clawing at their mouths, grinning like simpletons, shaking like they 'as the Saint Vitus dance. Can't have that. Can't go useless like that. Rather stick me rifle barrel in me mouf and pull the trigger meself." Then he asked shyly, "You 'elp me?"

I told him I would.

He hadn't expected it to be so easy. My agreeing moved him, and he blinked back a few tears. "A regular gent, you are, Stanhope."

Something in me knew for sure that if he didn't leave now, he never would. I didn't tell him that. I said I figured we were square, said I knew he'd have done the same for me. Said I never asked him, for he was such a lousy shot.

He nodded, hitched a sigh. "Don't duff it."

I promised I wouldn't. Then I got my rifle and my gear. We headed down the old firebay into the traverse. I checked to make sure the magazine was full.

"Crikey." Calvert was brave enough; but his voice shook when he joshed me. "Thought you was a sharpshooter. Shouldn't need but one."

I cocked that Lee-Enfield, made sure I had a bullet up the spout.

"Wait till the shelling picks up," he said.

It seemed for a while that the Boche artillery was planning on a cease-fire. We cussed them until the shells started coming faster. Thumping, thunderous whizzbangs. A nice flurry like a giant's scampering footsteps, ones that made the ground shake. I aimed one-armed, put my free hand on Calvert's shoulder. I looked into his eyes.

"I'll miss you," I told him.

"Don't duff it."

I fired. The recoil nearly flung the rifle out of my grip. I saw him go down. He fell so sudden, splashing into the standing water, hissing air though his teeth, "Bugger it. Oh, bugger it. Flaming 'urts."

I sat down in the flooded trench with him. The bullet had shattered the kneecap. His leg was turned wrong. Blood poured nice and even down his pants leg.

"A good, clean shot," I said. I pulled his arm around my neck. He grunted, and I knew he was hurting bad. "I can bring the litter down for you."

He shook his head. "Bloody shells."

I understood. He was tired, and it was time. I pulled him

up, hoisted him by his coat, and dragged him to the aid station. Uncle Tim, the new boy we named Ears, and the one we named Lack-a-bum stood when we came in.

"I shot him," I said. "Best get the med officer."

None of the officers believed us, but Calvert and me had got our stories straight. I was cleaning my rifle when it went off; and I had the oil can and the rag in my pocket to prove it.

Riddell eyed me. " 'As me doubts."

But Blackhall shook Calvert's hand. He shook mine, too. He whispered, "Nice shooting, Stanhope."

"Thank you, sir."

"Mind you don't muck wif me others."

"No, sir."

Uncle Tim and me and the two boys packed Calvert warm. We tucked him in, tied his leg so it couldn't move. We did everything right. When we picked the litter up, he didn't so much as murmur.

We carried him all the way to the hospital through the growing night, through the shelling. We put him down in the yard with a line of other wounded. I told him goodbye.

Snow was coming down like goose down, piling in drifts by the tents. The lamps were lit inside the hospital. One was burning a welcome at the door. It was so pretty, Bobby, the lamplight, the snow falling. The building seemed implausibly solid, the one thing left that was good and true. I wanted to grab hold of a clapboard corner and hang on for dear life.

"Always remember you, Stanhope," Calvert said.

"You'll cuss me every time you take a step."

In the yellow glow of the lamp snowflakes swirled like moths. Calvert was grinning. "Worth it." He seized my hand so hard that it startled me. "Got some chocolate in me pack. Want you to have that. All me gaspers, too. Some dirty postcards you might fancy."

Calvert's payment for services rendered. I guess it made him feel better about leaving me behind. The chocolate was tasty. The cigarettes were stale, but I'll smoke them, anyway.

Uncle Tim and me and the new boys made it back to the

trenches at dawn. The ground shimmered with fresh-fallen snow and not with vision. Still, it was going to be a pretty day. As morning came on, the mud fields turned cobalt, then pink. When the sun broke through, the frozen earth caught fire.

In the grandeur of that sunrise, I sat in the aid post and got out Calvert's dirty postcards: all heavy girls with big titties and meaty, gartered legs. I passed them to Uncle Tim, who studied them a long time, then somberly and diligently licked them. Reverent, he wiped them off with his sleeve, handed them back. I stuck them in Miller's volume of Shelley, and we tumbled into our sleeping bags. I went to sleep listening to Uncle Tim's soliloquy on whores he'd known. I finally dreamed.

The graveyard was empty. The sun was down, a full moon out. In all the lichened nooks and mossy crannies between the tombstones leaves glistened. Moonlight spilled over the bent shoulders and folded wings of the angels. Down in their graves, Marrs and Trantham glowed like paper lanterns. I ran up and down the steps, searching every glass-topped tomb, shouting Miller's name. I ran through the milky splashes of moonlight on the mausoleum's floor. Far away, through the spectral monuments and the dark, glittering trees, I saw a chalky flicker. Maybe the girl in the wedding dress, maybe O'Shaughnessy. I called out, but the flicker faded. I stood there and let the shimmer surround me. Beautiful, that graveyard. Perfect. So aloof that it scared me.

Travis Lee

DECEMBER 19, THE RESERVE TRENCHES

Dear Bobby,

I don't know why they don't move us forward, why they don't move us back. We stay here, pounded on by the Boche and by the weather. It's so cold that the new boys bring their braziers inside, even when they're told not to. Yesterday Uncle Tim and me found three of them curled in their funk hole, their faces serene. Lucky, drowsy boys. The charcoal fire had warmed them; it had seduced them into death while they slept. I wondered if they had been dreaming.

It's not all gentle. The Boche are hitting us with white stars. The new boys aren't fast enough with their masks. We find them white-eyed and blind, twitching and slobbering, coughing up scarlet blood and pink lung-lining. They cling to you tight as frightened children when you pick them up. They try to talk, and that's hard to watch. I wish I knew what they want so bad to say. To tell their mother they loved her? To ask that damned useless question: Why?

I keep hoping I won't find a familiar face in a funk hole. I keep hoping I'll see Miller in the graveyard. Between shellings, Uncle Tim and me sit around like old timers in front of the feed store, talking about the old days.

The new boys try to fill us in on newspaper stories from back home about the evil Kaiser, about a noble Parliament and King. They rattle on about glory and making the world a better place. They bore us shitless.

"Got to believe in the rightness of it," Lack-a-bum told us finally. "Otherwise, why be fighting?"

"Gor!" Uncle Tim said. " 'Cause they keep shooting at us!"

"If you don't believe in the cause, why'd you sign up, anyway?" Ears asked.

Uncle Tim considered it. He sat back, lit up a Woodbine. "Me girl—a ripe little piece—asks why all the rest of the boys was going, and I was staying behind. Figure I joined up to keep me cock happy." He turned to me. "Why'd you do it, Stanhope?"

"Damned if I know," I said.

Whatever our reasons for being here, the Boche keep punching us. Boys die in pieces. Boys die buried. Boys die coughing, begging us desperate—wordless as deaf mutes—for help. I'm no expert on it, but seems to me that the coughing is the worst.

Travis Lee

DECEMBER 20, THE RESERVE TRENCHES

Dear Bobby,

Last night I walked the corridor of home. The upstairs was all dim and shadowy. The wood floor gleamed like satin. The air smelled of floor wax and rosewater and camphor. Down the hall, morning sunlight flowed from Ma's open doorway, throwing a luminous square against the wall. It made the creamy paper glow and the painted rosebuds spark like flames. At her doorway, I stopped.

Ma's window was open and an autumn-scented breeze blew through. The lace curtains fluttered. Pa was sitting on her bed, on that ring-patterned quilt, in that cascade of light. His back was bowed, his head down. He was looking at the toy wooden horse he held in his hands.

Beside him sat Miller. His stare made my spine go cold. He knew everything about me—why Pa was waiting, why I wouldn't go inside. Beyond the window, the sky was all soft gray clouds, like a tender rain was coming. Forgiveness tugged at me with its small, insistent fingers. Pa looked so frail, so old. Wars wear you out, Bobby, even the personal ones like Pa fought. I stood there, my hand on the doorjamb, knowing that Miller expected me to come in. I couldn't. After a while, I walked away.

Travis Lee

DECEMBER 22, THE RESERVE TRENCHES

Dear Bobby,

Yesterday between shelling and carting wounded, I had tea in Riddell's dugout. For that short time the day was quiet. I sat on a crate and watched sun wink on the trench's standing water.

Riddell told me how he gets scared sometimes. How the shelling gets him down.

"I know you're going to make it home," I said.

He shrugged.

"I know you will. I seen you." I'd seen him walking down that tree-canopied path to his sister's house. It was late fall and the war was over. The path he was walking was strewn with leaves; but the sun was out in England, and the last of the late flowers bloomed. I knew the end of Riddell's story like I'd once known which shell holes to hide in. There's a lot of things I'm aware of. I know that when we die, we find kindness. I know that we sleep for a time, and someone watches over. I've been told the secrets of spirits. I'm a lucky kind of a man, that way.

Riddell nodded. "Father O'Shaughnessy always said you 'ad the gift." Politely, he asked, "You see the rest of 'em, lad? Mind telling me?" Riddell, still mother-henning his chicks. "Like to know about Lieutenant Blackhall. Man's been kind."

Blackhall would make it through with a pension and some pain. I knew that by the time the war was over he'd consider that to be reward enough—just a little calm, just the chance to hoist a few. Blandish would go home unscathed; and Uncle Tim, whose girl would still be waiting. For me, there was a compassionate mist. It would close over me the way the water accepted Miller. That's the part I didn't tell him.

Riddell broke out some candy his sister had sent. It was herb candy, and it had a bite to it. Wasn't as good as O'Shaughnessy's box of French chocolates, but it wasn't bad.

"Calvert?" he asked. "Would 'e 'ave made it, lad?"

"Don't think so."

Riddell nodded. "You was protecting 'im. Thought as much."

"We're all of us protected."

Saying it out loud that way made me finally understand. Even Marrs in the fire, even Foy's leaking and blistered body. No matter the pain, every story has a happy ending, if only because the letting go is sweet.

"I dreamed about Miller," I told him.

"A good man," Riddell said.

Miller, who knew forgiveness; who, despite it all, believed in justice. When I dreamed that dream again, I decided, I would walk down the hall that smelled of floor wax and camphor. I would stop in the gentle spill of light from the doorway, and this time I would go inside.

I know things, Bobby, so I know that when I take the toy horse from Pa's cupped hands, he'll raise his head. Our eyes will meet and we'll see each other for the first time.

Riddell said, "Nice to 'ave your gift. A comfort, like."

"I'm lucky that way."

It was homey there. Over the stink of the trench, Riddell's dugout smelled of pungent herbs and hay.

Nothing much happened that afternoon, Bobby, but I'm telling you about it because it was important. It helped me understand what had happened the night before. I woke up from a sound sleep and saw the calico girl standing before me, solid and as real as life. And I swear to God I wasn't dreaming.

Behind her stretched the graveyard. The moon was high there, and everything shimmered. Past the marble angels, a golden inferno went walking: O'Shaughnessy. Marrs and Trantham walked with him, bright and unknowable as stars.

The calico girl leaned so close that I could smell the lavender scent of her. *No*, I thought. I prayed hard to anyone who would listen: *Please not yet.*

She straightened, looked down at me a while. "Not quite yet," she promised.

She faded then. Everything faded until I was looking at the peeling door of the aid station and remembering her sad smile. I'd let us both down, you see? For despite everything I've been through, despite everything I've seen, I'm still afraid of the dark.

You listen careful now, Bobby, for I must tell you the most important secret: The black by the cypress looks threatening, but beyond waits a calm and sparkling place. And if I never bequeath you anything else, I give you this certainty: That shimmer I've seen is the power of the universe. It runs through me and you, through the dead men in the field and through the rats that eat them. It's love. Funny how simple

Mrs. Leon Stanhope
Box 56
Harper, Texas

December 24, 1916

My dear Mrs. Stanhope,

I regret to inform you that your son, Travis Lee Stanhope, expired of battle wounds yesterday. I did not know him well, but I have heard that he was a brave lad and acquitted himself well during the campaign. You should have been proud of him.

He was sitting in his dugout when a gas shell hit. It may be some consolation for you to know that he bore his injuries with extraordinary courage and with little complaint. All in all, he did not suffer long.

Enclosed please find his effects along with a stack of personal papers which were found in his haversack.

My deepest sympathies,

Roger Dayton Gilchrist

Roger Dayton Gilchrist, Captain, B.E.F.